Pride Publishing books by L.M. Brown

Single Books
To See the Sky
To Change the Stars
My Boyfriend's an Alien
One Perfect Wish
Falling into Darkness

Mermen and Magic
Forbidden Waters
Tempestuous Tides

Heavely Sins
Between Heaven and Hell
Between Good and Evil
Between Life and Death

I0692890

Mermen & Magic

TREACHEROUS SEAS

L.M. BROWN

Treacherous Seas
ISBN # 978-1-78651-845-3
©Copyright L.M. Brown 2019
Cover Art by Erin Dameron-Hill ©Copyright June 2019
Interior text design by Claire Siemaszkiewicz
Pride Publishing

TREACHEROUS SEAS

Prologue

Cari stood on the balcony of her private quarters in her palace on the Isle of the Gods. From her vantage point, she watched the two men sparring on the beach below.

"His form isn't too bad," Medina commented from beside her.

"No, it's not," Cari agreed. "His form isn't the problem, though, is it?"

Medina sighed. "I suppose not."

"There's a great difference between fighting another man—even a god—and battling a sea dragon. No matter how much he's improved, he still won't survive a battle with Urion."

"Maybe Caspian will talk him out of it," Medina suggested.

"I doubt he's even trying to," Cari muttered. If anyone could appreciate the thirst for vengeance, it was her brother.

Medina leaned on the railing. "I don't know. Caspian knows what will happen if Marin tries to fight Urion. Do you really think he'd let him face that fate?"

Cari closed her eyes and summoned a vision of Marin's future. Once again she saw him, trident in hand, facing the largest of Mariana's sea dragons, Urion. Urion dispatched the merman with frightening speed, burning him with sea fire until there was nothing left at all.

Marin's desire to avenge the man he loved would lead to his death, and no matter how many times Cari gazed into the future, she couldn't see anything different.

Chapter One

Marin glared up at the god from where he lay sprawled on the sandy beach.

Caspian held out his hand. "Perhaps we should call it a day?"

"It's still light," Marin argued, though he accepted the outstretched hand and let Caspian pull him to his feet.

"You're getting tired."

"I'm fine." He picked up his trident and took his fighting stance once more. "Come on. You're a god, you're not tired."

Caspian shrugged and placed his feet in the sand. "You need to work on your balance."

Marin snorted. "I'll be facing Urion underwater. What's the point of learning to balance when I'll be swimming?"

"Because I said so," Caspian replied as he thrust his trident at Marin.

Marin dodged the jab with ease and countered with a stab of his own. Caspian swung to avoid his attack, and with one sweep of his weapon, he sent Marin flying again.

"You're too tired," Caspian said. "When you're fresh and concentrating, you can anticipate that move with ease. Come. Let's get something to eat and call it a day. We'll practice again tomorrow."

Marin opened his mouth to argue but Caspian had already vanished from the beach.

With a frustrated sigh, Marin scrambled to his feet and walked over to the path leading from the beach to Caspian's temple and palace.

The temple was overgrown and sorely neglected. Caspian had told him that part of the building was forbidden to him. Marin had no problem with that. The place gave him the shivers.

The palace was in a slightly better state of repair, though not by much, and only a few rooms were habitable. The rest were dusty and unused and didn't beckon explorers at all.

Caspian had brought him here two days ago. He'd given him a quick tour of the rooms he could go into and had made it clear that everywhere else was strictly out of bounds. When Marin had asked where Caspian's own rooms were, in case he needed something, Caspian had told him he didn't live here, but the god wouldn't elaborate further.

Marin didn't press for information. It wasn't any of his business. He was here so Caspian could train him for his battle with Urion. He didn't need to know any more than that.

When Marin arrived back at his rooms, he found Caspian setting the small table. He'd clearly been somewhere to get what he told Marin was a takeaway while Marin had been walking back from the beach.

"What do you intend to do tonight?" Caspian asked after they had begun eating.

Marin shrugged. "Sleep and get an early start with our training in the morning."

"It's the solstice," Caspian said.

"Yes, I know." Marin had felt the heat of the mating fever rising throughout the day. He'd done his utmost to ignore it. It wasn't as if he had any intention of breaking his fever. It was his second solstice without Calder and the pain was already worse than the last, but he was trying as hard as he could to put it out of his mind.

"Would you like me to take you to the island that the mer from Atlantis are using?"

"No, that won't be necessary." Marin concentrated on his food and tried not to think about the mating seasons he had spent during happier times.

Calder.

Older and more experienced, Calder had known without being told what Marin needed on the night of the solstice. On their first night together, Calder had taken him to a secluded grove and initiated Marin in the ways of mermen who craved the touch of their own gender.

Big and strong, Calder had been the most powerful of the Atlantean guards, yet he had submitted to Marin without hesitation, spreading his legs for the younger merman with a willingness that had been as arousing as it was surprising.

They had never spent a solstice apart.

Until Calder had been cruelly taken from him.

"The pain from your fever will get worse if you don't break it," Caspian reminded him.

Marin glared across the table. "Do you think I don't know that?"

"Sorry, but I'm sure there are many mermen who would be happy for you to suck their cock."

"That's not my trigger," Marin replied.

"Oh. Sorry. I guess I just assumed. Well, even so, many mermen would be happy to fuck you, too."

Marin didn't bother to reply to that, annoyed that Caspian, like everyone else, automatically assumed that he would be the one taking another man up his arse. Truthfully, he didn't mind being on the receiving end of a good fuck, and he and Calder had often switched roles the rest of the year, but it wasn't what he needed during the mating season.

"It'll only take a few seconds for me to transport you to the island," Caspian continued. "I can collect you later and bring you back."

Marin pushed back from the table. "I have no intention of breaking my fever. Tonight I intend to honor Calder's memory by remaining abstinent."

Caspian stared at him, his expression unreadable, for several long seconds. "Even though you know it will bring you pain?"

"Yes," Marin replied.

Caspian nodded slowly. "I understand. Now, finish your meal and I'll say no more about the solstice."

Marin hadn't thought he would convince Caspian so easily. He pulled back to the table and picked up his fork once more.

It was going to be a long night, but he owed it to Calder to be strong and focused.

* * * *

"I'm ready," Marin declared.

"No, you're not," Caspian argued. "If you leave now, you'll die."

"You don't know that."

"Yes, he does." Cari appeared behind Caspian. "Calder was a fine merman and I'm truly sorry for what happened to him."

"Not sorry enough to do anything about that monster that murdered him," Marin pointed out. "And if you and the rest of the gods aren't going to bring him to justice, I will."

"Justice will be served," Cari said.

"When?"

"I don't know, but it will come to pass. I promise."

Marin paced away toward the edge of the water. "That's not good enough. I want him dead."

"Revenge isn't the answer."

"He murdered the only merman I've ever loved. I want justice for him."

"You want revenge. There's a difference."

"I don't care," Marin screamed.

"Urion's death won't bring Calder back," Caspian said.

Marin glanced over his shoulder to glare at Cari's brother. "For a God of Justice, you don't seem to be delivering it. I'd say you're somewhat slacking."

"It won't take away the pain of his loss either," Caspian added, ignoring Marin's jibe.

Marin choked out a bitter laugh. "What would *you* know about loss? You and the rest of the gods have never had to lose anyone. You've not had to hold your lover in your arms while he takes his last breath. You're immortal. How can you *ever* understand what I'm going through?"

"Enough!"

Marin flinched at the booming voice. The god who had shouted appeared a moment later.

"Grandfather." Cari bobbed a low curtsy that the god completely ignored.

"This is Antar," Caspian said. "He is our grandfather and the God of Space and Time."

Antar ignored Caspian's introduction as well. "You, merman, dare to raise your voice to a god?"

"It's fine," Caspian interrupted. "Marin is just a little upset."

"Entire armies have been destroyed for lesser insults," Antar continued.

Lightning flashed over the water, even though there wasn't a cloud in the sky.

"Grandfather, leave Marin be," Caspian said. "He's been through enough."

With a wave of his hand, Antar froze both of his grandchildren in place.

Marin took a step back.

"Yes, you should be scared," whispered Antar, the soft tone even more terrifying than when he'd shouted. "You show disrespect to those who have shown nothing but kindness to you. You aren't worthy of their attention."

A waft of perfume heralded the arrival of Medina, the Goddess of Love.

"Stay out of this, Medina," Antar warned, without turning his steely gaze from Marin.

"Marin is a merman who has lost the one he loves. His heart cries out to me."

"A broken heart is no excuse for disrespecting the gods."

"I'm sure he didn't mean to. Perhaps a second chance, before you do anything drastic?"

"Why does this insolent creature deserve a second chance?" Antar growled.

"Look into his eyes," Medina said. "See what Caspian, Cari and myself already have."

Antar seemed to take her at her word and stared right into Marin's eyes, searching for goodness knows what.

"Ah, I see," Antar finally said.

"If you punish him for his insolence, the repercussions will be disastrous."

"I presume your appearance here means you have another suggestion?"

"Marin needs to remember how to love," Medina said.

"I know how to love," Marin interrupted. "I love Calder."

Antar nodded. "He does have a point there. But he has forgotten so much. Perhaps it is time he remembered."

Marin felt rooted to the spot, unable to move his limbs or utter a word.

The wind howled through his ears, though not a hair moved on the heads of any of the immortals standing before him.

Lightning flashed over the ocean and the earth seemed to shake beneath his feet.

"Remember," Antar whispered. "Remember…"

Chapter Two

The Isle of the Gods
Before Records Began

Caspian blinked as he stared up at the seething goddess at the end of his bed. "I thought I made it clear several centuries ago that women weren't welcome in my bed."

"You did," replied Medina, her tone as icy as her glare. "You'll note that I'm not *in* your bed, unlike my priests."

Caspian smiled and stretched as he took in the delectable sight of his most recent bed mates. "They came to me willingly. It took very little persuasion to convince them that they might find the touch of men as satisfying as that of women."

"As my priests are specifically chosen because they are attracted to both genders, this doesn't come as a surprise to me. I have no issues with them seeking pleasure with each other when I'm *otherwise engaged*."

"You mean once you're bored with them," Caspian replied.

One of the priests stirred beside him and Caspian patted him on the rump.

"My priests can bed whomever they wish," Medina said, "just *not* when they're due to perform ceremonial duties in my temple."

"I'm not keeping them from their duties. They are free to leave whenever they wish."

Medina gave the nearest priest a shove, waking him from his slumber and nearly sending him to the floor.

"What the—?"

"Your goddess requires your presence," Caspian explained.

"The dawn blessing!" The priest darted from the bed, waking the other three occupants in the process.

There followed a mad scramble of arms and limbs as Medina's priests clambered to their feet and rushed around the room in search of their robes.

Medina ushered them out of the door before casting a final vicious glare at Caspian. "Do you think now that you've bedded *all* my priests, you might turn your attentions elsewhere?"

Caspian shrugged. "Maybe, maybe not. Your priests are most talented."

Medina snarled, her lovely face becoming ugly for a brief moment, before she disappeared through the archway, leaving only a lingering trace of her perfume in her wake.

Caspian chuckled and gave his cock a rueful glance. It was a shame—if not entirely unexpected—that Medina had charged in here so early. Maybe he shouldn't have deliberately enticed her favorites into his bed the night before the dawn blessing ceremony.

He'd have to track down one of his own priests to take care of him.

Thankfully, his High Priest appeared in the archway before Caspian had to move from his bed. "Rafe, you must have read my mind."

Rafe strolled over to the bed and sat on the edge. "Did you have an enjoyable night?"

"Yes, I did indeed. You?"

Rafe gave a half shrug. "It could have been better…if you'd invited me to join you last night."

Caspian frowned at the possessive chiding. Rafe had become quite vocal recently about his displeasure with Caspian inviting other men into his bed. "You knew when you swore to serve me that I'm not a man who'll ever stick to one lover."

"I know."

"But you thought you would be the one to change that," Caspian continued.

"Do you blame me?"

"No. You aren't the first to think so, and I doubt you'll be the last. Now, enough of your jealousy." Caspian gestured to his groin and Rafe dove onto his cock, swallowing him eagerly.

Caspian closed his eyes as he let Rafe bring him release. The priest teased him with his tongue and fingers, fondling his balls with a grip that was just a shade too aggressive.

His mind drifted as Rafe sucked him. After last night he had bedded every last one of Medina's priests, a quest that had taken several years, thanks to the Goddess of Love's own insatiable sexual appetite. Luring her priests into his bed when they had been largely satisfied in the goddess' had been quite a feat.

He wondered what his next challenge could be.

18

* * * *

Caspian took his place at the council meeting, bored as ever with the tiresome wittering of his fellow immortals.

He turned to whisper to his sister Cari, Goddess of Prophecy, before recalling that Medina had taken Cari's usual place at the table. He quickly looked away and tried to listen to his father reporting on the latest wars among the men who worshipped other pantheons. Once again, the Atlantean gods were relieved that they had protected their people by sinking Atlantis below the waves and gifting them with the ability to survive at great depths. While other pantheons were falling into chaos, their own continued to thrive.

"Wine?" a soft male voice beside him whispered.

Caspian nodded and the priest filled his goblet to the brim. From the corner of his eye, Caspian could see that the priest wasn't one of his own, and his robes revealed him to be one of Medina's. He couldn't remember bedding this one. Was he new?

The moment the meeting was over, Caspian made a beeline for the young priest. He was fair of hair with a clear and creamy complexion and Caspian was sure he hadn't had the pleasure of his company.

"And who might you be?" Caspian asked as he matched his pace to that of the priest, who was hurrying to keep up with his goddess.

"Bai," the young man replied with a hurried bow. "Your servant, sir."

"Have you been serving Medina long?"

"Just two days."

"And she already has you serving her at council meetings?"

"As you can see."

Medina looked over her shoulder. "Keep up, Bai. We have much to do today."

The priest scurried to catch her, but the goddess had come to a halt. She shooed him on past and waited for Caspian to reach her.

"Don't even think about it," Medina warned.

"He's most pleasing to the eye," Caspian replied. "Have you taken him to your bed yet?"

"Of course I have."

"What a shame. I would have enjoyed initiating him into the art of love."

Medina snorted. "What do *you* know about love?"

"I know as much as I need to."

"You know *nothing*!"

Caspian laughed. "For the Goddess of Love, you're equally ignorant in such matters."

"I know that you're leaving a trail of broken hearts behind you. I've had three of my priests begging me for help with capturing your heart."

"Really?"

"Yes."

"And what did you tell them?"

"The truth."

"Which is?"

"That you don't have a heart to be captured."

Caspian clutched his hand to his chest. "You wound me."

Medina smirked at him. "Not yet, but give me time."

Quick as lightning, Caspian grabbed Medina by the throat. "You dare to threaten me?"

20

Medina slipped from his grasp with ease. "You take men to your bed and once you're done with them, you cast them aside without a second thought. One day you'll feel the pain that they have suffered. There will come a time when the one you love will tear out your heart, and I cannot wait to see it."

"It'll never happen."

"Don't be so sure."

"I won't be falling in love, with anyone, so your threat will never come to pass."

Medina reached into her robes and pulled out a small vial held on a chain around her neck. "Are you sure about that? Bai is most handsome. I knew he would catch your eye from the moment I saw him in my temple. You couldn't take your eyes off him, could you? Tell me, Caspian, did you enjoy your wine?"

"Your love potions don't work on other gods," Caspian reminded her.

"Not usually," Medina agreed, "but this has a little something extra, especially brewed for you. Love is coming for you, Caspian. I've made sure of it, but you won't have it for long. You'll soon know what it's like to nurse a broken heart, and I will enjoy every second of your torment."

"You're bluffing," Caspian said, though he did recall a certain tang to the wine that he hadn't tasted before.

"I never bluff," Medina replied as she turned on her heel and strolled back to her temple, a jaunty whistle on her lips.

Caspian watched her walk away as he wondered whether she had truly managed to concoct a potion that would work on a god. Maybe his mother would know. She and Medina were close friends, after all.

Caspian found Odessa in her garden, pruning her roses. "Mother, do you have a moment?"

"Of course. Take a seat."

Caspian sat on the stone bench that was surprisingly comfortable for such a hard material. "Can I ask you a question?"

"Yes, what is it?"

"Is it possible for a love potion to work on a god?"

His mother whipped her head around to face him. "You don't have enough men in your bed already that you think to lure more in with magic?"

"No, of course not."

"Then why would you ask such a thing?"

"Medina was hinting that she'd slipped a love potion into my goblet at the meeting earlier."

"Oh, that's what it was, was it? I did wonder."

"You *saw* her?"

"Yes. I'm surprised you didn't, but you were rather distracted by her new priest."

"Damn. Do you think the potion will work on me?"

"Who knows?" his mother replied. "Most love potions are of short duration and merely invoke lust rather than the stronger and most lasting emotion of love. Even if she has brewed up a more powerful one for you, I doubt it would have any lasting effect."

"Good. The last thing I need is to fall in love."

His mother laughed airily. "I think it's long past time you fell in love. You need to find a nice young man to warm your bed for many years."

"I have plenty of men in my bed."

"And I'll bet you can't remember most of their names."

"Probably not, but what's the point, when their lives are so fleeting?"

"Perhaps you should look to finding a lover from another pantheon, if you truly cannot find someone among the Atlantean immortals—not that I imagine you've been trying very hard."

Caspian had no intention of doing anything of the sort. "The Egyptian gods are pretentious. The Norse are barbarians, and as for the Greeks and Romans—"

"You simply aren't looking hard enough," his mother interrupted. "If you got to know them, you'd find the gods of other pantheons are not so different from us."

"That may be true," Caspian agreed, "but it still doesn't change the fact that I have no intention of falling in love...with *anyone*."

"Maybe Medina's love potion, if she truly has slipped you one, will help with that."

"I doubt it. She said quite plainly that she wants me to fall in love and lose him."

His mother, who had been regarding him with mild amusement during the course of the conversation, paled considerably. "She's cursed you? I'll have her head!"

"Calm down, Mother. She didn't invoke her powers. She was just ranting."

"Still... A god or goddess should always be careful of their words. Let's hope that you *don't* lose your love."

"How about we hope I don't find him at all?" Caspian suggested.

Odessa sighed. "I don't understand why you're so opposed to finding a nice young man to share your life. Your father and I have been content for centuries, and I'd like to see you happily settled too. People do comment that I, the Goddess of Fertility, Family and the Home, have a son who openly shuns everything I stand for."

"Don't start…"

"I'm not," Odessa replied, even though Caspian could see that she definitely was.

"I need to head to my temple," Caspian said, making a quick escape before his mother could launch into one of her tiresome lectures on how he lived his life. He had heard it all before and had no intention of changing.

Chapter Three

Phoebus kicked the sand in frustration as his latest attempt to break his mating fever failed, just like the last.

"Maybe you *do* need a mermaid?" Ajax suggested. "I know you say you don't find the female form arousing, but it's not like you've ever tried to bed one of them."

Phoebus shook his head. "The trigger to break my fever is supposed to be what I desire the most. I think I'd know if I wanted a female. Can't you think of something else to try?"

Ajax held up his hand and marked on his fingers. "I've penetrated you and you've done me, though you couldn't release. We've tried you on all fours, on your back, on your side. Now I've tried using my hand on your cock, but nothing."

Phoebus glared down at his aching erection. What would it take to get rid of the wretched thing? There had to be something they hadn't tried, but he couldn't think what. He had hoped that Ajax, a year older than he was and having participated in three other mating seasons, all with different mermen, might have had a few ideas.

"How did you find out what your trigger was?" Phoebus asked.

"I just found a willing body to stick it in and the fever vanished," Ajax replied with a shrug. "I knew I wanted to do that with someone—I'd seen other mermen take their pleasure in such a manner—and it worked just as I expected it to."

"Well, it didn't work for me. Are you sure you can't think of anything else to try?"

"I saw a mermaid getting a good spanking in the coconut grove last season," Ajax suggested. "Do you want me to try that?"

Phoebus shook his head. "No, definitely not."

"Then I'm out of ideas. Perhaps you need to consult an expert."

"What do you mean?"

"The Atlanteans look to their gods when they have problems. They pray to them for help, and sometimes they answer."

"You're not suggesting I pray to them, are you?"

"Why not?"

"Well, for one thing, I'm not an Atlantean. I'm mer. Why would their god listen to me?"

"Goddess."

"God, goddess, what difference does it make? I'm still mer."

"The Goddess of Love, Lust and Carnal Desire has been known to show herself to the mer. They call her Medina, and she's invited several of the mer into her bed."

"Really?"

"Well, I don't know for sure, but that's what the gossips in the market say."

26

"And you think she'd want to help *me?*"

"Why not? You're a handsome young merman and those mismatched eyes of yours are most striking. I think she'll be only too happy to invite you into her bed."

"I don't know. Goddess or not, she's still female, and outside of the mating season, I've only ever felt desire for the male form."

"She has many priests," Ajax said. "If they're skilled enough to satisfy a goddess, surely she could spare one of them to help you."

Phoebus sighed. "I suppose it can't hurt to try calling to her. It's not as if I have any other ideas." His mind made up, he returned to the sea, where he transformed into his half-fish form for the long swim home.

Back in the sunken city, it only took a quick enquiry at the market to discover which temple belonged to the Goddess of Love. Even though he was a little nervous — and a lot skeptical — he swam into the building. The temple was surprisingly crowded. Two priests, dressed in robes with the flowered trident emblem of their goddess embroidered on the breast, swam among the other visitors, smiling and talking to those who had come to seek advice and help from the goddess they served.

One of the priests glanced his way and did an immediate double-take. Phoebus realized that he was the only mer in the temple. He wondered if the rumors of the goddess taking mer as lovers might be nothing more than tall tales.

"Why do you seek advice from the Goddess of Love?" asked the priest, his voice as clear in Phoebus' head as that of any of the mer.

"I, um, it's the mating season..."

"And you can't find a mate?"

27

"No, I went to land with someone, but we couldn't... I mean, I couldn't, um..."

"Ah, well, perhaps our goddess might be able to help you. If you call to Medina by name, she will hear your prayer, and if you're lucky, she might answer it for you."

Phoebus nodded, and at a gesture from the priest, he approached the statue of the Goddess of Love.

"Medina? Um, I don't know if you can hear me, but they say you might be able to help with my problem. I can't break my mating fever."

Phoebus felt a little foolish projecting his voice to someone who might not even be listening, especially when doing so no doubt alerted everyone in the room to his problem.

"There's no need to be embarrassed."

Phoebus gave a small cry as he fell to the ground in a room that was the same as the one he had been in a moment ago, except it was on land. He flopped on the floor in front of the goddess.

"Welcome to the Isle of the Gods, Phoebus. I must say that it's rare for one of the mer to seek my assistance." Medina tossed him a sheet of fabric, which he used to dry his fins and regain his legs. She sat on a nearby couch, her gauzy robe leaving nothing to the imagination. "Unfortunately, I can tell that my personal assistance is not what you need."

Phoebus ducked his head. "Sorry."

Medina laughed. "No need to apologize, my darling. No one can help who they find attractive."

"It's not that I don't find you beautiful," Phoebus hurried to assure her. "You *are*. It's just..."

"That you find the male body more arousing. Of course, this does present something of a problem for me in helping you to break your mating fever, since I obviously don't have what you need."

Phoebus hung his head. "Thank you for hearing me anyway. I guess I knew it wasn't likely to help."

"Now, now, don't be so hasty." Medina patted the seat beside her. "Come sit with me and tell me about yourself while I ponder which of my priests might be most suitable to assist you."

"They won't mind being forced to mate with me?"

Medina laughed. "Mind? Oh no, they'd be delighted to be given such an honor as to take you to bed to please me. Tell me, Phoebus, how many mating seasons have you suffered through without release?"

"This is my second. The first wasn't so bad, but the pain is worse this time."

"It will get worse every season you go without release. What did you try?"

"Everything we could think of."

Medina gave him a sly smile. "If you've only been trying for two seasons, I suspect that isn't much. The art of making love can take many forms, but you're young and inexperienced."

Phoebus' face heated, but the goddess patted his hand in a kindly gesture. "We were all young and inexperienced once, even me. Only with the passing of time can we learn."

"And you truly think one of your priests can teach me what I need?"

Medina gave him a considering look. "I think perhaps there might be another who can help you more than any of my priests. Have you heard of the God of Justice?"

Phoebus shook his head. "I don't really know any of the Atlantean gods. We mer don't worship you like the Atlanteans do."

"No, I suppose not, though many of us would welcome your devotion, if it were given freely and with love in your heart. Anyway, the God of Justice is named Caspian, and he, like you, is a lover of men. He knows as much about sexual desire between men as myself, but he has the cock I lack to put it into practice."

"Would he help me if you asked him to?"

Medina snorted in a most un-goddess-like manner. "If *I* were to ask him, he'd definitely say no. We don't get along."

"Oh, well, is there another god who might help me?"

"You misunderstand me," Medina said. "Just because Caspian won't do anything *I* ask him, it doesn't mean he might not assist you if you were to ask him personally."

"Thank you, Medina. Um, how do I get back to the sunken city to find his temple?"

"He has a temple here on the Isle of the Gods. You can approach him there. Let me find someone to escort you."

Medina led him from the temple and out into a beautiful garden. There were several handsome men in various states of undress stretched out on the grass. Two of the men were naked and rubbing up against each other with feverish moans of pleasure. Phoebus tried not to stare, but as they had to walk right by them, it was rather difficult to avoid watching.

"Did you try that?" Medina asked. "The pleasure to be obtained from frottage is a favorite among many of my priests."

Phoebus nodded. "I tried that my first mating season but nothing happened, save that my lover spilled over my body."

Medina waved over a handsome man in robes that bore a different emblem to that of her priests. The trident was the same, but it seemed to have some form of snake twined around it. "Isander, would your goddess spare you for a few moments?"

Isander grinned. "I'm sure she could. How can I serve the sister of my goddess?"

Medina urged Phoebus forward. "Isander serves my sister, Mariana, Goddess of Sea Creatures. Isander, this is Phoebus, who seeks the assistance of Caspian. Would you mind escorting him to Caspian's temple?"

"Of course. Do you wish me to provide him with a robe on the way?"

"No. Phoebus is mer, and Caspian is well acquainted with naked men. I'd take him myself, but I'm afraid I have other duties to attend to."

Isander gave a sweeping bow. "As always, I'm delighted to be of service."

Medina smiled and waved them on their way.

"So why do you want justice?" Isander asked as they strolled along a winding path.

"I don't," Phoebus replied. "I need help breaking my mating fever, and Medina thought Caspian might be able to assist."

Isander gave a booming laugh. "I have no doubt he'll give it his best. And if he fails, come find me and I'll try too."

Phoebus flushed at the blatant invitation from the handsome Atlantean. "Maybe I will," he said. "Do I call for you in Mariana's temple?"

"Goodness no!" Isander shook his head. "My goddess has no love for the mer at all. If you poke a fin into her temple, she'll be furious."

"But Medina said she was the Goddess of Sea Creatures."

"She is."

"The mer are creatures of the sea."

"I know." Isander glanced around, clearly checking they weren't likely to be overheard. "Mariana is most tiresome in her prejudices against the mer. Just take my advice and stay away from her and the rest of her priests."

"I will."

"Well, here we are." Isander pointed to the temple directly ahead. "Just go in and ask for him. There's sure to be at least one of his priests in there."

"Won't he wonder how I got here?"

"I doubt it. Many Atlanteans bring their lovers here to the Isle of the Gods. We're not really supposed to, but everyone does it. Good luck!"

Isander gave him a little nudge in the small of his back and Phoebus steeled himself to face the Atlantean God of Justice.

* * * *

Caspian looked up as a shadow fell across his face. Rafe stood in the doorway. "Yes?"

"There's a merman asking for you in your temple audience chamber."

Caspian frowned. "The only person in there at the moment is an Atlantean woman." The weaver, who had no concept of the difference between petty revenge and true justice, had been there for hours, praying to Caspian for him to send plagues of boils and other delights to the rival who had stolen her man. Caspian had been tuning her out as much as he could.

"Not the temple in Atlantis, the one here," Rafe explained.

"How did he get here?" Caspian asked. Immediately his thoughts turned to Medina and he wondered if this was her doing.

"I saw him approach with Isander, one of Mariana's priests."

"Ah." Caspian smiled. "That would explain it. No doubt Isander brought the merman here and now finds his goddess lingering around, so he can't send him home without incurring her wrath. Show them in."

"Isander has already left, but the merman waits in the audience chamber."

Caspian didn't like Isander's presumption that he would solve the problem of the wandering merman, but supposed he would have to go see him, unless he wanted to leave him hanging around in his temple, getting underfoot and making a nuisance of himself until such time as it was safe to return to Atlantis by the same method he had arrived.

The naked merman stood in the middle of the audience chamber. He stared at Caspian's statue, though Caspian doubted it was his rendition that had triggered such arousal in the merman. The solstice of the previous night was no doubt to blame for that. He wondered why Isander hadn't taken the trouble to give his friend the release he clearly needed before dropping him off at the temple.

Caspian strode over to his throne and sat on the cushioned seat. "I'm Caspian, God of Justice. What brings you here, merman?"

The merman, who Caspian realized was younger than he had first thought—perhaps only eighteen summers—stared at him from a pair of mismatched eyes, one dark blue and one light blue. Caspian found himself unable to look away.

"Do you seek justice?" Caspian asked when the merman continued to gaze at him silently.

He shook his head and flushed scarlet as his gaze traveled over the various priests who were working away in the room, clearing away the remnants of the feast of the previous night.

Caspian clapped his hands together and his priests jumped to attention. "I sense our guest is shy. Leave us."

The priests hurried to obey.

"Not you, Rafe. I may need you." Caspian pointed to the priest's usual spot in the room. "Now, merman, what is your name?"

"Phoebus."

"And what do you want from me, if not justice?"

"Um..." Phoebus hung his head and mumbled something too quiet for a mortal to hear, but which was no problem for a god.

"I see," Caspian replied. "A mating fever that won't break, and what makes you think I'm the one to help you with your problem?"

"I was told you were familiar with such matters."

"I am indeed," Caspian said. After the business with Medina earlier that morning, the day was looking up. He had bedded a few mermen over the years, but never one who was in the heat of a mating fever. "Well, what have you tried so far to break your fever?"

Phoebus gave a shrug and offered his pitifully short list of things. Caspian could immediately think of half a dozen things they might try.

"Rafe, what do you think our friend should attempt first?"

Phoebus gave Rafe a look of hope.

"Sucking?" Rafe suggested.

"How would you like that, Phoebus? Rafe is an expert at sucking a man to the brink of an orgasm."

"Sucking?" Phoebus asked.

Caspian chuckled. "How refreshing to meet such an innocent. Rafe, if you don't mind..."

Rafe walked over to Phoebus, turned his back to Caspian and dropped to his knees.

Phoebus stared down at Rafe with wide eyes as the priest took the merman's cock into his mouth and set to work.

Watching Rafe and Phoebus was as arousing as anything Caspian had ever experienced.

Rafe continued his attentions for several minutes before pulling away and looking over his shoulder. "It doesn't seem to be working. Maybe we should try something else?"

Phoebus nodded his agreement. "Rafe is right. This isn't working."

Rafe rose from his knees. "I could give him a good spanking."

Phoebus snorted. "No! And why does everyone seem to think hitting me will help?"

Caspian smiled. "No one will raise a hand to you without your consent, that I promise. There are, however, some men and women who find pleasure from pain."

"I'm fairly sure I'm not one of them," Phoebus replied.

"Then we will look at other methods."

Caspian shifted slightly in his seat, his own arousal shielded by his loose robes but no doubt obvious to both Rafe and Phoebus.

The merman licked his lips, his gaze locked on the tent of Caspian's robes.

"Ah, now you have the look of a man who knows what he wants." He crooked his finger to beckon Phoebus closer. "Is that what you need, Phoebus? To wrap your lips around another man's cock and suck him until he spills his seed into your mouth?"

"I don't know."

Caspian unclasped his robe and moved the material aside, revealing his erection. He could practically see the merman's mouth watering at the sight.

"Come kneel before me," Caspian said. He tossed a cushion between his feet, ignoring Rafe's brief flash of annoyance that he hadn't given him one when he had knelt before Phoebus.

Phoebus approached him slowly and knelt between Caspian's legs.

"You saw — felt — what Rafe did to you. Now it's your turn."

Phoebus leaned in and licked at the end of Caspian's cock. Then he slowly sucked at the head, his eyes closed in deep concentration. Caspian gripped the arms of his throne to keep himself from bucking into the young mer's mouth. He reminded himself that the man on his knees was inexperienced and may not want Caspian thrusting into his mouth with his usual wild enthusiasm.

He sensed Rafe watching them and looked up, offering him a smile. Rafe didn't seem to notice, his attention fixed on the merman, jealousy clear in his eyes.

Caspian sighed. He really must do something about that. He had made it clear to Rafe when he had first entered his service, some twenty years ago, that he would always have to share Caspian with other men.

Phoebus continued to suck him, making sounds of contentment.

"That's it," Caspian encouraged. "Are you sure you've never done this before? Oh my…yes, harder."

Phoebus took him at his word and sucked him in earnest.

Caspian moaned as he drew closer to the brink. He stroked Phoebus' face, his skin still hot to the touch.

Then he began to come and the merman's fever started to recede. Phoebus stiffened and stopped working his mouth up and down Caspian's cock. It seemed they had found his trigger.

When Phoebus pulled away, his face was still flushed, and he gestured at the foot of the throne. "I'm sorry. I seem to have made a bit of a mess."

"Don't worry about it," Caspian said. He waved his hand and cleared up the evidence of Phoebus' orgasm in an instant. "The advantages of being a god."

Phoebus sat back on his heels. "Thank you."

"No, thank *you*." Caspian held out his hand and pulled Phoebus to his feet. "I assume you'll want to return to Atlantis now?"

"Yes, please. Unless... Well...did you want something from me in return?"

"No, of course not." Caspian guided Phoebus to the crystal that would open the portal to Atlantis. "I hope you'll visit me again, maybe next mating season."

Caspian didn't know why he had suggested such a thing. The handsome young merman must have dozens of offers for company during the mating season, and it wasn't as if he, Caspian, had a shortage of willing men eager to join him in his bed if he were to click his fingers. One of them was Rafe, of course, who stood a few feet away, glowering with discontent.

Once Phoebus was on his way, Caspian gave his High Priest his undivided attention. He didn't say anything at first, but instead probed his mind for his thoughts.

Caspian didn't often read the minds of his priests. They were loyal to him and he rewarded their devotion with allowing them their privacy — most of the time.

"Jealousy is most unbecoming," he said. "It's an ugly trait, especially when there is no cause for it."

"I'm not jealous of *him*."

37

"You know you cannot lie to a god," Caspian told him. "I've lived long enough to recognize the signs, even without my powers."

"Why did you invite him back next solstice?"

"The next mating one isn't for another two seasons. I doubt he'll even remember my offer."

"Then you don't intend to have him suck you again?"

"I don't intend to track him down, but if he comes to me, I will not turn him away."

"He's a merman."

"I am well aware of that. Do you have a problem with mermen? Or is it just the fact that I allowed him to pleasure me?"

Rafe bowed his head. "I have no problem."

"Good."

Caspian disappeared back to his private quarters, content to relive the moment the handsome young merman had pushed him over the brink.

Chapter Four

Phoebus floated on the surface of the sea. A prod at his fins startled him and he flipped over as Ajax popped up beside him.

"Where have you been?" Ajax asked. "Did you talk to the goddess?"

Phoebus nodded and smiled as he stretched his arms and relaxed once more. "I did."

"And?" Ajax placed a hand on his brow. "Well, your fever's gone. Did you need a woman after all?"

"No," Phoebus replied, easing Ajax's palm aside.

"Then how did you break it?"

"Medina sent me to talk to Caspian."

"Who's he?"

"The Atlantean God of Justice."

"Ah, I see. *That* Caspian."

Phoebus' face heated as he recalled his wanton behavior in the temple of the god.

"Well, aren't you going to tell me what your trigger is?" Ajax asked. "It might be nice to know for next season."

Phoebus shrugged. "My fever broke when I sucked Caspian's cock."

"You *what*?" Ajax gaped at him.

"I sucked his cock." Phoebus shivered a little as the memory sent a fresh wave of desire through him.

Ajax continued to stare at him. "I've never heard of mer doing that before."

"Me neither, but neither of us is that old, and my partner during my first mating season was untouched as well. I guess I just needed to speak with someone who had more experience."

Ajax scowled. "I have more experience than you. I'm not some innocent who doesn't know what to do with his cock."

Phoebus rolled his eyes. "There's no need to be offended. Things will work out fine next season. You can bury yourself in my arse until you come, then later, when you're ready again, I'll be able to suck you until you climax again. The taste of your seed in my mouth will be as intoxicating as that of Caspian's."

Ajax swam in the direction of the beach. "Why wait for the mating season? Come on. You can educate me now."

Phoebus laughed as he darted through the waves, overtaking Ajax and arriving at the beach far ahead of him. He already had his legs by the time Ajax flopped down beside him.

There wasn't a soul on the beach, many of the mer only coming to land during the mating seasons and rarely during the hours of daylight, when there was much work to be done in the ocean.

Phoebus stroked his length as he waited for Ajax to dry his fins.

"What was he like?" Ajax asked.

"Who? Caspian?"

"Who else? He's a god and we've all seen the statues the Atlanteans build in honor of their deities. Are they true to life?"

"Caspian's is. I mean, the statue of him in the temple is bigger than he is, but it's an accurate representation of his features."

"From what I've heard, the God of Justice has many lovers, all men."

"Does he?"

"Yes."

Phoebus continued to play with himself, his body reacting to the thought of Caspian. Would the god have forgotten him already? Or maybe he was using his powers to watch them right now?

"Was he a good lover?" Ajax asked.

"I wouldn't say we were lovers at all."

"But he broke your mating fever."

"Yes, but all he did was sit there while I knelt between his legs and sucked his cock until he came in my mouth. At that point I came as well, and that was that."

"Did you kiss him?"

"Of course not." Phoebus snorted at the ridiculous idea of kissing the god.

"Why not?"

"I don't think it would have been appropriate."

"You've kissed me."

"That's different. We're friends as well as lovers."

Ajax made a noise of triumph as his legs and cock appeared at last. "I suppose you're right. Now, how about you show me what you learned from the god?"

Phoebus didn't need any further invitation. He dove on Ajax's cock and sucked him into his mouth. Now that his fever had gone and the desperation to find release had abated, he could take his time, and he intended to do just that.

Ajax moaned as Phoebus licked at his length, using his tongue to stroke his testicles. He tasted of saltwater, as did all mer after they'd emerged from the depths of the ocean.

"Ah, yes," Ajax moaned, "that feels so good."

Phoebus' hard shaft ached for attention and he rubbed himself against Ajax's leg, dividing his attention between pleasuring Ajax and driving himself closer to the brink.

"Turn around," Ajax ordered.

Phoebus released the tip of Ajax's cock and frowned at him. "What do you mean?"

"Exactly what I said," Ajax replied. "I want to suck you too. If you turn around, I can do that while you're doing me."

Phoebus nodded with eagerness and swiftly changed his position.

Even though he hadn't come when Rafe had sucked him, Phoebus knew that outside of the mating season, it wouldn't be a problem. When Ajax's lips touched his cock, Phoebus cried out and he began to shake with desire. Only Ajax's firm grip at the base of his shaft prevented him from humiliating himself by lasting no more than a couple of seconds.

He lowered his head over Ajax's cock once again and sucked him hard. If he was going to come so quickly, he wanted Ajax to do likewise.

Ajax copied his moves and Phoebus slowly pushed his way into his lover's mouth, easing in and out of the wet heat as he moved his mouth up and down Ajax's shaft at the same pace.

Phoebus could tell he wouldn't last long. His eagerness for sucking cock made him ache for release. Ajax fondled his balls and probed his arse with his fingers, each touch bringing Phoebus closer to the pleasure he craved. He lavished the same attention on Ajax, poking at his arsehole with a finger, causing him to buck his hips and push his cock right back into Phoebus' throat.

Ajax's mouth vanished from his cock as he screamed out his pleasure, spilling into Phoebus' mouth with such force Phoebus couldn't keep up with all his seed. It spilled from Phoebus' lips as he frantically swallowed what he could.

The taste of his lover sent a final wave of lust through his body and he came over Ajax's chest and neck. Ajax, too sated to do anything other than lie there, panted and moaned.

Phoebus collapsed onto the sand beside Ajax and rolled onto his back.

"I can see the attraction of such play," Ajax finally commented.

Phoebus chuckled. "Me too."

"Was I better than the god?" Ajax teased.

Phoebus laughed. "I don't kiss and tell."

"You didn't kiss him at all," Ajax reminded him. "Is he bigger than me?"

The temptation to say yes, just to see his friend's reaction, was almost too much to resist. Ajax was big and he knew it. He prided himself on having more below the waist than most other mermen and, at times like this, enjoyed having his ego stroked nearly as much as his cock.

"No, he's not," Phoebus admitted. His jaw still ached a little from their earlier activities, though thankfully the soreness in his arse from the night of the solstice had subsided.

"I didn't think so," Ajax replied, gloating openly.

Phoebus poked Ajax in the ribs. "Bigger isn't always better, you know."

"Better than being so small you can't even feel it when he shoves it up your arse."

Phoebus glanced fleetingly at his own cock, measuring it against those of other mermen.

Ajax laughed. "I wasn't talking about you. You're fine."

"Fine?"

"Adequate."

Phoebus glared. "That's not an improvement."

Ajax rolled onto his side and leaned on his elbow. "You have nothing to be ashamed of. Now, how about you give me all the details of your dalliance with the god?"

Phoebus' annoyance vanished and he told Ajax everything he could recall, which would never be enough to satisfy his friend's appetite for the dirty details. As he spoke, he considered that it might not be enough for him either.

Caspian had invited him back again next mating season, but that didn't mean the god would remember his suggestion when the time came. Still, the idea of seeing the handsome god again was deliciously tempting.

* * * *

"Caspian, there you are." Cari breezed into the room and settled herself onto the chaise. "I've been searching everywhere for you."

Caspian sipped his wine before answering his sister. "Well, now you've found me."

Cari helped herself to a glass of her own. "Since when do you travel to this part of the world?"

"I needed some time alone," Caspian replied. Rafe's jealousies had pushed him to his limit today, so he had escaped to a small province in Italia for a little peace and quiet. Hiding from his priest wasn't difficult, but avoiding his sister was another matter entirely.

"Rafe?" Cari asked.

"You know I don't like it when you poke into my head." He managed to block most of the immortals from his mind, but his sister appeared to have the ability to bypass all his defenses. He supposed it came from being the Goddess of Prophecy.

"I didn't," Cari replied. "But when I checked your palace, he was ranting about some merman you'd fucked. I simply drew my own conclusions."

"I didn't fuck him."

"Rafe seems to think otherwise."

Caspian rolled his eyes. "Rafe was present in the room the entire time. He is well aware of what we did."

Cari huffed. "Did you ever think that your priest might not get quite so jealous if you didn't make him watch you with other men?"

"The merman was having trouble breaking his mating fever. He came to me for help, we broke his fever and he returned to the ocean. That was it."

"What was his name?"

"Who? The merman?"

"Yes, him."

"Phoebus. Why do you want to know?"

"Just curious. I spoke to Mother this morning."

"And what did she have to say for herself?"

"She told me Medina had slipped you a love potion."

"Apparently. She added something to my wine, but I don't know what. She was probably bluffing."

Cari laughed briefly. "Don't you know by now that Medina never bluffs?"

"Well, it doesn't seem to have had much of an impact on me. Probably she isn't as good at brewing up mischief as she likes to think."

Cari sipped her wine. "You never did figure out the difference between a love potion and one that simply inspires lust."

"What do you mean?"

"I mean that if she'd given you the latter, which is what she hands out to most who seek her services, you'd be fucking that young merman right now. A true love potion, on the other hand, takes time to work, just like real love takes time to grow."

"What are you saying? You think I'm going to fall in love with someone? The merman?"

"Like it or not, you are about to discover what falling in love is like."

"I think I'll let that particular experience pass me by, thank you all the same."

"You seem to be laboring under the mistaken belief you have a choice in the matter."

"I do."

Cari finished her glass of wine and poured herself another. "I took a peek into your future after I spoke to Mother."

"I suppose telling you I don't want to know about my future would be pointless?"

"It would."

"Very well. Tell me what you saw, and if I don't like it, I'll do what I need to so I can change it."

"You can't alter course mid-stream."

"Says who?"

"Fate."

"I don't believe in fate."

"It doesn't matter what you believe in. You've met Phoebus, and been intimate with him, just hours after drinking Medina's concoction."

"He only sucked me."

"That's more than enough to trigger the potion. Chances are, if it's one of Medina's brews, the touch of your hand to his would have been enough."

"I'm probably never going to see him again," Caspian said, even though the thought of a second encounter with the merman made his heart race.

"I assure you, you'll be seeing him very soon. He's a nice man and I think he'll be very good for you."

"Why are you and Mother so eager to see me settled down with just one man? I'm perfectly happy as I am."

"Are you?"

"Yes."

Cari shook her head. "When you've fallen for him, when you're head over heels, desperately in love with him, you'll know what perfect happiness is."

"Oh, please." Caspian rolled his eyes.

"You'll see."

Caspian sighed and finished his wine. "I don't know why you're so eager for me to find someone to settle down with. You know that if I do, you'll be next in line for Mother's meddling in your love life."

Cari smirked. "I told Mother years ago that I've seen my soul mate and will embrace him when the time comes. That has kept her from interfering for centuries and will continue to keep her out of my business for many years to come."

"Have you really seen your soul mate?"

"Of course not. I haven't looked."

Caspian had to admire her guts at lying to their mother. He wasn't sure he would have dared.

Cari stood and straightened her gown. "Don't let your stubbornness keep you from Phoebus. Just do what you would normally do if Medina hadn't told you about the potion. Let nature take its course."

Caspian nodded, but the gesture was more automatic than agreement. When he looked up, his sister had vanished. He finished his wine and poured himself another, wishing, not for the first time, that it was possible for immortals to actually become intoxicated. Goodness knew that if anything called for it, his present circumstances surely did.

* * * *

Phoebus sat in the tavern listening to the Atlanteans talking about their days. The lives of the humans under the sea weren't so very different from those of the mer, yet they rarely socialized together. This evening, however, Phoebus wanted to listen to the bard who told stories of the gods for the entertainment of the patrons.

He had heard that stories about Medina, the Goddess of Love, were the most popular, with those of Caspian a close second. He was curious to know what the stories said about the god who had helped him discover his mating trigger.

Settling into a corner of the room, he nibbled on a piece of fruit as he waited for the bard to start.

It seemed his luck was in, and the storyteller had tales of Caspian to relay tonight.

"Caspian acquires lovers like no other immortal," he told his captive audience. *"Men flock to him like bees to a honey pot. He can satisfy a dozen men in a single night, and his bed is big enough to hold even more."*

Phoebus wondered how much he heard was true and how much was embellishment to satisfy the audience.

"Tell us of the night he bedded the muses!" someone called from the front of the room.

"Ah, the muses," the bard replied. *"Female in form, they were determined to discover the truth of Caspian's prowess, so they changed their forms to those of men in order to seduce him. But such spells cannot fool a god like Caspian. He saw through their disguises immediately and transformed his two highest ranking priests so that they took his form. Then he challenged the muses to figure out which of the three of them was him. If they correctly guessed, he would fuck them in their male forms, but if they mistook one of his priests for him, they would gift all of his priests with unique talents. Needless to say, the muses failed to identify Caspian, and from that day to this, Caspian has priests who are accomplished not only in bed, but also in music and the arts. It is said that one of his former high priests crafted the statues of Caspian that reside in his temples, so you can see for yourselves the talent they possess."*

Several patrons nodded to each other, clearly having seen the evidence for themselves. Phoebus had seen the statues as well, but he had no idea as to the truth of the story.

The bard took a short break and when he returned he started a new tale, this one focusing on a great battle between the Atlanteans and the Greeks, long before the city had sunk below the ocean. There was no mention of Caspian in the story and Phoebus soon found his mind wandering. He was so deep in his thoughts that he didn't notice Ajax swimming over to him.

"What are you doing here?" Ajax asked. "I thought you'd be up on the island tonight."

"It's not the solstice."

"No, but there's a party of guards celebrating the killing of those two sharks the other day. The gatherers are invited, so long as we bring some food for the feast. I thought you'd be there, but instead you're hanging around here."

"I was just listening to the bard," Phoebus explained.

"Ah." Ajax gave him a knowing glance. "Let me guess… He's been telling stories of Caspian?"

"Just one," Phoebus replied. "I think he's done now, if you want to go to the island."

Ajax made no move to swim toward the door. "Why are you so interested in hearing stories about him?"

"I don't know. I guess I want to know more about the god whose cock I sucked."

"If that's the case, why not go and visit him again? You'll find out far more from the man himself than you would listening to a hundred bards."

"I'm sure he's far too busy."

"Not too busy to fuck every man who offers up his arse," Ajax countered.

Phoebus toyed with his fins. "Do you really think he's that bad?"

"Everyone says so. Not that there are any complaints about his, er, performance. But the fact of the matter is, Caspian is the most promiscuous of the gods and only his priests hold his attention for longer than a few fucks."

"I wonder what makes his priests so special?"

"They probably aren't. Getting fucked by their god is considered a perk of the job."

"I wonder if he's ever had any mer priests?" Phoebus commented.

"You aren't thinking of offering to serve him, are you?"

"No!" Phoebus shook his head. *"I was just wondering. I don't worship the gods any more than you do."*

Ajax gave him a doubtful frown. *"You need to get him out of your mind – and fast. I suggest you go to his temple, spread your legs and let him fuck you now. Don't drag things out by waiting for the next solstice. Once he's bored with you, you can move on and find a merman to spend your life with."*

"You think he'll tire of me that quickly?"

Ajax nodded to the bard. *"You've been listening to his stories. You know Caspian's reputation. Just be prepared for him to cast you aside once he's done with you. Do not give this god your heart. He won't know what to do with it."*

Phoebus didn't want to be just another man Caspian fucked. Even though he knew it was foolish to hope for more, he couldn't seem to stop himself.

Chapter Five

Caspian lasted four days. Three and a half, if he had to be precise. Then the temptation to seek out Phoebus became too much.

Summoning the merman to his palace would be easy, though Caspian was reluctant to do so with Rafe glowering at him from every shadowy corner.

The island of the mer was more appealing, but Caspian preferred the comfort of a bed to the sandy beach.

Eventually, Caspian decided he would take Phoebus elsewhere, to show him something of the world. The mer had seen so little of the world of men, and he would enjoy showing Phoebus the delights to be found on land.

Caspian found a quiet glade on the outskirts of Rome and, after deciding it was suitable, searched with his mind to locate Phoebus and bring him there.

"Phoebus?" Caspian called to the merman telepathically.

"Who's that?" The reply sounded sleepy and Caspian belatedly realized he might have intruded on Phoebus at an inconvenient time.

"This is Caspian."

"Caspian?" Phoebus sounded slightly more alert, if a little confused.

"Yes. The Atlantean God of Justice. You came to my temple a few days ago."

"I hadn't forgotten." Laughter echoed through Caspian's mind. *"I just didn't expect to hear from you."*

"I invited you to seek me out at the next solstice."

"That's still two seasons away."

"I know."

Phoebus didn't say anything in response and Caspian contemplated how he might break the silence without sounding like a fool.

"Have you ever been to the Roman baths?" he finally asked.

"Of course not. I've never been to any land populated by humans."

"Would you like to?"

"I don't know. Humans can be dangerous. We mer try to avoid them."

"I would protect you from any who would do you harm."

"Perhaps somewhere else?" Phoebus suggested. *"Somewhere with less water."*

"I have the power to erase the memory of anyone who sees your fins. You need not worry on that account."

"You have that much power?"

"Yes. But if you'd rather go somewhere else instead, we can do that."

"Very well."

The moment Phoebus gave his consent, Caspian summoned him to his side.

The merman blinked up at him from the grass and Caspian crouched down beside him. He handed him a towel and waited for the merman to dry his fins.

Phoebus regained his legs and clambered to his feet.

Caspian took a moment to admire the form of the merman, before reluctantly providing him with suitable attire.

Phoebus plucked at the material with distaste. "Humans have such strange customs."

"They do indeed," Caspian agreed. "I much prefer you naked, but the locals might object. Well, some of them might. Others would no doubt appreciate the view as much as I do."

Phoebus blushed but didn't lower his eyes. Caspian liked his boldness.

"You can really make sure no one remembers seeing my fins?"

"Yes, though would it make any real difference if I didn't? Mer are often spotted by ships and more than one sailor has netted himself a mermaid for a wife. We aren't staying long, and I can whisk you back to Atlantis in the blink of an eye. They would never find you. They would just have a story to tell their friends of the merman they saw right here in the city."

Phoebus held out his hand for Caspian to take. "You promise to get me out of there if any danger arises?"

"I give you my word as a god."

"Then let us visit the baths."

Caspian hooked Phoebus' arm through his and they walked through the trees toward the city. "How have you heard about the Roman baths?"

"The Atlanteans. They often tell stories of other cultures in the taverns in Atlantis. I like to go and listen to them. Tales of what takes place in the baths are most popular among men like me."

"Ah, I see. Well, time may have moved on since we sank Atlantis beneath the waves, but the Roman baths have changed very little. I think we shall visit one that is frequented by men such as us."

"There are places especially for gods and mermen?" Phoebus asked.

Caspian gaped at him, before he glimpsed the twitch of Phoebus' lips and realized he was teasing him. He found he liked that.

"There are baths for men who seek the touch of other men. What happens inside those walls is a poorly kept secret."

The nearer they drew to the baths, the more aroused Caspian became. He asked Phoebus questions about him and his family in an attempt to distract himself from his increasingly painful erection. He was surprised to find that he enjoyed discovering more about Phoebus and his life.

"I grew up in Atlantis," Phoebus said. "My grandparents were from a clan who lived under the northern ice, but they came south because their parents didn't approve of their mating. My grandfather was from a family who believed in defending themselves from predators, while my grandmother's family thought that all creatures deserved to be left in peace. They wouldn't even defend themselves from bears or sharks. They would rather sacrifice themselves and give the rest of the family time to escape. So my grandparents fled south and settled in Atlantis."

"Are they still there?"

"No, my grandfather returned to the waters before I was born, and my grandmother about five years ago."

Caspian patted Phoebus' hand in quiet understanding. "I'm sorry to hear that."

"Thank you. What about you? Obviously your parents will still be alive, being immortal, after all."

"Yes, they are both still with us, though it is possible to kill an immortal. Just because we don't age and die from natural causes, it doesn't mean we're completely impervious to harm."

"I didn't realize that."

"We don't exactly shout it from the rooftops. Anyway, my father is the God of War and my mother is the Goddess of Fertility, Hearth, and Home. I have one sister, Cari, who is the Goddess of Prophecy. Do you have any siblings?"

"I'm the youngest of four," Phoebus replied. "I have one sister and two brothers, though my oldest brother prefers the rootless existence of traveling around the oceans."

"A dangerous way to live," Caspian said. "I will remember him in my blessings and hope he stays safe."

"That's most kind of you."

"Think nothing of it."

They continued on their way and the smells of the countryside were replaced by the stench of the city.

"What do you do to pass the time?" Caspian asked.

"I work in the fruit fields. It's not the most taxing of occupations, but it's a necessary job."

"There's nothing to be ashamed of about working in the fields. Not everyone can handle a spear or trident, and if every merman joined the guards, the inhabitants of the city would soon be starving."

"I know, but sometimes I think my parents would prefer it if their youngest son were a little more adventurous."

"Is your second brother in the guards?" Caspian guessed.

"Yes, and my sister, much to the dismay of our parents."

"I didn't realize the guards were allowing mermaids in their ranks."

"They don't usually, but she defeated every merman in the barracks, including the leader, so they didn't have much choice in the matter."

"They could still have refused her."

"I suppose, but she managed to talk them around. I think her final argument won them over."

"What was that?"

"That there was one opening and two applicants for the position. It was allow her to join them or be stuck with me."

Caspian gave Phoebus' hand a squeeze. "I'm sorry."

"I don't mind, not really. I'd only tried out to please my father. I'm much happier in the fields."

"I could teach you to fight, if you wanted to try out again," Caspian suggested.

"No, but thank you for the offer."

Caspian nodded and gestured to the building ahead of them. "Here we are. Last chance to change your mind."

Phoebus smiled up at him as they approached the entrance. "I'm ready. Just make sure to get me out of there if anyone looks like they may take offence at the presence of a merman."

"They will be delighted to have your company, just as I am."

"Flatterer."

Caspian chuckled and they entered the building.

As they walked through the main entrance, Caspian saw several men eyeing Phoebus with frank appraisal and appreciation. A stab of something like jealousy hit him in the gut. He brushed it aside with a reminder that Phoebus was *his* guest at the baths.

Phoebus gazed around in obvious wonder. A Roman with the physique of a soldier approached them, his gaze raking over Phoebus with blatant lust. Caspian glared at him and the man quickly departed.

"He was only looking," Phoebus whispered as they headed farther into the building.

"I would prefer he look elsewhere," Caspian muttered.

Phoebus chuckled. "It was your idea to come here."

"And I'm already regretting my choice."

"We can leave, if you wish?"

Caspian shook his head and sighed. "No, I'm just not used to feeling this way."

"What way is that?"

"I don't know, annoyed at other men looking at you as if they'd like to bend you over a bench and take you."

"Surely you aren't jealous?" Phoebus asked. "You have more men in your bed in a single night than I've had in my entire life."

"You've been asking about me?" Caspian questioned. He wasn't sure whether to be pleased that Phoebus had taken the trouble to learn about him, or worried about what he might have found out.

"Yes."

"And what else did you discover?" He really was a glutton for punishment.

"Very little, other than stories of your legendary stamina and the fact that no one holds your attention for longer than a few days — other than your priests, of course."

"Days? I'll have you know that many of my lovers have come back to my bed one season after another."

Phoebus laughed. "There's no need to become so defensive. With as many men as you've taken to your bed, is it so surprising that people cannot keep track of them all?"

Caspian shook off his grumpiness and guided Phoebus to the edge of the bathing pool. "I suppose not. Will it bother you if they gossip about you as well?"

"What would they have to say about me?"

"That you're one of the rare mermen that I've taken into my bed."

"You've bedded other mermen?"

"Yes. Not many, and I've never had the pleasure of breaking a mating fever, at least until you. People will notice you spending time with me, and they will surely talk about it."

"I don't mind. Do you?"

"No. I've never cared what people say about me."

Caspian unwrapped his toga and let the fabric drop to the floor. His cock, which had been twitching since before he had summoned Phoebus to the grove, was at full mast under Phoebus' blatant staring.

Phoebus didn't look away as he undressed. Caspian reached over to take hold of his cock and gave it a quick squeeze. Phoebus glanced around the room.

"No one is watching," Caspian said. "There are many men here enjoying the same pleasures we are about to. You'll find Romans are as open about sex as the mer."

Phoebus relaxed a little and gestured to the pool. "Have you ever been sucked underwater?"

Caspian frowned as he tried to remember whether he had. "No, I don't believe so."

"Would you like to be?"

Caspian nodded and released Phoebus' cock. "Yes, but not immediately. Once you enter the water, everyone here will see you for what you are. I want to enjoy other pleasures with you before then."

"Such as?"

Caspian picked up their garments and led Phoebus away from the water and into one of the rooms off the main one. He gestured to a high bench. "Climb on here and let me give you a massage."

Phoebus did as Caspian said and rested his head on his arms with a contented sigh.

Caspian started at his neck and slowly made his way lower, kneading the knots from Phoebus' muscles and causing him to moan with delight.

"Has no one ever done this for you before?" Caspian asked.

"No, never."

Phoebus closed his eyes when he felt the press of lips against his neck. He shivered in delight and his cock ached.

"You barely know your own body," Caspian said. "There are so many things I could teach you about the pleasures to be had between two men."

"Hmm?"

Phoebus felt Caspian's lips on his spine, inching lower with each soft kiss. When Caspian reached his buttocks Phoebus moved his legs apart without even fully realizing what he was doing.

"You *are* eager, aren't you?" teased Caspian, his breath warm against Phoebus' skin.

Phoebus let Caspian open his legs wider. He moaned when Caspian gently spread his cheeks. When the wet tongue touched him intimately, he nearly shot off the table. Only Caspian's firm grasp kept him in place.

"That's it, Phoebus," Caspian encouraged. "Moan for me, nice and loud. I want the Romans out there to hear you."

Phoebus had forgotten there was anyone else there.

Caspian continued to lick him, probing him with his tongue and fondling his buttocks.

"Touch me," Phoebus begged. "Please, Caspian, touch me."

Caspian chuckled. "I thought I already was."

"You know what I mean. My cock, Caspian, touch my cock." Phoebus gripped the edge of the table as he ground his groin against the hard stone.

Caspian, clearly seeing what his aim was, altered Phoebus' position so he was on his back and unable to bring himself to climax. "You are so young. You have yet to learn the joys to be found from prolonging the pleasure."

Phoebus reached down for his cock, but Caspian gently slapped his hand away.

"No, my impatient merman. You don't get to come yet."

Caspian climbed up onto the step, bringing his erection level with Phoebus' arse. "Do you want me to fuck you?"

Phoebus nodded.

"I didn't hear you," Caspian teased. "What was that?"

"Yes."

"Yes, what?"

"I want you to fuck me," Phoebus said. "Please, Caspian, fuck me now."

Caspian nudged his cock against Phoebus' opening and Phoebus moaned in eager anticipation.

"How badly do you want it?" Caspian asked.

"So much. More than anything. Please!"

Despite his pleading, Caspian didn't seem inclined to do as Phoebus had asked. He stepped back and leaned down, licking along the length of Phoebus' cock.

Phoebus bucked up, trying to thrust into Caspian's mouth, but the god moved out of his reach again.

He was on the brink, desperate for...something. He didn't know whether he wanted Caspian to suck him or fuck him, but he needed him to do something before he lost control.

Caspian lifted Phoebus' legs and rested them on his shoulders. "I find these surfaces the perfect height for this," he said as he lined up his erection with Phoebus' arse. "Breathe deep and relax."

Phoebus did as the god had told him and a moment later Caspian began to push his way inside. He opened himself to Caspian, letting the god claim him as his own.

His cock wilted only momentarily. Then Caspian touched him and the pain vanished instantly.

Caspian chuckled at Phoebus' surprise. "An advantage of being fucked by a god is that he can take away the pain of being breached, leaving you with only pleasure."

As Caspian thrust into him, Phoebus' cock hardened once again. He moaned and begged for more. He was vaguely aware of someone else entering the room, only to leave a few moments later. He didn't care if they stayed to watch. The mer had no aversion to public sex and there had been several witnesses during his first mating season, mostly offering advice as well as their own services in breaking his mating fever. Not one had made the suggestion that he'd needed to hear, each being fairly young and relatively inexperienced.

Not like Caspian. The god was the complete opposite of those fumbling mermen.

Caspian was everything Phoebus could have asked for in a lover.

And you know why that is, don't you?

The voice of reason reminded him of exactly why Caspian was such a skilled lover. He had no shortage of men eager to warm his bed.

"Is something wrong?" Caspian asked, his thrusts slowing a little.

"No, don't stop."

"You're tense. Try to relax again. You were doing so well."

Phoebus took several deep breaths and Caspian quickened his pace once more.

"That's it," Caspian encouraged. "Now let me hear you moan again."

Phoebus couldn't have stopped his noises, even if he'd tried. He had already been told he was a loud lover by two of the witnesses to his first mating season, who had heard his eager cries and come to see who was making them.

It seemed his moans now were having a similar effect, at least if the trio of Romans at the door were anything to go by.

Having an audience didn't usually excite him, but for some reason it did today. He wondered if they could tell that Caspian was a god and that he was a merman. Did humans have the same kind of stamina as the gods and the mer? Would a human be able to fuck him so thoroughly or would he have tired by now?

"Yes!" he shouted as Caspian changed his angle and hit something inside of him that he hadn't even realized was there. "Fuck! Caspian, fuck me!"

"He already is," commented one of the voyeurs, much to the amusement of his companions.

Phoebus laughed along with them. He gasped and moaned as he begged Caspian for more. "Harder, fuck me harder. Caspian, please."

"If Caspian can't satisfy you, come over here," another of the men shouted. "I've got a rod you can ride."

Caspian growled at the comment and leaned in to whisper into Phoebus' ear. "If you're even thinking of taking him up on his offer I'll remove your ability to understand him."

"Huh?"

"I gave you the power to speak and understand the languages of men before we left the woods. I can remove it just as easily as I can remove your clothes."

"You're enough for me," Phoebus assured him, "as long as you get on with it and stop talking."

"Demanding little mer, aren't you?"

Phoebus cast a cautious glance over at their voyeurs, but they didn't seem to have heard him. "Yes," he said. "Now fuck me."

Caspian laughed, but did as Phoebus had ordered.

Phoebus closed his eyes again and let himself feel the pleasure of being filled so completely. He cried out Caspian's name, over and over, as he met his thrusts. His arse began to ache, but not nearly as much as his cock.

He felt the heat of Caspian's release in his arse and his own cock pulsed in response. The moment Caspian touched his aching shaft, Phoebus screamed out, his climax robbing him of the ability to speak. All he could do was feel—and he did.

The soreness of his arse. The cramps in his legs. The rough stone beneath his fingers.

But most of all he felt the warmth of Caspian's embrace.

When he returned to his senses, he found himself curled up in Caspian's arms and their audience gone.

He moaned, this time at the stiffness of his limbs.

"Come on," Caspian said as he stood, holding Phoebus in his arms. "The waters in these particular baths are heated and known for their healing properties. A nice warm soak in them will cure those lingering aches and pains in no time."

"Are you really sure about this?" Phoebus asked as Caspian carried him back into the main room.

"If anyone thinks to harm you, I'll know, and I'll get you out of there before they get anywhere near you. Now, I believe you said something about sucking me underwater."

Phoebus glanced around the room. There weren't many people there. He thought he recognized one of the men as being part of the group who had been watching them earlier, but he couldn't say for sure.

He tried not to look at anyone as Caspian stepped into the water and lowered them both beneath the surface.

Phoebus' fins returned within moments of being submerged and he kept his eyes firmly on Caspian's the whole time. As his head broke through the water, he heard a gasp from someone nearby, but he didn't turn to see who it was. He couldn't believe he was here, in the middle of a human building, blatantly showing his tail and fins.

"You're beautiful," Caspian whispered. "Your tail and fins are unique. I've never seen a merman with two-tone fins before."

"They go with my mismatched eyes," Phoebus said.

"So they do," Caspian replied as he stroked the fins lightly.

Phoebus shivered as Caspian touched a particularly sensitive part of his fins and he gasped in pleasure when Caspian did it again.

"Now that's interesting," Caspian teased. "I thought the mer couldn't come when they were in this form."

"We can't, but we can still get quite excited when we're touched in certain places."

"Like here." Caspian rubbed his fingers over the place where his fins met his tail, and Phoebus squealed.

The whispers were getting louder and Phoebus ducked under the water so he didn't have to hear them. He trusted Caspian would get them out of there if he needed to. He just hoped the god could closely monitor the humans at the same time as being sucked.

Phoebus worked his way down Caspian's body until he reached his cock. As he stroked the stiff flesh, he guessed Caspian must have used his powers to clean them both while he had been recovering from his orgasm. Belatedly he realized that his arse hadn't hurt as it had done after the solstice and he guessed he had Caspian to thank for that too.

He took Caspian's cock between his lips and sucked hard. Phoebus had no doubt that his own erection would be back right now if he were in his human form.

He used his hands and mouth to bring Caspian to the brink, then pulled back and gazed up at him through the water.

"You're a tease," Caspian said, his voice clear in Phoebus' mind.

Phoebus nodded and grinned. He wouldn't apologize for that, especially when Caspian was just as bad.

He took him into his mouth again, licking and nipping at the length as he drove Caspian wild.

"So good," Caspian said. *"My beautiful cock-sucking merman."*

Phoebus chuckled and Caspian began to come. He drank down the god's seed, swallowing it all, making sure not a single drop went into the water.

Caspian tugged at his hair as he thrust erratically into Phoebus' mouth. *"That's it, Phoebus. Take it all."*

Phoebus had no intention of letting anything go to waste. Only when he was sure Caspian was completely spent did he pull away with one final lick of his cock.

He popped up out of the water and pulled Caspian into a messy kiss.

Around him he heard the sound of clapping and calls of encouragement, but he ignored them all. The only one he had eyes for was Caspian.

Eventually, Caspian eased them apart and climbed out of the pool. He held out his hand to Phoebus and pulled him up beside him.

Phoebus couldn't take his eyes off Caspian. The god had called him beautiful, but Phoebus knew he was just one of many men who he had given such compliments to.

"What now?" Phoebus asked.

"Now I take you home," Caspian replied.

"And then?"

Caspian shrugged. "My offer for you to come and suck me on the solstice still stands."

"Oh."

Phoebus tried not to be disappointed in Caspian's words. He reminded himself that the god had plenty of men to keep him satisfied. It would be selfish of Phoebus to want to monopolize his time.

Caspian gave Phoebus a quick kiss on the cheek. "Of course, it doesn't have to be the solstice for you to visit. As long as you don't interrupt any of the ceremonies, you can come and see me whenever you wish. And if I'm busy, I'm sure many of my priests would be happy to entertain you in my absence."

Phoebus nodded as he forced himself to keep smiling as Caspian casually told him he didn't care if he fucked one or more of his priests.

"What if you're, er, with your priests when I arrive? I mean, doing something like we just did?"

Caspian laughed. "It'll happen sooner or later. You can either join us or come back another time."

Phoebus hid his disappointment behind a bright smile. "Well, I have a shift in the fields soon, so you should probably take me home."

"Of course," Caspian replied, and a moment later Phoebus found himself back in the sunken city.

He tried not to be too upset at the abrupt ending to their fun. The thought of walking in on Caspian with another man — or men — made his stomach churn. Maybe he should just keep his distance from now on.

He told himself that his time with Caspian was a once-in-a-lifetime experience and he should just leave it at that. How many mermen could say they had visited the Roman baths and been fucked by a god? He should consider himself lucky that he had captured Caspian's attention for as long as he had.

He would be thankful for the experience Caspian had given him and set his mind to finding a nice young merman to spend the solstice and the rest of his life with.

Chapter Six

Phoebus could see Caspian on the beach as he swam to the shore onto the night of the next solstice. He wondered what the god was doing there. He had never seen him on the mating island before. *Surely he isn't here to see me?*

When he reached land, Caspian handed him a length of fabric to dry his tail and fins with. Phoebus told himself not to read anything into his actions. It was probably just a coincidence.

Ajax arrived just as Phoebus regained his legs. "You have to be the fastest swimmer in all the oceans."

"You're just slow," Phoebus teased. "Have you met Caspian?"

"No, I don't believe I've had the pleasure."

Phoebus let Caspian help him to his feet. "Then let me introduce you to the Atlantean God of Justice. Caspian, this is Ajax."

Caspian gave a small nod toward Ajax. "Any friend of Phoebus is most welcome. Now, if you'll excuse us, I would like to spend some time alone with Phoebus."

Ajax shrugged. "Far be it from me to stand in the way of true love. I think I see a likely prospect to break my fever just down the beach."

Phoebus shot Ajax a dirty look, which he returned with a wink.

"He didn't mean anything by that comment," Phoebus said. "When he talked about love, I mean. He was just trying to be amusing."

"I understand," Caspian replied. "After all, if you were in love with me, you wouldn't have stayed away for so long."

"I'm sure you've had plenty of company."

Caspian took his hand and transported them to a bedchamber Phoebus had never been in before.

"Where are we?"

"My private chambers on the Isle of the Gods."

Phoebus ran a hand over the silken fabrics of the bedspread. "Why did you come to the beach?"

"To see you, of course."

"But why?"

"Because I wanted to. Do I need any reason other than that?"

"I suppose not."

"Aren't you glad to see me?" Caspian asked. "I thought you enjoyed our time in Italia."

"I did, but I didn't expect to see you again after we... You know..."

Caspian guided Phoebus to the center of the bed and they stretched out, side by side. "There are many ways we can pleasure each other that we didn't do at the baths. I said I would wish to see you again. Didn't you believe me?"

"I suppose not."

Caspian leaned close to kiss him. "I never say anything I don't mean."

Phoebus sighed into the kiss as he sank into the pillows, Caspian pressing him down into the mattress. His cock ached and he could feel Caspian's hardness nudging his thigh. He opened his legs in blatant invitation.

Caspian chuckled against his lips. "I do love a man who makes it clear what he wants."

"Good, because I have no hesitation in making my demands known. And while I do want you to fuck me sometime tonight, you know I need something else first."

"Ah yes." Caspian sat back on his heels and stroked his length. "How remiss of me to have forgotten."

Phoebus crooked his finger and Caspian moved up the bed.

As soon as he was in reach, Phoebus took him into his mouth and sucked eagerly. His own erection had been paining him all day, but the work in the fields had prevented him from swimming to land any earlier.

Caspian moaned above him, thrusting into his mouth and giving Phoebus exactly what he needed to break his fever.

Phoebus drank down the god's seed, swallowing it all, while at the same time conscious of his own pulsing erection spilling over his belly and, quite possibly, Caspian's arse.

His fever broken, he released Caspian's cock and scrambled up into a sitting position so he could kiss him.

Phoebus moaned in pleasure. The kiss was frantic and messy and Caspian continued to spill between them. Phoebus joined him, rubbing his cock against Caspian's, searching for friction.

When Caspian reached between them to take them both in hand, Phoebus groaned and bucked into Caspian's fist.

"That's it," Caspian encouraged. "Make as much noise as you want. Let me hear you scream in pleasure."

Phoebus shouted encouragement as he thrust erratically while clinging to Caspian like a limpet.

Then he was on his back and Caspian was pushing his way inside him, stretching him and filling him with heat.

"Oh god," Phoebus yelled, barely conscious of the fact that in the heat of pleasure he was crying out a word he had never used before. He had never called to the gods, yet here, while one of those beings was buried in his arse, he couldn't seem to help himself. "Oh god, oh god, ooooh god!"

"Call my name," Caspian ordered. "Let me hear my name on your lips when you climax."

"Caspian," Phoebus moaned. "Oh my god, Caspian. More, oh god, more. Caspian, more. I need...more... Oh god...yes...Caspian... Caspian... Cas-"

Phoebus lost the power of speech as the heat of Caspian's release filled him, and he came again, spraying them both with his seed.

"Phoebus!" Caspian screamed as he shook violently and collapsed on top of him.

The merman couldn't move, not even to push the larger man aside. Caspian was still inside him, soft now, but nevertheless *there*.

Caspian moved to the side, easing out of Phoebus and flopping onto his back with a sigh of contentment.

Slowly, Phoebus reached down to his own groin and carefully touched his wilted cock. The sensitive flesh twitched in response.

"Phoebus, thank you," Caspian said.

"There's no need to thank me for that," Phoebus replied with a chuckle. "It was my pleasure."

Caspian propped himself up on his arm. "I want to see you again—regularly, I mean."

"You have the power to summon me whenever you wish," Phoebus reminded him.

"I know, but it might be nice if you would come to me of your own volition."

"Oh."

Caspian smiled and kissed him lightly on the lips. "A god might be able to summon a man to his bed, but sometimes I would prefer the one I desire to come to me without being called."

Phoebus kissed Caspian back. "I shouldn't have stayed away so long. I guess I thought that after you'd fucked me at the baths, you'd have lost interest in me. You made it clear to me that there were numerous other volunteers to warm your bed."

"Foolish merman," Caspian teased. "Come here and let me introduce you to the fine art of frottage."

"Hmm, I like the sound of that."

"You'll like the feel of it even more."

Phoebus pressed himself against Caspian. He mirrored the god's moves, letting the more experienced immortal set the pace, as he gave himself over willingly.

"I can't believe you kept away from me for so long," Caspian complained.

"Me neither," Phoebus replied between moans of pleasure. "Maybe you should keep me here until you're bored with me."

"I'll never tire of you," Caspian said. "But I do like the idea of you staying here on a more permanent basis. My palace has many rooms. I'm sure we can find you one that is suitable."

Phoebus stilled. "I wasn't hinting. I'm quite content with my home in the sunken city."

Caspian kissed his neck and sucked on the skin, hard enough to mark him. "I have many homes. You could keep your place in Atlantis as well as a room here in my palace."

"Maybe," Phoebus replied, though he suspected it wouldn't take much for Caspian to talk him into the idea. A few more kisses and the god could probably convince him to do just about anything.

* * * *

Phoebus managed to hold out for half a season before Caspian talked him into taking rooms on the isle. He followed Caspian into the chamber. The room was small and neatly furnished.

"This will be your room," Caspian said. "You can come and go from Atlantis as you please by using the crystal portal. As one of my favorites there's no need for you to make an offering in my temple. The door will always be open."

Phoebus walked over to the window and looked out at the garden. The neat flowerbeds surrounded a large fountain.

"That's my private garden," Caspian explained. "Even my priests stay out of there unless I invite them in with me."

"I'll be sure to stay away from it as long as you show me the entrance I need to avoid."

Caspian wound his arms around Phoebus' waist. "That wasn't what I meant. I just wanted you to know that if you need some time alone, you can go there. No other rooms, save my own, look out over the gardens."

"Thank you," Phoebus replied as he twisted in Caspian's embrace and wrapped his arms around the god's neck. "I'm not sure how much I'll be here, though. After all, you have perfectly adequate rooms of your own, don't you?"

"Yes, but sometimes they do become rather crowded."

Phoebus frowned at the reminder that he wasn't the only one to share Caspian's bed. "Is that often the case?"

Caspian's amused expression told Phoebus the god knew what he was really asking. "Haven't you heard the stories about the nightly orgies my priests and I engage in?"

"You're teasing me."

Caspian chuckled. "Just a little. You shouldn't believe everything you hear in the taverns."

Phoebus rolled his eyes. "*You're* the one who just said your rooms get crowded."

"Have you walked in on me with anyone yet?"

"No."

"And what does that tell you?"

Phoebus shrugged. "That your priests are nimble on their feet?"

"Or perhaps bedding a merman at his sexual peak is enough for me at the moment."

At the moment. Phoebus tried not to think about what that might mean for their future. "Well, if I should interrupt you when you have other men in your bed, I'll simply go to the sunken city and sleep on my own sponge."

Caspian shook his head. "You are remarkably stubborn."

"So I've been told," Phoebus replied with a smile. "But you know as well as I do that I don't really need these rooms. You should keep them for someone else."

"*You* need them. By providing you with rooms here in my palace, it shows everyone that I hold you in the same high esteem as my priests."

Phoebus didn't need reminding about the priests.

"I'll leave you to settle in," Caspian said. "I have duties to attend to, but I'll be back tonight."

Caspian disappeared out of the door, leaving Phoebus to watch him go.

The god had only been gone a moment or two when Phoebus heard the sound of footsteps approaching. When Rafe walked through the door, Phoebus could barely contain his sigh of frustration. Of all the priests in Caspian's service, Rafe was his least favorite. The high priest made no effort to hide his contempt for Phoebus or the mer in general.

Without invitation, Rafe stretched out on the circular bed. "It won't last, you know."

Phoebus ignored him, though it appeared Rafe didn't need a reply.

"He'll tire of you, just as he does everyone else. You're just a novelty—a merman to warm his bed and suck his cock."

Phoebus sighed. "I'm well aware of Caspian's habit of bedding any willing man who crosses his path. I know he'll become bored with me and move on. I don't need you to tell me this."

"If you know this, why are you still here?"

"Because I enjoy spending time with him. Don't you?"

Rafe snorted. "Not particularly. He's selfish in bed and ignores me — his high priest — most of the time."

"Then why act so jealous, if you don't care for him?"

"I'm not jealous."

"You act like you are."

"Well, I'm not. I'm just trying to warn you what he's like. As his high priest, I have served him in all things for many years. I have seen him bed more men than any other immortal, even the Goddess of Love."

Phoebus folded his arms across his chest. "Again, you tell me these things as if I don't already know. I have heard of Caspian's reputation for myself. I'll enjoy his attentions while I can, and when he's grown bored with me, I'll return to the sunken city permanently and find another lover. I assure you, I won't linger around here, watching him with other men, while all the time wishing he still wanted me."

Rafe's face turned red then white. "You are very outspoken for an uneducated merman."

"The mer don't need educating," Phoebus replied. "We are creatures of the sea and we learn only what we need to survive."

"Yes, I know, which is why Caspian will grow tired of you even more quickly than he does other men. Uncultured, ignorant, barely more than animals, the mer are unworthy of the attentions of a god. He wouldn't even be interested in you now if it weren't for Medina's love potion."

"What did you say?" Phoebus hated that he was rising to the bait, but this was the first he had heard of any love potion.

"Ah, Caspian hasn't told you about it. Everyone on the isle is aware of it."

"What are you talking about?"

Rafe gave him a nasty smile. "Medina, Goddess of Love, dosed Caspian with a love potion the day you met him. It had to be strong enough to work on a god, but even the most powerful spell doesn't last forever. When the potion wears off, Caspian will forget you. That's how love potions work."

Phoebus shook his head. "Love potion or not, sooner or later Caspian will lose interest in me and when he is done with me, I'll leave. Why don't you try doing the same?"

Rafe stood and sneered down at him. "Just remember... I *did* warn you."

Phoebus didn't need warnings from Rafe. He might be young, but he wasn't a fool. He knew his time with Caspian was limited. He would just enjoy it while he could.

* * * *

Phoebus ran his fingers down Caspian's hip, teasing him with the light touches.

Caspian sighed and stretched. "Again?"

Phoebus chuckled. "This close to the mating season, I'm always ready."

Caspian laughed and rolled Phoebus onto his back. "Lucky for you, we gods have remarkably fast recovery time."

Normally, at this point Phoebus would spread his legs for Caspian to take him, but tonight he didn't. "Caspian, have you ever been fucked?"

"What? Where did this come from?"

"Have you?"

"No, of course not." Caspian kissed his chest and flicked his tongue over a nipple. "I know where my talents lie."

"You might like it," Phoebus suggested in between moans at Caspian's attentions.

"I doubt it. I don't like giving up control. No god does."

"Then you don't like the idea of me being inside you? Filling you with my seed?"

"Not really," Caspian said. "Why do you ask?"

"I thought you might want me to."

Caspian gave him a quick peck on the lips. "You give me everything I want, so don't worry yourself."

Phoebus knew he should let things go, but he couldn't. "What if I *want* to fuck you?"

Caspian drew back. "Do you?"

"Maybe."

Phoebus waited for Caspian to say something — anything — in response. Finally Caspian climbed off the bed and walked over to the table.

"If you want to fuck someone, we'll need to invite someone else into our bed," Caspian said as he poured them each a goblet of wine. "I may enjoy watching you pound another man's arse, even if I have no wish for you to do that to me."

"I don't want anyone else," Phoebus said. "I love you."

Caspian snorted. "You're too young to know what love is."

Phoebus bristled and struggled out of the sheets. "I think I'll just head back to the city for a while."

He wasted as much time as he could in leaving, but it soon became clear that Caspian had no intention of asking him to stay.

* * * *

As Phoebus swam around his quarters he cursed himself. He shouldn't have said anything. Caspian had never given him any indication that he would ever spread his legs for another man. He shouldn't have mentioned it at all and he certainly should have kept his mouth closed when he'd said he loved him. *What was I thinking?*

He knew Caspian didn't love him and that his own growing feelings for the god were not reciprocated. Why in the world had he blurted out that he loved him?

Stupid, foolish merman!

He was so distracted he darted right into Ajax as he swam through the door.

"What are you doing back?" Ajax asked. *"I thought you'd be spending the night with Caspian."*

"I changed my mind."

"Uh-oh." Ajax descended to the seating and patted the sponge beside him. *"Come tell me all about it."*

"There's nothing much to tell."

"I'm sure there is. What happened?"

Phoebus joined Ajax on the sponge. *"I suggested that he might like me to penetrate him."*

"And since you're now moping around here instead of being buried balls deep in his arse, I'm guessing he said no."

"He suggested we invite someone else to join us if I want to do that."

"Well, there you are, problem solved. I'll even volunteer for the job if you haven't already got someone else in mind."

"You're not amusing," Phoebus said. *"Anyway, that's not all. After he suggested a third, I said something really foolish."*

"Which was?"

"I told him I loved him." Phoebus cringed again as he relived that moment, seeing once more the look of contempt in Caspian's eyes. *"I can't believe I said such a thing, to a god, of all beings. What was I thinking?"*

"I doubt you were thinking at all," Ajax replied. *"You simply told him what was in your heart."*

"I should have remained silent. Gods don't want mortals to love them, they want to be worshipped."

Ajax shook his head. *"This is what comes of getting involved with immortals. They just don't think like we do."*

Chapter Seven

Phoebus emptied his net of sea fruits into the large stone trough before swimming back out to the gathering fields. It was his fourth net of the shift, but his mind was not on the work.

He hadn't seen Caspian since his disastrous declaration of love. He still couldn't believe he had told the god his feelings. He didn't know what he had been thinking. And as for asking Caspian whether he could fuck him…

Phoebus silently cursed his stupidity.

Caspian was a god, a being of great power. Why would he ever want to give up even so small a part of that?

Maybe things would be different if Phoebus were a different kind of merman—stronger, a fighter, one of the guards perhaps. He glanced at the guards on the edge of the gathering grounds, who were keeping a watchful eye out for predators. If he were one of them, maybe Caspian would have felt differently about the idea of letting Phoebus take charge.

Instead, the god was stuck with a merman who did a mermaid's work, because he was too weak and inept to do anything else.

He snarled as he realized the fruit he had just picked was barely ripe. He tossed it aside and tried to concentrate on at least doing the job he had correctly.

All too soon his mind was drifting back to Caspian and the fool he had made of himself.

"You aren't concentrating today," Ajax commented as he swam near. "Are you still worrying about what you said to Caspian?"

Ajax wasn't actually a gatherer, but he sometimes kept Phoebus company in the fields when his own duties repairing and maintaining the buildings in the city were done.

"I can't believe I told him I loved him. I'm such a fool."

"Maybe you should end things with him, if he doesn't feel the same way as you do?"

"I've been thinking the same thing," Phoebus admitted. "I just don't know if I can."

Ajax gave him a sympathetic pat on the arm, grabbed a fruit from his net and took a large bite from it.

"Hey!"

"What? I'm hungry. I've been lifting heavy stones all morning."

"Are you working this afternoon?"

"Yes, I'm just taking a break to eat and check on you."

"I don't need watching over."

"I know, but I'm worried about you. You spend more time on land with Caspian than you do in the ocean these days."

Phoebus hadn't thought he had spent that much time on land, but now that Ajax had pointed it out to him, he realized his friend was right. When had Caspian become such a huge part of his life?

"Phoebus, what are you going to do?"

"I don't know."

"You aren't going to forget about him, are you?"

Phoebus shook his head. *"I wish I could, but it's too late for that. Whether he loves me back or not doesn't matter. I love him."*

Ajax gave him another pat on the arm, snatched a couple more fruits from Phoebus' net and returned to work with a wave.

Phoebus replenished the fruits Ajax had taken and continued to fill his net. Could he leave Caspian? Did he have the strength to end things with him? He didn't know, and he wasn't even sure whether he wanted to find out.

He pondered his options as he filled net after net, swimming through the fields and barely concentrating on his work. He stayed in the fields long past the end of his shift. He didn't want to go home alone and he had no intention of visiting Caspian without an invitation. For all he knew the god was glad to see the back of him and breathing a sigh of relief at a lucky escape.

"Shark!"

The warning from one of the mermaids screamed through his mind and he swam around to see which direction the danger was coming from and where the guards were.

He spotted the guards first and swiftly realized that they were heading directly for him.

"Behind you!" one of the guards yelled, waving his spear over Phoebus' shoulder.

Phoebus spun around to see where they were pointing, only to find himself face-to-face with the biggest and sharpest set of teeth he had seen in his life.

Frozen in terror, Phoebus couldn't seem to do anything but stare at the shark. Behind him, the guards shouted for him to swim to them or just get out of the way.

As the shark darted forward, Phoebus finally moved, but his reflexes were slow and he wasn't quick enough to avoid the teeth as they grazed his side.

The first guard reached him and pushed him roughly aside as they all turned on the shark, using their spears to force it back out of the gathering grounds.

They dealt with the creature swiftly and efficiently before returning to their posts.

"You should get that looked at," one of the guards advised as they swam away, pointing at the gash on Phoebus' side. *"You don't want to keep bleeding. It'll only draw even more sharks if you do."*

Phoebus clutched at his side to stem the flow of blood. His heart rate had just about returned to normal. He chanced a look at his injury. It wasn't too bad, but the guard was right. With sharks in the vicinity, they would be drawn to his blood.

Taking his half full net to the stores, he deposited his fruits, grabbed one to eat on his way and headed home.

Once he was safely in his own house, he settled down with a sponge on his hip to gather up the blood. He kept the pressure on the wound as he waited for it to stop bleeding. It wouldn't take long and the healing properties of the sponge would help take away the pain and seal the gash.

He cursed his own stupidity again. How could he let himself get so distracted by Caspian that he didn't see a shark circling around him?

Fool.

He had to get over Caspian—and soon.

* * * *

"Aren't you going to visit Phoebus?" Cari asked Caspian as she joined him on the beach near his temple.

"No, not today."

"Why not? I thought you were getting along rather well with him."

"I was."

"But?"

Caspian shrugged. "I think perhaps we've reached the end."

"The end of what? Your relationship?"

"Maybe."

"But you gave him rooms here on the isle. Why would you do that if you think things are ending?"

Caspian sighed. "I don't know if I might have made a mistake in suggesting he takes rooms here."

"What makes you think that?"

"He told me he loved me."

Cari stared at him for several long seconds. "And?"

"And what?"

"Well, did you tell him you loved him back?"

"Of course not."

Cari smacked him on the arm, hard. "What *did* you say when he told you?"

"I told him the truth, that he's too young to know what love is."

"You didn't!"

Caspian stepped back at the force of his sister's glare, but before he could say anything, she was already speaking again.

"He might be young, but he knows more about love than you do, for all your centuries of bedding every male who crosses your path."

"I know all I need to."

"You know nothing, not even the strength of your own feelings." Cari hooked her arm through Caspian's and walked him toward the edge of the water. "I had a vision earlier today."

"Of?"

"Phoebus."

"And me?"

"No. He was working in the gathering fields."

"It doesn't take a goddess of prophecy to see that. He works in the fields most days."

"He had company. A shark."

Caspian stumbled to a halt. "What happened? What did you see? When will this happen? Can you stop it?"

"No. The attack has already come to pass."

"Attack?" Caspian whispered as the world began to spin around him. "No."

Cari smiled at him as visions of Phoebus and sharks raced through his mind. Her calm demeanor was the only thing stopping him from panicking.

"Where is he?" he finally managed to ask.

"In his home in Atlantis."

"Then he wasn't hurt?"

"I didn't say that."

Caspian didn't wait a moment longer. He summoned Phoebus to his side with a thought.

"Phoebus?" He knelt beside the merman and drew aside the sponge at his hip.

"Caspian?" Phoebus glanced around at his surroundings before turning his attention back to him. "What did you bring me here for?"

"You were attacked by a shark."

"Yes, I know."

"How did this happen?"

"I wasn't concentrating on my surroundings," Phoebus admitted as he poked at the cut. "It was my own fault. Don't worry about it."

"Let me heal this for you," Caspian said. "Then we'll talk about how this happened."

"It'll heal on its own in a day or two," Phoebus replied.

"But it'll leave a scar."

Phoebus shrugged. "It'll be a reminder to me to take more care."

"And the memory of the shark won't be?"

"Memories fade over time." Phoebus took back the sponge and placed it over the wound again. "Now, are you going to send me back home or are you going to wait for me to get my legs back and walk to the temple myself?"

"You want to go back to Atlantis?"

"Of course I do. It's my home."

"You have rooms here now too."

Phoebus gave him a questioning look. "You haven't moved someone else into them yet?"

Caspian drew in a sharp breath. "You think I would have replaced you so quickly?"

"Why not? I'm just the latest fool to warm your bed, aren't I?"

"You're more than that. I've never moved anyone into rooms in my palace, save for my priests, of course."

"I don't need reminding that I share you with your priests. Now, if you'll excuse me, I've had a long and trying day, and I'd like to go home...to Atlantis."

Caspian had no intention of letting Phoebus out of his sight. He swept him into his arms and carried him toward the palace. He caught Cari's smirk as he passed her, but he didn't give her the pleasure of making one of her usual smart remarks.

Phoebus grumbled most of the way, but he didn't make any real effort to escape from Caspian's embrace.

By the time Caspian reached his bedchamber, Phoebus had regained his legs and was able to stand on his own two feet, not that he made any attempt to rise from the bed where Caspian had placed him.

"I didn't think you'd be inviting me here again," Phoebus said as he sat up.

Caspian sighed and sat beside him. He knew Phoebus deserved to hear words of love, but he couldn't bring himself to say them. "Let's not talk about what happened," he suggested instead. He brushed aside Phoebus' shoulder-length hair and kissed his neck.

He lowered Phoebus onto his back, but drew back when the merman cringed. "Can I at least stop you from bleeding?"

Phoebus nodded and removed the sponge. Caspian brushed his hand over the cut and sealed it. At Phoebus' insistence he didn't remove the lingering scar.

"Now, where were we?" Caspian murmured.

Phoebus moaned as Caspian slid his hand between his legs and eased them apart. He rubbed him intimately and Phoebus grabbed his hand to hold it in place.

"You like that?" Caspian teased.

Phoebus nodded as he guided Caspian's fingers away from his arse and toward his testicles.

Caspian took the merman's heavy balls in his hand and squeezed them gently. "Is this what you want?"

"Yes. Oh, yes." Phoebus gave another long moan of pleasure as Caspian licked and sucked and fondled him.

"I'm sorry I wasn't there to stop the shark," Caspian said.

Phoebus snorted. "I don't want to think about sharks right now."

Caspian chuckled and kissed his inner thigh. "Sorry. I'll try not to ruin the mood again."

"Did I just hear a god apologize to a mere mortal?" Phoebus teased.

"Maybe. It does happen occasionally."

Phoebus laughed. "I'll be sure to remember this moment forever."

"Do I detect a hint of sarcasm there?"

"Maybe."

Caspian pulled back and gave Phoebus a mock glare before diving on the merman's cock and swallowing him down.

Phoebus gasped and cried out something completely unintelligible.

Caspian hummed and relished each moan from Phoebus. He fingered the merman's arse and as Phoebus shook and quivered at his touch, Caspian knew it would be a while before his lover regained his power of speech.

His own cock ached to be stroked, but since he had his hands full playing with both Phoebus' arse and his balls, he had no chance of relief just yet. Unfortunately, the position they were in wasn't one that allowed Phoebus to lend him a hand either. With no other option, he ground into the sheets.

"Take me," Phoebus demanded. "Caspian, please take me."

He didn't need any more encouragement. He released Phoebus' cock and repositioned himself to do as Phoebus had begged. He nudged Phoebus' hole with the tip of his cock. "Is this what you want?"

Phoebus grabbed his arse with both hands and pulled him forward with enough force that Caspian was inside him within a moment. "This is what I want."

Caspian groaned and held steady while he tried not to lose control too soon. He was a god. He could do this. He wasn't some mortal who barely knew the limits of his own body.

Phoebus clenched around him and Caspian came undone.

Buried in Phoebus' arse, he came harder than he could ever remember doing in his life. And Phoebus was right there with him, his hand flying over his cock as he moaned with pleasure at his climax.

Later, Caspian watched Phoebus as he slept. He was safe now, here on the Isle of the Gods. No sharks could touch him here. He traced the faint line of the scar from the attack. He yearned to heal it entirely, remove the blemish from the merman's skin, but he knew Phoebus didn't want him to and he respected the merman's wishes.

Phoebus rolled over and opened his eyes. "Why don't you try to sleep?"

"Gods don't need sleep."

"Maybe not, but even gods might like to dream sometimes."

Caspian smiled and kissed Phoebus gently on the lips. "Perhaps."

Phoebus kissed him back and pulled him down on top of him. "What is it that troubles you?"

"I'm just worried about you. The life of a merman can be most dangerous."

"The shark attack was an isolated incident. Most of them never make it past the guards, and for one to get to the fields is unheard of."

"Not anymore."

"It's highly unlikely to happen again."

"Still, I would prefer you remain safe."

"I take care."

Caspian harrumphed and pulled Phoebus into his arms once again. "What do you think about the idea of staying here on the Isle?"

"I do stay here," Phoebus replied.

"No, I mean permanently."

"What?"

"You could live here, with me."

Phoebus shook his head. "I don't know. I like the ocean too much."

"There's water here for you to swim in. The Isle is surrounded by sea."

"A sea that isn't real," Phoebus reminded him. "There are no other creatures in it."

"Which makes it safer than the shark-infested waters around Atlantis."

"Lonelier too."

Caspian kissed Phoebus again. "You would never be lonely if you stayed here forever."

"You don't know that. Sometimes a person can be lonely, even when they are in a place filled with other people."

"I wouldn't let that happen to you."

"You say that now, but what about later?"

Caspian didn't want to argue, and with a few more kisses, he had completely distracted Phoebus. Still, the thought lingered in his mind of how close he had come to losing the merman.

Chapter Eight

Caspian found his sister consulting with her Oracles. They were in deep discussion and he was reluctant to interrupt them. He lingered in the outer chamber, waiting for them to finish.

When they were done, the Oracles left, each of them bowing respectfully to him as they passed.

Cari stood in the doorway to her private chambers, waiting for him to join her.

"What brings you here?" Cari asked.

"Phoebus."

"Your merman lover? What about him?"

"I want you to look into his future for me."

Cari frowned at him. "You are well aware that knowing the future means you risk changing it."

"Yes, I know, but what if there's another shark attack, like the one a few days ago?"

"You're worrying over things that might never happen. If I see something in the future that bodes ill for Phoebus, I'll make sure to tell you about it."

"You didn't tell me about the shark attack until after it had happened."

"Caspian, you are well aware that my visions don't always occur with enough time for me to prevent them, particularly when the vision shows no fatalities."

"Phoebus was hurt and it could have been prevented."

"Not by me. There simply wasn't enough time between my vision and the attack. Is he very shaken by what happened?"

"He doesn't seem to be. I suspect I'm more bothered about it than he is. His lack of concern is why I would see him safe."

Cari sat on her couch and put up her feet. "For someone who was considering ending things with him just a few days ago, you seem very concerned about him. Are you ready to admit you like him yet?"

"Of course I like him. I wouldn't bother asking about his future otherwise."

"No, I mean you *really* like him," Cari said. "You are considering keeping him in your life for longer than most of your other lovers."

"Very well. I admit it. He's a sweet young thing and I'm enjoying teaching him about the pleasures that can be found when two lovers share their bodies."

"Have you considered inducting him into your rank of priests?"

"No, of course not. He's mer. You know as well as I do that the mer don't worship us. I merely enjoy having his company in my bed."

"And is Rafe becoming accustomed to having Phoebus around?"

Caspian realized immediately that Cari had already been sneaking glimpses of his future. "Rafe is jealous, as usual, and needs to be reminded of his place. His future is not the one I'm concerned about."

"I've never seen you worried about any of your lovers' futures. What makes Phoebus so special?"

Caspian shrugged. "I don't know. I just want to know that he'll be safe."

"I'm sure he'll be fine for as long as he holds your interest, which probably won't be for much longer."

Caspian shot his sister a sour look. "I don't know why I bother asking you to look into the future. You never tell me what I want to hear."

"You ask me because you know I'll give you nothing but the truth."

Caspian knew she was right, even if he didn't want to admit it out loud. "There is one way I could ensure his safety."

"Such as?"

"I could petition the pantheon for permission to make Phoebus immortal. Would you support me in this?"

"Why would you want to make him immortal?"

"To keep him safe, of course."

"And you think making him immortal will accomplish that?"

"Of course. He would not fear sickness, and all but the most serious of injuries could be cured with only a thought."

"Did Phoebus ask you to petition on his behalf?" Cari questioned quietly.

"No. He probably doesn't even know there's a possibility of such a thing. As one of the mer, he's not accustomed to Atlantean ways."

"Are you saying you haven't talked about this with him?"

"Not yet. I would not wish to raise false hopes."

"His—or yours?"

"Both."

Cari took Caspian's hands in her own. "Brother, why do you really want to make Phoebus immortal?"

"I told you, to keep him safe."

"Immortality is not the only way to do that. He could live here on the Isle. If he were to swear loyalty to you and serve you as one of your priests, no one would question his presence in your home."

"Do they question it now?" Caspian asked.

"There are those who have noticed that he is your latest favorite. They talk of how he has lasted longer than most of your lovers. The Atlanteans have a wager on how long he will be warming your bed."

"They *what*?" Caspian glared at his sister as he snatched his hands from her grasp.

"I believe the shortest odds are that you will have lost interest in him before the next solstice."

"How dare they?"

Cari laughed airily. "You know the Atlanteans wager on anything and everything. This has always been their way. It never bothered you before."

"They weren't betting on my love life before."

Cari smirked at him.

"What?" he asked. "What's so funny?"

"Nothing, my brother, nothing at all. Tell me, why have you never considered offering immortality to one of your priests?"

"I assume you mean Rafe?"

"Yes. After all, he has been asking you to make just such a petition for some years now."

Caspian grimaced. The thought of an eternity with Rafe at his side was not one he wished to contemplate.

"Your high priest won't be pleased when he hears you wish to make Phoebus immortal."

"These days, he's never pleased about anything."

"Can you blame him?"

"As my high priest, he is sworn to serve me. As a former lover, he is most troublesome."

"Former?"

"I have not taken him into my bed since Phoebus. His jealousy is most unattractive."

"What of your other priests?" Cari asked. "Have you bedded any of those since the merman?"

"No. Phoebus is a most satisfying lover."

"Hmm. I seem to recall you saying how no single man could ever be enough for you."

"For the moment, Phoebus is enough."

Cari frowned at him. "For the moment? And if he were to join us in immortality and was no longer enough for you, what then?"

"I..."

Cari rose and stared down at him. "If you want to make him immortal because you cannot bear the thought of eternity without him, then, yes, I will support your petition. But if you wish to give him this gift for any other reason, then I cannot give you my vote."

She left the room, leaving Caspian alone. He needed the support of the other immortals if Phoebus were to drink from the cup of eternal life. They each had one vote on his petition and the majority had to vote in his favor. If he couldn't even persuade his own sister to side with him, what hope did he have of convincing the rest?

* * * *

"Phoebus, how would you like to stay with me permanently?" Caspian asked.

"I already told you, I like the sea too much to leave it for a life on land."

"You could still visit Atlantis or any other part of the ocean, but you would be safe from harm."

Phoebus kicked at the sand as they strolled down the beach. "You're not making sense. I can already do that."

"Not safely."

"It's safe enough. Besides, if I stay here forever, I can't visit the ocean."

Caspian drew Phoebus to a halt and sat them down on the dunes. "If you accept my offer, you would be safe. You would be immortal."

"What do you mean? How is that possible?"

"There is cup that has a never-ending supply of water from the fountain of life. It is strictly guarded, but any god or goddess can petition the rest of the pantheon for permission to make someone immortal."

"Have many humans become immortal in this way?"

"A fair number, but none in the last few centuries."

"And how many mer?"

"None."

"Not all of the Atlantean gods are accepting of the mer. They would never agree to making me, or any other merman, immortal."

"They wouldn't have to. As long as the majority agrees, then you could drink from the cup."

Instead of being delighted at the prospect, Phoebus appeared troubled.

"What is it? Don't you want to stay with me?"

Phoebus sighed. "I don't know. I never even thought about the possibility of living forever. What would I even do for all that time?"

"You would remain at my side, of course."

Phoebus laughed, short and harsh. "Until you get bored and want someone else. Is there a second cup to reverse the effects of the first?"

"No, if you tired of immortality, you would have to find a way to take your own life or have another take it from you."

"So being immortal isn't entirely safe anyway."

"It's an improvement on your current state."

"I notice that you didn't contradict me when I said that you would become bored with me."

"Ah. No, I didn't, did I?"

Phoebus sighed and rested his chin on his raised knees. "I don't know if I want to live forever."

"Not even to be with me? You said you loved me."

"I shouldn't have said that."

"Why not? If it's what you feel, then you were merely being honest with me."

"Honesty isn't always recommended."

"I think you'll find that in most circumstances, it is."

"It doesn't matter. It's not like I can take the words back."

"No, and I'm glad you said them. But if you love me as you say you do, why wouldn't you wish to be with me forever?"

Phoebus shook his head. "Because you don't love me. If I wanted to spend eternity with someone, it would be with a man who loved me back."

Caspian could tell Phoebus wanted him to say the words, but he couldn't do it. He cared for Phoebus, more than he could recall caring for anyone else in all his long life, yet he didn't love him. He wasn't sure he had ever loved anyone.

"I might grow to love you," he offered. It was the best he could do, and even as he spoke the words, he knew they weren't enough.

"No, you won't," Phoebus replied. "If you thought there was any possibility of that, you wouldn't keep reminding me that I'll always have to share your bed with other men."

"I haven't been with another man since the day I took you to the baths."

"Well, that explains the hostility of your priests."

Caspian grabbed Phoebus' arm. "Have they said anything to you?"

"Nothing much," Phoebus replied. "Just reminding me that you'll soon tire of me, and I knew that already."

"You don't have much faith in me, do you?"

"I'm not Atlantean. I don't have faith in any of you gods."

"That's not what I meant. Faith in me as a man."

Phoebus shook his head, but there was a smile on his lips. "You have more priests than any other god or goddess, save Medina, and you've fucked all of them and cast them aside for the next man who catches your eye. It would be rather arrogant of me to believe that you'll treat me any differently."

"What would it take to convince you to accept the gift of immortality?" Caspian asked, hoping from the bottom of his heart that it was a price he could pay.

"I don't know."

"What if I give up all other men?"

Phoebus raised an eyebrow, skepticism written all over his face.

"No other man will share my bed from this day forth."

"It's easy to say that now, but what about next season? No, Caspian, you know as well as I do that you'd never manage to keep that promise."

Caspian bristled at the—probably justified—insult that he could not keep his word. He held out his hand and a silver dagger appeared in his palm. He took the blade in one hand and sliced the tip across the palm of the other, drawing a thin line of blood.

He tugged aside his robes and placed the wounded hand over his heart.

"By this blood oath, I swear to you that no other man will know my touch as long as you live."

Phoebus stared at him silently.

"Do you believe me?" Caspian asked. "Tell me you trust my word."

Phoebus nodded. "I believe you, but why would you make such an oath?"

"Because I want you at my side, forever. Will you allow me to petition the pantheon on your behalf?"

Phoebus glanced out over the waves for several long minutes. "Yes, Caspian."

"And if they grant my request, you'll join me in immortality?"

Phoebus shivered visibly. "I don't know. I need time to think about it."

"You can take all the time you need."

Caspian healed and cleaned his hand with his powers before lowering Phoebus back onto the sands. "Phoebus, don't return to the ocean tonight. Stay here with me."

Phoebus nodded and captured Caspian's lips in a heated kiss.

Caspian would have liked to keep Phoebus on the Isle until the petition was heard and voted on, but such matters took time.

* * * *

Caspian looked around the table where the rest of the gods were staring at him as though he'd lost his mind. It was unusual for him to call a council meeting at all, and he had certainly never called the pantheon together for a reason such as this. Several immortals looked at him as if they were waiting for him to tell them it was some kind of joke.

"Are you sure about this?" his father finally asked. "I mean, you're not exactly known for fidelity."

Odessa turned to her husband with a glare. "As my son, it's about time he was. I think it's wonderful that our Caspian has finally found someone worthy of his love."

Caspian frowned, but he knew the wisdom of holding his tongue. Telling his mother he wasn't in love would do nothing to help win the support of the other gods.

Cari kept her eyes on her goblet, clearly lost in her thoughts.

"We'll need time to consider your petition," Antar, Caspian's grandfather, said. "And your merman will need to decide if he can make the sacrifice necessary as well."

"Merman?" Mariana interrupted. "This Phoebus is a merman?"

"Yes, he is," Caspian replied.

"You failed to mention *that*."

"I didn't feel it was relevant."

Antar coughed loudly. "Actually, his being mer does pose another problem."

"What do you mean?" Caspian asked.

"Not only will he have to watch his family and friends grow old and pass from this world, he will have to make an additional sacrifice."

"I don't see why."

Antar shook his head. "This is not my rule. The properties of the waters of life cure all ills, remove all scars and, in the case of the mer, transforms them into humans, permanently."

"What are you saying? Phoebus would have to give up his fins?"

"Yes. It isn't something we can change. The waters of life have only been drunk by one mer before, and the effect on the mermaid was immediate."

"I didn't know any mer had become immortal," Caspian said. "Are you sure?"

"It was before you were born. Unfortunately, the loss of her fins was too much for her and she chose to end her life."

Shivers ran up and down Caspian's spine. "Would this happen to Phoebus?"

"I don't know. There was no cure for what ailed her, the malady being entirely in her mind."

"I'll have to talk to Phoebus about this." Caspian couldn't keep it from him, even though he dreaded the thought of Phoebus changing his mind. His merman loved the sea and his mer form. To give that up was a sacrifice Caspian had not anticipated.

* * * *

The potted plant smashed against the door jamb and Phoebus ducked to avoid the shards and dirt as they flew in all directions.

"You devious little whore," Rafe snarled. "How did you do it? How did you talk him into it?"

Phoebus had known word would get out about Caspian's petition, but he hadn't expected it to reach Rafe's ears quite so quickly.

"I knew nothing about such things until he raised the possibility with me," Phoebus said. "I'm mer. You know we know little of the Atlanteans and their customs."

Rafe stalked across the room and pushed Phoebus into the wall. "You lying little worm. I've served Caspian since I came of age. Everything he's ever asked of me, I've done it, willingly, and in the hope that one day he might wish me to join him for eternity."

Phoebus stepped out of Rafe's reach. "You've served him in the hope of what you might gain from him. I thought the priests were meant to serve their gods without conditions."

"You dare to speak to me like that?"

"I don't have to listen to this. These are my rooms, and I want you to get out of them."

"As high priest of the God of Justice, I have the right to enter the quarters of any of the lesser priests."

"I'm not a priest and I'm telling you to leave."

"No, you're not a priest. You're just a whore."

"Whores get paid for their services."

"And what is immortality but the price Caspian is paying for the pleasure of your arse?"

Phoebus clenched his fists and resisted the impulse to smack Rafe in the mouth. The mer were generally a peaceful race, but there was something about the high priest that angered him to a point where he nearly forgot himself.

"Are you that good a fuck?" Rafe asked.

With lightning-fast moves, he grabbed Phoebus and flung him onto the bed.

Phoebus twisted to scramble off the bed, but Rafe was suddenly on top of him. For the first time in his life, Phoebus wished the mer wore clothing, so there would be something between him and Rafe.

He screamed at the top of his lungs, but Rafe only laughed.

"Caspian is meeting with the rest of the gods, putting forward his petition. There's no one to hear you except the other priests, and they hate you as much as I do."

"Get off me," Phoebus shouted as he bucked his hips to try to dislodge the larger man.

Rafe thrust a hand between Phoebus' legs and shoved them apart. "Let's see what you have that he finds so fascinating."

"Caspian will kill you when he finds out about this," Phoebus warned.

"I'm his high priest," Rafe whispered into Phoebus' ear. "I'm untouchable…unlike you."

Phoebus struggled in earnest. He scratched and bit any part of Rafe's body that he could reach. He screamed until his throat felt raw, desperate for someone to hear him.

No one came, and he realized for the first time that he might be in real danger.

With strength he didn't know he had, Phoebus clawed at Rafe's eyes, causing the other man to pull back in pain. Fast as an eel, Phoebus slid from the bed and raced out of the room.

He only stopped running when he had travelled through the portal and back to Atlantis. He swam from the temple and headed to his home—his *real* home. The rooms in the palace were just that. His home was in the water, with the rest of his people.

* * * *

Following the meeting of the pantheon, Caspian found Phoebus in the ocean—*where else?* He watched him for a while before he made his presence known. The merman seemed so happy in the water. Could he really ask him to give up his fins?

A shark swam in the distance and Caspian's mind was made up. If the only way to keep Phoebus safe was for him to become human, then so be it.

He got the merman's attention and took him to land. Rather than risk interruption by Rafe or one of the other priests, Caspian took them to a deserted island where no one would bother them.

"I didn't expect to see you today," Phoebus said as he dried his fins. "I thought you were petitioning the other gods."

"I have been. That's what I wanted to talk to you about."

Phoebus stilled for a moment. "I haven't made my mind up whether I want immortality yet."

"I know. The gods will need time to cast their votes as well. There's something else you need to know, though."

"Yes?"

"If you were to drink from the cup of immortality, you would become human." Caspian bit his lower lip as he tried to read Phoebus' expression.

"You mean permanently, don't you?" Phoebus asked.

"Yes."

"Why didn't you tell me that before?"

Caspian bobbed down so they were on a level. "I didn't know. I only found out at the meeting. No mer has taken the route of immortality in my lifetime, but apparently one did before I was born."

"They did? Who is it? Can I talk to him...or her?"

"I'm sorry. She is no longer with us," Caspian replied, hoping Phoebus would leave it at that and not question him further in that regard. He didn't want to tell him about the mermaid's depression at leaving the sea unless he absolutely had to.

"Oh." Phoebus looked out at the sea. "Then I suppose that's another thing I must take into account when I make my decision."

Caspian nodded, even though Phoebus wasn't looking at him. At least this latest issue hadn't convinced Phoebus to turn down the offer of immortality.

If only I knew how to talk him into accepting it.

Chapter Nine

One moment he was swimming from the fields to the storage cave, his nets full of sea fruits. The next he found himself flopping around on the ground and breathing air. He stared around, wondering where he was. The garden was beautifully tended but unfamiliar.

"Phoebus, welcome," a woman said from behind him.

He twisted around easily, maneuvering his tail so he faced the goddess. She was too beautiful to be a mere mortal, and even though he didn't recognize his exact location, he was fairly sure they were on the Isle of the Gods.

The woman passed him a length of fabric, which he used to dry his fins and regain his legs.

"I'm sorry. Do I know you?" he asked. He hoped his question came across as politely confused and not rude. The last thing he needed was to get on the wrong side of one of the more tempestuous immortals.

"No, my dear. I'm Odessa, Caspian's mother."

Phoebus stared at the goddess in awe. "You don't look old enough," he blurted before he could stop himself.

"Ah, mortals." Odessa laughed. "You should know by now that we don't age like you do. Those who are born immortal stop ageing when we reach maturity."

Phoebus flushed. "I knew that. I just didn't think."

"It's of no matter. You'll soon learn the way of things, especially if you are allowed to join us."

Phoebus still hadn't made his mind up about that and he hoped Odessa hadn't brought him here to try to force him to make a decision. Caspian hadn't been pressing him for an answer, for which he was grateful.

"I'd never do such a thing," Odessa replied in answer to his unspoken thought. He supposed the reading-minds thing was a habit of all immortals.

"Yes, it is. Sometimes we can't help it."

"It's annoying from my point of view," Phoebus muttered. He stood up so they were at eye level.

"Sorry. I'll try not to."

"Thanks."

"You're probably wondering why I've brought you here," Odessa said.

Phoebus nodded and picked up his net of fruits. He didn't want his hard work in the gathering fields to go to waste.

"I thought it was long past time I met the young merman who has captured the heart of my only son." Odessa smiled brightly and swept him into a tight hug.

"Um, I can't breathe," Phoebus managed to gasp.

"Oh, I'm sorry." Odessa released him and he took a deep gulp of air. "Now, come and sit with me. I want to hear all about you."

Phoebus cringed and tried to imagine how he must appear to the goddess. He wasn't a warrior or anyone of importance in the sunken city. All he did was gather fruits, one of the most menial of tasks. There was no possibility of advancement and the mermaids far outnumbered the mermen in the fields.

Caspian didn't seem to mind what he did to earn his keep, but he doubted his lover's parents would be impressed with his choice of partner.

Odessa frowned at him and he wondered whether she had just read his mind again.

"You appear to be worried about something," the goddess said. "I'm trying not to intrude in your thoughts, but when you look at me in the same way a minnow faces a shark, it's rather hard not to pry."

Phoebus sighed. He might as well tell her the truth. She would certainly know if he tried to lie or attempted to evade her questions.

"I suppose I'm worried that I'm not what you would have wanted for your son."

"Why ever would you think that?"

Phoebus shrugged. "Caspian told me that you're the goddess of Family."

"I am, among other things."

"Doesn't it bother you that Caspian has chosen a merman to spend his life with?"

"Do you ask because you're mer or because you're male?"

"Both, I guess."

Odessa smiled. "I have had many centuries to reconcile myself to the fact that Caspian won't be producing any grandchildren for me. It comes as no surprise at all to find that now he has finally decided to settle down, it is with a man. Families can take many forms, and you and Caspian becoming one brings me great joy."

"And my being mer?"

"I won't pretend that all the immortals are accepting of the mer. I am sure you already know they aren't. I think you'll find, however, that I have welcomed the mer into my temples and have always answered their calls as much as the Atlanteans. Maybe even more so, because I would like more of the mer to seek my counsel."

"I've never worshipped any of the Atlantean gods," Phoebus admitted. "I don't think I ever will. My family has never sought the help of the gods."

"It's of no matter. It is enough that you love my son and that he loves you in return."

Phoebus sighed. "I'm not so sure that he does love me."

"But of course he does. He's petitioned the pantheon to be allowed to make you immortal."

"He's done that because of fear."

"What do you mean?"

Phoebus pointed to the healing scar from the shark attack. "He never thought of making me immortal until I got too close to a shark."

"It seems to me as if you got *very* close," Odessa commented. "When you become immortal, all such blemishes will be erased. You will be young and beautiful forever."

"Caspian said that too. I don't care about the scar."

"I can assure you that Caspian would not care about it either. I know my son, and he has not made the petition just to fix that. In fact, he could remove it without making you immortal."

"He offered. I told him not to."

113

"Why?"

"I don't know. Maybe I like having the reminder to keep an eye open for sharks instead of daydreaming."

Odessa laughed. "Were you dreaming of Caspian?"

"Maybe." Phoebus flushed and ducked his head. "I can't seem to get him out of my head."

"That's only natural when you're in love, especially when it's all new and exciting for you."

Phoebus frowned at the use of the word 'love' again. Even though Caspian had put forward the petition to keep him by his side forever, he had never actually used the word.

"Caspian does love you," Odessa assured him. "Oh, sorry. I forgot again. I'm just so used to being around other immortals day after day and we all read each other's minds, mainly to save on time."

"What do you know about the Goddess of Love?" Phoebus asked.

"Ah, I see you've heard about the love potion she slipped into Caspian's wine."

"Is it true?" If anyone had reason to lie to him about such a thing, it was surely Rafe.

"Yes, I believe so. She certainly slipped something into his goblet. I don't know for certain what it was, but if Medina says it was a love potion, I see no reason to doubt her word."

"How long do such potions last?"

"It depends on how strong they are brewed. Most are of short duration and simply invoke lust."

"And the one Caspian drank?"

"I don't know, though I imagine even the strongest spell would have fizzled out by now."

"Would it? It concerns me that he might still be under the influence of Medina's magic. What if I become immortal and the potion wears off? What am I supposed to do with eternity then?"

Odessa took his hand. "Caspian is one of the most stubborn men I have ever known. He is not the sort of weak-willed fool to let himself be overpowered by a love potion for long, especially when Medina has been foolish enough to brag about it."

"Then you think he might really care for me?"

"He loves you."

Phoebus was still dubious. "He's never said he loves me."

"That's because he's stubborn as a mule," Odessa replied. "He doesn't want to lose you, not to a shark or a curse or anything else."

"A *curse*?"

Odessa paled and suddenly wouldn't meet his eyes. "Forget I said anything. It's not important."

"What curse?" Phoebus pressed. "Tell me, please."

"I didn't realize you were unaware," Odessa replied. "I shouldn't have said anything. Caspian will be furious if he discovers I've spoken out of turn. You should probably forget it."

Phoebus glared at the goddess. "You can't just say something like that and leave me wondering."

"Don't worry about it."

"I'm already worrying about it. What curse are you talking about?"

"It's probably nothing."

Phoebus wasn't accepting that. Everything about the demeanor of the goddess told him that this was something—a big something. "If you don't tell me about this curse, I'll refuse Caspian's offer, even if the pantheon says I can become immortal."

Odessa stared at him, open-mouthed. "That's blackmail!"

"I know."

"You dare to blackmail a goddess?"

"Yes, I do."

Odessa's lips twitched, as though she fought back a smile. Then she sighed and shook her head. "My son has certainly met his match with you."

"The curse," Phoebus prompted. There was no way he was going to allow her to slyly change the subject before he discovered what she was talking about.

Odessa mumbled something under her breath that sounded rather uncomplimentary before seeming to come to a decision. "You'll know that Caspian has never been short of company?"

"Is that the polite way of saying he's had a lot of lovers?"

"Yes, I suppose you could say that."

"Then yes, I know. What does that have to do with a curse?"

"Caspian decided to bed Medina's priests—all of them—and the goddess wasn't very happy about it."

"But Medina has dozens of priests."

"Yes, and Caspian took each and every one of them into his bed. He wasn't exactly discreet about it either. You might say he flaunted his conquests, mostly because he knew it would infuriate Medina."

"They don't get along, do they?"

"You've noticed that."

"It's rather hard not to."

"Yes, well, Medina doesn't handle rejection well and Caspian turned her down."

"But Caspian never takes women to his bed."

"I know, but Medina didn't know that at the time. This was many centuries ago. Caspian rejected her, but instead of doing so privately and with tact, he did so in public, humiliating her in the process."

"Oh dear."

"They have been fighting and squabbling ever since. Caspian's main method of annoying Medina seems to be to lure her priests into his bed. Every time a new one takes his post, Caspian makes his move and Medina loses her temper. Why the silly woman doesn't just hire females is beyond me. A few decades of women serving her and Caspian would forget about their feud. I doubt he would go so far as to try to lure women into his bed. But who am I to interfere? Anyway, they have been carrying on in this immature manner for centuries. Recently, however, Caspian not only bedded a number of Medina's current priests, but in doing so they missed an important ceremony of their goddess. Medina was furious and spoke words in anger that might amount to a curse."

"What did she say?"

"She told him that he would find love but lose it after a short time. It may not be a true curse. Caspian doesn't think she invoked her powers. Unfortunately, gods and goddesses can curse others without actually meaning to. Unlike mortals, our words have power, and as such Medina may well have cursed Caspian to lose his love—to lose you."

"*If* he loves me," Phoebus said.

"He *does*. I have no doubt on that point. When the shark attacked you, it probably reminded him of Medina's words and he realized how close he was to losing you. By making you immortal, he need not fear her curse."

Phoebus nodded, understanding what the goddess was saying, even as his temper rose. Medina was the one who had sent him to Caspian that first time he had called for her help. Had she already cursed him at that point? Was he simply a pawn in the centuries-old feud of two squabbling gods?

He had to know the truth.

He couldn't make a decision about eternity without having all of the facts. He guessed he would be making another visit to the Goddess of Love.

* * * *

Odessa had no hesitation in giving Phoebus directions to Medina's temple. He had the distinct impression she was looking forward to seeing what happened when he confronted the goddess.

As he approached the building, he realized he would probably have recognized it anyway. No other temple had quite the same number of men sprawled about on the lawn outside.

He searched the crowd for a familiar face, but he didn't see anyone he knew.

One youth caught his eye as he picked his way through the masses. He winked at Phoebus and rubbed his groin suggestively. "Can I help you?"

"I'm searching for Medina. Is she here?"

"She's around somewhere," the man replied. "How about you come and sit with me while we wait for her to appear?"

Phoebus shook his head. "No, thank you."

"Are you sure? You look like a man who knows what a cock is for."

"Oh, he does," another man remarked from a short distance away.

"You know him?" the first man asked.

"Yes. He's the merman Caspian has petitioned the pantheon to make immortal. You don't want to be infringing on the God of Justice's territory."

Phoebus didn't like being referred to as Caspian's 'territory', but he didn't get the chance to say anything further.

Everyone around him suddenly jumped to their feet and hurried into the temple. He hadn't seen or heard anything to signal the priests had been called inside, but clearly they had been summoned.

Guessing that Medina was the one who had called them, Phoebus followed behind, hoping to find the goddess that way.

Inside the temple was a hive of activity. The priests all seemed to be engrossed in their tasks with no one paying him any mind at all.

He didn't see Medina at first, but suddenly there she was, standing just a few feet away from him.

"Good afternoon, Phoebus. What can I do for you today?"

"I wanted to talk to you about something," Phoebus said. "Is there somewhere we can speak privately?"

Medina replied by transporting them into what he guessed were her private chambers. "What is it you wish to ask me? Obviously your mating trigger has been found, so I can't imagine what else you might want, unless Caspian isn't enough for you?"

"He is everything I could have wanted in a lover," Phoebus replied.

"I'm so happy for you."

"Are you?" Phoebus asked. "Because I've heard otherwise."

Medina frowned, her face the image of confusion.

"Am I cursed?" he asked.

"Men know when I've cursed them," Medina replied with a laugh. "They usually find themselves with limp cocks that won't perform, no matter what they try. Your own is clearly in full working order."

Phoebus suspected she might be deliberately avoiding his question. Perhaps another tactic was in order. "Did you curse Caspian to find love and lose it?"

Medina waved away his question. "I might have said something to that effect. You shouldn't let it trouble you."

"Not let it trouble me?" Phoebus shouted. "I love him and you've cursed him to lose me!"

"It's not as bad as you think."

"Did you know you'd cursed him when you sent me to his temple?"

"Yes," Medina confirmed. Phoebus formed the distinct impression she wasn't bothered about this in the slightest.

"You deliberately sent me to him, knowing you'd cursed him and knowing it wasn't just his life you were interfering with. It was mine too."

Medina, who had been perfectly calm just moments before, rose from her seat, her eyes blazing in fury. Phoebus had never seen anything like it and cringed at the unnatural gaze.

"You dare to speak to me that way?"

Phoebus shrank back against the archway.

"Caspian needs to learn a lesson, and yes, I sent you to him to help with that. He has found love and he was destined to lose it."

"Was?" Phoebus squeaked.

"He seeks to avoid the curse by making you immortal," Medina said. "And it will work, if the pantheon votes in his favor."

Phoebus didn't think she sounded too pleased about the prospect.

Suddenly all the heat went out of her eyes and she sat back down with a sigh.

"Non-specific curses, like this one, are hard to predict. They don't always play out as I intend them to."

"What do you mean?"

"I mean I thought you'd reject Caspian. There you were, an innocent merman, faced with a god who has bedded so many men he lost count centuries ago. I never imagined you would develop any feelings for him, least of all love."

"But I did," Phoebus said. "I love him, but because of your curse, I'm going to lose him."

"Not if you become immortal," Medina reminded him. "If it helps to make amends, I will cast my vote in your favor. I'll also do my best to convince those gods who value my opinion to do likewise."

"You know I'll have to give up my fins to become immortal?" Phoebus asked.

"Yes, that's something that can't be helped, I'm afraid."

"Mer is what I am. I've never known anything else."

"When you've lived as a man for a few centuries, you'll barely remember what it was to have fins."

"That's what worries me. I don't want to forget who I am."

Medina shrugged and the sound of someone calling her from outside distracted her from his contemplation.

She was gone in a flash, leaving him to wonder what in the world he was going to do.

Chapter Ten

Phoebus floated on the water, letting the comfortable familiarity of the sea ease his troubled mind. He flipped his fins, wondering if this might be one of the last times he did this.

Could he really give up being mer and embrace life with only one form?

He didn't know.

It wasn't just the lack of fins that troubled him. He wasn't sure he wanted to live forever, not when it meant losing his family and friends to the ravages of time.

Caspian had assured him that he would still be able to visit Atlantis, survive under the ocean and communicate with the mer telepathically. It wasn't as if he would become a mortal human. As an immortal, he would at least have powers that would enable him to do as the Atlanteans did.

He wondered if Caspian would let him live in the sunken city. Somehow he doubted it.

Phoebus would be much happier in the ocean than sharing the palace with Caspian's priests.

"There you are," Caspian said, startling Phoebus, who still wasn't quite used to immortals appearing out of thin air. "What are you doing out here?"

Phoebus recovered his composure and settled back again. Caspian floated alongside him. "Just thinking."

"You shouldn't really swim so far from the guards," Caspian warned. "It can be dangerous out here on your own."

"I'm perfectly fine."

"Still, all it takes is one shark and—"

Phoebus flipped and swiped at Caspian with his tail, sending the god spinning under the water. "I'm not *completely* helpless, you know."

Caspian spluttered as he righted himself. "I never said you were. I just couldn't bear to lose you, not when we're so close to the vote."

Phoebus sighed and swam into Caspian's arms. "I know. Medina's curse really has you worried, doesn't it?"

"You know about that?" Caspian asked. "Who told you?"

"It doesn't matter. I'm not worried about it."

"I'm probably scared enough for both of us," Caspian admitted.

Phoebus kissed him, light and brief. "The vote is just two days away. I think I can manage to stay out of trouble until then."

Caspian raised an eyebrow, his expression dubious.

A moment later Phoebus found himself on his back in Caspian's bed, the god hovering over him.

"Much better," Caspian said. "I think I'll just keep you right here until the vote."

Phoebus tried to give him a stern glare, but with Caspian teasing his fins, he couldn't quite manage it. "You do remember that I've not made my mind up yet?"

Caspian frowned at the reminder. "Why wouldn't you want this?"

A pointed cough in the archway provided one of the reasons. Rafe glared at them, though quickly schooled his features into a more neutral expression the moment Caspian turned to face him.

"What is it, Rafe?"

Rafe dropped to one knee. "Caspian, my god, I bring news of the offerings made in your temple in the city."

"You can report on that later. Just distribute the offerings as normal. You know the procedure."

Rafe continued to linger in the entrance.

"What *is* it?" Caspian repeated.

"Do you want some company?" Rafe asked. "It has been some time since you requested my services, and I understand you've not been inviting your other priests to your bed either."

"I have all the company I need," Caspian replied. "Please deal with the offerings and spread the word that I'm not to be disturbed for the rest of the day."

"Very good," Rafe said before disappearing through the archway.

Phoebus shivered, unable to shake the uneasy feeling Rafe always left him with.

"Now, where were we?" Caspian said.

Phoebus stopped his progression back down on top of him with a firm hand. "Caspian, why do your priests have to live here in the palace?"

"They have always lived here," Caspian replied. "It's the custom."

"Andaman's priests don't live with him."

"Andaman has never fucked his priests, so he doesn't need them close by."

Phoebus pushed Caspian off him and swung around. With his fins still slightly damp, he couldn't yet rise from the bed and storm out of the room, but the lack of legs was the only thing stopping him.

"What did I say?" Caspian asked, sounding confused.

"You really have no idea, do you?" Phoebus frantically dried his tail with the sheet.

"Apparently not. Would you care to enlighten me?"

"You want to keep Rafe and the others close by, so they're near at hand to warm your bed."

Caspian leaped off the bed and towered over him. "Didn't you just hear me send him away, telling him I have all the company I want?"

"Yes, I heard."

"Then what's the problem?"

"Why can't they live in Atlantis?" Phoebus asked. "If you truly want me by your side, to share your life and build a home with you, why can't you send them away?"

"This palace is their home."

Phoebus finally regained his legs and he rose to stand face-to-face with Caspian. "You're asking me to make this my home too. Don't I get a say in this?"

"It seems that you're already having that say," Caspian retorted.

"I might be having my say, but you're not exactly listening to me. If I accept your offer—if your petition is passed—you're expecting me to share your home with a dozen other men. Half of those hate me because I'm mer, and the other half because they think I've stolen your affections from them."

"They don't hate you," Caspian said. "If they did, I'd know. I *can* read their minds."

"And they've had plenty of time to learn how to bury their thoughts," Phoebus argued. "You can be right there in the room when they send their insults directly to me without you ever hearing them."

Caspian appeared taken aback and Phoebus wondered whether he had said something he shouldn't have.

"My priests say inappropriate things to you in my presence?" Caspian asked.

Phoebus sat back on the bed with a sigh. "I shouldn't have said anything."

"Do they?" Caspian pressed.

"Yes."

"Which ones dare to do this?"

Phoebus shrugged. "It doesn't matter. I don't take any notice of them. It's only words."

"Clearly you do take notice or you wouldn't mention it. Now tell me who?"

"It would be easier to tell you which of them *don't* taunt me," Phoebus muttered.

Caspian sat beside him and took hold of his hand. "I'm sorry, Phoebus. I have always tried to give my priests privacy within their own heads. I dislike it when other immortals pry into my thoughts, so I try not to do it to others. I see I have been remiss in my duties though. Come. Put on a robe and follow me."

"What are you going to do?" Phoebus asked. He made no effort to find a robe or even move from his spot on the bed. He had a bad feeling about this. The last thing he needed was for the priests to have another reason to hate him.

Caspian fetched him a robe and pulled him to his feet. He pulled the robe around him, tying the sash and straightening the fabric with a fastidiousness that Phoebus had never seen before. When he was presentable, Caspian changed his own robes with nothing more than a thought, the wet ones disappearing and his best dry ones taking their place.

"Why didn't you make my robe appear like that?" Phoebus asked, partly from curiosity and partly to stall for time.

Caspian smiled and gave him a quick peck on the lips. "I like dressing you nearly as much as I like undressing you. You should know by now that I don't always consider speed to be a good thing. Now come along. I've summoned all the priests for an audience in the temple."

"You really don't have to do that," Phoebus said. "It might make things worse."

Caspian ignored him and transported them immediately into the temple proper.

All of Caspian's priests had gathered, most appearing rather confused as to what they were doing there.

Caspian sat on his throne and gestured for Phoebus to stand beside him.

"I would like your attention, please," Caspian said, his voice echoing unnaturally throughout the room.

The priests all faced him, save for Rafe, who stood with his head bowed but his eyes trained firmly on Phoebus. He didn't need to meet the high priest's gaze to feel the malevolence in it.

Caspian said nothing and Phoebus began to fidget, wanting him to hurry things along.

"I see," Caspian finally said, drawing Phoebus' attention back to him. He raised his hand to Phoebus, who took it and let the god draw him near. "I have always tried to give you all privacy. Unlike some of the other immortals, I don't routinely poke into the minds of my priests. Perhaps I should have done so."

Several of the priests shifted their feet, heads bowed and faces flushed.

Caspian maintained his grip on Phoebus' hand as he rose from his throne. "Phoebus is not a passing fancy. He is not a whore. He is the man I intend to spend my life with. As such, you will all treat him with respect. If you don't feel you are able to do this, then I would recommend you renounce me right here and now and return to Atlantis, permanently."

Phoebus drew in a sharp breath but Caspian wasn't finished.

"If the only reason you remain in my service is because you desire my body, then again, I tell you to renounce me and find another lover. From this day forward, Phoebus is the only man I will take into my bed. If anyone here thinks they can convince me otherwise, leave now."

Caspian raised Phoebus' hand to his lips and kissed his palm. "From now on, I will be routinely checking in with each of you, and I will see anything you try to hide from me."

"Caspian, you don't have to do that," Phoebus whispered, but his lover ignored him.

"If you cannot accept Phoebus in my life, leave my service. For if I discover any one of you disrespecting him again, my fury will know no bounds. You will be cast from my temple, and you will find no work with any other immortal in the Atlantean pantheon. You will treat Phoebus as you would me or you will pay the price for your deceitfulness. Now, get back to work, all of you, and remember that your thoughts are no longer your own."

They scattered like a flock of birds, hurrying from the room to escape their chosen god's temper. Even Rafe appeared taken aback at Caspian's speech.

When the room had emptied, Caspian turned back to Phoebus. "I'm sorry I didn't notice how my priests were treating you."

Phoebus shrugged. "You do know that the worst of them won't change their ways? Wouldn't it just be easier to put some distance between them and the palace now, rather than have to dismiss them later from your service entirely?"

"They know not to cross me," Caspian said.

"But—"

"No." Caspian raised his fingers to Phoebus' lips. "The palace is their home, just as it is yours. They have been given fair warning of what they must do from now on. If any of them step out of line, I will see them gone from here, but until then, I will not send them from their home. Do you understand me?"

Phoebus nodded. He wasn't asking for them to be dismissed. He just wanted to have a home that was for the two of them, without Caspian's entourage. He supposed that it was too much to ask for and the price of immortality and loving a god.

"A compromise," Caspian said.

"Did you just read my mind?" Phoebus asked.

"Yes, and I make no apologies for it this time."

"What sort of compromise?"

"In future, when priests enter my service, they shall live on Earth, not on the Isle of the Gods."

"That's a compromise?"

"Yes. In time, those who serve me now will come to the end of their lives. You will have me to yourself for eternity. Surely you can share our home with them for a little time."

"They could live another hundred years!"

Caspian laughed. "You are mortal still. You think a hundred years is a long time. You will soon find that it is gone in the blink of an eye. And for as long as you are sharing your home with my priests, I will be watching them carefully. I promise I will protect you from their hostility."

Phoebus wasn't entirely convinced, but the compromise was clearly the best offer he was going to get.

Now all he had to do was make the final decision about whether he accepted immortality or not.

As he always did when he needed to think things through, Phoebus returned to the ocean and his mer form. He couldn't put off the decision much longer.

He swam back and forth in his small house at the edge of the city as he weighed his options. He knew Caspian wanted him to live on the Isle of the Gods, but perhaps he might allow him to keep this place, at least until his current priests were no longer living. Surely, with all the compromises he was making, he could ask Caspian for this one.

Ajax found him there and swam down to sit on one of the sponges. *"You're not still fussing about whether to become immortal, are you?"*

"Yes, of course I am."

"Why is it such a hard decision to make? I'd have thought after your recent brush with death, you'd be eager for it."

"It was hardly a brush with death," Phoebus replied. *"The shark barely grazed me."*

"If it was close enough to touch you, it was a brush with death. I'm surprised Caspian has even let you back into the water while you're still vulnerable."

"He doesn't know I'm here," Phoebus said.

"Uh-oh."

"I don't need his permission to come to the ocean. I'm not his prisoner."

"I know, but he does seem rather protective of you. If it's already annoying you after so short a time, how do you think you'll handle eternity living with him?"

"He won't worry so much if I become immortal. I just don't know whether his reasons for making the petition are the right ones."

"What do you mean?"

Phoebus swam down onto his own sponge. *"If I was sure of his love, I'd not be hesitating to give up my fins at all."*

"Give up your fins? What are you talking about?"

Phoebus cursed his slip of the tongue. He hadn't meant to mention that part, though perhaps it was for the best. Ajax was mer and it might be good to have his opinion too.

"If I drink from this cup and become immortal, I will also become human, completely human. I'll no longer be mer."

Ajax stared at him, his mouth hanging open. *"Are you telling me that you'd give up your fins for him?"*

"If I thought he was doing this out of love, then yes."

"But you're mer. It's part of who you are. You could never give up the sea."

"For the right man, I would. I just don't know if Caspian is the one."

"He seems to favor your company above all others."

"For the moment, but what about in years to come? Just because he hasn't tired of me yet, doesn't mean he won't."

"He does have something of a reputation, but you knew this anyway. At least he doesn't flaunt his other lovers in front of you."

"He has promised not to take any other men into his bed," Phoebus admitted.

*"Well, there you go. He **must** love you."*

"He's never said the words, and when I told him I loved him, he wasn't exactly thrilled to hear me say it."

"Do you mean to tell me that the only reason you aren't flipping your fins in delight at the idea of immortality is because Caspian hasn't said he loves you?"

"Well…"

"You do realize that many men, both mer and human, say those words without ever meaning them?"

"Yes."

"Then why is it so important to you that Caspian says them? Surely you don't need those words to be sure of his feelings?"

"I guess not."

Ajax gave a firm nod. *"What you need to be asking yourself is not whether Caspian loves you, but whether you love him enough to give up such a huge part of what you are for him. I don't think I could do it."*

Phoebus closed his eyes and rested his head on the sponge. *"I think I could."*

* * * *

Later that night, Phoebus stood in the doorway to Caspian's bedchamber, watching the sleeping god. There were no other men in his bed and Phoebus realized that he had never doubted that would be the case. Caspian had given his word and he knew he would keep it.

As quietly as he could, Phoebus slipped across the room and slid beneath the covers.

"Phoebus," Caspian murmured sleepily as he tugged him into his arms.

"Who else?" Phoebus whispered back, ridiculously pleased that even in his drowsy state, Caspian had known who was crawling into bed with him.

Caspian opened his eyes and smiled. "You've been in the ocean. You smell like the sea."

"I'll probably always smell like that, even when I'm human."

"When?"

"Well, providing the petition is successful."

"Does that mean you've made your decision?"

"Yes." Phoebus kissed Caspian and pressed their bodies together. "I love you."

Caspian didn't say the words back, but this time Phoebus didn't let the lack of response bother him. Caspian's kisses told him all that he needed to know about the god's feelings for him.

Chapter Eleven

Caspian didn't think he had ever been so nervous in his entire life. He paced back and forth along the path outside the council chamber, waiting for the rest of the gods to answer his grandfather's summons. In just a few more minutes, he would find out whether Phoebus would be allowed to join the immortals.

Even though Phoebus was the kindest and most deserving man he knew, Caspian still wasn't sure how the vote would go. There were too many immortals who were prejudiced against the mer, so the vote would be close.

"Nervous?" Odessa asked as she met him coming down the path as she was on her way up it.

"Terrified," Caspian admitted. "What am I going to do if the vote is no?"

"From what I've heard, that's very unlikely to be the case, but even if it is, you can always petition again in a few years."

"You know as well as I do that if the vote is no now, it'll be exactly the same then."

"Stop worrying so much. It's not fitting for a god."

"Sorry, Mother. I can't help it. I don't think I could stand it if I lost Phoebus."

"Medina's curse may not come to pass, even if it is a true curse and not just her blustering."

"I know, but I don't want to take any risks with his life."

"You assume that the curse means he would die," Odessa said. "He might just leave you for another."

"That isn't helping, Mother."

"Or it could be simple old age and a normal mortal death that will take him from you, many years from now."

"No, it won't be that." Caspian shook his head. "Medina said I would only know love for a short time before I lost it."

"Mortal lives *are* only a short time when compared to immortality."

"I know, but I don't want to lose him at all."

Odessa linked her arm through his and steered him toward the chamber. "I don't want you to lose him either. I've never seen you so happy. It's like I've been telling you all these years… Loving one man is far more fulfilling than bedding many men who you don't even care for."

Caspian nodded. He still didn't know whether what he felt for Phoebus was love, but his feelings were certainly stronger than anything he had ever felt before. He also had the sense to know that saying he wasn't in love right now would be a sure-fire way to persuade any immortal in earshot to vote against his petition, and he couldn't risk that happening. He just hoped they didn't delve into his mind to ascertain the depth of his feelings for Phoebus.

Inside the chamber, most of the gods were already gathered. The final few arrived shortly after Caspian had taken his seat.

"We all know why we are here today," Antar said. "To vote on Caspian's petition to make his lover Phoebus immortal. We have all had time to consider his request and I am aware that some of you have spoken to Phoebus to see what sort of a man he is. Now we will cast our votes. All those in favor of Phoebus becoming immortal, please raise your hands."

Caspian quickly counted the votes, noting that his parents and sister all had their hands raised, along with Medina, which came as something of a surprise. More predictably, Mariana and her friends had not voted in his favor.

"Making a merman immortal is an insult to every god and goddess here," Mariana complained.

Caspian ignored her. She had cast her vote the same as everyone else and she had been outnumbered.

"I'm so happy for you," Odessa said as she swept Caspian into a hug. "I'm sure you can't wait to tell him the good news."

Caspian nearly shook with relief. Phoebus would be safe from the curse and he never had to risk losing his merman to illness, sharks or even old age.

His father patted him on the shoulder. "I haven't spoken to Phoebus myself, but I hope to get to know him soon. I hope he makes you as happy as your mother makes me."

"I'm sure he will."

Cari gave him a smile and a nod. "I won't keep you from going to tell him the news. I'll just step aside so you don't trample me in your rush through the archway."

Caspian laughed and stepped around her. Unfortunately, while his sister had anticipated his eagerness to leave, there were others who were not so astute. It seemed as though the news would have to wait a little bit longer after all.

* * * *

Rafe had waited until Caspian was at the council of the gods. The god had barely left before the high priest was hovering in Phoebus' doorway, his usual sneer on his face.

"Get out," Phoebus said as he climbed off the bed. He wasn't going to give him a chance to overpower him again like he had done the last time he had entered his rooms uninvited.

"I hear the petition is likely to go against you," Rafe said. "What are you going to do then?"

Phoebus had no idea which way the various gods would be voting and he doubted Rafe knew either. Most gods rarely confided in their own priests, and they certainly weren't going to be telling their private business to the devoted follower of another god.

"Aren't you going to answer me?" Rafe pressed.

"No, I'm not," Phoebus replied. "What I do with my life is none of your business. Becoming immortal is not my only ambition in life."

"From what I've heard, you have no ambitions at all," Rafe said. "I heard the guards hired your sister rather than allow you into their ranks. That is truly pitiful. What's it like to spend your life doing women's work while a mermaid took the job you truly wanted?"

"I'm perfectly happy with the job I have, which is more than you are." Phoebus gave the priest a cold smile. "At least I assume you're unhappy in your position, considering the amount of complaining you do."

"I was content in my duties until you came along," Rafe snarled. "I still don't know what Caspian sees in you. No merman is that good a fuck."

Phoebus rolled his eyes. "You seem to be quite obsessed with my performance in the bedchamber. I'd say that's a sign of your own insecurities more than anything else."

"I'm not insecure. I know what to do with my cock—unlike a pathetic merman who couldn't even figure out his own mating trigger because he was so inexperienced."

Phoebus bristled at the insult but there was nothing he could really say in response. Rafe was right about his ignorance and the high priest would always have more experience than he did.

Rafe stepped closer. "I hear you wanted to fuck Caspian."

Phoebus cringed as he realized Rafe had probably been eavesdropping on their conversations.

"He'll never let you do that. I fucked him once, but he won't allow any of the other priests to do so."

"You're lying," Phoebus said. Caspian was a lot of things, not all of them good, but he wasn't a liar. Rafe was simply trying to goad him, and he refused to rise to the bait.

"You can't be sure about that," Rafe taunted.

"Yes, I can, and even if you had fucked him—which you haven't—it is of no consequence to me."

Phoebus walked past Rafe and into the corridor. He would go to the sunken city until Caspian returned with the result of the petition. He had no reason to wait around here, listening to Rafe's insults and jibes.

"Going so soon?" Rafe asked as he grabbed Phoebus' arm and pulled him to a halt.

"Let go of me."

"No, I don't think I will," Rafe said. "I want to know what you have that has my god acting so besotted."

Phoebus yanked himself free of Rafe's arm, only to be pushed into the wall, with Rafe pressed against his back. "Get away from me!"

"Why? A whore doesn't care who fucks him, as long as he gets paid."

"I'm not a whore."

"I say you are."

Phoebus twisted free once more and raced for the temple and the portal back to Atlantis.

"Caspian!" he yelled, hoping the god might be able to hear his call, even if he weren't close by.

Rafe was right behind him when Phoebus arrived in the main temple. If he could just get to the crystal and open the portal, he could escape to the sea where he'd be safe. Rafe could follow him, but as a merman, he had an advantage in the water, and there was only a short swim into the city where the rest of the mer would be able to help him.

One of Rafe's fellow priests was suddenly in front of him. Phoebus tried to duck under his arm but the bigger man blocked his path, the grin on his face making it clear he was doing it deliberately.

"Surely you don't want to leave us so soon?" Rafe asked. "After all, Caspian wants you to become one of the family. A permanent member."

"Let me past," Phoebus ordered the priest in front of him.

The priest laughed and stepped aside, offering a sweeping bow toward the portal.

Phoebus bolted across the room but it was too late. The priest had stalled him for too long and he was still several feet away from the crystal when Rafe grabbed him from behind, bringing him crashing to the stone floor.

His knee twisted painfully, but he forced himself to ignore the pain as he continued struggling to free himself.

"Caspian," he yelled.

"He can't hear you," Rafe hissed. "No god can hear the prayers of their followers when they're in a council meeting. The gods don't like to be interrupted with trivialities when they have important things to discuss. Not that you're important. I'm only telling you this so you can cease your whining for your lover."

"Rafe, don't you think that's enough?" the priest who had stalled Phoebus asked.

"Help me," Phoebus begged, hoping that common sense would prevail.

"Get out of here," Rafe shouted. "This is not your concern."

"Rafe, you know Caspian favors this merman."

"Favors him over the priests who have served him their entire lives," Rafe replied. He twisted Phoebus' arm behind his back, and Phoebus screamed in pain. "I intend to sample this whore before I get rid of him once and for all. Unless you want to add your blood to his, you'll walk away, right now."

"Please help me," Phoebus tried again. "Please don't let him do this."

The priest shook his head but didn't step forward. Instead, he turned and walked away, leaving Phoebus alone in the temple with Rafe.

Phoebus felt as though he were suffocating under the weight of the heavier man on top of him. He squirmed and shouted, hoping the priest would come back or that someone — anyone — would hear him and come to his rescue.

"Be quiet or I'll cut out your tongue," Rafe snarled, and Phoebus saw the flash of a blade in the corner of his eye. He had no doubt Rafe would carry out his threat.

"Just get it over with," Phoebus whispered. He closed his eyes and tried to imagine he was anywhere else but here.

Rafe pulled his head back and Phoebus whimpered in pain. "I will not watch my god brought to ruin by a whore."

The moment the blade touched his skin, Phoebus renewed his struggles, but Rafe was bigger, stronger and had the advantage of a weapon — a knife that pressed into his flesh every time he tried to release himself from his tormentor's grasp.

"Don't do this," Phoebus said. "You know Caspian wouldn't want you to do this."

"Once you're gone, Caspian will come to his senses."

Phoebus could tell there was no reasoning with him, but he had to keep trying. Surely someone would come to the temple sooner or later. If he could just keep him talking until help arrived.

"Did you know that in the olden days, the Atlanteans used to make sacrifices to the gods?" Rafe whispered into his ear. "*Human* sacrifices."

Phoebus' heart raced, blood rushed to his head and the room swayed around him.

"Personally, I always thought it a tradition that should be revived. You should be honored at the thought of being sacrificed to the gods."

Phoebus struggled again, lashing out wildly and frantically as he tried to break free.

He didn't know how much time had passed. His throat was raw from screaming, but no one answered his cries. He hoped Caspian returned soon and used his powers to take away the pain Rafe had inflicted upon his body. He knew he couldn't take much more of this.

Pain erupting in his chest was the last thing he felt as he slumped to the ground.

* * * *

Caspian departed the meeting with a good feeling about the future. He had left Phoebus in his bed this morning and he had high hopes of finding him there when he returned. Now that the council meeting was over, he had the rest of the day to enjoy time with his lover, then tonight, he would take Phoebus to the glade where the cup of immortality was kept, and once he had drunk from it, everything would be fine.

As he approached his temple, he spotted most of his priests lingering around outside. This wasn't entirely unusual, but they weren't normally standing on the path as though hesitant to enter.

"What's happening here?" Caspian asked as he approached the priests.

None of them seemed to want to meet his eyes, which was odd in itself since he had known all of them intimately at one time or another.

"Seth?" Caspian approached the nearest of the men and the one he considered most likely to cave under pressure if he was forced to demand answers from them.

Seth shuffled his feet and nodded toward the entrance. "You should probably go inside."

Caspian looked from one priest to another as he waited for someone to say something. He didn't know why he wasn't going into the temple as Seth had said. Something he thought might be fear seemed to be preventing him from taking that step.

"What's happened?" Caspian demanded.

Seth dropped to one knee and bowed his head. One by one the rest of the priests followed his example.

Caspian had never demanded subservience from his priests and to see them all on their knees before him sent a shiver down his spine. "Where's Rafe?" he asked when he realized his high priest was the only man missing from their number.

Seth pointed at the door.

Caspian could see they weren't going to tell him what was happening. He could read one of their minds and find out immediately what troubled them, but that same fear of what he might find stopped him. He forced himself to enter his temple.

He saw Rafe immediately. His high priest knelt on the floor, facing Caspian's throne. He wore his dress robes with the long wide sleeves and his arms were spread wide.

"Rafe?" Caspian asked. He was vaguely aware of the other priests entering behind him.

His high priest stood and turned to face him. It was only when he rose Caspian saw what his robes had previously hidden from view.

"Phoebus!" Caspian ran across the room and dropped to his knees beside him.

It was too late. He knew it immediately.

He recognized Rafe's knife, still buried in Phoebus' chest, and he pulled it out and tossed it aside.

"Do you accept my sacrifice, my god?" Rafe asked.

Caspian screamed at the top of his lungs, his powers reverberating through the temple. The ground moved as an earthquake shook the island. The sight of Phoebus' dead body sent his powers spiraling out of his control for the first time in his life.

"Caspian, what is it?"

"Caspian?"

"Son?"

The voices were echoing through the temple but Caspian didn't pay any attention to them. He couldn't. The rage he felt wouldn't allow for him to do anything right now.

Caspian gathered Phoebus into his arms and gently brushed his hair back from his face.

Cari knelt down on the other side of him. Tears streamed down her face. "I'm so sorry. I'm sorry I didn't see this coming."

"It isn't your fault, my daughter," Odessa said as she drew nearer. "You know your powers can never show things that will happen in the temple of another god. It is the way it has always been."

"Still, I knew there was tension and jealousy between Phoebus and the priests. I should have seen something of what would happen."

Caspian's father shook his head. "Your mother is right. It's not your fault that your powers are limited."

The island finally stopped shaking as Caspian brought his powers back under his control.

He took in a long deep breath and forced himself to calm the storm raging outside the temple. Standing close by, Medina shuffled her feet and wouldn't look at him.

"You did this," Caspian shouted at her. "Your curse has played out. Are you happy now?"

"No," Medina whispered. "I didn't want him to die."

"I don't care what you intended!"

"Phoebus was a sweet young merman. I would never have wished him harm."

"Your damned love spell is the cause of all of this."

"No. It can't be."

"Undo the magic," Caspian demanded. "You've made your point."

Medina nodded and raised her hand toward him. A glow emanated from her palm and her hair whipped about her head as though she were standing in the wind. "I cannot," she finally said, her voice coming from a distance.

"Why not?" Caspian snapped. "You made me love him, now make it stop."

"I opened your heart and your mind to the possibility of love," Medina said. "The spell has already run its course. Your feelings are not a result of my magic. They are real, and as such, I cannot remove them."

Caspian blinked as Medina faded in and out of view. It was almost as though she was having difficulty maintaining her corporeal form.

Caspian's father placed his hand on his son's shoulder and Caspian acknowledged the gesture with a small nod.

"To murder the chosen consort of a god is unprecedented," Cynbel said. "This cannot go unpunished. Caspian, what do you suggest?"

Caspian shook his head. "Not now, father. I can't deal out justice right now."

Cynbel squeezed his shoulder. "Then I will do so for you. From this day forth, Atlantis will no longer be home to the Atlanteans. They will be banished from the city and will walk on land with no memory of their heritage."

"You would punish an entire people for the crime of one man?"

Caspian recognized the voice of Mariana, goddess of sea creatures. Several immortals were agreeing with her.

Cynbel banged his trident on the floor. "This isn't just *any* crime. This is the murder of a god's consort, in that god's own temple."

"It was a sacrifice," Rafe argued. "You used to accept sacrifices."

Cynbel shook his head. "This was no sacrifice. You didn't kill the merman to appease your god. You did it to satisfy your own jealousy. You will be the first to be sent from this place."

"No!" Caspian shouted. "Banish whoever you wish but not him. I will punish him myself — but not right now."

"Of course, my son," Cynbel said. "The rest of the Atlanteans will be gone from the city before sunset."

"What of our priests and priestesses?" one of the goddesses asked. "Are they to be banished too?"

"They are," Cynbel replied. "The discord between the Atlanteans and the mer has been escalating for many years. This will end today."

"I thought you'd be all for war," Mariana commented. "It is your specialty, after all."

"This is not a war among men," Cynbel said. "The mer are peaceful. They do not crave land or power or anything else that humans kill each other over. The mer have done nothing to earn the hatred of the Atlanteans."

Mariana sneered. "Just because they're too weak and foolish to fight back."

"It isn't weak to want to live in peace. It isn't foolish to desire a life without war."

"Coming from the God of War, I find that a rather strange attitude to have."

"There is no glory to be found in defeating an opponent who has no wish to fight," Cynbel said.

Caspian carefully picked up Phoebus and carried him away from the arguing immortals. His mother and sister followed him.

"Can you see him?" Caspian asked Cari. "When will I find him again?"

Cari closed her eyes for several long moments, but when she opened them again, she shook her head. "I'm sorry. I do not see him."

"But you must," Caspian said. "He'll be reborn sooner or later. Even if his body is different, his soul will be the same. You can see that, can't you?"

"The mer are not reborn in the way of humans," Cari said. "Their essence returns to the ocean when they die. They become a part of the waters."

"Then he's gone forever?" Caspian didn't want to believe it.

"Not yet," Odessa said. "As long as his body remains here, his soul will linger. When you send his body to the ocean, so too will his essence depart this world."

"What if I were to bury him instead?"

"Then his tormented spirit would remain here in your temple."

Caspian didn't know which idea he hated more — losing Phoebus to the ocean or leaving his spirit in torment.

"I have to let him go, don't I?" Caspian whispered.

"I'm sorry," Cari said. "I will help you to send him to the waters. I know the words the mer use and will say them for you, if you wish."

"Let's not be so hasty," Odessa said.

"I won't force him to stay here in spirit," Caspian replied.

"No, of course not," Odessa agreed, "but there may be another way."

"What do you mean?"

"The mer are not so different from humans. They are half human, which means it might be possible to change things."

Odessa tapped at her lips with her finger as she paced the floor. She mumbled under her breath as she thought over whatever it was she had in mind.

"Mother, what are you thinking?" Cari asked.

"If the mer were to reincarnate, as humans do, Phoebus would one day return to Caspian."

"But you said yourself, they don't."

"No, but they could. It would only take a small tweaking of their species. It's been done with others to a much greater extent. Just look at all the hybrids the other pantheons have created over the years."

"But you're not talking about creating a hybrid. The mer are already hybrids."

"Yes, which means this should be easier to accomplish. The mer are already half human and half fish. It is their fish half that compels them to return to the waters after they have passed from this life. It would be just a small thing to let their human halves decide."

Caspian wasn't sure whether he should allow himself to hope, but he turned to Cari anyway. "If she changes the mer, would Phoebus be reborn?"

Cari closed her eyes and this time when she opened them she nodded. "Yes, but not right away."

"I'm immortal. I can wait." Caspian took Phoebus' hand in his and held it tight. "Do it, Mother."

Odessa did as he asked and Caspian watched as she, like Medina, began to fade in and out of view.

"What's happening to them?" Caspian asked.

"We're losing our followers," Mariana shouted. "Cynbel, it's not too late to reverse your edict. You see what is happening to your own wife. Will you see us all reduced to shadows just because your son wanted to fuck a merman?"

Cynbel banged his trident on the floor again. Sparks shot from the tips. "The Atlanteans are gone. Only those bound to the gods remain. Summon them to your temples and let them know what is happening. Those who have been most loyal to us deserve that much."

Caspian glared at his own priests. "Get out of here, all of you."

They all hurried to the door, Rafe included. Caspian raised his hand and used his powers to stop the high priest in his tracks. "Not you," he said. "You will remain here until I've decided how to deal with you."

The other immortals hurried to their various temple, leaving Caspian with his parents. "What about your followers?" he asked. "Are they banished too?"

"They will be," Cynbel said. "Odessa, stay here with Caspian until I've sent my priests on their way. Don't leave him alone. You can go talk to your own after I've returned."

"I don't need a minder," Caspian argued.

Both his parents ignored him as though he hadn't spoken.

Caspian didn't have the energy to press the issue, so he sat quietly, holding Phoebus in his arms, as he wondered how long it would take for his lover to return to him.

His mother seemed to be recovering from casting her spell, and by the time his father returned, she appeared more like her normal self.

"Mariana is going to be difficult," Cynbel said.

"Isn't she always," Odessa replied. "I'll go speak to my priests and say my goodbyes."

Cari returned shortly after Odessa had left. "I've appointed new Oracles from the mer," she said. "I also sent Fabian to his mother's temple. As a demi-god, I do not believe he should be banished."

"A loophole I didn't foresee," Cynbel commented, "but I suppose you are right. As the son of a goddess, Fabian is part of the pantheon. You did the right thing."

Cari returned to Caspian's side. "Are you ready to say goodbye to him now?"

Caspian didn't think he would ever be ready, but he gave a nod.

He let Cari speak the words that would send Phoebus on and he choked out a sob when his lover vanished from his arms.

A few moments later, Cari gave a small squeal and Caspian realized she had had a vision.

"What is it?" he asked.

"Mariana is about to defy Father's edict."

"How?" Cynbel questioned.

"She's transforming Fabian and her priests into sea dragons."

"I'll stop her," Cynbel said.

"It's too late," Cari replied. "It's happening right now."

"Then I'll make her undo this."

"Do you have the power?" Cari asked. "I feel weaker without my followers. Also..."

"Also what?"

"I don't sense Mother any more. It's as if she's no longer a part of this world."

"Cari's right," Caspian said. "I can't sense her either—or Medina, or Tempest. Father, what happens to gods who have no followers?"

"When we have no followers, we can no longer remain a part of this world until such time as someone calls on us again. Do not fear, my son. There are always those who call for justice, just as there are always those who crave war. We won't cease to exist. We just need to be careful about using our powers. If we should drain them entirely, we'll go into a form of stasis."

"Is that what's happened to Mother?" Cari asked.

"Yes," Cynbel confirmed. "The magic she performed to alter the physiology for the mer people might have been simple, but to change it for all the mer is still tiring. She would have done better to alter it for Phoebus alone, but it's too late now. Her priests kept her in this world, but now that they are gone, her foothold has been lost."

"Will she return?" Cari's voice quavered as she asked her question.

"In time. Now, let us go see what trouble Mariana is brewing. Caspian, are you coming with us?"

Caspian shook his head. He was barely keeping a rein on his powers as it was. If he were to get involved in an altercation with Mariana, he knew he would lose control.

Cynbel and Cari hurried to Atlantis to confront Mariana, leaving Caspian alone in the temple, with only his thoughts for company.

Or not quite alone, he amended. Rafe, frozen mid-stride, still remained there.

"And what shall I do with you?" Caspian asked with a sigh.

He rose from his seat and went to pick up the knife from where he had thrown it across the floor. The murder weapon in his hand, he stood before Rafe and wondered how he could have failed to see his vile nature all these years.

With a wave of his hand, he unfroze his high priest. "Why?" he asked.

"That creature didn't deserve your attention," Rafe snarled. "He wasn't even human."

"He was kind and caring, and he loved me for myself, not for what powers he might get from serving me. He was prepared to give up his fins to stay with me. What sacrifices have you ever made for another?"

Rafe remained silent. Caspian wasn't surprised. He had never done anything without it being advantageous to himself.

Caspian raised the knife to Rafe's throat, causing the priest to flinch at the touch of the blade to his skin.

"A quick death is too good for you," Caspian said. He gestured toward the door at the back of the throne. "Go downstairs."

"To the catacombs?"

"Of course. Now move."

Rafe kept one eye on Caspian as he headed down the stairs.

"To the cell at the end." Caspian pointed with the dagger, and when Rafe didn't step into the room, he prodded him with it.

Caspian conjured a lamp to hang from the ceiling and surveyed the room briefly.

"Your new quarters," Caspian said. "Enjoy them. You're going to be here for a long time."

Caspian closed and locked the door behind him.

He walked up to his private garden and knelt before the fountain in the center. Cari found him there when she returned with the news that both Mariana and their father were drained of their powers.

"It wasn't your fault," Cari said as she sat on the edge of the fountain.

"I swore I would protect him," Caspian said. "I promised to keep him safe. I failed."

"You couldn't be with him every single moment."

"I'm a god. We're supposed to be omniscient. How did I fail to see what was right before my eyes?"

Rafe's knife rested on the stone in front of him, still stained with Phoebus' blood. Caspian picked it up and sliced the blade across the palm of his hand.

"Caspian, what are you doing?"

"I swear no other mer will suffer while I have the power to prevent it. I failed Phoebus, but I won't fail again."

"You cannot watch over all the mer. You're just one man."

"One *god*."

"Even so, you cannot be everywhere at once."

Caspian sighed. "You are right, of course."

"Phoebus was going to give up the sea for you," Cari said. "Perhaps you could focus on those mer who choose to do likewise. Mer on land are rare, but they are in more need of help than those who choose to dwell in the water."

Caspian nodded. "I think Phoebus might like that."

"I'm sure he would."

Caspian drove the knife into the stone, embedding it to the hilt. "I swear it."

A few minutes after his oath had been sworn, Caspian heard the sound of his first charge arriving on land. He transported himself from his temple to the merman, ready to begin his work.

Chapter Twelve

Present Day

Marin could still feel the blade in his chest and he had to look down to check that there was no blood.

"It's okay," Caspian assured him as he knelt in front of him. "There's nothing there now. It's over."

Finally he stopped shaking and gathered his wits together.

Medina and Cari stood behind Caspian, but Antar had vanished.

Marin shook his head as the memories of his current life battled against those of his past. There was so much to remember, as well as forget.

"Marin," Medina said as she carefully sat down on the sand and handed him a goblet. "Drink this."

"What is it?" Marin asked.

"Just wine."

Cari took the goblet from Medina and tossed the contents away. "Really, Medina, you know the mer cannot handle strong drink. Here... Try this, Marin."

Marin stared at the fine china cup. He had no idea what it contained either.

"It's just tea," Cari said.

Marin didn't know what tea was, but he took a cautious sip of the hot beverage anyway. He recognized it as something he had tried in England during his short time there. It didn't really help with his problem, but at least the trio of immortals weren't staring at him as though he might have some sort of mental breakdown at any moment.

"Was it real?" Marin asked.

"Yes," Caspian replied. "We all remember you from before. Now you remember us too."

"What if I want to forget again?" Marin shied away from the memory of the knife piercing his flesh. He had no doubt he would have nightmares about it for years to come.

"The bad memories will fade in time," Cari assured him. "Take this from someone who has seen in her visions many deaths and tragedies over the years."

"That's not the same thing though, is it?" Marin said. "Watching something and living through it personally are different experiences."

"Yes, but let me ask you this. Which did you find most horrifying, the loss of your own life or witnessing Calder's death?"

Marin closed his eyes and gave a small nod. Watching his lover die *had* been worse than the pain of his own death. The pain of the blade was fleeting compared to the ache in his heart when Calder had been taken from him.

"I need to be alone for a while," Marin said.

"You aren't going to do anything foolish, are you?" Medina asked.

Marin shook his head. "I won't leave this beach. I promise."

The immortals left him alone as he'd requested and Marin tried to get all the jumbled thoughts in his head straight.

The longer he sat there, the more dreamlike his life as Phoebus seemed.

"But it wasn't a dream," Marin said, even though a small part of him wished that it had been.

He glanced over his shoulder and saw Caspian sitting against a tree, some way down the beach. At least he knew now why the moody god had taken an interest in his life.

He wondered how much of a resemblance he bore to Phoebus. There were no mirrors in Atlantis and few on the isle of the gods. He knew his eyes and tail colors were the same, but he had no idea about the rest. He thought he might be a little taller now—and maybe more muscular. His hair was darker as well, though the shade wasn't entirely dissimilar. He was certainly close enough in appearance that those who had known him as Phoebus recognized him in his new life.

Long after the sun had gone done, he felt the presence of someone standing behind him and he turned to see Caspian gazing down at him.

"You should come eat," Caspian said.

"I'd rather stay here."

Caspian sat beside him and produced a bowl of what appeared to be some kind of soup.

"I'm not hungry."

Caspian sighed. "You never used to be this stubborn."

"I used to be a trusting fool."

Caspian held up the spoon and guided it toward Marin's mouth.

"I'm not a child," Marin muttered, though he didn't try to avoid the spoon. It tasted good, perfect in fact — just what he would expect from something produced by a god. He took the spoon from Caspian and fed himself.

When the bowl was empty, he put it to one side. "I owe you an apology, don't I?"

"No." Caspian frowned as though Marin's question had confused him.

"Yes, I do. I said you'd never lost anyone and couldn't understand what I was going through. I'm sorry. I shouldn't have said that."

"You couldn't have known."

"I know, but it still must have hurt."

Caspian snorted. "Forget it. They were words spoken in the heat of the moment."

Marin took Caspian's hand and gave it a quick squeeze. "Still, I am sorry I said it. I shouldn't have presumed."

Caspian smiled. "Apology accepted. And I'm sorry too."

"What are you sorry for?"

Caspian gave a humorless laugh. "It would be easier to list what I'm *not* sorry for. I promised to protect you, and I failed. I dismissed your concerns about my priests, and you lost your life because of it. I should have listened to you. Can we start afresh?"

"I'm no longer Phoebus," Marin reminded him.

"A part of you is," Caspian replied.

"I know, but that doesn't mean I have to like it."

Caspian let go of Marin's hand and turned around so he too was facing the ocean. "I shouldn't have asked you to give up your fins for me either. You're mer. It's a huge part of who you are, and I should never have asked that of you."

"You wanted to keep Phoebus with you, and that was the only way. I understand that. He was prepared to give up the ocean and I don't believe he would have regretted his choice. He was happy with you and he knew that being immortal would have made you happy too."

"Still…"

Marin shook his head. "It doesn't matter. The past is done. Phoebus is dead and we've both moved on. You have your life and I have mine. You have your duties and I have my own."

"You're talking about avenging Calder?"

"Yes, of course. Did you think that remembering my life as Phoebus would make me forget him?"

"No."

"Good, because I haven't. I want you to continue training me to fight Urion, starting tomorrow morning. Will you do that?"

Caspian nodded. "Yes, though I still wish you'd reconsider."

Marin didn't bother to reply to that. Caspian knew as well as he did that it wasn't going to happen. He had told him enough times.

* * * *

Three days later, Marin was out of patience with training again. He wasn't going to let Caspian put him off facing Urion any longer. He had tried every argument he could think of before his time reliving the past, but now he had a new one to swing things in his favor.

Marin glared at Caspian. "You complete bastard!"

Caspian stepped back a pace and raised his hands. "Many have called me such. Would you care to explain why *you* think so?"

"You're a hypocrite."

Caspian snorted. "I am many things, but I'm not a hypocrite."

"You fucking well are!"

"Why would you think that?"

Marin raised his spear and pointed it at Caspian's throat. "You took your revenge on Rafe, yet you deny me justice for Calder's murder."

Caspian grimaced. "Urion will kill you if you face him."

"I don't care."

"Well, *I* do!"

"Because you think I'm Phoebus?" Marin snarled. "Well, I'm not him."

"Yes, you are, whether you believe it or not. You could not have relived his memories otherwise."

Marin faltered slightly. "Maybe I was him once, but now I'm me—Marin—and I won't let you stop me from avenging Calder's murder. You did the same for Phoebus, so don't you dare talk to me about the difference between justice and revenge."

Caspian flushed and stared out over the waves.

"You took your revenge on Rafe and you have no right to deny me the same."

"Yes, you're right, I did take revenge on Rafe," Caspian finally said. Marin shivered slightly at the coldness in his voice. "I gave him exactly what he had craved for so long."

Marin frowned. "What do you mean? Cari told me you prevented your father from banishing him with the rest of the Atlanteans."

"Yes, I did. A new life on land, with no knowledge of what he had done, was hardly suitable punishment for his crime."

"And what did you think was?"

Caspian held out his hand. "Come with me and I will show you."

Marin hesitated a moment, but when he placed his hand in Caspian's, the firm grip was familiar and welcoming.

Caspian led him away from the beach and along the path toward his temple.

Marin's sense of foreboding increased the nearer they approached.

"You feel uneasy in my temple, don't you?" Caspian said. "Not just now that you know what happened there, but before as well."

"Yes."

"It's because your soul remembered, even if your mind didn't. Don't worry. No one in my temple with harm you again."

"You promised me protection once before," Marin reminded him. "Or should I say you promised Phoebus?"

"Yes, I did, and you will never know how I have cursed myself for my failure."

Marin supposed he should tell Caspian that it wasn't his fault, but a part of him thought it was, and he held his tongue.

"I won't ask your forgiveness," Caspian said. "I don't deserve it."

They reached the main entrance to the temple, where Caspian opened the doors with a wave of his hand. Everything inside was covered in dust, and weeds had sprung up through cracks in the floor and walls.

Marin's gaze was drawn to the place at the foot of the steps and his heart raced. The world around him began to spin and spots appeared at the edge of his vision.

"Deep breaths," Caspian said. "It's all right. Breathe in, breathe out, breathe in, breathe out."

Marin blinked and realized he was on the floor with Caspian crouched in front of him.

"Perhaps it was a mistake to bring you here," Caspian said.

"You think?" Marin snapped. "Why did you imagine I'd want to set foot in this place again?"

"For your revenge," Caspian replied.

"Unless Urion has got a lot smaller, I doubt he's in your temple."

"No, he's somewhere in the Atlantic right now. I brought you here to see Rafe."

"What?"

"Rafe is imprisoned in the catacombs of the temple."

"He's alive?"

"He wanted immortality and to stay here with me for eternity. I gave him what he wanted."

The grim expression on Caspian's face sent another shiver down Marin's spine.

"Can you stand?" Caspian asked, holding out his hand for Marin to take again.

Marin nodded and let Caspian help him to his feet. He deliberately avoided looking at the place where he had drawn his last breath as Phoebus.

"Do you want to leave?" Caspian asked. "You don't have to see him if you don't want to."

Marin was torn. He wanted to get out of here so badly, to return to the sea and the form he felt most comfortable in. Yet he wanted to see Rafe too. He had dropped his spear on the floor and he bent to pick it up. He held it tight. "Take me to him."

Caspian steered him around the back of the throne and through the doorway leading to the palace and priests' quarters. The stairs down to the catacombs were dark until Caspian produced a torch, the flame casting flickering lights on the walls.

"Why not use a human torch?" Marin asked as they slowly made their way down the stairs. During his brief time on land, he had seen many wonderful inventions that the humans had made and he wondered why Caspian didn't embrace them here.

"Habit, I guess," Caspian replied.

They reached the bottom of the stairs and headed down the long, bleak corridor until they finally reached a thick iron door.

"Here we are," Caspian said. "Rafe is chained to the wall with manacles made by Andaman himself. They are unbreakable. You will be perfectly safe in his presence."

"The other gods know he's down here?" Marin asked.

"Andaman knows what I wanted the chains for. I don't know whether he realizes Rafe is still here now. He hasn't asked about him and I certainly haven't offered the information."

"What about the rest of the gods?"

"They may suspect, but no one has ever had the courage to ask me about him outright."

"I wonder why," Marin muttered sarcastically.

"Am I *that* unapproachable?" Caspian asked.

Marin shrugged. "You do kind of give off a 'don't come near me' vibe—or you do now, at least."

"I prefer to be left alone," Caspian said. "But not by you."

Marin couldn't meet his eyes.

Caspian cleared his throat. "Come on. Let's see what Rafe has to say for himself today."

The door swung open and Marin took a tentative step forward.

The small room was lit with a single lamp that hung from the center of the ceiling. The room contained no furniture at all and the floor and walls were hard stone.

The sole occupant sat on the floor at the far side of the room. There were manacles around his ankles and wrists and the chains were secured to the wall behind him.

"It's been a long time," Rafe said quietly. "How many years have passed since you last visited me?"

Marin glanced at the lamp, having assumed Caspian must visit daily to replace the candle.

Caspian followed his gaze. "The lamp is enchanted to remain lit during daylight hours and go dark during the night. It is all Rafe has to mark the passage of time."

"And when did you last come in here?" Marin asked Caspian.

"I don't know. Not since I found you again."

Rafe turned his attention to Marin and a familiar sneer appeared on his face. "Ah, the merman who captured the heart of a god has returned. Hello, Phoebus. It's been a long time."

"Not long enough," Marin said as he stepped forward.

"Marin has only recently regained his memories of his life as Phoebus," Caspian explained.

Rafe shrugged and gave the impression of being entirely uninterested.

Caspian leaned against the wall near the door. "As you can see, Marin, there are worse fates than mere death. Rafe dreamed of immortality, and now he has it."

"You know this isn't what I had in mind," Rafe snarled.

"Yes, I know," Caspian agreed. "You thought you would spend eternity in my bed."

"If you'd given me a chance, I could have made you love me," Rafe said.

"No one can make someone love another," Caspian replied.

"I think Medina might disagree with that," Marin interrupted. "She certainly managed to work her magic on you."

"Medina had nothing to do with my feelings for you," Caspian said.

"Are you sure about that?" Marin asked. "You said yourself that she'd slipped you a love potion."

"Later," Caspian said before turning back to Rafe with that same cold stare. "How many times do I need to say it before you believe me? I will *never* love you. There is nothing you can say or do that will ever erase your crime."

"That half-human didn't deserve immortality. For one such as him to dare to touch a god was an insult to me and every other priest who had sworn devotion to you. He never prayed to you. He never worshipped you like I did."

"I didn't want his prayers," Caspian said. "I had followers, those who devoted their lives to me. I didn't want that from him. He made me happy like no one else did."

"You didn't give me a chance," Rafe argued. "I could have won your heart in time."

Caspian shook his head. "Even after all these centuries, you still don't understand. But it doesn't matter. I'm not here today to listen to the same false words."

"Why are we here?" Marin asked.

Caspian gestured to Rafe. "This man took your life. He took his ceremonial dagger and used it for the most vile of crimes. This man murdered you. I give you your vengeance."

Marin gripped his spear tight. "What are you saying?"

"From the moment my mother worked her magic to ensure you would be reborn to this world, I knew you would one day return to me. It was inevitable. For all that time, I have kept him here, ready for you to face him."

Marin stepped back until he hit the wall. "You want me to *kill* him?"

"Why are you so shocked?" Caspian asked. "You seek to kill Urion for what he did to Calder. Why should it come as a surprise to discover that I would wish the one who killed the man I love to die?"

"But you said he was immortal."

"He does not age, he cannot starve to death and illness cannot touch him. But just like any of the gods, he can be killed."

"He won't do it," Rafe said. "He always was a spineless little half-breed."

"Quiet." Caspian waved his hand, and although Rafe continued to open and close his mouth, no sounds came out.

Marin stepped forward again and pointed his spear at Rafe. "Not today," he whispered. "I think you should live a little longer."

Without another word, Marin left the room and practically ran down the corridor and up the steps. He didn't know if Caspian was behind him or not. He didn't care. He had to get away.

Once he was outside, he gulped in air and threw the spear to the ground.

Then he ran again, heedless of where he was headed, until he collided with a hard body.

"Steady there," the Atlantean said.

"Isander!" Marin fell to his knees, shaking violently. His stomach lurched and he thought he might vomit.

Isander rubbed his back, the gesture comforting and familiar. "Feeling better?"

Marin nodded. "I remember you."

"We former sea dragons are rather hard to forget," Isander replied with a grin.

"No, I mean from before."

"Before?"

"From when I was Phoebus, in a former life. You escorted me to Caspian's temple."

Isander stared at him for several long seconds. "Is it going to sound really bad if I say I have no idea what you're talking about?"

Marin smiled and shook his head. "It was a very long time ago."

"Perhaps you'd like to refresh my memory then?"

"There's not much to say. I had asked Medina for help in breaking my mating fever. She asked you to take me to Caspian's temple. You escorted me, flirted a little and that was pretty much it."

Isander smiled. "Well, that certainly sounds like me. I never could resist a handsome man. I presume Caspian helped you with the mating fever?"

"Yes, he did."

"Well, that's good. And now he's helping you again."

Marin looked at him curiously.

"I've seen you training with him on the beach," Isander explained. "You're planning on taking on Urion, yes?"

"Yes."

"You do know he'll kill you almost instantly?"

"So everyone keeps telling me."

"That's because they're right. If sea dragons were easy to kill, we wouldn't have lived as long as we have. Many a time a ruler of Atlantis has decided we're too dangerous to have around and thought to destroy us."

"They have?"

Isander settled himself on the grass and Marin made himself comfortable beside him. "Not for a hundred years, but yes, they have. Even bound and defenseless, the sea dragons were practically invincible."

"Practically?" Marin focused on the word that gave him a tiny sliver of hope.

"While we were collared, we couldn't breathe sea-fire, but even without our main defensive mechanism, they could not destroy us. Before the mer forgot how to conjure sea-fire from the tridents, there was a time when the guards tried to take out one of our more troublesome members."

"Urion?"

"No, not that time. Every mer in Atlantis fired tridents at the dragon at the same time. They aimed for the eyes, the mouth, the joints, everywhere they thought they might find a vulnerable spot."

"What happened?"

"They were reminded that sea dragons are not so easy to kill. They eventually gave up, at least until another king decided to give it a try. That was the only time they even came close to killing one of our kind. The prolonged attack weakened him, and it might, in time, have killed him, but it didn't. It *did* remind us that we weren't immortal, though, and after that, we tried not to draw too much attention to ourselves. To remain useful, if you like, so the mer would keep us around."

"But it is *possible* to kill a sea dragon?"

"It is, but you're forgetting something most important."

"What do you mean?"

"When we were collared, we could not summon sea-fire. Urion is no longer a prisoner of the mer and his greatest weapon is in full working order. It was nearly impossible to kill a captive sea dragon, so how much harder do you think it would be now?"

Isander spread his arms and gestured for Marin to look over his body. "Not a single scar mars my body, because no weapon can break the skin of a sea dragon. The eyes and mouth might be vulnerable, but you'd never get close enough to find out."

"There has to be a way to kill him."

"Not while he stays in his current form," Isander replied. "You cannot face a sea dragon and live, but—"

"But if he were to become human again..."

Isander smiled. "Now you're getting it."

"But what if he doesn't become human again?"

Isander laughed loudly. "He will."

"What makes you so sure?"

"Because inside that dragon's body is a man, and that man will be as horny as the rest of us after centuries of abstinence. Sooner or later he will resume human form again. Take my word for it."

"What's to stop him becoming human and turning back into a sea-dragon again as soon as someone tries to attack him?"

"It doesn't work like that. Mariana is the one who has the power to change our forms. She turned back those of us who renounced her, rather than risk us defeating her loyal priests. She isn't going to give Urion the power to change back and forth at will."

"Why would she turn him back into a human at all? Surely it serves her purpose to keep him as a sea dragon?"

"It does."

"Then it's hopeless. I *have* to find a way to defeat a sea dragon. They must have a weakness somewhere."

"They don't. I told you. Urion will want to take human form eventually, and when he does, you'll have your chance to take your revenge."

"That could be years away."

Isander laughed. "I give him six months at the most — less if he finds out Mariana has taken another lover. He always was the jealous type and a dreadful complainer."

Marin sighed. "Are all priests of the gods and goddesses the jealous types?"

"No. I never cared who Mariana was fucking. I only shared her bed once and I could barely manage to perform my duties at all."

"I suppose preferring men might be something of a hindrance."

"Yes. Thankfully she soon realized what the problem was and never bothered me again. If I had known my initiation into her ranks involved bedding her, I'd never have sworn myself into her service. Actually, with the benefit of hindsight, that's not the only reason I should have stayed clear."

Isander shook his head and gave Marin a rueful smile. "Just be patient. Urion will walk on two feet again soon and you'll have your chance."

Marin wasn't so sure, but he supposed if anyone knew about Urion, Isander would be the one to ask.

"So, what has you racing around the isle like the place is about to sink into the sea?" Isander asked.

Marin sighed. "Did you know Caspian has one of his priests imprisoned in the catacombs below his temple?"

"No. I've only been in his temple a handful of times, and I've never been in the rooms beneath it."

"It's Rafe, his head priest."

"I wasn't aware he still had any priests."

"Rafe held the position when the Atlanteans were banished," Marin explained. "He killed me."

"What?" Isander gaped at him.

Marin rubbed at his bare chest, feeling once again the sharpness of the blade as it tore into his flesh. "Phoebus," he corrected. "He killed Phoebus."

Isander took Marin's hand and gave it a squeeze. "I'm so sorry. Do you want to talk about it?"

"He was jealous of me, so he decided to get me out of the way forever."

Isander gasped. "*You're* the merman Caspian fell in love with, the one he petitioned the pantheon to make immortal."

172

"Yes." Marin gestured to the decaying temples around the isle. "It's all my fault that the Atlantean gods are now reduced to this."

"No," Isander replied. "Whatever happened, you were not to blame."

"If I had never accepted Caspian's offer, the Atlanteans would still live in the city alongside the mer. Your gods and goddesses would be powerful still. Mariana wouldn't have turned her priests into sea dragons to avoid them being banished. Urion would be long dead and Calder would be alive."

"You don't know that. Some things are destined to happen, no matter what we do."

Marin shook his head. "I *chose* to accept Caspian's offer to join him in his bed. I should have turned him down."

Isander snorted. "You're an idiot."

"What?" Marin thought he might have misheard.

"You're an idiot," Isander repeated. "Caspian loved you. This was a god who slept with more men in a week than some might bed in a lifetime."

"That's hardly something to be proud of."

"I'm not saying it is, but he was going to give that up for you. He was prepared to devote eternity to just one man...you. He loved you and you're sitting here saying that you think you should have broken his heart."

"He'd have got over it," Marin said. "He *has* got over me."

"You think so?"

"Of course. It's been centuries."

"Centuries that he has devoted to protecting the mer," Isander said. "I wonder why that was?"

"Because he couldn't protect me," Marin whispered.

"Yes, exactly. I'm not saying he's been celibate all this time, but you only have to see the way he looks at you to know that his heart is still broken. He isn't getting over you any time soon."

"Well, he'll have to sooner or later," Marin said. "I'm not Phoebus any more. He died in the temple, and he's not coming back."

"There's a part of Phoebus inside you," Isander said. "His soul lives on."

Marin heard the sound of someone moving in the shrubbery behind him and glanced over his shoulder. It came as no surprise to see Caspian watching him silently.

"I think you should talk to him," Isander whispered. "Properly."

Marin nodded. He guessed an honest conversation was long overdue.

Chapter Thirteen

Caspian didn't say a word as he transported them away from the Isle of the Gods and into the world of men.

Marin grimaced as he realized Caspian had provided him with clothes.

"Would you prefer a different style?" Caspian asked.

"All clothes are restrictive and annoying. These will do as well as any. Where are we?"

"England. Come on. Let's go talk."

Marin turned to follow Caspian and immediately recognized the home of Jake and his two mermen lovers.

"They no longer live here," Caspian said as they walked down the path.

"Are you reading my mind?"

"No."

Caspian let them into the house and turned on the lights.

The living room was still furnished as it had been when he'd last been there. *How long has it been?* With the memories of his past life so fresh in his mind, it was hard to tell how much time had elapsed.

They sat on opposite ends of the sofa. Marin didn't know where to start.

Caspian didn't wait for him to gather his thoughts. "Medina tried to reverse the magic caused by the love potion she had slipped into my wine."

"What?"

"You believe my feelings for you aren't real, that they stem from magic. That's not true. Medina wanted to teach me a lesson about love. She wanted me to find love and lose it because she didn't like the way I treated men."

"I can't say I found it one of your better qualities myself."

Caspian gave him a small smile. "She concocted a love potion powerful enough to work on me, and it worked only too well. I fell in love with you and I was never happier than when we were together."

"That sounds to me like the potion talking."

"I thought so too, but after I lost you I begged Medina to reverse her magic."

"I'm surprised she would, if she thought she were teaching you a lesson."

"Me too, but she was quite fond of a particular young merman and had no idea that her curse upon me would have such devastating consequences for him—for you. She never believed that a merman would give up his fins to be with me, not with the reputation I had. She thought you would either leave me to find another or simply die of old age, leaving me alone to mourn you. She only meant to punish me, not you."

"I was—what do humans call it?—collateral damage?"

"Something like that. After your murder, the pantheon sank into chaos. The loss of our followers did lasting damage, and even the smallest of spells sent immortals into stasis. Medina was lost because of trying too hard to undo the spell she had put me under, not realizing that she was attempting the impossible. My mother's spell to ensure you were reborn was her undoing. That one caused a whole new set of problems, as if there weren't enough to deal with already."

"What do you mean?"

Caspian squeezed the bridge of his nose and sighed. "Until that day the mer didn't reincarnate. They returned to the waters and continued their journey that way. My mother's spell caused the mer to be reborn in a way similar to humans, so that you would one day come back to me in a form I would recognize."

"Do I look a great deal like Phoebus?"

"Yes, you do. I first saw you the day you tried out for the guards and I knew it was you right away."

"Even though I look like him, I'm still Marin."

"I know." Caspian raised a hand toward Marin's face, but lowered it again before they touched. "Anyway, my mother's spell had a rather unexpected side effect."

"What do you mean?"

"Mer are only *half* human," Caspian said. "The spell didn't take that into account. We didn't even realize what had happened for several generations, and by then, my mother was sleeping and it was too late."

"What happened?"

"Each time a merperson dies they are reborn, but they are not all reborn as mer. A third of the mer come back in this form, while another third come back as humans and the final portion as fish. With the mer no longer returning to the water the way they used to, the magic that allows them to thrive is dwindling."

Marin felt bile rise in his throat as the implications of what Caspian had told him sank in. "*I'm* the reason why our numbers are falling? It's *my* fault the mer are on the brink of extinction?"

Caspian grabbed his hand. "No. This is not your fault. None of this is down to you. You are not responsible for the mistakes of the gods."

Marin pulled his fingers out of Caspian's grip and steadied his breathing once more. "Your mother isn't sleeping now. She's awake. She can reverse what she did."

"I have already asked her to."

"And?"

"She refuses to do so."

"Why? Does she hate the mer so much she wants to wipe us out?"

"No, she has no prejudices against your people. You have met her yourself and know this to be true. But she is aware that if she undoes her spell, you will one day return to the water and I will never find you again."

"I'm right here," Marin pointed out.

"Yes, but you and I aren't..."

"Ah, I see."

"I'm trying to convince her to reverse her magic," Caspian assured him. "Unfortunately, she is most stubborn."

Marin shook his head. "This is all too much. Can we get back to Medina?"

Caspian nodded. "There isn't much more to say. I begged her to remove the spell from me and played on her guilt over what had happened to you. When she tried to reverse the spell it drained her powers almost entirely, because my feelings were true and not magically induced. Her attempt to do the impossible, combined with the loss of her priests, sent her to sleep."

"It took that much effort?"

"You have to remember that my father had just banished all the Atlanteans and erased their memories of Atlantis and the entire pantheon. We were all weak without our followers. Magic that might once have come easily with little effort on our parts drained us. I would have welcomed oblivion myself, but I held off from using my powers too much, knowing I didn't deserve the luxury of sleep. I soon accepted that what I felt for you wasn't as a result of magic."

"Maybe Medina didn't really reverse the spell?"

"I wondered the same thing, but as time passed, I accepted the truth. No potion or spell can truly move the human heart."

"And a god's heart?"

"A god in human form," Caspian reminded him. "Even though I'm immortal, a part of me died in that temple with you. My heart works the same way as any other man's."

"Then what did Medina's potion do?"

"It opened my eyes to the possibility of love. When I was under the effects of her potion, I didn't reject the very idea of falling in love, as I had in the past. When I asked her to remove the spell, I thought it would stop the feelings but it didn't. She had her revenge on me, not that she was around to enjoy it. My feelings for you are true and not the result of magic. I swear it."

"Phoebus," Marin said. "Your feelings for *Phoebus*."

"You are Phoebus reborn."

"Yes, I know, but we're not the same person."

Caspian rolled his eyes and Marin's temper rose. "We're not!"

"I have no intention of arguing with you about this," Caspian said. "I know you've had different experiences and that your life as Marin is nothing like your life as Phoebus."

"Exactly!"

Caspian brushed Marin's fringe back from his eyes. "I'd like to get to know you again, if you'll let me."

"What if you don't like me as Marin?"

"I already like you, so it's too late for that."

"You know what I mean."

"Yes, I know. All I'm asking for is a chance."

Marin still felt highly skeptical, but he found himself nodding in agreement. He was rewarded with a bright smile from Caspian, something he hadn't seen since his previous life. He liked it.

"No spells or potions," Caspian said. "Just two men getting to know each other after a long time apart, right?"

Marin smiled back. "Okay."

* * * *

"No." Caspian wasn't going to budge from his position, that much was clear.

"I'm ready to face Urion," Marin argued. "You said yourself that I've improved."

"You have, but that doesn't mean you've managed to change your fate."

Caspian sat down and tugged Marin onto the sand beside him. "I know you think you're ready or you simply don't care if you die, as long as you're avenging

Calder, but I'm certain that Calder wouldn't want you to sacrifice yourself."

"What would you know about Calder?" Marin muttered.

Caspian smiled. "I know more about him than you think."

"You do?"

"Yes. He wasn't a friend, since we both know I don't have those, but we talked."

"I never knew that. Why didn't he mention you to me?"

"It was before you and he met," Caspian explained. "He would have been about the age you are now and was a very angry young merman."

"Are you sure you're talking about the same Calder?" Marin asked. Fierce and protective as he was, Calder was one of the most relaxed and easy-going mermen Marin had ever met. He wasn't sure he had ever seen him lose his temper completely, not for any reason.

"I'm sure," Caspian said. "The Calder I knew hadn't met you. You were very good for him and he mellowed a lot after your first mating season together."

"You weren't spying on us, were you?"

"No!" Caspian appeared genuinely appalled by the suggestion, much to Marin's relief. "Why would I want to see the man I love being fucked by another?"

Marin rolled his eyes at the comment. It wasn't the first time Caspian had assumed Marin was the one on the receiving end. At least now Marin knew why Caspian had made the assumption.

Caspian didn't seem to want an answer to his question and continued. "You never knew Calder's brothers."

"I knew he had several. They were all older than him."

"Yes, and they were all what humans call straight. That is, they preferred the company of females on the solstice."

"Many mermen do," Marin replied.

"Calder, of course, desired men. His brothers tried to convince him to try with a mermaid — or ten — rather than let him trust his own instincts. They would foist mermaids on him, one after the other, in the hope that he would change his mind."

"It doesn't work like that," Marin reminded him. "His brothers should have known better."

"Probably, but there are still mer out there who believe that the only way to break a mating fever is with someone of the opposite sex. Calder's birth clan were of that opinion."

"His clan had come to Atlantis before Calder was born."

"But you know as well as I do, newly arrived clans tend to stick together in the sunken city. It takes a few generations before a clan is fully integrated. Calder, because of his preferences, struggled to fit in. The laws preventing same-sex relations were in place and the solstices were hard for him."

"They were hard for all of us, at least until King Nereus repealed the law."

"I'm sorry either of you had to suffer during that time."

Marin snorted. "We didn't suffer that much. I never went a solstice without release, regardless of that stupid law."

Caspian gave him a grim smile. "Calder, unfortunately, did. Between his brothers' efforts and the law, he went through quite a few of them without breaking his fever. He also found that his quick rise through the ranks of the guards resulted in him being closely watched by those who sought his downfall."

"But where do you fit into this?" Marin asked. "How did you come to meet him?"

"On an island partway between Atlantis and the land of humans. He intended to go to land and find a new life among humans. I'd sworn to protect all mer, especially those who went to land, and when he collapsed on that beach, my powers alerted me to his presence."

"He tried to leave the sunken city?"

"Yes."

"How did I not know this?"

Caspian shrugged. "I don't know for sure why he didn't tell you, but I suspect it is because he loved you so much. He wouldn't have wanted to do or say anything to cause you unhappiness. I feel the same way, but unlike Calder, I seem to be failing at making you happy."

"It isn't your place to make me happy," Marin said. He raised his hand to stop Caspian's next words. "I know you want it to be, but it's not."

Caspian acknowledged his words. "Calder stayed on that island for nearly two weeks. I kept him company, listened to what he had to say and waited for him to decide what he wanted to do."

"Why did he choose to go back to the city instead of to the land of humans?"

"That was Cari's doing. My sister came to us on the island on that last day and showed him a vision. I don't know what of. I didn't ask or pry. I suspect you might have been there somewhere, but I cannot say for sure.

Whatever it was, he chose to return to Atlantis and stayed there for the rest of his life. I visited him on occasion. We talked a little. Or rather, he talked and I listened. You'll know by now that I'm not the most talkative of men."

Marin raised an eyebrow.

"Well, not until now," Caspian amended.

"I don't remember you visiting him."

"After he met you, I thought it best to stay away, for all our sakes."

"I'm surprised you didn't try to fight him for me, or seduce me yourself, before he had the chance to."

Caspian gave a soft chuckle. "I thought about it— fighting him for you, that is. I didn't see you until after you'd already met and fallen in love with Calder."

"What stopped you fighting him for me?" Marin asked.

"You were happy with him," Caspian replied immediately. "Far happier than you were with me, if we're being brutally honest today."

"Calder did make me happy," Marin whispered. "I want him back."

"You know that is outside of my powers."

Marin nodded. "I know he's gone, and that I'll never see him again. I don't need the reminder. What I *need* is help in seeing his murderer brought to justice."

Caspian sighed. "I'm already helping you train for this suicide mission you're determined to go on."

"I know your sister says I'll die if I face Urion, but Cari doesn't know everything. Besides, she says herself, the future can be changed if we know our fates in advance."

Caspian stood and glowered down at him. "I assure you, there is no possible future for you at all if you try to fight Urion. He's a sea dragon."

"He'll take human form again eventually, and I intend to be ready for him when he does."

Caspian crouched down in front of him. "Marin, you're not a murderer. No matter how angry you are at what he did to Calder, you don't have it in you to take the life of another."

"You don't know that. You aren't giving me a chance."

"Marin, if you could kill another, you would have killed Rafe by now."

"Rafe is immortal."

"Even an immortal can be killed if you know how." Caspian materialized a trident in his hand and held it out to him. "A direct blast of sea-fire right between the eyes will render an immortal unconscious for between twenty and thirty seconds. That is time enough for a killing blow to be delivered."

Marin didn't take the trident. "I thought the gods had the power to heal themselves?"

"We do, as does Rafe. But not if he's unconscious."

"That seems rather an easy way to kill someone who is supposed to be invincible."

"Easy if you know the weak spot." Caspian tapped the bridge of his nose. "And if you have access to a weapon that produces sea-fire, as well as know how to summon it. You also need the immortal in question to remain still enough for you to take aim or be exceptionally gifted at hitting a moving target that may vanish in the blink of an eye. And, if you manage all that, you need to be able to summon a second blast of sea-fire almost immediately. Tell me, Marin, how quickly can you do it?"

"About five minutes between blasts," Marin replied. He had been timing himself.

Caspian nodded. "You're getting faster, but you're not there yet. When you are, I want you to face Rafe. I want to see if you can avenge your own murder before I see you go within a thousand miles of Urion."

"What are you saying? You want me to fight Rafe?"

"No, not fight," Caspian replied. "He is secure in his cell and I intend to keep him that way. When you're ready, I'm going to take you to him, hand you a trident and stand back and watch."

Marin ran his finger down the center point of the trident. "You want me to kill him, in cold blood?"

"I want to see if you can," Caspian replied.

"You don't think I can do it," Marin said. He could tell from Caspian's tone and expression that the god didn't believe he'd go through with it.

"No, I don't." Caspian vanished the trident back to wherever he had summoned it from. "I am the Atlantean God of Justice. I swear to you, justice will be delivered, both for your murder and Calder's. But I have no doubt it will be delivered by a hand other than yours."

Caspian vanished from sight, leaving Marin to his thoughts.

* * * *

Twenty-nine seconds. Marin punched the air in triumph. He had finally managed to conjure two bursts of sea-fire less than half a minute apart. If only Caspian had been around to witness it. Unfortunately he hadn't seen the god all day. He had left him practicing shortly after dawn and hadn't returned.

Can I do it again?

Marin aimed the trident at the tree he had been using for target practice. His aim had been improving as well, though he still missed his mark more than he hit it.

He told himself that Rafe would be closer. He wouldn't have to aim far.

No, you'll just have to look him in the eye when you do it. He pushed the unsettling thought aside and concentrated on summoning another blast.

The sea-fire hit the tree and he started to summon a second blast right away, counting down the seconds until the spark ignited.

Thirty-four. *Damn it.* He was getting slower—or more likely, he was tiring.

Perhaps he should take a break and try again in a little while. When he faced Rafe, he would be refreshed.

His heart raced at the thought of seeing the man who had murdered him. Last time, he hadn't been prepared. This time, he would be ready.

Caspian still didn't think he could kill Rafe, but Marin knew the god wouldn't allow him to face Urion until he had. He wouldn't let Rafe be the one to stop him from avenging Calder.

* * * *

"There… That's three times I've managed to conjure sea-fire in under thirty seconds." Marin stuck the trident into the sand and shot a smug look at Caspian.

"Your aim is still diabolical," Caspian replied. "The last shot barely skimmed the tree at all."

"You never stipulated that my aim had to be perfect," Marin argued. "You can't change the rules now."

"No, I suppose not."

"Besides, Rafe won't be as far away as the tree is."

"True."

"I'm ready," Marin declared.

Caspian nodded silently. "Very well. Let us go visit Rafe."

"Really?"

"Yes, I want to see whether you have what it takes to go through with this."

"I have!"

Caspian sighed. "That's what worries me."

Marin let Caspian lead him back to the temple and down the stairs to the cell within the catacombs.

Rafe, Marin wasn't surprised to see, was in a similar temper to the last time he had seen him.

A movement behind him distracted him from Rafe's malevolent stare.

"Where are you going?" he asked when he realized Caspian was walking back out of the door.

"I'll be upstairs in the throne room."

"Aren't you going to stay? I thought you wanted to watch."

Caspian shook his head. "I've changed my mind. This is between you and him. I made my peace with what Rafe did a long time ago."

Rafe snorted. "You've been ignoring me for so many years I can't even count them."

Caspian didn't bother saying anything in response to Rafe's comment.

Marin shivered as he realized he was going to be on his own in this.

"Rafe murdered you," Caspian said. "For a long time I considered killing him for his crime, but I didn't. I knew that one day you would return to me, and that when you did, you would deserve to have the opportunity to kill him yourself. That was when I let go of my hatred for him."

"You've forgiven him?" Marin asked.

"Never, but hating someone for so long can be tiring. You, of all men, should know this."

Marin knew that only too well.

Caspian clasped his upper arm and gave the muscles a squeeze. "Now we'll see if you have the cold determination revenge requires."

Marin watched Caspian until he was out of sight before turning back to Rafe.

"If you're planning on killing me, do get on with it," Rafe said. "I have long since grown tired of my captivity."

Marin raised the trident and took aim. The blast lit up the cell and struck Rafe true, squarely between the eyes.

"One… two… three…" Marin counted out loud, the trident pointed at the unconscious Rafe.

He *could* do this. He *had* to do this.

Yet now that the time had come, he found himself doubting. His grip on the trident eased and the staff of the weapon slipped a little.

The seconds passed. Rafe's eyelids fluttered as he came around.

Marin dropped the trident and fell to his knees.

"Couldn't do it, huh?" Rafe said. "I can't say I'm surprised. You always were a pathetic little whore."

Marin felt a renewed burst of temper, but even that wasn't enough to see his mission through to the end.

"I never understood what Caspian saw in you," Rafe continued. "At first I thought it was your innocence. I remember you standing in his temple that first time like it was yesterday. Practically a virgin—or at least without any clue as to what he could do with his cock. Then I speculated it might be because you're mer. After all, your kind are known for your sexual appetites during the solstice. Yet even outside of the mating season he sought your company over mine. I waited for him to grow bored with you, but instead he decided to keep you."

Marin could hear Rafe's jealousy—still strong after all these centuries—in every word he uttered.

"That he chose to gift a sexually inexperienced merman—over me—with immortality is as incomprehensible now as it was then. I served him from the day I came of age. I shared his bed more than any other priest—and yes, more than *you* ever did—but it wasn't enough for him."

Rafe closed his eyes and leaned against the wall. "For the love of the gods, what will it take for you to kill me?"

Marin drew in a sharp breath. "You *want* to die?"

"Of course I do," Rafe replied. "Eternity in this cell isn't living."

Marin picked up the trident and took aim, but he couldn't even summon a first burst of sea-fire, let alone a second. He actually felt sorry for Rafe, and he had no idea how *that* could have happened.

Swearing loudly, Marin stalked out of the room, up the stairs and into the audience chamber.

Caspian sat on the steps in front of his throne. He looked up as Marin approached and opened his arms.

Marin tossed the trident aside and threw himself into Caspian's embrace. "Why couldn't I do it?"

Caspian stroked his hair. "Because you're not a murderer. *Now* do you understand why I can't let you face Urion?"

"That's different," Marin argued. "He's not chained up in a cell."

"Are you telling me that if I released Rafe from his manacles, you'd be able to go through with it? If I gave him a fighting chance, it'd be different?"

Marin shook his head and sighed. "Probably not. How can I hate Urion more than I hate Rafe? I can still feel the sharpness of the blade as he drove it into my chest. He shows no remorse for what he did and despises me as much as he did Phoebus."

"Urion killed the one you love," Caspian replied.

"And Rafe did the same to you," Marin said. "I'm amazed you've let him live all this time."

"It's as I've told you before. There are worse things in this world than death. I didn't want him to die and be reborn. I wanted him to suffer."

"And now?"

Caspian sighed. "Now? Now, I try not to think of him at all."

Marin didn't want to think about Rafe either. He curled into Caspian's side and let the god hold him.

"The other Atlanteans were banished, right?"

"Yes," Caspian confirmed. "My father sent them out into the world of humans with no memory of Atlantis or their heritage."

"Could he do the same to Rafe?"

"I suppose so. He is awake now and it wouldn't take much power to banish one man."

Marin sat back and faced Caspian. "I think you should ask him to do that. I don't want him here, and I can't seem to kill him. Let him be gone from our lives."

"Are you sure?" Caspian asked.

Marin nodded. "I am."

"I'll speak to my father today," Caspian said. "Now, what about Urion?"

"I..." Marin didn't know. He still hated Urion, but what if he couldn't kill him either? What if he froze when he faced him?

"You don't have to be the one." Caspian cupped his face with his hand and stroked his cheek with his thumb.

"I know."

"Urion will pay for what he has done, but it doesn't have to be at your hand."

Marin placed his hand over Caspian's. "You can't protect me from everything."

Caspian gave a bitter laugh. "Believe me, I learned that lesson when I held Phoebus in my arms, knowing it was too late to save him. I wish I *could* shield you from all the evils in this world. I would keep you safe here in our home and do everything in my power to ensure no harm ever came to you."

Marin didn't bother to remind him that his murder had taken place in this very room. He let Caspian hold him close once more, and for a few blissful minutes, he let himself believe he was safe.

Chapter Fourteen

Caspian stood before the council of the gods, feeling a strange sense of déjà vu. The last time he had stood here like this, they had told him that he could make Phoebus immortal.

Not everyone had been happy about the result, but in Atlantis, the majority ruled. Democracy, the cornerstone of many modern cultures, had been the way of the Atlanteans long ago.

"Father," Caspian began once everyone had settled down around the table, "I would seek your assistance in the matter of Rafe."

"Rafe?" Cynbel replied. "Who is that?"

"He's my former high priest," Caspian explained. "I would now wish you to banish him and remove his memories, just as you did the rest of the Atlanteans."

Several of the immortals around the table began to whisper to each other. His father remained silent, a strange look on his face.

Caspian shifted his feet, trying to pick up on what the various whisperers were saying. He caught the odd word here or there, but most were speaking telepathically and carefully shielding their thoughts.

His father banged on the table with his fist, drawing the meeting to order once more. "Caspian, I allowed Rafe to remain here for you to deliver justice as you saw fit. As the God of Justice and the life partner of the victim, that was your right. Are you telling us that Rafe lives?"

"Yes, Father."

"His natural life should have ended many centuries ago. How is it that he is still alive?"

Odessa patted her husband's arm. "Perhaps he has rediscovered Rafe, just as he has Phoebus."

"No, Mother," Caspian said. "Rafe has remained my prisoner in the catacombs beneath my temple from that day to this. I trusted in your powers and knew that one day Phoebus would return to me, and that when he did, he should have the opportunity to face his murderer."

"Nevertheless," Cynbel said, "it does not answer the question as to how."

Caspian met his father's eyes. "I think you already know the answer to that question."

"No doubt, but we need to hear you say it."

Caspian braced himself. "I let him drink from the cup of immortality in place of Phoebus."

Several immortals gasped at his words but Caspian ignored them, remaining focused on his father.

"You know it is forbidden to let a mortal drink from the cup without the permission of the pantheon?"

"I do." Caspian gestured around the table. "But with all due respect, most of you were asleep, and unable to debate the issue."

"That is not the point!" Cynbel rose from the table, his voice booming through the whole island. "This action cannot go unpunished."

Caspian tried not to cringe in the face of his father's fury. He supposed he had known that what he was doing was wrong. Even as he'd placed the cup in Rafe's reach, knowing the priest would drink it, he had wondered what repercussions he would have to face when the rest of the gods found out what he had done.

"I accept whatever punishment you see fit," Caspian said. Thankfully, his voice remained steady.

"We will need to think on this and consider," his father replied. "As for Rafe…"

The Atlantean appeared at Caspian's side, still chained.

Andaman rose to stand beside Caspian. "I made the manacles that hold Rafe, and I did so knowing what Caspian intended for him."

"You don't have to do this," Caspian said. "I never told you I intended to make him immortal. You only suspected."

Andaman shook his head and clasped Caspian's shoulder. "No, my friend. I knew, because if I had been in your place, I would have done the same thing. Had you called for a vote, I would have found in your favor."

Caspian hung his head, overwhelmed at Andaman's words. That the other god considered him a friend came as something of a surprise. Yes, they were among the few who had remained a part of the world, while the rest of the pantheon had been in stasis, but it wasn't as if they went down to the tavern for a drink in the evening or out to a club in the modern world.

Andaman had always been a loner and had never taken the trouble to hide his contempt for Caspian's promiscuous lifestyle. They had little in common, and after losing Phoebus, Caspian had done nothing to encourage others to keep him company.

Maybe we have more in common than I thought.

Caspian turned to his sister. "What about you? How would you have voted?"

Cari wouldn't face him. "I don't know. I am torn because I would have wished to support your decision, but I, of all people, know how little can be achieved by focusing on the past."

"It doesn't matter how any of you would have voted," Cynbel said. "The fact of the matter is that Caspian didn't tell anyone what he intended to do."

"Better he makes an Atlantean immortal than one of the mer," Mariana commented loudly.

Caspian glared at her. The Goddess of Sea Creatures really should have learned to keep her mouth closed and her opinions to herself.

Cynbel ignored her and turned his attention to Rafe. "To send an immortal out into the world with no memories is asking for trouble. Sooner or later he — and those around him — will realize that he does not age and heals unnaturally quickly."

"Can't he be stripped of his immortality?" Andaman asked.

"No," Cynbel replied. "If he were born immortal, as the gods are, our powers can be removed by one of our parents. But Rafe drank from the cup, which poses something of a problem."

Rafe remained silent as the gods debated his fate.

"I say we send him out there and let him deal with the consequences," Andaman suggested. "What difference does it make to us if the humans discover what he is? It's not as if he has any god powers...other than the ability to heal and not age, of course."

Several of the immortals around the table nodded in agreement.

"Humans no longer believe in us," Cari said. "Even the raising of Atlantis did little to change this. They talk of earthquakes and climate change, and search for scientific explanations for what we did. Even if Rafe were to be discovered, they would not think of us. They would study his genes to find the reason for his longevity."

"Cari is right," Medina said. "I say we erase his memory and toss him down in the middle of a random city...naked."

Caspian tried to hide his smile at Medina's final comment, but his lips twitched of their own accord. He didn't like Medina. He never had and he suspected he never would, but in this they were of one mind.

"This is hardly constructive," Cynbel said.

Medina shrugged. "That vile creature murdered an innocent, a sweet young merman who had just found his true love. He does not deserve anything from us except our contempt. He should be castrated and—"

"Thank *you*, Medina," Cynbel shouted, while Rafe struggled to cup his groin, despite the manacles.

Cynbel walked over to Caspian and Rafe and stood before them. "Caspian, is there anything you wish to say to Rafe before I remove his memories and banish him?"

"No, thank you, Father. I have already said all I wish to say to him."

"And Marin?" Odessa asked. "What does he have to say about this?"

"Marin is the one who suggested this," Caspian said.

"That weak creature couldn't even kill me," Rafe snarled.

"Silence." With a wave of his hand Cynbel forced his command on Rafe.

"Leave him like that," Medina suggested. "Mute, naked and with no memory. Hmm, I like that. Where are you going to drop him? Might I suggest somewhere in New York?"

Cynbel rolled his eyes and, with another wave of his hand, Rafe vanished.

"Where did you send him?" Caspian asked.

"Does it matter?"

"I suppose not."

Medina made a noise of mild annoyance. Caspian had a feeling she wanted to know more than anyone else in the room. She really was not a goddess to cross, and he should know.

Cari smiled smugly across the table toward Medina. Caspian could tell she had already seen where Rafe had been deposited. He had no doubt she would tease Medina with her knowledge for months.

"Is there anything else you would ask of the pantheon?" Odessa asked. "While we are all gathered here."

"No, Mother," Caspian said.

"You do not wish for Marin to be made immortal?"

Caspian shook his head. "No, or at least not yet. Maybe not ever."

Odessa gave him a sad smile. "Come, my son. Let us talk privately."

The meeting broke up, leaving Caspian and his mother alone.

"What is it you wish to say to me?" Caspian asked.

Odessa hooked her arm through Caspian's. "How are things going with Marin?"

"Slowly," Caspian admitted. "He loved Calder very much, and it will take time before he's ready to move on. Sometimes I wonder if he'll ever be able to. They were together for far longer than Phoebus and I were."

"You do realize that while they are of one soul, Marin is a different person from Phoebus?"

"Yes. He is much more forceful than Phoebus—and stubborn. Times have changed and Marin is a modern merman."

"I wasn't aware that the mer had changed that much over the centuries. What little I have seen of them since my return does not seem so different to how they were before."

"They have not changed as much as humans, but there are some differences. Or maybe it's just that I didn't see what was there."

"You mean with regard to Phoebus?"

"Yes. I loved him so completely, but I'm no longer sure that he felt the same. He said the words, but he was very young and inexperienced."

"He was prepared to give up the sea for you," Odessa reminded him. "Only one who loves you with his whole heart and soul would make such a sacrifice."

"I know, but—"

"But what?"

"I wonder whether he would have agreed to that if I had not pushed him into it. He was also aware of Medina's curse, and like any other young mortal, he did not wish to die."

"The curse has run its course," Odessa reminded him. "If you were to ask him now, he would not be swayed by such fears."

"If I were to ask him now, he would say no. He does not love me."

"Not yet, perhaps."

"Maybe not ever."

"In time, his feelings for you will grow, providing you don't give up on him."

Caspian didn't want to, but neither could he push Marin into accepting him. He wanted his love to be given freely.

"Do you think he could ever give up his fins?" Odessa asked.

"I don't know. Phoebus was reluctant, and I suspect Marin will be even more so. It's a pointless question anyway. The pantheon will never allow me to make such a petition again."

"Of course you can."

"Even though I allowed Rafe to drink from the cup?" Caspian hadn't forgotten his father's decree that he would be punished for his actions.

"That was a foolish thing to do, but you know as well as I do that it was done on the spur of the moment. Had you thought things through, I doubt you would have made the same decision."

"I did think things through," Caspian argued. "I only gave him the cup when I had talked myself out of killing him there and then. I never considered how I might feel centuries later—or what Phoebus would say."

"Did Phoebus ever tell you I talked to him before I made my decision on your petition?"

"He told me he'd met you but not what you'd talked about."

"Mostly we talked about you. It was I who told him about the curse. I didn't realize he wasn't aware of it."

"It's not your fault. I should have told him myself. He deserved honesty and I failed to give it to him. I'm determined to do better this time around."

"Even the gods have lessons to learn."

"I just hope it isn't too late."

"I will speak to Marin, if you think it will help."

"Thank you, but no. He needs time, and I intend to give it to him."

As they rounded a corner, Caspian saw Isander and Dolph ahead of them. The two Atlanteans still hadn't decided where they would settle among the humans. He should probably have a private word with them before his father ran out of patience with their stalling.

"Cynbel will not push them," Odessa told him, in answer to his thoughts. "They are making themselves useful around here with cleaning up various temples."

"They are?"

"Medina and Cari set them to work. Neither of them likes to see idle hands."

"Maybe I'll have them come around to my temple," Caspian suggested. "It could use a little work."

"You've let it fall into ruin," Odessa chided.

"It wasn't as if I was living there all these years," Caspian pointed out. "I have made my home among humans for centuries now."

"What's that like?"

Something in his mother's tone gave Caspian reason to pause. "Why do you ask?"

Odessa gestured to the buildings around them. "Look at what has become of us. We have no followers, no one to worship us. What is there left for us here?"

"You're thinking of living on the mortal plane?" Caspian hoped she didn't intend to move into his spare room. He quickly buried that thought deep inside and reassured himself that Marin was now in that room and not likely to move into the master bedroom any time soon.

"Cynbel rejects the idea, but I would like to see what has become of the world. Medina enjoys her time among humans and is already increasing her followers. She even has a new priest."

"One she tricked into the post," Caspian reminded her.

"She still sees the advantages to be gained from spending time in the world, rather than hiding out here on this isle of ghosts."

Caspian could see his mother's point. The island had once teemed with life, but now it was almost deserted.

"Why do you not seek followers?" Odessa asked.

"I have no wish to return to that life."

"I'm not talking about taking lovers. Goodness knows, I never understood why you insisted on having sexual relations with *all* your priests. It would never have happened if you'd hired a few young maidens."

Caspian rolled his eyes. "I wasn't talking about that either. I have no wish to be worshipped. I don't want power or followers. I already hear the calls of so many humans who seek justice. The last thing I want is to be deafened by billions of calls to me personally. With so many humans alive today and so much injustice in the world, I'm not sure I could handle it."

"You underestimate yourself."

"I'm tired, Mother. Sometimes I feel that I've lived too long."

"All immortals feel that way at some point. You are at a crossroads in your life. You are on the brink of regaining your love and beginning a new chapter in your story. It's only natural that you would question the direction in which you're traveling."

Caspian sat down on a stone bench and his mother, after cleaning the dust and weeds from it with a wave of her hand, joined him.

"What if Marin never loves me as Phoebus did? What will I do then?"

"He will live his life, be reborn and you will find him again. Perhaps next time he will come into your life before finding another love."

"No, Mother. It won't happen. This is my last chance, my *only* chance."

"My magic is strong. He will be reborn."

Caspian shook his head. "I want you to undo your spell."

"But if I do that, the mer will no longer reincarnate. They will do as they did before, and you'll never find Phoebus again."

"It has taken hundreds of years for Phoebus to be reborn as Marin. The mer won't last that long. Their numbers are falling with each generation. You *must* undo your magic, or their entire race will be lost."

"But—"

Caspian took his mother's hands in his own. "Phoebus was mer. Marin is mer. They are a peaceful, loving race who, through no fault of their own, are on the brink of extinction. I know neither Phoebus nor Marin would wish to see the end of their people. That's not who they are."

"You would give up your chance for love for the mer?"

"I still have one more chance," Caspian said. "And if I cannot win his love, then I don't deserve him."

"You know that if I do as you ask, I cannot later change my mind and cast the spell again? I haven't the strength to manage it, not even for a single merman. It took all of my powers the last time."

"I understand."

"Then I will do as you ask," Odessa said.

"Thank you, Mama."

Odessa teared a little at his use of his childhood name for her. She closed her eyes and Caspian watched the concentration on her face. Her power rippled through him where they touched. A gust of wind blew across the island, a cloud passed over the sun and it was done.

"Now, go win the heart of your merman," Odessa said.

Caspian wished it was as easy as she made it sound.

Chapter Fifteen

The mating season was just around the corner again. Marin couldn't believe it had arrived so quickly, but the fever was unmistakable.

From the expression on his face that morning, Caspian had noticed the heat as well.

Marin sighed and stared out over the ocean, watching the tide ebb and flow. "Calder, help me. What should I do?"

No answer came, not that he expected one. Calder was gone and he was never going to return. The one man who Marin had always turned to was out of his reach forever.

The sun had disappeared below the horizon some time ago, but Marin hadn't moved from his spot. Caspian could find him if he wanted to. The god had the power to transport himself to Marin's side, no matter where he was in the world.

He wondered what he would do if Caspian showed up on the beach now. They had become closer in recent months, but they hadn't started a physical relationship, not even sharing so much as a kiss. Marin could tell Caspian wanted to progress things between them, but he had respected Marin's wishes to go at a pace the merman found comfortable.

Tonight was different, though. The mating fever was upon him and the pain was worse than last time. He knew the ache in his guts would only increase with each season he endured without seeking release.

For the first time since Calder's death, Marin considered the possibility of breaking his fever with another man. The thought was fleeting, but the guilt that followed lingered. How could he even think about betraying Calder's memory?

He sighed again and picked up a handful of sand, letting the grains run through his fingers.

Calder wouldn't want him to experience such discomfort, nor would he want him to spend the rest of his life alone. His lover had suffered through several mating seasons without release during his younger days, and he had never wanted to see other mermen go through the pain. The two of them had often invited mermen without a lover of their own to join them on the night of the solstice. They had never been jealous or begrudging of their occasional third.

This was different, though. This wasn't inviting someone to join them, nor was it simply doing what he needed to break his fever. His growing feelings for Caspian meant that if anything did happen, it could never be just sex.

Marin pushed aside the surge of warmth he felt when he thought about Caspian. It was becoming harder each day to remember where Phoebus ended and he began. He wished he could shut out the memories of his past life and concentrate on the here and now. Maybe then he wouldn't be so confused and he could figure out how much of what he felt was real and what were just remnants of what he had felt as Phoebus.

Phoebus had loved Caspian. He had fallen for him completely and had been prepared to give up his fins to spend eternity with him. Marin couldn't imagine loving anyone that much. He wouldn't have given up the sea, even for Calder, not that a fellow merman would ever have asked for such a sacrifice.

Thoughts of Calder made him ache even more as he recalled their last time together. His strong and powerful lover had never hesitated to give Marin what he needed, opening to him without question from their first night together to their last.

An image flashed across his mind as he thought about taking Caspian in the same manner. For once he knew that the image wasn't one of Phoebus' memories. Caspian's refusal to allow Phoebus — or any man — to penetrate him meant that Marin only had his imagination in this regard.

Marin hadn't bothered to enlighten Caspian as to the trigger to break his mating fever. Caspian had assumed his trigger was sucking cocks because that had been Phoebus' trigger, but when Marin had corrected him, he hadn't bothered to ask for clarification, merely jumping to the next conclusion, that Marin needed someone to fuck him.

The annoyance at Caspian's assumption returned again and he picked up a stone from the beach and threw it forcefully into the sea.

Bloody arrogant god!

He picked up another rock and pulled back his arm to throw, only to find someone standing right in front of him.

"Hello, Marin," Cari said. "I thought I'd see how you were doing."

"I'm fine."

"Hmm." The goddess didn't sound as if she believed him, but he didn't care whether she did or not.

"Did you want something?" Marin snapped.

"No, I just thought I'd take a little stroll on the beach."

"And you just happened to pick this one?"

Cari smiled. "I thought you'd be spending tonight with Caspian."

"Did you?"

"Yes."

"Well, as you can see, I prefer to spend the night alone. I'm honoring Calder's memory."

"Rubbish," Cari replied. "You're hiding from Caspian and being needlessly stubborn."

"What would you know about it?" Marin glared at the goddess. "Many mer honor their deceased mate by remaining abstinent."

"Yes, they do," Cari agreed. "And until this mating season you were doing that too. But tonight we both know that this is not the case."

"How dare you?"

"How dare *you*," Cari retorted. "Do you have any idea how long Caspian has been waiting for you?"

"He's been waiting for Phoebus," Marin replied. "I'm not him. I'm Marin, and Caspian needs to understand that."

"My brother can be blind in some matters but he isn't stupid. He is well aware of who you are. He knew you for his love reborn from the first time he saw you."

"He recognized my face and fins. That doesn't mean he knows me."

"That's why he wants to get to know you—to learn who you are and discover how much of Phoebus lives within you."

"Not much," Marin muttered.

"That's not true," Cari said. "Even I can see the similarities in your personalities."

Marin frowned. He hadn't thought himself much like Phoebus at all. "What do you mean?"

Cari shrugged. "You both fall in love very quickly. Phoebus gave his heart to my brother the first time he met him. You were the same with Calder, weren't you?"

Marin gave a slow nod. He had been with Calder since his first mating season, and he had loved him from that night.

"You are both loyal and honest and brave to the point of being foolhardy."

"That's not true."

"You still insist on facing Urion yourself. That is the height of foolishness."

"So you all keep telling me, but Phoebus didn't take risks like that."

"No, but he didn't tell Caspian as soon as the jealous priests were becoming problematic. He remained silent, thinking he could handle them himself, and we both know how that ended."

"That wasn't bravery."

"Then what was it? Why didn't you tell Caspian and ask him to deal with them?"

"Caspian did know."

"Eventually, but you could have told him sooner."

"It wouldn't have made any difference. Caspian made it clear that he wouldn't dismiss the priests from his service, that I had to learn to live with them."

"Had Caspian known what would happen, he would never have let you remain in danger."

"Well, he didn't know, did he? For some reason, the Goddess of Prophecy failed to see my murder before it happened."

Cari shook her head. "Unfortunately, the power that enables me to see into the future cannot show me anything that takes place in the temple of another god. Had Rafe attacked you anywhere else, I would certainly have seen his actions in time. To my eternal regret, I was unable to save you."

"I didn't realize that."

"No god or goddess likes to broadcast their weaknesses," Cari said. "I am truly sorry I wasn't able to stop him."

"It wasn't your fault any more than it was Caspian's."

"Then you know he feels guilt for what happened?"

"Yes, of course I know that. Anyone with eyes in their head can see he does."

"Actually, very few do see that. Until Phoebus, my brother was carefree and open about his feelings, the good and the bad. He hid nothing, even when he tried to. His love for Phoebus was obvious to everyone except Caspian himself. I had never seen him happier than he was when he was with Phoebus. Then he lost him and closed himself off from the world. He has been a shadow of his former self for centuries. I thought when he found you, after all this time, he could finally be happy again."

Marin shook his head. "Maybe if I was more like Phoebus it would be possible, but we're just too different."

"You're the same person."

"No, we're not, and that is what none of you seem to understand. I don't doubt that Caspian loved Phoebus, but that doesn't mean he could ever love *me*."

Cari hooked her arm through his and steered him casually down the beach. "Please give him a chance. My grandfather gave you the memories of your past life so you would remember your love for Caspian. Please don't forget it again."

The goddess vanished mid-step, though Marin felt her hand on his arm for a second or two longer before it too disappeared.

Perhaps he should go talk to Caspian. They certainly couldn't continue on like this. It wasn't fair on either of them.

Marin found Caspian in his apartment, right where he had left him earlier in the evening.

Caspian turned off the television and tossed the remote onto the coffee table.

"You didn't have to do that if you were watching something," Marin said.

"Just a documentary on the rising of Atlantis. No new theories, just the same old nonsense they've been reporting all along. Did you want something to eat?"

Marin shook his head. "I'm not hungry. I think we should probably talk."

"If you like," Caspian said. "About anything in particular?"

Marin sat down on the sofa and pulled up his legs, tucking his feet under him. "I'm not Phoebus."

"I know that."

"I'm not sure that you do. I keep telling you, but I think there's still a part of you that sees him every time you look at me."

"I can't help that you share his image."

"I know. I just..."

"What?"

Marin stared out of the window at the lights of the city. "Why wouldn't you let Phoebus fuck you?"

"Where did that come from?"

"The one time he — I — brought it up, you refused. You suggested we invite another into our bed if I wanted to fuck someone."

"I've never let any of my lovers take control in that manner. It wasn't any reflection on you."

"Even after all these years, you *still* haven't let someone top you?"

"No... I..."

Marin turned back to Caspian to see him staring at his hands. "What is it?"

Caspian rubbed his nose and wouldn't meet his eyes. "There hasn't been anyone since you," he finally said.

"But it's been centuries!"

"I know." Caspian grimaced. "I'm just thankful gods don't get mating fevers."

"You've really been celibate all these years?"

Caspian shrugged. "I swore to you that no other man would know my touch for as long as you lived."

"Um, I was dead, though. I wouldn't have expected you to remain faithful all this time."

"I couldn't face being with another man. Goodness knows my sister tried her best to set me up with any number of men, but while I dated, I never took any of them into my bed."

"Oh."

"You believe me?" Caspian asked. "Most men would doubt my word."

"You've never lied to me, even when you've told me things I would probably rather not hear. If you say

212

you've been faithful to me since the day I died, I believe you."

Caspian gave him a smile. "Just don't tell anyone."

"You're worried about your reputation?" Marin stared at him incredulously.

"No, I've never been concerned about such things. It's just rather embarrassing."

Marin smiled. "I don't think you should be embarrassed at all. I like that you waited for me, even though I think perhaps you shouldn't have."

"I'll wait for you forever," Caspian said. "You're it for me. Don't you know that by now?"

The intensity of Caspian's gaze was more than he could stand. Marin turned away.

"Marin, what is it?" Caspian asked. "What did I say?"

"I think you should consider letting Phoebus go," Marin replied, his voice barely more than a whisper. "He and I are just too different."

"You keep saying that, but I don't see it."

Marin gave Caspian a sharp stare. "You wouldn't let Phoebus fuck you. What about me? Would you let me — Marin — fuck you?"

"I told you… I don't let anyone do that."

"Then you need to find someone else to spend eternity with."

"What? I don't want anyone else. I want you. I *need* you."

Marin stood and walked to the door of the guest room. He hesitated, but he had to at least tell Caspian why he couldn't be with him. "I need someone else," he finally said. "The only way to break my fever during the mating season is for me to fuck another man."

Caspian didn't know what to say, but Marin didn't wait for him to respond. He disappeared into his room, closing the door softly behind him.

How could I have been such a fool? Marin had said himself that his trigger wasn't the same as Phoebus', and he had just assumed that Marin needed to be taken and overpowered to break his fever. He hadn't even considered that he might need to be the one in charge.

What in the world am I going to do?

Closing his eyes, he leaned back on the sofa and tried to process what he had just heard.

Phoebus had never been happier than when he was on his knees, giving pleasure to him. He had let Caspian take him and had only once raised the possibility of them changing places. When Caspian had refused, Phoebus hadn't mentioned it again.

Now Marin hadn't just brought up the subject. He'd made it clear that he needed what Caspian had always refused to give anyone.

Can I give that to Marin?

Caspian didn't know. He felt the unfamiliar need to talk to someone about this, but his choices were rather limited. His family was out of the question, and he wasn't exactly surrounded by friends. Before Phoebus, he'd had lovers but not friends, and since he'd lost him, he'd had no one. For the first time, he felt lonely and isolated.

He searched his mind for someone who might understand. There was Jake, a human who was very familiar with mermen and mating triggers. With two lovers with fevers to break, he was surely an authority on the subject. Unfortunately, it was the night of the solstice, which meant any discussion would have to wait, because he would have his hands full with his mermen tonight.

Or maybe not.

Caspian glanced at the clock and belatedly remembered the time difference. Jake and his family were on the other side of the world. Perhaps he would have time for a quick chat after all.

He transported himself to Jake's island before he could think it through too much.

He found Jake working in his vegetable patch. His efforts to be as self-sufficient as possible seemed to be going quite well. Treacle, the family dog, barked at him and left off *helping* Jake to run and greet him.

Caspian had never really understood the concept of keeping animals as pets, but he was quite fond of Treacle. "Hello, boy," he said as the dog jumped up at him, leaving muddy paw prints on his trousers.

Jake, alerted by Treacle, put down his spade and came to greet him. "Caspian, what brings you here? Hopefully not more trouble in Atlantis?"

"No, the island is crawling with scientists, but nothing new to report in that regard. I'm here on a different matter. Do you have a few minutes?"

"Sure. What's up?"

Caspian looked at the house. "Where are Kyle and Finn?"

"They're in New Atlantis at the moment. I expect them back later. Did you need to see them?"

"No, but I didn't want to intrude on your time, especially with it being the solstice."

"It's fine. They broke their fevers before dawn this morning."

"Ah, good. Um, that's what I wanted to speak to you about, actually."

"What? Mating fevers?"

"Yes." Caspian gestured to the house and Jake led him along the path, calling Treacle to come to heel before he got into more mischief.

"Do you want a drink?" Jake asked once they were inside.

"Sure. I think I need one."

Jake poured them each a large whisky and they sat in the living room.

Caspian took a swallow of his drink as he tried to think where to begin.

"How's Marin?" Jake asked, before he had gathered his thoughts.

"Better than he was," Caspian replied.

"Is he still determined to track down Urion?"

"He's prepared to wait until the high priest returns to human form, but I suspect his patience will run out sooner or later. He has other things on his mind at the moment, though."

Jake cringed in sympathy. "How much can one merman be expected to handle?"

Caspian shook his head sadly. "Unfortunately, the additional burden he has to bear is my fault."

Jake waited for him to say more, not prompting or encouraging him in any way. Caspian rather wished he would, though he suspected he might know why he didn't.

"Jake, do you consider me a friend?" he asked.

"Um, I guess...maybe. You've been very good to me and my guys. You know we can never repay your generosity."

Caspian shook his head. "I'm not talking about that. I mean...am I someone you would talk to, confide in?"

"Er..."

216

"I see that I'm not," Caspian concluded for himself. "I know I'm not really approachable. I haven't been for a long time." He gave a bitter laugh. "I didn't used to be like this. I would throw parties that were the envy of the entire pantheon. I fucked more men in a week than most humans would in a lifetime. Then I met Phoebus and everything changed."

Jake refilled their glasses and sat back without a word.

Caspian hadn't realized how much he needed to talk about what had happened all those years ago. The words poured from him as they never had before. Jake listened to it all.

They got through an entire bottle of whiskey—or he had, Caspian thought ruefully. He would have to buy Jake a bottle to replenish his stock.

Finally he reached the end of Phoebus' tale and swallowed the last of his drink in a silent toast to his lost love.

"I had no idea," Jake said quietly. "I'm so sorry."

Caspian acknowledged his sympathy with a nod. "Marin is Phoebus reincarnated."

Jake gaped at him. "Marin? Calder's Marin?"

"Yes."

"Wow."

"He is exactly like Phoebus in appearance, even his mismatched eyes and two-toned fins."

"I'm sensing a *but* here."

"Phoebus and Marin have different triggers when it comes to the mating season."

"So?"

Caspian looked at Jake out of the corner of his eye. "Phoebus needed to suck off another man. Marin needs to fuck one."

Jake shrugged. "I'm not seeing the problem here. I know there have been a few problems with the mer who have incompatible triggers, but you're not mer."

"What do you mean about incompatible triggers?" Caspian asked. He hadn't heard of such a thing, though he had to admit his knowledge of mermen sex was somewhat limited.

"Kyle and Finn have mentioned some mer who have had issues of that nature. There were a couple of mermen who both needed to be fucked, to feel the heat of release inside them, but neither could come in the other until they had broken their fevers by having someone come in them. I understand that in those circumstances another steps in to assist. The mer are always willing to help out others in that regard."

Caspian nodded. "I see what you mean. I suppose I hadn't really thought about that possibility."

"I can't say I had until they mentioned it. I still don't see what your problem is, though."

Caspian guessed he had to say it out loud, even though he had told no one except Marin of his anal virginity. "I've never let anyone fuck me."

"You mean to tell me that in all these orgies you used to host, you never once let a man near your arse?" Jake snickered and Caspian reflected that perhaps they should forgo any more refills.

"Not once," Caspian replied, still sober and regretting his godhood. "I like being in control. I *need* to be in control."

"Maybe Marin does too," Jake suggested. "I can't say I would blame him if he did, especially after being murdered. Who wouldn't be reluctant to give up control in those circumstances?"

"I never thought about it like that. Do you really think what happened to him in his past life could have such an effect on this one?"

"I don't know. Until this afternoon, I never really thought about reincarnation at all. It was just one of many afterlife theories I'd heard about and not given much thought to—kind of like gods and mermen. Until you're face-to-face with the reality, you don't really consider it."

"We've thrown a lot at you these last few years, haven't we?"

"Oh, yeah. But I get Kyle and Finn out of it, so I'm definitely not complaining."

Caspian chuckled. "You're really happy with them, aren't you?"

"More than I ever thought I could be with any man," Jake replied. "I don't know how I ever lived without them."

"I'd like that too." Caspian sighed. "I nearly had it once, and it slipped through my fingers. It was my own damn fault, and I've cursed myself every single day for failing to protect him."

"Phoebus is why you now protect the mer who come to land, isn't he?" Jake guessed with his usual astuteness.

"Yes."

The sound of a door opening made Caspian jump. A moment later Kyle and Finn appeared in the doorway, laughing and tussling with each other, at least until they saw Caspian and jumped apart, startled.

"Not *more* trouble?" Finn said in lieu of a greeting.

Caspian frowned. *Do I really only come here when there's a problem?* He thought back and realized he did. Maybe he should make an effort to rectify that.

"Nothing for you to worry about," Caspian assured him. "I just came here to get some advice from Jake about mermen and mating triggers."

Finn laughed. "If you want advice on those, why ask the human instead of the mermen?"

Caspian shifted uncomfortably in his seat. "I wasn't sure whether it would be considered rude to talk about mating triggers with a merman. Such things are rather personal, aren't they?"

Finn flushed bright red and Caspian found himself wondering what Finn's trigger was. He bit his tongue rather than ask.

"Most mer are pretty open about their triggers," Kyle said as he sat down in the large chair opposite the sofa. Finn flopped down onto his lap with a contented sigh. "Hell, most of them have sex on the beach out there, in full view of everyone. They aren't all lucky enough to have a house like this with a nice comfortable bed in it."

"What did you want to ask about triggers?" Finn asked.

"I was wondering if you knew of anyone whose trigger changed during the course of their life?"

Both mermen frowned, thought about his question for a few moments then shook their heads in response.

"Why do you ask?" Kyle questioned.

"I was just curious."

The mermen gave him twin glances of open skepticism, but it was Jake who spoke.

"You're wondering if Marin's trigger might change in time?"

"Yes."

"I've never heard of such a thing," Kyle said. "My trigger has never changed and I've not known another's to either. Admittedly, I haven't had that many lovers, so I could be wrong, but I suspect that Marin's trigger will remain what it is now for the rest of his life."

"I thought that might be the case, but I wanted to ask. If there's any chance it might change, I'd like to know. Before I..."

"Before you what?" Finn asked. "Are you and Marin fucking?"

Caspian shot him a glare and Finn blanched and shrank into Kyle's side. Caspian immediately regretted his temper and tried to school his features into something less forbidding. He didn't want Finn to be scared of him. "I'm sorry, Finn. I'm still rather—what do they call it these days?—socially inept. No, Marin and I aren't fucking. He's only just beginning to get over Calder. I'm not sure it isn't too soon for him to be thinking about a relationship with anyone. But tonight is the solstice and the subject of mating fevers and triggers came up."

Finn seemed to ease a little. "We talked about inviting Marin to join us on the solstice to break his fever but he refused our offer. He said he wanted to remain abstinent in honor of Calder."

"Yes, he told me the same thing last solstice," Caspian said.

"Don't push him if he's not ready," Jake warned. "It may take years for him to truly lay Calder's memory to rest. You, of all people, should know how hard it is to let go of someone you love."

Kyle and Finn stared at him curiously, but Caspian couldn't bear to tell his story again. He would leave it for Jake to fill them in after he had left.

"I know," Caspian said quietly. "I just had the feeling tonight that he might have been close. If not for a relationship, at least for some relief during the solstice. I was prepared for it to just be sex, meaning more to me than it did to him. I just wasn't expecting his trigger to be what it was."

Kyle gave him a knowing glance, and Caspian didn't need to ask to know that Kyle was well aware of Marin's trigger. He suspected Kyle had easily put two and two together and figured out what he was struggling to say.

Finn, a little slower on the uptake, made a sound of astonishment. "You mean you've never...?"

Caspian shook his head. He supposed it was better that they all knew his secret now. That way he wouldn't have to wonder if Jake had told them after he'd left.

Jake patted his arm. "The way I see it, Marin's trigger is set for life. He needs someone who's willing to let him fuck them each solstice. If you can't do that, perhaps you need to let him go."

"What if I can't?" Caspian asked. Losing Phoebus had torn him apart. If he lost Marin too, he didn't think he'd be able to stand the pain.

Jake took his hand and squeezed it. "If you love Marin as much as you loved Phoebus, you'll give him what he needs."

Caspian wanted to, he really did, but could he actually give up control to someone, not just once but on a regular basis?

If the alternative was losing Marin, he thought perhaps he could.

He supposed there was only one way to find out. It was time to face his fears, if Marin would let him.

Back at his apartment, the place was in darkness. He couldn't hear Marin in his room, but he doubted the merman was sleeping. The pain from the solstice was always at its height at this time and Marin would be having a very restless night.

Caspian knocked on Marin's door, waiting for the invitation to enter.

Marin's call of 'come in' was barely audible, but Caspian, as a god, could hear it without difficulty and he let himself in, closing the door behind him.

The merman sat on his bed, a pillow against his chest and a painful grimace on his face.

"What is it?" Marin asked. "Is something wrong?"

"You could say that," Caspian replied as he unbuttoned his shirt. "I find it very wrong that there's a merman in great pain in my home, especially when there's something I can do about it."

Marin stared at him and Caspian knew he wasn't imagining the naked lust in his gaze.

"You wouldn't..." Marin whispered. "You said yourself, you never give up control."

Caspian tossed his shirt onto the floor and unzipped his trousers. "Until tonight."

"Are you serious?"

"Yes, I am." Caspian stepped out of his clothes and stood naked before another man for the first time in centuries. "Do you want to break your fever? If you'd rather honor Calder's memory by staying untouched again, I'll leave you in peace. You only have to say the word."

Marin shook his head and moved across the bed, making room for Caspian to join him.

Caspian sat down next to him and took hold of Marin's hand. "I know you don't love me, and I don't ask that from you. I'll not push for more, and if tonight is all we have, I will accept that."

Marin flashed him a quick smile. "The solstice comes around every six months."

Caspian chuckled. "So it does."

"I remember Phoebus' love for you," Marin said. "Perhaps one day I'll learn to love again and come to care for you as well." Marin shook his head. "No, I already care for you. I'm not sure when it happened, but I do. And if I can care, maybe one day I'll love."

Caspian raised Marin's hand and kissed his palm. "That's enough for me."

Marin eased Caspian onto his back and ran his hands over his chest and abdomen. "I'll try to treat you with the same gentleness that you once showed Phoebus."

"Phoebus wasn't untouched," Caspian reminded him.

Marin snorted. "As good as."

Caspian didn't argue the point. It wasn't as if it mattered. The past was over and done with. He let Marin open his legs and slip his fingers between his thighs.

"Do you have anything to ease my entrance?" Marin asked.

Caspian shook his head, before remembering he could summon lube with a thought. He managed to concentrate long enough to produce some and pass it over. "This is what humans use."

"Is it any good?" Marin questioned as he opened it and sniffed at the contents.

"Well, it certainly helps with easing the pressure," Caspian replied, moving his hand in a timeless gesture to illustrate his meaning. "I presume it works well enough for fucking as well."

Marin shrugged and poured some of the lube into his hand. "I guess we'll soon find out."

Caspian closed his eyes as Marin prepared him, teasing him as much as his fingers stretched him.

Marin clearly knew what he was doing, and Caspian pushed the thought from his mind that Marin had done this with Calder many times during their years together. Jealousy had no place in his heart tonight.

He moaned as Marin took hold of his balls and squeezed them. His cock hardened and his eyes flew open when he felt a damp swipe along its length.

Marin gave him a wicked grin as he used his tongue to lick at his tip. "You taste nice."

"I'm glad to hear it," Caspian replied. "Perhaps you'll let me return the favor sometime."

The moment the words left his mouth, he realized what he had said and cringed. Marin needed to fuck him and he wouldn't be able to come until he did. No amount of sucking and licking on Caspian's part would bring Marin pleasure tonight. His words, spoken without much thought, hinted that he wanted more than the solstice. Even though he had promised not to push him, he was already breaking his word.

Marin seemed to understand his discomfort and smiled at him from his spot between his legs. "It's all right, Caspian. I think I might like that too."

"No pressure," Caspian assured him.

"I know."

For a second, Caspian thought Marin might kiss him, but then the moment passed. Marin licked at his balls as he continued to move his fingers inside him, each press a little deeper, stretching him and readying him for Marin's cock.

He closed his eyes, only opening them again when Marin removed his fingers and replaced them with the blunt head of his cock.

"You're sure you want to do this?" Marin asked. "You can still back out and change your mind."

"I'm sure," Caspian replied. He clutched at the sheets and braced himself.

"Try to relax," Marin said. "It'll go easier if you do."

"Easy for you to say," Caspian muttered.

Marin chuckled. "I'm a lot smaller than you. If I can take you—and you remember that I did—then surely you can manage me."

Caspian glanced down at Marin's cock. "You seem bigger now than when you were Phoebus."

Marin frowned down as he prepared himself with lube. "You think so?"

"Yes. Or maybe I'm just thinking you are because you're about to shove it into me."

Marin laughed and shook his head. "I don't know. I don't remember."

Caspian smiled at the sound of Marin's joy. "Go for it."

Marin took him at his word and slowly pushed his way inside. Caspian tried to relax, he really did, but still he tensed at the intrusion. He took a deep breath and forced his muscles to relax again.

"That's it," Marin encouraged. "Let me in."

Caspian used his powers to take away the pain of Marin's entrance, even as he mentally chided himself for *cheating*. He raised himself up to meet Marin's thrust and moaned as the merman slid inside.

He reached around and grabbed Marin's buttocks, pulling him nearer.

"Are you okay?" Marin asked. "I'm not hurting you?"

Caspian shook his head. "I used my powers to ease the pain."

Marin halted his thrust and stared down at him. "All this time you've had the power to erase your own pain and you still refused to let anyone fuck you?"

"It was never about the pain," Caspian replied. "It was about the control. I like being in charge."

Marin nodded and with one hard thrust he buried himself in Caspian's arse. "So do I."

Caspian gasped and moaned as his body adjusted to the feel of Marin inside him. His erection had subsided, but when Marin moved within him with short, barely there jerks of his hips, the friction sent vibrations through his entire body and it rose once more.

"Move," Caspian said. "Please, please, move!"

Marin didn't hesitate. He fucked him with an expertise that only came from experience and Caspian shouted his encouragement as he met his thrusts with an enthusiasm that he never thought he would have.

It was the night of the solstice and Marin didn't last long. All it took was a few minutes before he came, the heat of his release filling Caspian, even as the mating fever abated and Marin's temperature returned to normal.

Marin collapsed across his chest with a groan. "Fuck."

Caspian wasn't sure how to answer that comment, so he held his tongue.

After a short time Marin rolled off him, pulling out of him as he did.

"You didn't come," Marin said.

Caspian gave a half-hearted shrug. "It's fine. You've broken your fever, and that's what's important."

"Calder always came when I fucked him," Marin said. "He enjoyed it."

Caspian rolled onto his side. "I enjoyed it too."

"But you didn't come."

"No, but I think if we'd carried on a minute longer, I would have. You know as well as I do that on the solstice it's harder for a merman to hold back and make things last."

"I suppose so."

Caspian sat up and stretched his arms over his head. "I'll leave you to get some sleep."

He had gathered up his clothes and was halfway to the door when Marin spoke.

"Don't you want me to take care of that for you?"

Caspian smiled and shook his head. "I'll take care of it."

"Are you sure?" Marin asked, though even Caspian could tell he was only asking out of politeness.

"I'm sure," Caspian replied. "Goodnight, Marin."

He closed the door behind him and headed into his own room. Secure in the knowledge that he was alone, he settled himself on the bed and took himself in hand.

No stranger to the fine art of self-pleasure, Caspian slowly stroked his length and cupped his balls.

He closed his eyes and tried to conjure up the image of the merman who had haunted his dreams for centuries. For the first time he failed and instead of Phoebus, he saw Marin, his face captured in the bliss of his orgasm. Two mermen, so similar in looks, and yet also so different. Both had striking mismatched eyes, but the fire he saw in Marin's was something he had never spotted in Phoebus' — the glint of wickedness, the desire to dominate and the teasing confidence of a man who knew how to please a lover. Marin had those in abundance.

"Marin," he whispered, cautious in case his guest heard him.

He wanted Marin as much as he had ever wanted Phoebus. More, he realized. He liked the fire that burned within Marin. It drew him like a moth to the flame. He could only hope that it didn't consume him.

"Oh, Marin," he moaned as he increased his speed. "Marin, my Marin." *No, not* my *Marin. Not yet. Maybe not ever.*

Still, it didn't stop him from imagining that the merman in the other bedroom might one day touch him like this.

He came hard, spilling across his abdomen and chest. He panted and gasped with the force of his climax. As a god, he didn't need to breathe to survive, but still, he always felt short of breath when the orgasm hit him.

Sticky, yet sated, Caspian idly stroked his chest with one hand while exploring his arse with the other.

He squeezed his nipples as he fingered himself. Marin hadn't found his prostate earlier, and now he found himself curious as to what it would be like to feel a touch there.

Exploring slowly, he slid a second finger inside with ease.

He wondered why he hadn't done that centuries ago.

Sighing deeply, he fucked himself with his fingers. His cock rose again and he gripped the base to stave off a second orgasm.

When he found the spot he was searching for, his hips bucked involuntarily.

"Oh fuck." He touched it again, sending shockwaves of pleasure through his body. "Marin, fuck!"

A knock on the door startled him from his work.

"Caspian, did you call me?"

"No. You go back to bed." Caspian did his best to sound normal.

"Are you okay in there?" Marin asked.

"Yes. I'm fine." He choked out the words as he removed his fingers from his arse, the movement brushing his prostate one final time.

"Are you sure?"

Caspian cleaned himself with a thought and pulled on a robe. Once he was certain he was presentable, he opened the door. Marin stood outside, a concerned frown on his face.

"As you can see, there's nothing wrong." Caspian shrugged and tried not to look as though he'd just been caught pleasuring himself to thoughts of his guest.

Marin took him at his word and returned to the guest room.

Caspian sighed and closed his door once more. *What in the name of Atlantis am I going to do about this?* He couldn't throw Marin out to fend for himself. He had offered him a home for as long as he wanted it. Yet the longer they remained in close quarters, the harder it became to ignore his growing feelings.

Chapter Sixteen

Marin stared at the object called a television. He still didn't understand how the device worked, but he didn't need to. The picture on the screen showed Atlantis and the science teams who were reporting back on their explorations of the mysterious island that had risen from the depths of the ocean.

"You won't find out anything new about Urion on the television," Caspian told him as he passed him a mug of coffee.

"You don't know that."

Caspian sat down beside him. "If the sea dragons had been spotted by humans, Mariana would have made us all aware of it."

"Are you sure about that?"

"Oh yes, I'm sure."

Marin turned back to the television. "Isander seems to think Urion will want to turn back into a human sooner or later."

"He probably will. Despite his current appearance, inside he is still a man, with a man's needs and desires.

Of course, he can't turn back without Mariana's help, and she seems determined to keep her priests in this form. They give her a certain advantage over the rest of us immortals."

"Why would she need that?" Marin asked.

"Because the Atlantean gods and goddesses have never seen eye to eye on anything. They have always sought to increase their powers, and right now, Mariana is the only one of them with priests. Well, save for Medina and Cari. My sister has her Oracles, and Medina has Jake."

"Jake is a priest?" Marin wondered whether Caspian even realized he spoke of the other immortals as if he were no longer one of them.

"A somewhat reluctant one, but yes," Caspian confirmed. "None of the others have bothered to enlist anyone yet. They hoped that raising Atlantis would increase their powers, but it wasn't to be. We no longer have a place in the world of men."

"You sound resigned to that."

"I suppose I am."

"The mer still believe in you."

"Unfortunately, it isn't enough. It might have been once, but your numbers are so few these days..."

Marin sighed. "And that's my fault, of course."

"No, it's not. Anyway, my mother has undone her magic, so the mer will no longer decrease in numbers with each generation. We hope that will save your people from dying out completely."

"Why did she undo it?" Marin asked.

"Because I asked her to."

"Even knowing that it means this life I live now will be the last one for me? That I'll return to the ocean in the way of the mer, instead of being reborn some day in this form?"

"Yes."

Marin lowered his eyes. "What if I never grow to love you in this life?"

"Then so be it," Caspian said. "I want you to love me. I don't deny that. But I don't want your people to suffer any longer."

"Thank you," Marin said, and he kissed Caspian on the cheek.

* * * *

Caspian arrived at the council meeting just as it was starting. He had no idea what it was about, but no one seemed to be taking much notice of him, so he guessed they hadn't yet decided on his punishment for making Rafe immortal.

He took his seat and waited for the meeting to be called to order.

When Mariana stood to address the gods, Caspian was surprised. He couldn't recall a time when she had been the one to summon everyone together. He supposed it must have happened on occasion, but it was infrequent enough for him to have forgotten.

"I wish to petition the pantheon for the most loyal of my priests, Urion, to drink from the cup of immortality," Mariana said. "My high priest has served me longer than any other and I would see him rewarded for his devotion."

Caspian stared at the goddess in silent horror. Around the table, several immortals were in a similar state of muteness. Others, like Medina and Odessa, made choking sounds. He wondered whether they were choking on their wine or trying to smother their laughter.

"You aren't serious?" Cari asked. "Your high priest should have died centuries ago and is currently on a murderous rampage through the Atlantic Ocean. You can't imagine that we would ever allow such a man to be made immortal."

"Urion is obeying my orders, just as he has done for centuries, even when I was not around to guide him."

"I vote against it," Cari said.

Antar stood and raised his hand for silence. "We cannot vote on this immediately. Urion, whatever his faults, should be judged in the same way as any other mortal, before we cast our votes."

Caspian could tell that Cari had already made up her mind, but there was something he was curious about. "I have a question."

"Yes?" Antar replied.

"If he becomes immortal, what form will he take?" Caspian asked. "Will he be human or a sea dragon?"

"He will be human," Antar confirmed. "He will have to take human form before he drinks from the cup, and he will not be able to change back again once he is immortal."

Mariana made a noise as though she meant to argue, but Antar halted her with a glare.

"You don't have the power to transform him again and you know it. And even if you did, it is forbidden for an immortal to take such a form."

"Not in other pantheons," Mariana said.

"You're not in another pantheon," Antar snapped back at her. "In *this* one, the immortals only take human form."

"And how would you prevent him from taking another form?" Mariana asked with a sly smile.

Antar shook the room with his roar. "You are doing nothing to convince me to vote in your favor right now. And to answer your question, it would be a simple matter to make Urion immune to all forms of magic if he is made immortal. If you wish him to become immortal, then understand that he will be in human form."

"Very well," Mariana replied with bad grace.

As the meeting broke up, Caspian wondered whether Mariana's request was such a bad thing. Urion in human form was a lot less destructive than a sea dragon. He had to talk to Marin about this new development.

* * * *

"Immortal?" Marin stared at Caspian in horror. "Are you telling me that instead of being punished for his crimes, the gods and goddesses are considering making him immortal?"

"Yes."

"What sort of warped reasoning do they have?" Marin shouted. "They should be killing him, not making sure he stays around forever."

"The pantheon didn't decide this," Caspian explained. "The request has been made by Mariana, just as I once requested the same for Phoebus."

"Then they have to vote, as they did before?"

"Yes."

"When will that be?" Marin asked.

"Probably in a couple of weeks," Caspian said. "It doesn't usually take long to come to a decision about such things."

"Even less time when the one in question is a monster like Urion," Marin muttered.

Caspian gestured for Marin to take a seat at the table. "The decision isn't as straightforward as you might imagine."

"What do you mean?"

"If Urion becomes immortal, he'll be forced to give up being a sea dragon."

"Oh. And he's prepared to do that?"

"I don't know. Mariana wasn't happy to hear about that condition and I doubt Urion will be either. He seems to like being one. I never thought he'd stick to that form for so long."

"Me neither," Marin said. "Isander thought he'd want to change back to have sex long before now."

"Me too."

"So, you think some of the gods might vote to make him immortal, just so that he has to turn back into human form?"

"Yes, I'm considering it myself."

Marin glared at him. "But if he's immortal, how am I supposed to kill him?"

"Well, there're a couple of options," Caspian replied. "The same way I instructed you when it came to Rafe, though you'd need a lot more practice since Urion won't be chained in a dungeon waiting for you to strike the blow."

"And the other option?"

"There will be a short period of time where Urion is human and mortal," Caspian said. "During that time, he will vulnerable in a way that he hasn't been for hundreds of years. You could strike him then."

"The gods would allow me to do that?"

"It isn't a question of whether they would let you or not. You have free will, after all."

Marin nodded. "I guess I need to think about this."

"Yes, you do. It may be that Urion will eventually tire of his sea dragon form anyway. If that happens, you'll get a much longer window of opportunity to fight him."

Caspian left Marin to consider what he had told him. He didn't want Marin fighting Urion at all, but he knew there would be no way to talk him out of it. He just didn't know if it would be best to wait indefinitely for Urion to revert to human form, or whether to speed things along by voting for him to be made immortal and give Marin the chance to kill him before he drank from the cup.

Chapter Seventeen

The next summons from the council came through before Caspian had finished drinking his morning coffee. It was tempting to wait until he had, but this time he knew what he was being called for. Since he was being summoned to face his punishment, he thought it perhaps better to go immediately.

"What is it?" Marin asked from across the table.

"I'm being summoned by the pantheon," Caspian replied. "I should go and see what they want."

"Is something wrong?"

Caspian guessed he hadn't kept his voice as casual as he had hoped. "No, there's nothing for you to worry about. I'll be back soon."

He didn't give Marin time to question him further.

All the other gods had gathered already. From the look of them, they had been there for some time.

Caspian gave a bow of respect to his parents, but he didn't take his usual seat.

"You know why you have been summoned today?" Cynbel asked.

"I presume you have decided on my punishment."

"That is correct." Cynbel took his seat and turned to his own father.

Antar rose and gestured for Caspian to come forward. "I won't keep you in suspense, other than to say that we have not come to our decision easily. For making Rafe immortal without the consent of the gods, you will be stripped of your own immortality."

The room swayed around him as his grandfather's words registered in his mind.

"You will have one day to put your affairs in order, then tomorrow at dawn you will present yourself here for your father or mother to remove your powers."

Caspian frowned. "But what of justice?"

"The world will be as it was before you were born, at least until such time as a new god is born and appointed to that position. It will not be the same as if you were killed in battle."

"Will I retain any of my powers?" Caspian asked. He knew from discussions with Fabian, a former demi-god, that he had retained the power to communicate with sea creatures, though he had lost the rest. Caspian suspected that Mariana letting him keep that ability was nothing more than an oversight on her part. She had, after all, removed his demi-god status in the midst of an underwater battle, with the intention of killing her rebellious son.

"No," Antar confirmed. "You will live as a mortal."

Odessa coughed delicately. "You will still be able to visit this isle—however, you'll have to do so the same way mortals do, via the crystal portals. I will see a crystal installed into your home, wherever you choose to live."

Caspian nodded. He wanted to argue his case, but he knew it would be useless to do so.

"What of when I die?" he asked quietly. The words nearly choked him. He had never once truly considered his own mortality. Even in the midst of battle, the concept of death had seemed far removed from his reality.

"We believe you will be judged and move on in the same way as the Atlanteans once did, though we cannot say for sure since this is unprecedented."

"I see." Caspian pushed aside the thought of his impending death, which would hopefully be many years from now. He had a life to live before then and no idea what to do with it.

The room swayed once more and he stumbled forward. His mother leaped from her seat to catch him and guide him to a chair. "Leave us a moment, please," she said.

Caspian took a deep breath, trying to stem his rising panic.

Mortal. Fuck.

As the panic receded, he heard his mother humming softly to him and a feeling of calm washed over him. He could tell it was his mother's magic.

"Will you be the one to do it — or Father?" he asked.

"Who would you prefer?" Odessa replied.

Caspian put his head in his hands. "I don't know," he mumbled. "Either way, I'll be losing a part of myself, something I've had my entire life."

"Yes, you will," his mother confirmed. "But you'll be gaining a lot as well."

"Such as?"

"Um..."

Caspian chuckled but without much humor. "You know as well as I do that there is nothing to be gained from mortality that we don't already enjoy as immortals."

"Only the ability to grow old with the one that we love."

"I happen to like being young," Caspian muttered.

"As do we all, but how would you feel about remaining forever young while Marin aged and died?"

Caspian hadn't thought about that. *What am I going to tell Marin?*

"You said yourself that you were unsure about offering immortality to Marin. Like Phoebus, he is mer and would have to give up that part of himself if he were to drink from the cup."

"Marin and I aren't a couple," Caspian said.

"Not yet, but in time you will be."

"Since when do you see into the future?"

Odessa smiled. "I don't, but I have faith that you will one day win the heart of your merman."

Caspian wished he shared her optimism.

"Where do you think you'd like to live?" his mother asked.

"I have no idea," Caspian replied. "But if Marin is going to be a part of my life, it must be somewhere near the ocean."

"You'll have to make your mind up quickly," Odessa warned. "As of tomorrow, you'll lose your ability to magically move to any location you wish."

"Bloody hell. I'm going to have to conjure up official papers to live as a human. I'll have to learn to do things the mortal way."

Panic washed over him again as thoughts of all the things he didn't know how to do popped into his head.

He wasn't even sure he could make a decent cup of coffee without his powers.

"You'll do fine," his mother assured him. "You've been more a part of the human world than any of us. You even dress as modern men do."

"I'll have to get a job. What the fuck can I do?"

"Well, you could watch your language for a start."

"Sorry, but I've never worked a day in my life."

"You'll find something and you'll learn. Now, I suggest you go speak with Marin. He needs to know too."

Caspian nodded, but he didn't return home at once. Marin was expecting him to help deal with Urion. How was he going to tell him that he could no longer do so?

Instead, Caspian transported himself to the island where Jake and his lovers lived. Perhaps the human in this ménage could give him some advice.

He found Jake making lunch and realized he would have to learn how to cook as well.

"Caspian, come on in," Jake said when he spotted him at the door. "What can I do for you?"

"Can we talk?" Caspian asked as he stepped into the kitchen.

"Sure. Is something wrong?"

Caspian frowned. "Do I really only ever come here when something has gone awry?"

"Pretty much," Jake replied. He waved Caspian to one of the stools at the counter and sat down too. "Help yourself to a sandwich."

"Thanks, but I'm not hungry right now." He would be soon. Tomorrow he would have to eat and drink to survive. He made a mental note to ensure that wherever he ended up living, he stocked the cupboards with easy-to-make meals that didn't require any form of effort.

Jake studied him as though he were some form of strange creature he had never seen before. "What brings you here?"

Caspian drummed his fingers on the counter. "Is it hard to live as a mortal?"

Jake snorted. "I can't say I've ever really thought about it. It's not like I've lived as anything else to have a comparison. Why do you ask?"

Caspian shrugged. "As of tomorrow, I'll be living as one."

There, he'd said it.

Jake stared at him in silence. "What's happened?"

"I did something I shouldn't have done and the other gods have decided to strip me of my powers. Today is my last day as an immortal."

Caspian expected Jake to ask what he had done to incur their wrath, but he didn't.

"What will happen to justice?" he asked instead.

"It will be as it was before I was born," Caspian explained. "Don't worry. Justice won't be gone from the world. I just won't be able to help keep the balance."

Jake breathed a sigh of obvious relief. "And what does Marin think about this?"

"I haven't told him yet. I must, of course, but he's not going to be happy about it."

"What makes you think that?"

"I promised to help him deal with Urion. Now I'm not going to be in a position to do so. I'm not even sure how I'm going to deal with day-to-day life, let alone murderous sea dragons."

"Well, I'd offer to help, but there are limits to what I can do from here on the island. Er, this island isn't going to vanish or anything, is it? It'll still be here, powered and invisible to the rest of the world?"

Caspian nodded quickly, eager to reassure Jake, who appeared more concerned by the minute. "I'll speak to my mother about ensuring the magic continues. It should anyway, at least until my death. After that, I'm not so sure."

"Your death?"

Caspian gave him a weak smile. "Yes. I will be living—and dying—as a mortal man."

"I'm sorry." Jake reached out and squeezed Caspian's hand. The gesture nearly brought tears to his eyes.

"Thank you. I suspect the truth hasn't sunk in yet. I thoroughly expect to have a nervous breakdown the minute I get a paper cut."

Jake chuckled and opened a drawer. "Plasters are our friends." He placed a box on the counter. "Anything else I can help with?"

Caspian opened the box and pulled out one of the plasters. He stared at it, trying to figure out how the thing worked. For the first time in his life, he felt like a dunce.

Jake, seeming to understand his confusion, plucked it from his fingers, deftly undid the wrapper and applied the plaster to his face, right across his mouth.

Caspian smiled and reached out to pull it off. Jake cringed when he did.

"I would advise ripping the plasters off quickly," Jake said. "Kyle is a bit of a baby about them, but don't tell him I said so."

Caspian gazed around the kitchen. "I didn't even know these existed. How much more am I unaware of?"

"I thought you had a pretty good range of knowledge of humans?" Jake asked. "Better than Medina's anyway."

"I've learned as time has passed, but I've never needed to use these before. Human medicines aren't something I've ever needed. Because of that, my knowledge of such things is limited."

"I see." Jake picked up his phone and waggled it in front of Caspian. "Make sure you have one of these, with my number programmed into it. That way I'll be contactable when you no longer have the ability to pop in here by magic."

Caspian laughed. "At least I know about phones. Justin educated me on those, as well as other modern technology."

"I think he misses them now that he lives underwater," Jake remarked. "Every time he visits he makes a beeline for the computer so he can check his social media accounts. He's set up one for what he calls his 'merman persona' that's really popular."

"He's what?" Caspian didn't need the additional headache of exposure of the mer right now. The merman he had raised on land should know better.

"Oh, don't worry," Jake hurried to assure him. "No one thinks he's a real merman. They just assume he's one of these people who buys a fake tail and learns to hold their breath underwater for a long time. He got the idea when Kyle told him about that fiasco at the aquarium staff party."

Caspian had no idea what had happened at the party and he thought it better not to ask.

"We'll have you surfing the Net in no time," Jake teased. "Er…"

"What?" Caspian asked.

"Have you thought of maybe living here on the island?" Jake suggested. "You conjured up this house — hell, the entire island. What's to stop you from building another one here? Think about it. If Marin is going to be staying with you, then it's certainly close to the ocean. He can reconnect with his friends from Atlantis and visit whenever he wants. I know Justin would like to see more of you. I'll be on hand if you have any difficulties and — "

"And?"

Jake shrugged. "It'd be nice to have a neighbor or two. I mean, this place is great, and you'll never know how thankful I am for what you've done for us, but Finn and Kyle are mer, and while the colony is settling into their new homes, they spend more time in the ocean than on land. I guess what I'm saying is that it gets lonely sometimes. Treacle isn't a great conversationalist."

The idea had some merit — a lot, in fact. He wondered what Marin would think about the idea. In his quest to find Urion, he had isolated himself from the mer. Spending more time with his people could only be a good thing.

"You don't have to, of course," Jake continued. "It was only a thought. You'll probably want to be somewhere closer to civilization — in a city, perhaps."

Caspian smiled. "I think that after so many years of hearing the cries of mankind for justice, I might like a little peace and quiet."

"You hear them all?" Jake asked.

"Not if the human is calling upon another deity, but the general ones or those directed at me, yes. Not that anyone calls upon me personally any more. The

Atlantean gods are long since forgotten by man. Our time has passed."

"It still sounds noisy to me."

Caspian smiled. "You get used to it after a few centuries. You learn to filter out all but the most important."

Jake nodded and Caspian looked out of the window, recalling the layout of the island. There was certainly room for another building here.

Using his powers, he scanned the island for anyone who might be around. Other than a couple of mermaids sunning themselves on the beach, there was no one on land save for himself and Jake.

He smiled at Jake. "How would you like to see a house created out of thin air?"

Jake grinned back. "You mean you like the idea?"

"Yes, I think it's perfect. Though whether you'll think that after having me for a neighbor for a few years is debatable. Come on. I think I know a suitable spot."

They traipsed through the trees and bushes, with Caspian using his powers to create a stone path as they walked.

"Might as well set up a proper walkway now," Caspian said. "I won't be able to use my powers to come over after today."

He continued to move bushes, trees and rocks until they reached a clearing.

"Here?" Jake asked.

Caspian nodded. "I think so. The north beach is just through those trees. There's soil for planting, if you'll teach me how to grow our own vegetables."

Jake snorted. "That's likely to be the blind leading the blind. I research on the Internet, but I haven't yet figured out the cycle of the seasons here."

"Ah, that's probably due to the magic I used. This place is part of the real world but not entirely. I'll have to see about getting some sensible weather patterns set up. Tempest may help me with that."

"Tempest?"

"She's Goddess of the Storm, but she can summon and control most forms of weather. Once she's set up a cycle, she won't have to bother about it again."

"You think she'll agree to help?"

"If she doesn't, I'll get my mother to talk her into it. They've always been friends."

"That sounds great. And at least you won't have Treacle *helping* you. He digs up my vegetable garden every chance he gets."

Treacle barked as if in agreement.

Caspian resolved to make sure his own garden had a nice secure fence circling it before he got started with his own planting.

"Keep hold of Treacle," Caspian warned. "Menace as he is to your self-sufficiency efforts, I don't think you want him to get stuck in the foundations or anything."

Jake dutifully called Treacle to heel and kept a hold of his collar.

Caspian stepped into the center of the clearing and tapped into his powers. Beneath his feet, the grass transformed into stone, spreading out in all directions until he had set the boundaries of the house.

When he'd judged the size to be adequate, he raised the walls, deciding two levels would be enough. Like Jake's home, he made sure there were plenty of windows to let light into the building.

Piece by piece he added stairs, floorboards and doors. He added a balcony to the master bedroom and a veranda around the lower floor.

Once the house was structurally complete, he set about decorating it. He kept it plain and simple, telling himself that Marin might like to put his own touch on the place, if he were to make it his home.

At that point he summoned Jake to take a look around and see if anything was missing.

"I didn't omit any rooms in your house, did I?" he asked.

"No, there were plenty spare for whatever we wanted. Finn has his office and Kyle has his home gym."

"Good. Now the appliances." Caspian headed into the room he had designated as the kitchen. "Cooker, fridge, freezer... What else?"

"Dishwasher?" Jake suggested.

Caspian frowned. "I don't remember putting one of those into your house. Did you want me to add one now, while I still can?"

Jake laughed. "Sure. But let's get your new place set up first. How about putting a sink near the window?"

Caspian let Jake guide him as he installed everything the kitchen would need.

"Don't forget lights." Jake pointed at the ceiling. "I still don't understand how we have plumbing and electricity here, but unless you plan on sitting around in the dark, you'll need lights."

Caspian added some overhead lights and—at Jake's suggestion—a smoke detector.

"The place would probably burn to the ground before the fire service got here," Caspian pointed out. "Even if they could figure out where to come, which is highly unlikely, it would take forever for them to get here."

"In that case, may I suggest a sprinkler system?"

Caspian frowned. "You don't have much faith in my ability to cook, do you?"

"Having seen the disasters resulting from Kyle's and Finn's attempts, I doubt you and Marin will do much better."

Caspian laughed and dutifully installed a small sprinkler system in the kitchen. He found that he was enjoying himself, as well as Jake's company.

Once the kitchen was set up, Caspian filled the cupboards with enough food to feed a small army for a month. Hopefully by the time the supplies were running low, he'd have figured out how to cook as well as order in more.

"How are you managing for supplies?" Caspian asked.

"Pretty good. I head to the mainland once a month and stock up. I'm hoping that, in time, we can cut back on that. Kyle and Finn bring back some sea fruits from the new colony, but they don't like to take much, at least until the new fields are producing regularly, which I understand won't be for another year or two."

"I'll no doubt be coming with you on your shopping spree," Caspian said. "Which reminds me of something else I'm going to need—a bank account and an identity."

He sighed as he produced for himself all the papers he would need. "I hope this will be enough," he said as he looked at the bank statement.

Jake laughed as he spied over his shoulder. "Yeah, more than. Perhaps some papers for Marin too, just in case he needs them later?"

"Good idea." Caspian whipped them up and tucked them into a drawer with his own.

"Now, shall we tackle the rest of the house?" Jake asked with an enthusiastic grin. He was clearly enjoying this as much as Caspian.

They worked their way through each of the rooms. Some took longer to sort out than others. The living room was finished relatively quickly, while the bathroom took longer. There would be no more instant haircuts or clean-shaven faces in Caspian's future. Cursing his own folly after checking the sharpness of his new razor, Caspian healed the cut instantly and materialized a fully stocked first-aid kit, which he had Jake check through.

By the time the house was in order, it was mid-afternoon.

"I think I need a drink," Caspian said as he dropped into one of the chairs.

"Me too," Jake agreed. He pointed to the alcove in the corner. "I think you need a bar over there."

Caspian waved his hand and one appeared.

Jake laughed. "I was only joking. If you're going to be human, you might want to limit your alcohol intake."

Caspian walked over to the bar and poured them each a drink. "I'll enjoy my lack of hangovers while I still can."

They drank quietly, and Caspian knew he couldn't put off speaking to Marin much longer.

Jake placed his empty glass on the table. "I should be heading back to my place before Kyle and Finn get back and start wondering where I am."

Caspian saw him to the door. "Thank you, Jake. You've been a great help to me today."

Jake gave him an odd look. "You don't need to thank me for this. It's what friends do for each other. I hope you'll come to see me as a real friend one day."

Caspian nodded. "I already do."

They stood awkwardly on the veranda until Jake gave a short laugh and threw his arms around Caspian, enveloping him in tight hug. "Welcome to the neighborhood," he teased.

* * * *

Marin was training with the trident in the living room when Caspian found him. He had moved the furniture to the sides of the room and was currently working his way through the basic training moves. Caspian had ordered him not to conjure sea-fire in the flat and he was glad to see nothing had been scorched or set alight.

"How's it going?" Caspian asked.

"Good. Any word yet on whether Urion will be allowed to become immortal?"

"Not yet. Last I heard, they were still considering it. Urion hasn't exactly endeared himself to most of the pantheon, but if it means one less sea dragon in the oceans, they may agree, just on that basis."

"You'll let me know as soon as you hear?" Marin asked. "I don't want to miss my chance, and there'll only be a short period between his taking human form and becoming immortal."

Caspian gestured to the sofa. "You'd better sit down, Marin. I have something to tell you."

Marin gave him a curious glance but took a seat anyway. "You aren't going to make some ill-timed declaration of love, are you?" he asked.

"No. It's nothing like that." Caspian paced back and forth across the rug. "I don't know the best way to break this to you, so I'm just going to have to blurt it out. After today, I'll no longer be immortal."

"What?" Marin stared up at him in confusion.

"The pantheon has decided to strip me of my powers and make me mortal."

"They can do that?"

"Yes. I have to present myself to them at dawn tomorrow."

"I thought it wasn't possible to reverse immortality."

"Not for those who gain it through the cup. For those like me, who are born to immortality, our parents can take it from us, and tomorrow one of my parents will."

"Why would they do that?"

"It doesn't matter why." The last thing Caspian wanted was for Marin to feel unjustified guilt for Caspian's own actions. "What concerns you is what I intend to do now, and where you will go."

"They're throwing you out of your home here as well?"

Caspian shook his head. "No, this is mine, though I intend to sell it rather than live here. My temple on the Isle of the Gods is the only home I'll actually lose, but I've not lived there properly in centuries anyway."

"Where do you plan on living, if you aren't going to stay here?"

"I'm going to move to the island where Jake and his lovers are living. I built a house this afternoon and I'd like you to come there with me."

Marin opened his mouth but Caspian raised his hand to signal that he hadn't finished.

"The island is magically hidden from the world, as well as being close to the new mer colony. If you'd rather not live with me, you can return to your people. There is plenty of room in the new cave network and they could certainly use an extra set of hands."

"What about Urion?" Marin asked. "Will you know when they've reached their decision?"

"I may find out later, but it's unlikely the news will reach me in time for you to face him. I'll be allowed to visit the Isle of the Gods, but only via the crystal portals of other gods. My mother intends to install one such device in my new home, so I can still visit her."

Marin hung his head and sighed. "Then my one chance to kill Urion is lost already."

"I'm sorry," Caspian said. "I never thought the pantheon would do this. It didn't even occur to me."

Marin glared at him. "No, I don't imagine that it did. Still, as the God of Justice, you've done nothing to help get justice for Calder, so I suppose it was only a matter of time before you were removed from the post. Maybe your replacement will help me."

Caspian reeled at the venom from Marin. "I'll deliver you to the new colony. What you do from there is your own choice."

Before Marin could say anything else, Caspian sent him to the colony, depositing him in the middle of King Nereus' audience chamber.

Alone in his flat, he decided what he wanted to take with him to his new home—mostly just his books and music—and once that was done, he emptied the place of the rest.

Marin's trident was still on the floor and he picked it up. He'd find somewhere to keep it safely out of the way, just in case Marin ever decided to forgive him and wanted it back.

He transported himself to his new house and looked around him. The place suddenly seemed too big for just him, the quiet eerie rather than peaceful.

For the first time in a long time, he opened his mind to the cries of mankind. He might not be the God of Justice tomorrow, but for today, he still had the power to make a difference. He set to work, determined to get as much done as he could in the time he had left.

Chapter Eighteen

Marin swore when he realized he was suddenly underwater. He transformed immediately into his mer form and let his eyes adjust to the darkness of the ocean.

There were several mer swimming nearby and he recognized one of them as Justin, the young heir to the throne of the sunken city. He wasn't sure what he was heir to now, Atlantis being miles away on the other side of the world.

He turned in the water and saw King Nereus sitting on a large sponge shaped into a throne. Prince Finn hovered beside him, an annoyed expression on his handsome face.

Ah, this must be the new colony Caspian mentioned.

At the thought of Caspian, he searched the room for the god, but he was nowhere to be seen. *Has he just dumped me here without giving me any choice in the matter?*

When the god failed to appear after a few minutes, it seemed that he had.

"*Marin?*" Finn spotted him and swam over with a wide smile on his face. "*When did you get here?*"

"*Just a moment ago,*" Marin replied. "*Caspian sent me here – or at least I think he did. He didn't say anything, but I was talking to him right before I ended up here.*"

"*He didn't tell you before transporting you here?*"

Marin shook his head then stopped. "*He was saying something, but I guess I wasn't listening. I was too angry with him to take any notice of what he was telling me.*"

Finn took his arm and steered him into one of the side chambers. "*Come on. Let's go find some food and you can tell me what he's done to upset you.*"

Marin let Finn guide him through the caves. "*So this is the home of the refugees from the sunken city.*" It didn't seem much compared to the luxurious buildings of Atlantis. He supposed this was going to be his home now. "*Are there any empty caves here?*"

"*Oh yes, there are hundreds. The network is massive. We've not even explored it all yet. I'm sure I can find you a nice cozy cave to stay in. You can get a soft sponge to sleep on from Malka's clan. If you want rejoin the guards, they'll be happy to have you.*"

"*I doubt that,*" Marin replied. "*They all thought I was useless as a guard.*"

"*They'll soon discover you aren't,*" Finn said. "*You forget. I've seen you training back on land. You'll do fine.*"

Marin followed Finn into a cavern that seemed to be set out for a large feast. "*Are we celebrating something?*"

"*No, the food is always set out like this,*" Finn explained. "*With so many people coming and going at different times, we have a buffet of sorts set up. Anyone can come and grab a bite to eat whenever they want. The gatherers are working on shifts to make sure there's always plenty here.*"

Marin recalled his own time doing that job during his life as Phoebus. He had enjoyed the work and the camaraderie of the gatherers. Maybe he should look at doing that again.

He ignored the little voice at the back of his head, reminding him that he could have been starting a life with Caspian.

"*How are you doing?*" Finn asked.

Marin shrugged. "*Okay, I suppose. It's just a bit of a shock to be here. An hour ago I was practicing with the trident, preparing to meet Urion. Now I have no idea what I'm supposed to do.*"

"*You* still *want to face Urion?*" Finn asked.

"*Yes, of course. Someone has to see Calder's murderer brought to justice, and the god whose job it is certainly doesn't seem to be bothered about doing it.*"

Finn cringed. "*I hope you didn't say that to Caspian's face.*"

Marin shrugged. "*I might have said words to that effect.*"

"*Oh, Marin.*" Finn shook his head.

"*What?*"

"*You do realize Caspian is hopelessly in love with you?*"

"*Yes, I'd noticed. How did you know?*"

Finn snorted. "*It was pretty obvious before we left England. He always asked after you and he came by far more frequently when you were staying with us. I saw it in his eyes every time he looked at you.*"

"*I didn't realize.*"

"*When did you figure it out?*" Finn asked.

"*When his grandfather gave me the memory of my previous life,*" Marin muttered. "*Apparently, back then Caspian and I were a couple. He's been waiting for me to be reborn so he can pick up things where he left off.*"

"*I take it you aren't thrilled about that idea?*"

"*Not really. I remember my life as Phoebus – that was my name back then – but I was a different person. I've lived a different life this time around, and I'm not going to forget*

258

Calder so easily. Caspian just doesn't seem to understand that."

Finn patted Marin's arm. *"Calder wouldn't want you to be lonely for the rest of your life."*

"I know that, but I can't move on while his murderer walks free."

"I understand," Finn said. *"Just don't spend your whole life seeking vengeance instead of living."*

Marin privately considered that that was easier said than done.

"Why did Caspian send you here?" Finn asked. *"It sounds like you had an argument."*

"He promised to help me with Urion, and now he says he can't."

"Did he say why?"

"Yes. He told me he won't be a god after today. He's going to be mortal and he won't have any powers."

"What?" Finn stared at him in shock. *"Are you sure?"*

"Yes. He'd have no reason to lie to me about it, unless he thought telling me so would deter me from fighting Urion."

Finn shook his head. *"I don't know Caspian that well, but I don't believe he'd lie to you about something like that."*

Marin considered the possibility. *"No, you're right."*

"Do you know why?" Finn asked. *"Is it something he's decided to do himself, or is there something happening to all the gods?"*

"He said the pantheon had decided to strip him of his powers, but he didn't say why."

"That sounds like he's being punished for something," Finn said.

"Maybe not doing his job," Marin suggested.

Finn didn't say anything to that and Marin hoped he planned on dropping the subject.

They finished eating and went to explore the caverns. Finn found Marin a suitable corner to move into and they set about getting it furnished with sponges and crockery. Marin had forgotten how little the mer had in the way of furniture when compared to humans.

"I think I'm going to see about joining the gatherers," he told Finn after he was set up in his new home. *"Just until I figure out what to do about Urion, anyway."*

And what was he going to do about the sea dragon who aspired to become immortal? He truly had no idea.

* * * *

Caspian spent his last night taking advantage of the different time zones, working through the hours until his internal clock told him it was approaching dawn on the Isle of the Gods. He wondered whether he would still be able to sense the time there after he lost his powers. He supposed that was the least of his problems, all things considered.

He expected to find the council chamber filled with members of the pantheon, but it seemed not everyone was bothered about seeing his punishment carried out.

His parents were there, but of course they had to be. Andaman was also present, along with Medina and Tempest.

"You asked for me to come," Tempest said.

Caspian walked over to her. "Yes, thank you. I was hoping you could set up a permanent weather system over the island I'm going to be living on, if it's not too much trouble?"

"It doesn't have one already?"

"No, the island was magically created to help protect the mer."

Tempest nodded in understanding. "I see. I'll go set it up right now, unless you need me here?"

260

"No," Caspian said, "and thank you."

Tempest vanished, leaving the five of them to wait for the dawn.

"Cari couldn't make it," Odessa said. "She's been bombarded with visions the last few days."

"Anything relating to Urion, or the mer?" Caspian asked.

"Not this time. More human disasters, storms and fires—things she has no control over and cannot change. You know how those drain her."

"Can't Tempest do anything about the storms?" Andaman asked. "That is her area of expertise, after all."

"She's doing what she can, but she cannot prevent it all."

Caspian had a feeling Cari wouldn't have been here regardless of what was happening in the world. He wasn't sure he'd want to witness her being stripped of her powers either.

He looked over at Medina. "And what are *you* doing here?" he asked, knowing he was being rude but unable to help himself.

Medina shrugged. "I can't help feeling that a lot of this is my fault."

Caspian snorted. "That would be because it is. If you hadn't sent Phoebus to me, this whole chain of events wouldn't have happened."

"Well, you shouldn't have slept with all my priests," Medina retorted.

"And you should learn to handle rejection better." Caspian's lips twitched as they fell into the old habit of bickering. He burst out laughing and pulled her into a hug. "Oh, come here, you infuriating goddess."

Medina stayed in his arms for only a few seconds before she pulled away. "What was that for?"

"For sending Phoebus to me," Caspian replied. "Thank you."

Medina sniffled and gave him a watery smile. "You're welcome."

"It is time," Cynbel announced as the sun crept over the horizon. "Kneel, my son."

Caspian knelt before his parents. They each placed a hand on his shoulders and a green light spread out from their palms, surrounding him until he had to close his eyes against the brightness.

"It is done," Cynbel said.

Caspian opened his eyes and faced his mother. She had tears running down her face and he realized that this would be hard for her too. Immortals had never had to see their children age and die until now.

He stood and let her hold him for several long minutes.

"I'll install the crystal today," she said. "You have to visit at least once a month or I'll want to know the reason why."

"I promise."

His father nodded but said nothing. Caspian acknowledged his gesture with one of his own.

Andaman and Medina hovered to one side. Caspian turned to them. Medina, like his mother, was crying. Andaman glanced at Medina and rolled his eyes before stepping forward.

"Caspian, I hope you will visit me too," Andaman said. "I do not see that the loss of your powers should also result in the loss of our friendship."

Andaman held out his hand and Caspian shook it.

"You will be welcome to visit me in my new home," Caspian assured him. "Just don't expect too much in the way of edible meals at first."

Andaman laughed. "I won't, and if it's too bad, I'll whip up something magically myself."

"And on the bright side, at least I'll be able to get intoxicated now."

"Really, Caspian." His mother sighed and shook her head. "Just don't expect me to magic away your hangover the next morning."

"I won't."

Medina seemed to have recovered herself and stepped closer. "As you know, I visit Jake quite frequently, so I'll be able to check in with you whenever I'm on the island."

"There's no need to visit me *that* frequently," Caspian assured her. "I wouldn't wish to intrude on your time with your family."

Privately he suspected Jake didn't enjoy her popping in so frequently either, but he held his tongue. He hoped he was still shielding his thoughts from the gods but declined to say anything. The last thing he needed was to remind any of the immortals that it was probably easier to read his mind now than it had been before.

They all stood around awkwardly for a few minutes until Caspian figured out that they were waiting for him.

"You do remember I can't get home without some assistance?" he asked.

Odessa recovered first. "Of course, but I thought you might wish to ask about Urion?"

"What about him?"

"Didn't you hear the summons to all immortals to be here for the decision this morning?"

Caspian shook his head. "No, I must have missed it. I've been concentrating on those seeking justice since yesterday afternoon. I've been tuning out everything else."

"I see. Well, we'll be casting our votes this morning, so we can't deliver you home just yet. You'll only have to be brought back in an hour."

"Why would I need to be here?" Caspian asked.

"To cast your vote, of course," Cynbel replied, in a tone that said he thought Caspian's question rather stupid.

"But I'm no longer a god."

"You were immortal and the God of Justice when the petition was called. As such, you are entitled to vote this morning."

"I thought my right to vote would be forfeit along with my powers."

"On any future petitions, yes. However, I reminded Mariana and her allies that their votes to strip you of your powers might be considered a way of ensuring that her own petition passes."

Caspian frowned. "I thought the vote to remove my powers was unanimous?"

"Not at all," his father said.

Odessa stepped forward. "You thought we voted to remove your powers too?"

"Well, yes." Caspian shrugged. "I did break the law."

"Yes, but the method of punishment didn't have to be as harsh as this. There were other options, but we were outvoted."

Cynbel nodded. "Your mother is right."

Medina also assured him that she too had voted against his punishment. "The vote to make Urion immortal is likely to be just as close. Mariana's high priest has done little to endear himself to the gods and much to anger some of us."

Caspian sat down in one of the chairs at the table. "I have no idea how to vote on this."

Cynbel joined him and gave him a stern look. "I thought your intention would be to vote to allow it, then assist your lover in striking him in the interim between taking human form and drinking from the cup."

"You knew about that?" Caspian cringed.

"Yes, of course. It is what I would have done, and you are, after all, my son."

Caspian supposed he was. The God of War played a tactical game, and as his son, Caspian had picked up a few tips over the years.

"Unfortunately, that isn't an option now."

"No, it's not. I must admit that I am unsure how to vote on the issue myself. If we vote no, he remains a sea dragon, terrorizing the oceans and causing trouble with the rest of the priests. If we vote yes, he becomes human...but immortal."

"Immortality seems to be the less destructive of the options," Odessa commented. "Not that it makes a great deal of difference as Mariana has other sea dragons to do her bidding."

"Is there no way to force her to turn them all back?" Medina asked. "She did it to avoid the edict that they be banished. Surely that merits some form of punishment?"

The rest of the immortals made various noises of agreement.

"To undo her spell, she would have to be stripped of her powers or die," Cynbel said. "I doubt any petition to remove her powers would pass. She has too many friends among the gods."

"I would be reluctant to vote to remove my own sister's powers," Medina admitted. "No matter what she has done, she is my family."

"I understand," Odessa said. "Family is important to all of us."

Caspian nodded. "She needs to be forced into a position where she has to turn them back into human form. Once that is done, she won't be able to change them back again. None of us have the power we commanded when the Atlanteans worshipped us."

"She won't change them back while they give her such an advantage," Medina said. "There are few mer left in the Atlantic, thanks to her priests, and it's only a matter of time before she turns her attention to other bodies of water. It's clear she wishes to drive the mer out of her domain entirely."

Caspian banged his fist on the table. "She can't be allowed to do that. The mer are creatures of the sea. They cannot survive on land. Even Kyle and Finn, two mer with strong ties to humans, struggled and yearned for the sea. There is also the fact that any mer who lives on land risks exposure. The more who go to land, the greater the chance that one or more will be discovered and all the mer will be in danger."

"Their numbers will also increase now that I've undone the magic that enabled them to be reborn in the manner of humans," Odessa added.

"Does that mean the curse is broken?" Medina asked.

"Yes," Caspian replied. "Not that it was a curse — or at least not in the purest sense. The falling numbers of the mer was an unfortunate side effect of the magic."

"Um, has anyone told Cari and the Oracles?" Medina questioned. "When I spoke to her a few days ago, they were still searching for a solution to the decrease in the population." "I'll speak with her when she arrives for the vote," Odessa said. "While it is not obvious yet, as time passes, the number of mer will increase again and they will no longer struggle to carry their young to term."

Tempest returned, looking rather flushed and windswept. "Your weather system would appear to be working." She magically dried and cleaned her gown with a grimace. Caspian just made out the muddy imprint of a paw on the hem before it vanished. He guessed she had met Treacle.

They sat around making small talk until the rest of the pantheon arrived.

Finally, everyone was assembled and they took their seats.

"And how are you this morning?" Mariana asked Caspian. "You look a little under the weather. Are you catching a cold?"

Caspian shot her a dirty look. Trust her to make some snide comment about his loss of powers, while at the same time appearing caring to everyone else. Though, looking around the table, most of the gods were ignoring her anyway.

Antar took control of the meeting this time and called everyone to order.

"Have we all decided how we are going to vote on the issue of Urion, High Priest of Mariana, being allowed to become immortal?" he asked.

Most of the gods nodded.

"I have a question before I make my decision," Medina said.

"Go ahead," Antar said.

"The sea dragons have lived for centuries without ageing. Do they age now that Mariana is awake?"

"Yes," Mariana confirmed.

"Then they will one day die of old age?" Medina asked.

"Of course, though not for many years. My priests, you'll recall, were young. They were also all male, so no further sea dragons will be born of their lines."

Medina rolled her eyes. "At least I didn't retire my own priests the moment they hit thirty years of age."

Caspian hoped they weren't going to start bickering or he would be here all day. He was tired already, which was a new experience for him and not a pleasant one. Maybe he should have slept a little last night after all. *No*, he told himself, he'd had a job to do, and he had done it to the best of his ability.

As the women continued to squabble, Caspian thought the matter of Urion over in his mind. As a sea dragon he was troublesome, but as was just noted, he would eventually die. As an immortal he would be around for a very long time, and who knew how much chaos he could cause in those years.

He knew Marin wanted Urion to take his human form, but at what price?

Even if Marin did come face-to-face with him as a human, Caspian doubted he would be able to take his life. He had been unable to kill Rafe in cold blood, and as far as Caspian could see, this was no different. Marin might want justice for Calder, but he wasn't a murderer.

Antar brought the meeting to order again. "All those in favor of granting Urion immortality, raise your hands."

Mariana and her friends immediately did so.

Caspian wavered. Part of him felt as though he were betraying Marin, but he had to do what his conscience felt was right. He couldn't vote for someone as vicious and self-serving as Urion to be allowed to live forever.

"Caspian, are you voting yes or no?" Antar asked.

"I vote no," Caspian said as he placed his hovering hand firmly on the table.

A quick count of the raised hands told him at once that Urion was not going to be around any longer than his natural life permitted.

"You cannot do this!" Mariana screamed. "When Caspian wanted to make one of those mer creatures immortal, you allowed him to do so."

"Phoebus was far more deserving of immortality than Urion," Medina commented. "He wasn't a murderer, for one thing."

"Urion has been loyal to me, serving his goddess for longer than any other priest of the entire pantheon."

Medina snorted. "Only because you turned him into a sea dragon with an abnormally long life. Had events not happened the way they did, you'd have tired of him and moved on within a couple of years. You were already growing bored with him."

"That is not the point. Urion deserves to drink from the cup."

"The decision is final," Antar said. "He remains mortal. You may all return to your duties."

"You'll all pay for this," Mariana warned as she stalked from the chamber.

Caspian sighed and shook his head. *Bloody drama queen.* Even those who had supported Mariana's petition appeared taken aback at her fury.

Odessa approached him and patted him on the shoulder. "Would you like to go home now?"

"In a moment," Caspian said. "I just want a quick word with Cari."

He turned to his sister, but she had already vanished. An uneasy feeling settled in the pit of his stomach. *Is she avoiding me? And if so, why?*

"I guess I'll speak to her another time," he said, before letting his mother take him home to the island.

The sunny weather was noticeably absent. Tempest had done her job well and a steady downpour was currently soaking him through.

"You couldn't have deposited us *inside* the house?" he asked his mother as he ran for the door.

Odessa used her powers to stop the rain from hitting her, as she strolled leisurely toward the house. "This is quite a pleasant little island. Isn't it going to be a little lonely though?"

Caspian smiled and shook his head as he let himself into the house. "I'll be fine. I promise." Truthfully, he was already enjoying the quietness that came from not hearing the cries for justice.

His mother took him at his word and, after installing the crystal portal, she left him to return to her duties.

Caspian wondered what he should do first. He had so much to learn if he was to survive as a human. He hoped he was up to the challenge.

Chapter Nineteen

Caspian wasn't sure his cooking skills were good enough for a dinner party, but he was fairly confident that he wouldn't actually poison his guests.

Jake arrived early, brandishing a bottle of wine. "I thought you might need some help. Kyle and Finn will be here soon."

He waggled his eyebrows, making it clear to Caspian just precisely what the hold-up was.

"What about Marin?" Caspian asked. "Did Finn pass on my message?"

Jake nodded. "I'm sorry. He spoke to him, but he refused to come tonight."

"I suppose I can't blame him."

"He just needs time."

Caspian had every intention of giving him that, no matter how much it tore him apart to do so.

Jake tactfully changed the subject by gesturing to the kitchen. "Something smells good."

"Thanks. Let's hope it tastes all right too. This is the first time I've tried making something that isn't a meal that just needs heating up."

"I'm sure it'll be great. So, how are you finding life as a human?"

Caspian gave him a rueful smile. "This is the first morning I haven't managed to cut myself shaving, so I guess I'm improving."

Jake laughed. "If it makes you feel any better, I still occasionally nick myself. Finn and Kyle have it lucky. They don't need to bother, thanks to their mer genetics."

Caspian laughed. "You're right there. The only mer who have a need to shave are those who have a full human in their family tree, where the human genes are dominant. Finn has had a narrow escape. With a human father, he could have been much hairier than he is."

"Is there anything I can help with?" Jake asked.

"No, thanks. I have it covered. Just sit down and relax."

Caspian left Jake in the living room and returned to the kitchen. As soon as he was alone, he swore under his breath and punched the nearest cupboard. *Would it have killed Marin to come here for dinner?* He immediately regretted his burst of temper as pain shot through his knuckles. *Damn it.* He missed his powers nearly as much as he missed Marin.

He concentrated on finishing preparing dinner and was nearly done when Kyle and Finn arrived, their timing perfect.

"How are you finding life as a human?" asked Finn once they were all seated at the table.

"Tiring," Caspian replied with a rueful smile. "I never realized until now how much you all sleep."

Finn chuckled. "Just wait until you have Marin moved in here. He'll exhaust you even more."

Kyle hissed and Finn jumped. Caspian suspected Kyle had just kicked him under the table.

"It's okay," Caspian said. "You can talk about him. I'm not going to fall apart or anything."

"He's just being stubborn," Finn said. "He knows very well that Calder wouldn't want him to be alone. They even invited Kyle to have sex with them his first mating season in the sunken city. So he certainly wasn't opposed to the idea of Marin having sex with someone else."

"It isn't about the sex," Caspian replied. He didn't bother telling them that he and Marin had actually had sex during the last mating season. "It's about Urion, and Marin avenging Calder's murder."

"At least he isn't going to be made immortal," Kyle commented.

"No, he's just going to carry on terrorizing the inhabitants of the ocean as a sea dragon," Finn said. "We've had reports from clans who have come to us from the Atlantic waters that the sea dragons are moving south."

"You think they might be heading to the new colony?" Caspian asked.

"We hope not, but we'll soon find out if they are. Sea dragons are fast, and while they don't seem to be in any hurry, it won't take them long to reach us."

"Would they be able to get into the caverns?" Jake asked. He turned to Caspian to add, "Even though Medina assures me I can survive at depth under the water, I've been reluctant to test the theory. I like my feet to remain firmly on the land."

Kyle chuckled. "We'd take care of you."

Jake rolled his eyes. "You're never going to talk me into it."

Finn toyed with his food, a frown on his face.

"Did I add too much seasoning to the lasagna?" Caspian asked.

"Hmm, no, this is good. I was just thinking about the sea dragons."

"What about them?" Jake asked.

"It's just a shame that they have the power of invisibility," Finn said. "If they couldn't do that, the humans exploring the oceans might spot them."

"They'd just kill the humans," Kyle pointed out.

"Not if they caught them on camera rather than in person," Finn argued. "None of the priests will have any idea about human technology like cameras and things."

Caspian nodded. "He's right about that. Maybe it's something worth considering."

"You have an idea?" Jake asked.

"Maybe."

Finn leaned forward. "Tell us more. Perhaps we can help."

Caspian pushed aside his plate, too excited to continue to eat. "Sea dragons can't remain invisible while they're breathing sea-fire. Both tasks require too much concentration to be done at the same time. So, if we can get them to breathe sea-fire—not the most difficult of tasks—they can be filmed."

"Then what?" Jake asked. "We send the film to the press? Any reputable journalist will just think it's fake."

"Maybe an ocean exploration company?" Finn suggested. "I bet Mariana would have them changed back into human form in a flash if she thought they might be captured by scientists for studying and dissection."

"They'd just kill anyone who tried to capture them," Caspian reminded them. "Human explorers of the ocean would be even more disadvantaged against the sea dragons than the mer are. No, capturing them is not an option."

"Then what are you thinking?" Jake asked.

Caspian shook his head, hesitant to speak his thoughts aloud.

"What is it?" Kyle pressed.

Caspian gestured to the trident hung on the wall. "Mer weapons are next to useless against the sea dragons, but humans have far more destructive methods these days."

"You're thinking of exposing the sea dragons to the humans so that they can shoot them?" Jake asked. "It would take a missile or something, if they're as big as you say."

"It's not like we have access to anything like that anyway," Caspian replied. "We need a way to force them to become human again. That way they can't cause any more mischief."

"We'll figure something out," Kyle said.

Caspian gave him a smile. That they were prepared to help him with the problem meant more to him than they would ever know. Perhaps, together, they would find a solution.

* * * *

275

Marin stared at the house and seriously considered running straight back to the sea. He was only here at all because Finn had been pestering him relentlessly to at least hear Caspian out.

The former god appeared to be building some form of fence around a small garden. He didn't seem to have seen or heard Marin approach.

Marin coughed and Caspian finally looked up.

"Hello, Caspian," he said.

"Marin," Caspian replied, tossing aside his hammer and hurrying to meet him. "I'm so glad to see you. How are you enjoying life in the new colony? Do you have everything you need?"

"I'm fine," Marin interrupted the barrage of questions. "Finn said you wanted to speak with me."

"Thank you for coming. Would you like something to eat or a drink?"

"No." Marin shook his head. "I said I'd hear you out, so say your piece."

Caspian appeared unsure where to start, so Marin decided to help him out.

"Why did you vote against Urion being made immortal?"

"Because he causes enough trouble as a sea dragon. The last thing the world needs is for him to be around any longer than necessary."

"Did your vote make the difference?"

"No. Even had I voted for the petition, it would not have been passed."

"And yet you still decided to go against my wishes, knowing it was my only chance to see Calder's murderer brought to justice."

Caspian rounded on him with a glare. "You know as well as I do that you'd never have been able to kill him."

"That's not true."

"You couldn't kill Rafe."

"That's different."

"Is it? Because I don't see how. Both are murderers and you froze. You couldn't take his life, no matter what he had done. I know you say you want to see Urion pay for his crime, but it won't be at your hand, and if you were honest with yourself for just one minute, you'd know that."

"How dare you!"

"I dare because it's the truth," Caspian yelled.

Marin cringed and took a step back. Caspian stepped forward as well.

"Do you think I don't know about losing someone and wanting revenge on the one who took him from me? I spent years stopping myself from going down those stairs into the catacombs and strangling Rafe with my bare hands."

"That wouldn't have killed him," Marin pointed out. "It's hardly the same thing."

"You think I gave him the cup to drink from straight away?" Caspian asked. "Didn't you notice he'd aged years from the last time you saw him?"

"No, I didn't."

"Well, he had. I only gave him immortality when I knew I could not kill him myself. Only when I let go of my hatred and thirst for vengeance did I give him the cup to drink from."

"At least *you* had the chance to face Rafe. Everyone is doing their damned hardest to keep me away from Urion."

"Because he'll kill you and any mer on sight."

"I don't care."

"Well, I do!" Caspian roared. "I will *not* watch the man I love be murdered again. If it's in my power to stop it, I will. I won't watch you throw your life away."

"You don't get to have any say in how I live my life. You gave up that right when you let Rafe kill me."

Marin clapped a hand over his mouth the moment he realized what he had said.

Caspian didn't seem to know how to respond.

"I'm sorry," Marin said. "I didn't mean that."

"Yes, you did," Caspian said, his voice barely more than a whisper. "And you're right. I promised to protect you forever, yet I failed almost at once."

"I know it wasn't your fault."

Caspian gave a short, bitter laugh. "Of course it was. If I'd sent the priests to live in Atlantis like you asked, you'd have been safe in my temple."

"Rubbish," Marin argued. "Even if you'd sent them away, they would still have been able to travel there through the crystal portals whenever they wanted."

"I should have known that Rafe had such a black heart," Caspian continued. "If I'd routinely read their minds, I'd have known his intentions."

"You did read their minds when you brought them before you," Marin reminded him. "Anyone can shield their thoughts with a bit of practice, especially those who have spent a considerable amount of time with either the gods or the mer."

Caspian kicked aside a plank of wood. "There is nothing you can say to me that will ever convince me that Phoebus' murder wasn't my fault. You have every right to despise me for my failure. You can never hate me as much as I hate myself for what happened to you."

Marin didn't know what to say when Caspian gathered up his things and headed into the house. He wanted to erase the guilt he had seen in the former god's eyes, but there was nothing he could say that would do that, especially after his thoughtless outburst.

The scent of perfume on the breeze made him turn around, where he found Medina watching him.

"How long have you been there?" he asked.

"The sound of your screeching shattered my crystal earrings," Medina replied. "I thought I should come and see what the problem is."

Marin shrugged. "Just a disagreement between me and Caspian."

"So I saw. Can I ask you something?"

"If you like."

"What exactly is it that you want Caspian to do for you?"

"I…" *What do I want?* Truthfully, he wasn't too sure. He wanted Urion to pay for his crime, but what was he expecting Caspian to do about that?

"That's what I thought," Medina said. "You have no idea what you want from him, yet you still shout and rage because he's not able to give it to you. It was hard enough when he was a god, but as a human, he's even more limited in what he can do."

"That's not my fault."

"No, it isn't," Medina said. "Well, not if you disregard the whole reason why he's now mortal."

"What do you mean by that?"

Medina gave him a sly glance from the corner of her eye. "Haven't you asked Caspian why he was stripped of his powers?"

"No. I thought if he wanted me to know why, he'd tell me."

"You think so? Maybe if he didn't want you to feel guilty about it, he would."

Marin had no idea what Medina was talking about, and he had a feeling he didn't want to know either. It therefore came as something of a surprise to hear the next words from his treacherous mouth. "Why did he lose his powers?"

Medina smiled briefly. "Why, Marin, I'm so glad you asked. He was stripped of his powers as punishment for making Rafe immortal without the permission of the rest of the pantheon—something he did so that you would have the opportunity of facing him when you were reborn."

Marin stumbled over to a large rock and sat down heavily. "But he only did that so I could have my revenge on him."

"Yes. Not that you did, of course."

"He's lost his powers and his immortality because of me."

Medina sighed. "No, because of his own actions. I'm not telling you this to make you feel guilty but to show you how much Caspian has already done for you. There is nothing he won't give you, if it's in his power to do so. It's just…"

"I'm asking too much from him, aren't I?" Marin said.

Medina pinched her finger and thumb together. "Just a little. Caspian would do anything for you that's within his power, but you are asking too much and blaming him when he cannot deliver the impossible."

"I should go apologize to him."

Medina shook her head. "Not if you don't mean it or if you're going to lose your temper with him again.

He's having a difficult time at the moment, and the last thing he needs is for you to make it even more so."

The goddess vanished as quickly as she had appeared.

Marin didn't care what she'd said. He owed Caspian an apology and there was no use in putting it off.

He hurried to the house and knocked on the door. When no answer came, he tried the handle and let himself in.

"Caspian?"

He heard the sound of someone moving a chair in the kitchen and headed in that direction.

Caspian looked up from where he sat at the table. He didn't say a word.

"I'm sorry," Marin offered.

Caspian simply stared at him.

"Medina just paid me a visit," Marin said. "She told me the reason you've been stripped of your powers."

"Did she?" Caspian didn't appear bothered about the goddess' interference.

"She said it was because you'd made Rafe immortal."

"That's right."

"And you did that so that I would have the chance to face him and make him pay for what he had done."

Caspian rubbed at the spot between his eyes.

"Are you all right?" Marin asked.

"Headache," Caspian replied. "One of the more annoying human afflictions."

"I believe there are medicines you can take for them."

Caspian shook his head. "It's fine. Just something I'm not yet used to."

Marin didn't bother asking whether what Medina had said was true. He knew already that it was. Instead, he sat down beside Caspian and glanced at the computer screen to see what he had been doing. "What is this?"

"Nothing." Caspian made a move as though to shut down the computer but Marin stopped him.

"These pictures are from under the ocean."

"Yes."

Marin read the text. "You put cameras in the Atlantic ocean?"

"Not personally, no," Caspian replied, sounding quite testy. "I'm not able to survive at such depths now."

"Sorry," Marin said again. "But who has put them there?"

"Various human science exploration teams. There are a lot of them out there exploring the oceans these days. I've been searching the Internet for as many as I can find."

"To what purpose?"

"In the hope of seeing Mariana's sea dragons captured on camera. We—that is me and the various immortals allied against Mariana—thought that if they are at risk of being exposed to humans, Mariana might turn them back to human."

"The pictures don't seem to show much."

"Unfortunately, the distance human cameras can see in the depths of the ocean is limited. If we do manage to catch any on film, it'll be a total fluke. We thought that with the additional exploration teams around the location of Atlantis, it might be worth a shot to check their cameras. What we really need is a computer expert to get access to the camera feeds that aren't in the public domain."

"Have any of the priests been filmed at all, even a distant glimpse that doesn't really show what they are?"

"No, they're remaining stubbornly invisible at the moment. One of the problems is that they are only becoming visible again when they're attacking with sea-fire, and the only ones they're attacking are the mer."

"I see."

"Do you?"

"Of course. You don't want to expose the mer at the same time, right?"

"Yes."

"You said *one* of the problems. What others are there?"

Caspian sighed. "I guess you'll find out sooner or later anyway. They're moving south, and we suspect they're heading for the Pacific. Since they're heading away from Atlantis, they're going into waters which aren't exactly teeming with humans and their cameras."

"You think they might go to the new colony?"

"Yes. Mariana wants to drive the mer from the ocean, and she is using her sea dragons to do so."

"Why does she hate us so much?"

"Because she cannot control you. She can bend every other creature of the sea to her will but the mer are immune to her powers."

Marin thought that was a stupid reason to hate an entire race of beings, and from Caspian's tone, the former god agreed with him.

"We will find a way to stop them before they get here," Caspian said.

"You promise?" Marin asked.

Caspian hesitated. "I try not to make promises I might not be able to keep."

A crack of thunder overhead made them both jump.

"You should probably head back to the colony," Caspian said. "You don't want to be caught out in the storm."

Marin didn't move from his spot. "Can I stay a while longer?"

Caspian shrugged. "If you like. Don't expect anything exciting on the cameras though. The most interesting thing to happen on them all week is an octopus taking up residence right in front of one, and it has moved on now."

"I didn't mean I wanted to sit here watching obsessively for Urion."

Caspian gave him a look of skepticism.

"I didn't," Marin insisted. "I thought maybe we could spend some time together. I mean, we did enjoy that…before."

"Marin, I'm too tired to teach you anything with a trident today. I'm not inexhaustible now. I'm still learning the boundaries of my strength and I've already spent the morning working in the garden and building the fence to keep Jake's dog out when they come around."

"I didn't mean training," Marin said. "That wasn't all we did together, was it?"

"Pretty much," Caspian replied.

"Not when I was Phoebus though."

"No, not when you were him," Caspian agreed. "We spent most of our time in bed back then, which is just as draining, even if I was foolishly optimistic enough to believe that was what you meant."

Marin's heart rate sped up and his blood went south. Unfortunately, since he, like most of the mer, rarely bothered with clothes, there was no hiding his body's reaction from Caspian.

"It's not the solstice," Caspian commented.

"I know." Marin shifted on his seat a little and willed his erection to go away.

Caspian pointed toward the staircase. "I find a cold shower helps. The bathroom is upstairs if you want to use it."

Marin shook his head.

Caspian didn't make any effort to touch him and Marin was surprised to find he was disappointed at that.

"Are you sure you're too tired for sex?" he asked before he could second-guess the wisdom of making such a suggestion.

Caspian stared at him, his mouth hanging open. "Marin, if you want to fuck me when the solstice arrives, you know where to find me."

"Maybe I don't want to wait for the mating season."

Caspian rose from the table and began to pace the kitchen. "You don't know how tempting your offer is, but we both know it would be a mistake."

Marin crossed his arms over his chest. "I don't know anything of the sort."

Caspian stopped walking and stood at the other side of the table. He placed his hands on the surface and leaned over. "Marin, I love you. No, let me finish. I love you, but unless you feel the same way about me, it would be a mistake for us to have sex."

"But last solstice…"

"That's different," Caspian said. "You're mer and needed to break your fever. I'll help you with that, if you want me to, but that's just sex."

"And what would it be if we went to bed right now?" Marin asked.

"For me, it'd be more," Caspian said. "Sex right now would only complicate things between us. You've frequently accused me of treating you like you're still Phoebus and I think maybe you're right. I love— loved—him, and I've transferred those feelings onto you, without any regard for who you are now. I need to forget that you were once him."

Marin walked around the table. "You know that's never going to happen."

"If we're to have a future together, it *has* to." Caspian side-stepped Marin as he approached. "Other than on the solstice, I won't have sex with you unless you tell me you come to my bed out of love."

Marin drew in a sharp breath. Could he ever love Caspian as he clearly wanted him to?

"I know you don't love me," Caspian continued, "so don't try to convince me you do. Your heart still belongs to Calder and I can't fight a dead man for you."

"I care for you," Marin said. It was the best he could offer.

"I know you do. But it's not enough for me to take you to bed. We both need to be sure of our feelings for each other before we take that step. You need to know that I love you for yourself and not because you once shared my bed as Phoebus."

"And you?"

Caspian cupped Marin's face and leaned in as if he were going to kiss him. "I need to know the same."

Marin nodded and placed his hand over Caspian's. "You also need to know I've let Calder go, don't you?"

"I know he will always be in your heart," Caspian replied, "just as Phoebus will always be in mine. We each need to learn to live with the ghosts of our former lovers."

Another crash of thunder shook the house and broke the tension between them.

"Come on," Caspian said with a wave toward the living room. "Let's sit down and talk. You can tell me what you're doing in the colony and I can amuse you with stories of my incompetence as a mortal."

Marin liked the sound of that. He followed Caspian after sparing one final rueful glance at his cock. He supposed he should be grateful for Caspian's hesitation in taking their relationship any further, but it didn't solve his current predicament. Maybe he should take up Caspian's offer of a cold shower after all.

Chapter Twenty

Caspian found life on the island to be refreshingly peaceful. He soon settled into his new home and the routines of daily life.

Weather permitting, he spent his mornings gardening. Jake came over to help him every two days, and on the alternate days, Caspian went to his house to return the favor.

Marin came to visit him every few days and they spent the afternoons getting to know each other. Marin didn't ask for any more training with the trident and Caspian didn't offer. Marin stayed overnight on a couple of occasions, but only after falling asleep on the sofa. Caspian thought their relationship was progressing nicely and he was confident that he was able to separate his memories of Phoebus from the man with him now.

Odessa came to visit him, mainly to ensure he didn't forget his invitation to the Isle of the Gods for her monthly dinner party. Caspian didn't really want to go and listen to the immortals bemoaning the loss of their status, but he could see no way out of it. He would much rather have a nice cozy meal with his parents and sister.

Cari hadn't been to see him at all. Caspian wondered what was keeping her away, but he hadn't reached the point where he wanted to track her down to ask. He supposed he couldn't put that off much longer.

Relations with his adoptive son were much better and Justin visited him nearly as frequently as Marin did.

The island dwellers also found that they had surprising new neighbors who had appeared overnight.

Fabian, the disowned son of Mariana, and his merman lover Delwyn had taken up residence as well. Finn was delighted to have his best friend so close by, even if it meant that they were all roped into what seemed to be a constant stream of building repairs.

Medina was no architect and while the house she had magically constructed appeared to be structurally sound, there were some quirks to the property in the form of dodgy floorboards, drafty windows and a perpetually leaking roof.

"So, why did you decide to come here to live?" Jake asked as he, Fabian and Caspian worked on the roof.

"Delwyn missed the ocean and his friends, especially Finn," Fabian replied. "So I spoke to my aunt about it and she thought you might not object to a couple more neighbors."

"She was right," Jake said. "It was pretty lonely around here — before Caspian moved here, that is. You know the mer are happiest in the ocean, so I was on my own a lot."

"I'm sorry," Caspian offered. "I guess I didn't think about that when I moved you all here."

"There's no need to apologize," Jake assured him. "I have my guys close and they're far happier than they were in England. I didn't realize how much they missed the ocean and their people until we came here. I'm sure you'll see a difference in Delwyn too."

"I already have," Fabian replied.

Caspian hoped their little community would soon include an equally happy Marin, but he didn't say anything to the others. He couldn't bear to see the sympathy in their eyes if things didn't work out between them.

Almost as if his thoughts had summoned him, Marin appeared at the edge of the clearing where Fabian's house stood.

"I think someone is looking for you," Jake said, having seen Marin arrive through the trees as well.

Caspian nodded and handed over his tools to the others. "Sorry. I wasn't expecting him to visit until tomorrow."

"He couldn't stay away, huh?" Jake teased.

Caspian ignored the insinuation and climbed down from the roof. He waved goodbye once he was safely on the ground and went to meet Marin.

"Another leak in the roof?" Marin asked with a nod to Fabian's home.

"Yes. Medina had good intentions but would never make an architect. It's a wonder her temples have lasted as long as they have."

"I suppose being underwater, no one would notice a leaking roof," Marin replied.

Caspian laughed. "You have a point there. So, what brings you here today?"

"You were right about the sea dragons moving into the Pacific," Marin said. "A clan arrived today from the southern seas. They reported the loss of two of their warriors to a group of sea dragons. The sea dragons didn't follow them north to the colony, but they've definitely moved out of the Atlantic."

"They will head to the colony in time," Caspian said. "I'm sure of it. The reports I've heard from the other immortals who are monitoring them is that they're moving slowly so they don't miss any other large colony on the way."

"Are there many?"

"No, but they are unlikely to know that. They haven't left Atlantis since their transformations. They won't necessarily know about the decreasing mer population and the loss of so many of the larger clans. We have a little time before they reach the colony."

"And when they do?"

"I don't know," Caspian said. "I wish I did. If they aren't stopped, they won't rest until they've driven all the mer from the ocean."

"Or killed us," Marin added with a visible shiver.

Caspian didn't bother to confirm that would happen. It was obvious to them both.

Marin hissed and hopped on one foot.

"What is it?" Caspian asked.

"I trod on something sharp," Marin replied as he tried to examine the sole of his foot. "Fabian needs a better path."

"I know. It's on our list of chores to do once his house is in order." He guided Marin to a large rock and sat him down. "You've cut it, but I don't think it's too bad. It'll heal as soon as you transform again."

"Um, okay."

"What is it?" Caspian asked. "We're nearly at the clearing where my place is and I have a nice soft path leading to the beach. I think you can make it that far."

"I know. It's just…"

Caspian sighed. "You forgot I've lost my power to heal, right? It's okay. I forget myself sometimes. Old habits die hard, and I do have to stop myself from trying to heal various scrapes and bruises I seem to accumulate on a daily basis."

"That's not what I was going to say," Marin said. "It's just I was hoping to visit with you for a while."

"Oh, of course. Well, since you're here anyway, there's no real point in you swimming back to the colony, only to come back again tomorrow. I'll see what I have in the first aid kit to clean up your foot."

"Thanks."

Caspian hooked Marin's arm around his shoulder so he could lean on him and avoid making the minor injury any worse. "Come on, and don't expect me to carry you."

"I wouldn't dream of it," Marin replied. "Well, unless you're carrying me into the bedroom to throw me down and ravish me."

Caspian snorted. "Ravish you? You've been spending too much time with Finn and Delwyn."

Marin laughed as he hopped alongside Caspian. "They do love the stories that were told on the walls of the sunken city, and there was a lot of ravishing going on in those tales."

"Well, I can't fault Delwyn's translations."

At the house, Caspian grabbed the first aid kit, noting as he did that it needed replenishing, and settled Marin on the sofa so he could tend his foot.

"You're pretty good at that," Marin commented.

"I've been getting quite a bit of practice," Caspian replied. "I swear I never used to be so clumsy, but since becoming mortal, I seem to get more injuries in a week than I used to in a decade."

"Or maybe you're just noticing them more."

"Perhaps." Caspian placed Marin's foot down on the floor and sat back on his heels. "There you go."

He moved to rise, but Marin stopped him with a nudge of his foot. "I like you down there."

Something in Marin's voice sent a shiver down Caspian's spine. He glanced at Marin's groin, saw he was hard and swiftly looked away. There were times when he did rather wish the mer would wear clothing.

"Caspian, I want to have sex with you."

"Marin..."

Marin placed a finger over Caspian's lips. "I know what you said before, and I think we're ready."

"What makes you think so?" Caspian asked.

"Don't *you* think we are?" Marin replied.

"I'm not sure. Sometimes I think so, then you'll say something or look at me a certain way, and suddenly I'm thinking about Phoebus and remembering how he'd use the same phrase and had the same glint in his eye."

Marin smiled and shook his head. "Perhaps I'm looking at you the same way because I'm feeling the same as he did."

Caspian lowered his gaze, his hopes rising along with his cock. It was on the tip of his tongue to ask about Calder, but he couldn't bring himself to say the words that might shatter this moment.

It seemed that Marin had anticipated his concern. "I've not forgotten Calder, and I don't need to tell you that I never will. But I'm ready to love you too."

Caspian rose on his knees to meet Marin's lips as he leaned down.

For a brief moment the memory of the last time he'd kissed Phoebus flitted across his mind. The ghost of his former lover was banished when Marin slipped his tongue into Caspian's mouth and took control of the kiss.

Caspian moaned as Marin pulled him up onto his lap and tugged at his clothes.

"Damn it, Caspian, robes were so much easier to remove."

"They aren't exactly in fashion these days," Caspian pointed out.

"Which hardly matters here on the island," Marin replied as he fumbled with the buttons of Caspian's shirt.

With no such obstacles in his own path, Caspian wasted no time in running his hands over Marin's chest. *So familiar and yet also different.* He rubbed his thumb over the nubs of Marin's nipples, causing Marin to moan loudly in response.

"You like that?" Caspian whispered.

"Yes!"

Caspian pinched the nub, squeezing it tight. "How about that?"

"Fuck!"

Marin pulled back and swatted Caspian's hands away. "I need you naked, now."

Caspian chuckled and climbed off him so he could undress. "How would you like to take this upstairs?"

"Is there something wrong with the living room?"

Caspian nodded to the portal crystal. "Only that this is where unexpected guests appear."

"Ah, I see. I guess I'm not the only one to have changed over the centuries. You didn't used to be so shy. I remember when you whipped out your cock right there in the temple so I could suck it."

"That was before I understood what it was to love someone." Caspian held out his hand for Marin to take.

They went upstairs and Caspian guided Marin over to the bed. "What do you want to do?" he asked.

Marin took hold of Caspian's cock. "I want to suck this."

"You know I'd never have a problem with that idea," Caspian said as he sat on the edge of the bed and tossed a pillow onto the floor.

Marin knelt before him and smiled. "It might not be what I need to break my fever, but I do like the feel of a stiff cock in my mouth and the taste of a man's pleasure when he comes."

"No one ever sucked me quite as well as you did."

"Never?" Marin gave him a skeptical frown.

Caspian took Marin's face in his hands. "*No one.*"

With a wicked grin, Marin dove on Caspian's cock, taking it deep into his mouth, and sucking with such enthusiasm Caspian worried he might embarrass himself.

He didn't need to worry. Marin knew what to do to hold him on the brink. He gripped him at the root until the desperate need to come had passed, before beginning the process all over again.

Caspian let Marin set the pace. He moaned encouragement but without thrusting into his lover's mouth.

As Marin licked and teased him, Caspian could tell he was using his knowledge from his time as Phoebus to give him the most pleasure he could. It was strange that even though they were taking their first real steps to becoming lovers, Marin knew his body so well already.

"Marin, I'm going to… Marin…"

Caspian's warning went ignored. Marin sucked him down to almost the base. Caspian came with a shudder, filling Marin's mouth with his cum. Marin hummed contentedly as he drank him down before letting him go.

"Good?" he asked.

Caspian snorted. "Like you even need to ask. Now, come up here and kiss me."

Marin hopped up and pushed Caspian down onto the mattress.

"I like it when you take charge," Caspian said as he grabbed Marin's buttocks and pulled him closer.

"Good, because I like being the one on top."

Marin wriggled around until he was straddling him, his arse nudging Caspian's cock, which hadn't yet got the message that he was no longer an immortal with incredible stamina and seemed to want to participate in the next round too.

Caspian waited for Marin to settle down, eager to see what he had in mind now. He wasn't kept waiting for long. Marin stroked his cock as he met Caspian's eyes.

"You like watching me?" Marin asked.

"Yes."

Marin grinned and raised himself up a little. "How about touching me?"

Caspian didn't need any more encouragement. He slid his hand between Marin's legs and stroked him.

Marin moaned and rocked against Caspian's hand, his own hand still on his stiff length. "I need you in me."

"I can't get it up again just yet," Caspian said with a laugh.

"Use your fingers," Marin ordered. "Fuck, Caspian, I should have asked Finn to order some of his toys for us."

Caspian nearly choked. "What do *you* know about Finn's toys?"

"Enough to know I should have put an order in months ago," Marin replied. "That's it, Caspian. You feel so good inside me. I need more, give me more."

Caspian inserted a second finger into Marin's arse and was surprised to find the merman stretched more than he would have expected. "Are you sure you've not been borrowing one of Finn's toys?"

Marin shook his head and moaned loudly. "No…fuck…just been doing a bit to prepare myself the last few days."

"It sounds like you've been planning this."

Marin gave him a *what a stupid question* sort of look. "I have. Fuck!"

Caspian stroked Marin's prostate, causing him to cry out as he began to spill over his chest. "That's it, Marin. Let me see you come."

Marin didn't need Caspian to do much. He fucked himself on Caspian's fingers with the determination of a man who knew what he wanted and had every intention of getting it.

"More… fuck… more," Marin pleaded, until Caspian eased a third finger inside, and Marin lost the power of speech altogether.

Watching his lover lose control was as thrilling to Caspian as anything else they had done, and he cursed his lack of stamina. He yearned to be inside Marin, watching his merman ride his cock with the same abandon he now rode his fingers.

Marin cried out as he came, collapsing onto Caspian's chest, his breathing ragged and short.

"Caspian?" Marin whispered a short while later.

"Yes?"

"Are you sure you can't persuade your parents to at least give you back your power to come a dozen times a night?"

Caspian laughed. "Sorry, darling, but I'm afraid you're going to have to put up with a mere mortal from now on."

Marin propped his chin on Caspian's chest. "Darling?"

Caspian's face heated. "Sorry. It just slipped out."

"It's fine. I like it. I'm just worried about the solstice."

"Why? I told you. Whatever you need from me, you can have it. I let you fuck me last solstice, remember?"

"I know… It's just…"

"Marin, whenever you want to fuck me, you only have to ask, and on the solstice, you don't even need to do that. I'll be right here, my legs spread, ready for you to give my arse a pounding."

"I know. It's not that that's worrying me."

"Then what is it?"

"I'm mer and you know what our sex drives are like during the mating season. What if I wear you out?"

Caspian couldn't help it. He laughed loudly until Marin smacked him on the chest.

"I'm serious. When we were together — when I was Phoebus, I mean — we fucked *all* the time. I'm just as horny now."

Caspian got his mirth under control, though not without some difficulty. "Marin, just across the island there is a human named Jake. He lives with two mermen who both go through the mating season, the same as you do. As far as I've seen, he manages to keep up with them, satisfy them and even do chores around the house. I'm pretty sure that if he can keep up with two of you sex maniacs, I can manage one."

"Then you're not missing your powers right now?"

Caspian sighed. "I'm always missing my powers but there's nothing I can do about it, so why worry about something I can't change?"

"Is there no chance they could be restored to you? I mean, is it even possible?"

"Oh yes, it's possible but highly unlikely. Besides, I'm not sure I'd even want to be immortal again, not now."

"Are you crazy?"

"Probably, but I would rather not watch the man I love grow old and die while I stay forever young. I'm quite fond of the idea of sitting out there on the veranda with you beside me, watching the sun go down during the twilight of our lives."

"That was very poetic," Marin teased. "Have you been reading those stories in Atlantis too?"

"There's no need for me to read them. I was alive when the events they portray were happening."

Marin chuckled as he snuggled into Caspian's side. "You can't fool me. You're a closet romantic."

Caspian harrumphed and declined to comment. He supposed there were worse things to be.

Chapter Twenty-One

Of all the things Caspian missed about being immortal, being summoned to attend a council of the gods definitely wasn't one of them. Admittedly, there had been relatively few meetings during the centuries while the vast majority of the immortals had been sleeping. During those years, Andaman had taken on the role of leader of the pantheon. As a bit of a loner, he'd only called a meeting when he absolutely had to. After the rest of the gods had woken, the meetings had occurred with annoying frequency.

Having been stripped of his powers, he'd thought that would be the last time he'd have to hear the call to come and sit through one of the wretched things.

"What is it?" Marin asked.

Caspian smiled down at the sleep-rumpled merman. "Nothing to worry about, just a summons from the gods. They probably didn't mean to include me in it. Just go back to sleep."

Marin nudged him with his morning wood. "I'm wide awake now."

"So I see," Caspian replied as he dove under the covers and took Marin's cock into his mouth.

He ignored the second summons, just as he had the first. When he visited his mother, he'd ask her to mention to the pantheon that he was still being included in the general call, and hopefully they would figure out a way to take him out of the loop.

"Caspian!"

The sound of his mother yelling his name was enough to kill his erection entirely.

"Maybe they *did* mean to include you in the summons," Marin suggested with a sigh of annoyance.

Caspian didn't blame him for his irritation. He was similarly frustrated right now.

"Caspian, didn't you hear the summons?" Her voice was closer now, right at the bottom of the stairs. Caspian supposed he should be grateful that she hadn't materialized right in the bedroom.

"Yes, I heard it," Caspian called as he staggered out of bed and pulled on a bathrobe. He covered himself just in time for his mother to appear in the doorway.

"Then what are you still doing in bed?" Odessa asked.

"Sucking Marin's cock," Caspian replied with a wink at Marin, whose face was turning various shades of red.

"You know that's not what I meant. When the council summon you, you have a duty to answer the call immediately."

Caspian shrugged. "I thought I was included by mistake. It's not like I have any say in the matters of the gods now."

"You have a say in this one," his mother stated. "Now get dressed and present yourself in the council chamber."

Caspian walked over to the dresser and pulled out a pair of jeans and a T-shirt.

"You aren't going to wear those, are you?" Odessa frowned critically at his chosen clothing.

"They're clean," Caspian replied, right before his mother ripped them out of his hands and tossed them aside.

"Let me see," she said as she rifled through his wardrobe, tutting and huffing as she discarded one outfit after another. "How is it *my* son has no taste in clothes at all?"

"I have plenty of taste," Caspian argued. "I just happen to have moved with the times."

His mother gave up on his clothing collection and dressed him herself with a wave of her hand.

"Urgh," Caspian moaned when he realized what she had put him in.

"What are you complaining about?" Odessa asked. "It's modern."

"I don't wear *suits*," Caspian muttered.

"You're attending a meeting of the Atlantean pantheon. You can put up with it for an hour or two."

"How long is this meeting going to last?" The thought of a couple of hours listening to the immortals squabbling wasn't pleasant and certainly not how he'd intended to spend the morning. He glanced at Marin. So much for a lazy morning in bed with his lover.

His mother ignored his question and grabbed him by the arm. A moment later they stood in the council chamber. Caspian tried to hide an ill-timed yawn. *Damn it.* Had they always called these things at the crack of dawn?

"It's about time," Antar said. "Did you think that being mortal meant you could show up here whenever you felt like it?"

Caspian sat down in his usual seat. "I thought it was a mistake."

"The gods don't make mistakes."

"Of course you do," Caspian replied. "You just don't admit it."

He stifled a second yawn while silently cursing his lack of coffee. His father, seated on his right, produced a steaming mug and placed it in front of him. Caspian thought he had quite possibly never loved his father more than he did in that moment. It was funny how he was fully alert when he'd been going down on Marin, but now that he had to sit through a meeting, he could barely keep his eyes open.

"Now that we're all here," Antar said, "let's get down to business. We all know what the problem is."

Caspian didn't have a clue, but he had no intention of prolonging the agony by asking. He'd no doubt figure it out as the meeting dragged on, along with why he'd been summoned.

It seemed Caspian was the only one in the dark. Everyone else around the table nodded and there was a fair amount of whispering. Unfortunately, he no longer had the power to pick up anything of what they were saying.

Antar gestured to Cari for her to take the floor. "Granddaughter, if you'd like to tell us what your Oracle reported to you."

Cari stood and faced the room. She didn't meet Caspian's eyes and seemed to be focusing at the opposite end of the table. He should have tried to pin her down and find out what the problem was before now. He had just been so busy, learning how to be human, as well as getting to know Marin. He guessed he had been neglecting his sister, but in fairness, she hadn't made any effort to see him either and appeared to be avoiding him.

"Ula, my current Oracle of the future, had a prolonged and distressing vision last night. She saw an attack on the new mer colony by Mariana's priests. There were many casualties, caused by the destruction of the caverns the mer are currently inhabiting."

Cari sat down.

"Thank you," Antar said. "Mariana, explain yourself."

"What's to explain?" Mariana replied.

"You stated that as long as the mer vacated Atlantis and the surrounding waters, they would be left in peace. Why are your priests now heading for the new colony?"

"My priests go where they please. I do not seek to restrict them in how they carry out their duties."

"Their duties appear to be terrorizing the mer. This isn't the first time we've had to call a meeting regarding the actions of your sea dragons. For the last two months, they have been dangerously close to discovery by humans, risking the exposure of not only themselves, but also the mer."

"I really don't see the problem," Mariana said.

"The problem," Cari snarled, "is that your priests seem to have made it their mission in life to drive the mer from the oceans, and when they meet with resistance, they murder whoever stands in their way."

"Those mutants are not fit to live in my domain. If you all love them so much, find them somewhere to live on land."

"The mer are creatures of the sea," Caspian pointed out. "They need the water to survive."

Mariana glared at him. "You stay out of this. As a mortal, this has nothing to do with you. I don't even see why you've been brought to this meeting."

"That makes two of us," Caspian said. "But since I *am* here, I might as well offer my opinion."

Antar banged on the table. "You're here, Caspian, because you have close ties with the mer and because the majority of the gods feel you should be allowed to participate in the forthcoming vote."

"What vote?" Mariana asked, echoing Caspian's own thought.

Several of the immortals appeared uncomfortable. He had a feeling he wasn't the only one to have missed some recent meetings. Something was going on here that Mariana didn't know about either.

Antar gave Mariana a harsh stare, one that Caspian was thankful he wasn't on the receiving end of.

"Mariana, it is the determination of this pantheon, by majority vote, that you return your priests to human form immediately — and permanently."

The goddess laughed loudly. "You aren't seriously trying to order *me*, are you?"

"You will do this at once. The pantheon has voted."

Mariana merely laughed again. "None of you have the power to order me to do anything. You don't even have followers anymore. Other than Cari and her precious Oracles and Medina's reluctant human priest, none of you have anyone from which to draw your powers. My priests serve me loyally, and thanks to their devotion I am stronger than anyone here."

"Do you refuse to abide by the decision of the pantheon?" Antar asked.

"Yes, I do." Mariana sat back with a smug smile on her face.

Antar didn't appear surprised at her answer. "You will transform them back to humans or the pantheon will vote today on whether to strip you of your powers. Do you still refuse to obey?"

Mariana hesitated. "Ah, that's why you've summoned Caspian here."

It took Caspian a moment longer to figure out what she meant. Then he realized that his vote might be needed in the event of a tie.

"Go ahead," said Mariana with an airy wave of her hand. "I'm not concerned. Unlike *him*, I have committed no crime or broken our laws."

Caspian supposed she had a point there, but he already knew how he would vote if it came to a tie.

"If the vote was a tie for Caspian when he had flouted our laws for his own selfish purposes, by rights you should all vote for me to retain my powers and forget this nonsense."

A tie?

Caspian let Mariana's words sink in. At first he had thought the vote was unanimous, until his parents had confirmed otherwise. He supposed it was nice to know that not everyone in the pantheon had agreed with his punishment. Not that it made any difference, since the final vote had obviously tipped the scale in favor of making him mortal.

"Oh yes," Mariana said. "You didn't know how close the vote was?"

"Get out of my head," Caspian snapped.

Mariana chuckled. "I'm sure it won't come as a surprise to find out that I voted to remove your powers."

"I'm shocked." Caspian put as much sarcasm into his response as he could.

"Not as shocked as I was when the last goddess voted. I thought for sure you'd be getting away with your crime. How wrong I was." Mariana shifted her gaze to Cari.

Caspian knew exactly what that look meant, even if he didn't want to believe it. "Cari?"

His sister met his eyes for the first time since he had lost his powers.

"Is it true?" Caspian asked. "Did you break the tie?"

Cari stared at him in silence.

"Is it true?" he roared as he rose from the table.

"Caspian, sit down," his mother said as she placed a hand on his arm.

His father urged him to take his seat as well. No wonder his parents had decided to flank him at the table today. They must have known there was a risk that Mariana would say something of this nature as soon as the question of her own immortality was raised.

Caspian shook himself free from his mother's grip. "Is it true?"

"Yes." Cari offered no explanation or apology for what she had done to him.

He sat down with a thump. He felt sick to his stomach, and for the first time in his life he wondered if he might actually vomit. For so many centuries it had been just the two of them, best friends as well as siblings. They had even raised Justin together. The betrayal of his sister cut deep in his soul and he couldn't bear to look at her right now.

He realized Antar was still speaking and that Mariana was being asked to leave the chamber while the vote took place. Clearly she had only been present at the start of the meeting in order to give her one final chance to do the right thing and rein in her sea dragons, once and for all.

"Now we vote," Antar said. He turned to the goddess on his right, who happened to be Medina.

The Goddess of Love rose and faced the table. "The mer do not deserve to be wiped out. They are peaceful and loving, and more than that, they can boost our powers just as much as humans did."

"Thank you, Medina," Antar interrupted before she could get carried away. "We are all well aware of the mer and their nature. How do you vote?"

Caspian recalled that Medina was Mariana's sister. Would she betray her sibling, just as Cari had betrayed him?

Medina sighed. "I would give her one last chance to transform her priests back. If she refuses, even knowing we can remove her powers and thus force her magic to be reversed that way, I'm afraid I must vote to strip her of her powers."

Antar nodded. "Very well. We will give her one final chance to reconsider. If she refuses, your vote will stand."

Medina sat down and the god next to her stood to vote to let her keep her powers. He offered no explanation and wasn't required to.

One by one each of the immortals cast their vote. Cari, unsurprisingly, voted for her powers to be removed, as did Andaman, who added the comment that even if he were to provide armor to every merman and mermaid in the new colony, it would not be enough to save them if the cave network collapsed.

The goddess who spoke after him was one of Mariana's friends and countered his remark with the comment that the mer should simply move on from the caverns and find somewhere else to live.

"Since the sea dragons have traveled around the world to attack them, where do you suggest?" Medina asked with a fair degree of sarcasm.

No answer was forthcoming and the voting continued.

Caspian's mother stood to quickly vote for her powers to be removed and everyone turned to Caspian.

"I thought I was just here in case there was a tie?" he asked.

Antar shook his head. "You may vote now, as you would have before."

Caspian was surprised, but not even Mariana's staunchest supporters objected. "The mer need to be in the ocean to survive. I know mer who have tried to live on land, and they all return to the sea eventually. I vote the same as Medina. If she refuses to return the sea dragons to human form, she should be stripped of her powers."

He sat back down and let out a long breath. A part of him felt bad for helping to inflict on another immortal the same punishment that he had been given. He pushed the uneasy thought from his mind and waited for everyone to finish voting.

His father voted the same as Odessa, after which Mariana's own father's turn came.

The God of the Sea shook his head as he stood up. "The sea is my domain as much as it is my daughter's. I wish I could find a way to protect the mer from the sea dragons without the need to resort to such measures."

"Is there a way?" Medina asked. "Have you tried ordering them?"

"I have. Unfortunately, they do not heed me, and with no followers or priests of my own, my daughter's powers outweigh mine. I vote for her to be given one last chance, but if not, I will strip her of her powers and immortality, if that be the will of the pantheon."

"What if she resists?" Cynbel asked. "Unlike my son, who accepted his punishment without a fight, I suspect your daughter might not be so compliant."

Antar stepped in at this point. "If she should refuse our authority, her powers will be forcibly removed, which will be much more painful but just as effective."

The God of the Sea took his seat again and the rest of the pantheon cast their votes.

Mariana's mother, Goddess of the Moon, voted for her daughter to keep her powers but reluctantly confirmed she would abide by the decision of the pantheon and would not try to stop her husband from removing her daughter's powers. By this point it was already clear that Mariana would be losing her powers if she didn't comply with the order to return her sea dragons to human form.

"Mariana, you can return now," Antar called. His voice echoed so she would hear him wherever she was.

She took her time coming back into the room.

"Are you done?" she asked as she took her seat.

"We are," Antar said. "It has been decided that you should be given one more opportunity to return your sea dragons to human form —"

"Absolutely not," Mariana interrupted.

"Or you will be stripped of your powers. By majority vote of the pantheon, this is our decision."

Mariana didn't appear surprised or bothered by Antar's words. "You don't have the power to take me on."

Antar materialized a trident in his hand and banged it on the floor. Sea-fire shot from the prongs, lighting the chamber with an eerie blue light. "You forget who you are speaking to."

"I've not forgotten at all," Mariana replied as she conjured up a trident of her own. "You are a forgotten god, old and unworthy of the name."

"I am of the oldest of the immortals," Antar reminded her. "I was eons old before your parents were even born. Do not think you can challenge me."

"You are not of my blood," Mariana said. "Only my parents can remove my powers, and they would never betray me in such a way."

She turned to look at her parents and a flicker of doubt crossed her face. "You wouldn't?"

"Yes, we would," her father said. "It will pain us to do so, but we will obey the edict of the pantheon, just as you should have done when it was decreed that all Atlanteans were to be banished."

Mariana's trident glowed and she aimed it at one god after another, finally settling on Antar. "You will not take my powers, and my priests will retain their present form for as long as it takes to destroy the mer."

Antar moved too fast for Caspian to see. He wasn't sure he would have caught his move even if he still had his powers. The God of Space and Time could manipulate both in any way he chose.

One moment he was at the opposite end of the table, the next he was at Mariana's back, divesting her of her trident and encasing her in a pair of manacles. Even from halfway down the table, he could recognize Andaman's handiwork.

Mariana struggled and screeched.

Her parents joined Antar at the other end of the table and placed their hands on her shoulders. She tried to shake them off, twisting and squirming against her captors.

"Get your hands off me," she yelled. "You can't do this."

A strange green aura appeared around her, and Caspian recognized it as the same glow that she had aimed at Fabian when she had removed his powers and disowned him. That she had done so while he was underwater, rendering him mortal and nearly killing him in the process, had been nothing short of monstrous. At least she could be thankful that she wouldn't be risking death in the next few seconds.

Finally it was done and Mariana collapsed to her knees.

"You will all pay for this," she warned.

"What of the priests?" Odessa asked. "Are they restored to human form?"

Cari closed her eyes, opening them a couple of minutes later with a nod. "They are human again. As they are also Atlantean, they are in no danger of drowning. They are currently fleeing from the mer they were fighting a few minutes ago. I do not believe they will be troubling the mer much from now on, and if they do, the mer should be able to handle them."

Caspian breathed a sigh of relief.

Mariana's parents escorted her from the room, promising to get her set up in a new life among humans. Caspian hoped they chose a location well away from anyone he knew.

Odessa took hold of his arm as he stood to leave. "Now, how about you come home with me and let me know how you and your young merman are getting along. From what I saw this morning, we have a lot of catching up to do."

Caspian knew there would be no avoiding the third degree and decided to succumb to it without a fuss.

They were halfway to the door when Cari stepped in front of them.

"Don't," Caspian said before she could speak. The shock of her betrayal was too raw for him to listen to what she had to say in her defense. "I'll come and find you when I'm ready to listen."

"I'm sorry," Cari offered.

Caspian nodded and let his mother lead him out of the room. He knew he would have to hear Cari's side of things eventually, but he just couldn't handle that right now.

Chapter Twenty-Two

When Caspian arrived back on the island, Marin had gone to start his shift with the gatherers. Caspian stripped out of his suit and pulled on the more comfortable jeans and shirt as he pondered what to do.

Caspian wondered how Marin would take the news of Urion now being vulnerable. They hadn't spoken of him in a while, but Caspian wasn't fool enough to believe Marin had forgotten his quest for revenge.

A tiny voice in his head suggested that maybe he wouldn't have to tell Marin anything. The former sea dragons were a long way south, many miles from the new colony, and it would be a dangerous journey for the Atlanteans, if they intended to continue on their current route at all.

They might never reach the new colony. They could head for the nearest land mass and start new lives, as they should have done the day his father had banished the rest of their people.

Unfortunately, common sense told him that sooner or later Marin would find out, and if he thought Caspian had kept it from him, he would never forgive him.

Instinct told Caspian that the Atlanteans would head for the new colony, following the orders of their goddess. It wouldn't be hard for them to acquire basic weapons and even tridents weren't entirely outside the realm of possibility.

A knock on the door announced Jake's arrival.

"Hey, there you are," Jake said as Caspian opened the door. "Are we working today or what?"

"Sure. What time is it?"

"After eleven," Jake replied. "I've dug out a couple of rows for seeds, but I wasn't sure what you wanted to plant."

Caspian checked the seed supply in the cupboard. He still wasn't sure what to plant when. Tempest might have set up a weather system, but the seasons didn't necessarily follow any pattern he was familiar with. All he could do was hope she hadn't included a hurricane season.

Grabbing a couple of packets, he followed Jake back outside.

"So, Marin said you'd been summoned to a meeting of the pantheon," Jake commented as they set to work. "Have they restored your powers?"

"No, that's never going to happen. Did Marin think that was the reason I'd been called?"

"He feels it's his fault you were made mortal. I think maybe he's hoping if you get your powers back, he can let go of that guilt."

Caspian wished there was some way to ease his guilt, but he suspected there was nothing he could do, other than live his life to the fullest and show Marin he had no regrets.

"So, are you going to tell me what the meeting was about?" Jake asked. "Or is it top secret classified information?"

Caspian laughed. "No, it's not. I'm sure you'll find out sooner or later anyway. The situation with Mariana and her sea dragons reached the breaking point. The pantheon stripped her of her powers and immortality this morning."

"Does Fabian know?" Jake asked. "Even though she disowned him, she's still his mother."

"I suspect Medina will be stopping by to tell him."

Jake gave him a dubious look. "She's not exactly tactful. Are you sure you don't want to go tell him first?"

Caspian wasn't sure he wanted to be the one to tell Fabian, but Jake had a point. "Come on. Let's go see him."

They arrived at Fabian's house only to find Medina had already beaten them to it.

"I see you're here to tell Fabian the news," Medina said. "I'm afraid you're a little late."

Fabian nodded. Caspian didn't think he appeared overly upset at hearing that his mother had been stripped of her powers.

"How are you taking it?" Caspian asked as he sat down in a nearby chair.

Fabian shrugged. "I can't say I'm surprised. Save for her priests and a handful of humans, the mer are all who are left who believe in the Atlantean gods. The more of those who die, the weaker every immortal in the pantheon grows."

"Except for Mariana," Medina concluded.

Caspian hadn't even thought about it that way. He supposed he shouldn't be surprised that the gods were just as concerned for themselves as for the mer. Still, if it helped the mer, he couldn't really say anything. Besides, it was too late now. The decision had been made.

"How's Marin taking the news?" Fabian asked. "Is he eager to go track down Urion?"

"I haven't told him yet," Caspian replied. "He'd already gone to work by the time I returned."

"You know he's going to want to swim off and find Urion as soon as he knows."

"I'm hoping I can talk him out of it."

Fabian raised an eyebrow.

"I know. I know," Caspian muttered. "I won't be able to stop him or keep him safe."

"I will watch over him on his journey," Medina offered.

"Thank you, but I'm hoping that he'll at least wait and see if they come here, rather than facing the hazards of the journey as well as the priests."

"You believe Marin has the patience for that?" Fabian asked.

"I don't know."

"Even if he does agree to wait, what happens if Urion and the others decide not to come to the colony?"

"His patience will run out eventually," Caspian said.

Medina nodded. "It seems to me that we need a way to bring Urion here, and since two of you are human and Jake has some strange aversion to deep water, I guess it's up to me."

"Aunt Medi, what are you suggesting?"

Medina smiled. "I believe the priests will head to the colony on their own, but I don't think any of us need the stress of a prolonged wait for them to swim all this way. I can have them all brought here in the blink of an eye."

Caspian was well aware that she had the power to do that. He would have been able to do the same himself before his powers were taken.

Fabian nodded thoughtfully. "I have an idea."

"Yes?" Caspian asked. He was open to any suggestions that would keep Marin safe from harm.

"Urion is Atlantean, and as such, he should respect the traditions of our people. Whether it is justice or vengeance Marin wants, he could get both if he challenged Urion to single combat."

Caspian wasn't sure he liked the idea of Marin fighting Urion at all, but the Atlantean tradition would at least impose some rules on them.

"If Marin challenges, Urion would get the choice of weapons," Medina said. "What do you think he would pick?"

"Tridents," Fabian replied. "His aim with any type of throwing weapon was never very good. His talents lie with swords and tridents, and he will prefer the trident for its ability to produce sea-fire."

Caspian nodded. "Marin did improve his skills with a trident a great deal, but he hasn't been practicing recently."

"He'll need to," Fabian said. "Urion was a great fighter, and while he won't be at his best after all these years, he shouldn't be underestimated. If he does intend to continue driving the mer from the sea, he'll be refreshing his skills every day."

Caspian nodded as he mulled over the various possibilities in his mind. Where would Marin wish the fight to take place? As a merman, he was more comfortable in the water, but he had been doing most of his training on land. If he chose to fight in the water, Caspian would be able to do nothing except pace on the beach and wait for the outcome.

Urion hadn't been on land or in human form for years. Marin might have a slight advantage there, even if he was more at home underwater the rest of the time.

"I have to talk to Marin before we decide anything," Caspian said.

"You would let him challenge Urion?" Jake asked.

"I wouldn't like it, but I'd rather he face him in a ruled fight that he's prepared for than be ambushed somewhere."

Caspian didn't want Marin to fight Urion, but he couldn't stand in his way either. Marin deserved his support and nothing less.

* * * *

Marin stored the sea fruits he'd brought home in the fridge. The fact that he was starting to think of Caspian's house as his home wasn't lost on him. Caspian sat at the table, looking as though he wanted to say something but seemed hesitant to do so.

"What is it?" Marin asked. "Does it have something to do with the meeting this morning?"

"Yes."

Marin closed the fridge, hung up his net on the wall hook and slid into Caspian's arms. "How about we don't worry about the gods and just pick things up where we left off this morning?"

Caspian chuckled. "It's tempting, but I have something to tell you and it probably shouldn't wait."

Marin sighed. "Is this something that's going to kill my erection?"

"Probably."

Marin rubbed up against Caspian's leg, humping him gently. "Then I guess I'd better hurry up with this before you ruin the mood."

"I'm serious," Caspian said as he tried to slip out of Marin's range. "It's about Urion."

Marin glanced down at his wilting cock. "Yeah, that'll do it. What about him?"

"He's human again."

Marin stumbled and gripped the edge of the table. "Are you sure?"

"I've not seen him with my own eyes, but yes, I'm as sure as I can be. Mariana was stripped of her powers this morning, and as such, her magic has been undone."

"She's mortal?"

"Yes. Her parents are going to be relocating her somewhere on land, just as I have done. Unlike me, she didn't agree to her punishment, so she had no time to prepare or build her home in advance."

"And her priests can't turn back into sea dragons on their own?"

"No. The power came from their goddess and now she no longer has it."

"Are you sure? I mean, you created this island and home magically, but it's still here after you've lost your powers."

"That's because the pantheon had no objection to this use of my powers and my mother has ensured the continuation of my spells here."

"Where's Urion now?"

"Somewhere in the Pacific, headed toward the colony, the last we heard."

"Do you think they'll still come here, now that they're human again?"

"I don't know. They may decide to go to the nearest stretch of land. Only time will tell what their plans are."

Marin wondered what he would do if he were in their position. "They'll try to contact their goddess."

"Maybe, but they won't get very far. She won't hear their prayers any more than I can now hear those who call out to me."

Caspian took hold of Marin's hands, and Marin realized he was shaking. "Marin, you know you don't have to see him, not ever, if you don't want to."

Marin didn't know what to say, but Caspian wasn't finished.

"If you do still intend to face him, we've been talking about it."

"Who's *we*?"

"Me, Fabian, Jake and Medina."

"And?" Marin prompted. "Oh, let me guess. What's the best way to stop me from killing him?"

Caspian shook his head. "No, I wouldn't do that to you. I know how much you want to see him pay. What we thought was that you might challenge Urion to single combat. That way the other priests can't interfere in the fight and there will be rules you'll both have to follow."

"What sort of rules?"

"Well, if you challenge Urion, you get to pick the location of the fight, but he chooses the weapons. Fabian thinks he'll pick tridents, and I have to say that I agree with him."

"Would I be allowed to kill him?" Marin asked. "Or is one of the rules that if the loser concedes defeat, the victor has to allow him to walk away?"

"You get to decide whether you fight to the death or to first blood. But be warned, you cannot change your mind partway through. If you say it is to the death, that is what you fight to."

Marin nodded. "And how would I find him to issue the challenge?"

"Medina could bring him here, though I think we should do a little more training before you fight him."

"I should have been practicing daily," Marin scolded himself. "Instead I've been—"

"Getting on with your life?" Caspian suggested.

Marin walked over to the wall and took down the trident that hung there. "Can we practice now?"

Caspian grabbed a second trident and gestured to the front door. "Not in here. I can't magically fix the damage now."

Marin nodded and they headed outside. The sun was still high. They could get a few hours practice in before the light was gone.

They worked on balance and footwork, conjuring and aiming sea-fire and combat that was both up close and from a distance.

Marin could tell Caspian was tiring, but he didn't ask to stop.

Finally, Marin brought things to a halt and the two of them collapsed onto the grass of the clearing.

"Am I good enough to take him on?" Marin asked. He wasn't sure he wanted to know the answer.

Caspian didn't answer straight away, and when he did, it wasn't the answer Marin wanted to hear. "I don't know. I've never seen Urion fight. I don't know his strengths or weaknesses."

"At least his strength is no longer being a sea dragon," Marin offered.

"Good point." Caspian sat up and rubbed at his arms. "Cold?"

"A little."

"Sorry. I tend to forget that the mer don't feel the cold as much as humans do."

"I'll soon warm up once we're back inside," Caspian assured him. "Come on. Let's call it a night, and tomorrow I'll ask Fabian to come over and join our practice. I might not have seen Urion fight, but he has. He might have some tips to offer."

Marin nodded and they went home together. There was no longer any question of Marin returning to the colony at night. Even though the Atlanteans wouldn't reach the area for some considerable time, Caspian didn't want to risk him running into Urion before he was ready.

Chapter Twenty-Three

Marin stood between his trainers as they each gave him their expert opinion on his ability and chance of survival.

"Are you sure you're ready?" Caspian asked. "Remember… While you pick the location, Urion chooses the weapons and the time. He could say he wants to battle you then and there."

"It's not likely," Fabian said. "In the two weeks since he's been in human form, he hasn't had time to reach any land. He'll need some time to get his land legs."

"The time he picks has to be no longer than the date of the full moon after the next one," Caspian added. "The next full moon is in two days."

"Which is why I should challenge him now," Marin explained. "If I wait until after, it will give him two months on land to prepare, if he chooses to put off the battle as long as possible. I'd rather challenge him right before the full moon and limit his time on land as much as I can."

Caspian nodded. "Very well. And you're sure you remember all the rules? Once the battle begins, a barrier will rise over a ten-meter-diameter area. It will remain there, trapping you both within until one of you draws first blood or dies, depending on what you decide."

"To the death," Marin interrupted. "I'm not going to change my mind on that."

"I know. I'm just warning you. The barrier is powered by the God of War, my father. It's unlikely he'll show himself in person, but he will be monitoring the battle and making sure the rules are followed. If either of you breaks a rule, he *will* strike the culprit down."

"I won't. I promise," Marin assured him. Even though he hadn't said it outright, Marin knew Caspian wanted him to fight to first blood, but he simply couldn't. Calder hadn't stood a chance against Urion in his sea dragon form. He was dead, and Marin intended to see Urion join him.

"And you're definitely decided on land for the location?" Fabian asked. "I mean, you *are* mer."

Marin nodded. "I've done most of my practicing on land, and besides, I don't think Caspian could bear to wait here on land while I'm fighting underwater."

Caspian snorted. "Like it'll be any easier to watch."

"Where would you prefer me to fight then?"

"Wherever you think you have the best chance of winning," Caspian replied.

"On land," Marin decided. "I've just not done enough work in the water with a human opponent. I don't know your moves or capabilities as well as I do the mer."

"As long as you're sure?" Caspian asked.

"I am."

325

"Then I guess we should summon Medina, so she can go and bring him here." Caspian turned to Fabian. "If you don't mind?"

Fabian nodded. "Aunt Medi, can you come down here?"

The Goddess of Love appeared a moment later. She frowned at her nephew. "Please?" she prompted. "I'm sure I did teach you manners."

Fabian gave her a kiss on the cheek. "I'm sorry, Aunt Medi."

"That's better," Medina replied. "Now, what can I do for you?"

"We're ready for Marin to challenge Urion," Caspian explained. "Can you bring him here?"

Medina frowned at Marin. "Are you sure you don't want to wait a few more years? You really haven't lived that long. You could just as easily challenge him in fifty or sixty years' time."

"Thanks for the vote of confidence," Marin mumbled.

"I'm sorry, darling." Medina patted his arm. "It's just that I'm quite fond of you, and I do hate to see you throw your life away."

"You're not helping," Fabian said. "Can you just bring Urion here? Please?"

Medina sighed, but a moment later Urion appeared, along with the rest of the former sea dragons.

One of the priests spotted Medina and he went to his knees before her. "Great Goddess of Love, sister of our own beloved deity, thank you for hearing our prayers."

Medina nodded but didn't smile.

"Can you tell us what has happened to our goddess?" the priest continued. "We have called for her, but she no longer answers us."

A brief flash of panic crossed her face. Clearly no one had told the priests what had happened to Mariana.

Medina coughed. "I'm afraid I am the bearer of bad news. Your goddess has been stripped of her powers by democratic vote of the pantheon. That is why you have returned to human form and why my sister no longer answers you. She cannot hear your calls."

The priest rose and returned to where Urion and the others were congregating. There followed a lot of whispering and black looks sent in the direction of Marin and the others.

Medina raised her eyebrows and gestured to Marin to go over to the priests.

"You don't have to do this," Caspian whispered.

Marin took his hand and squeezed it tight. "Yes, I do."

He let go of Caspian and approached the priests. He realized he actually had no idea which of them was Urion, having only ever seen him in sea dragon form. "Urion?"

He supposed he wasn't surprised to see the man who responded was the largest and most muscular of the priests. It was just typical of his luck.

"You wish to speak to me?" Urion asked, in a tone that made it clear he thought Marin far beneath his attention.

Marin nodded and stepped closer. "I, Marin of the mer, hereby challenge you in single combat to a fight to the death."

Urion stared at him for several seconds before bursting out laughing. "You're not serious?"

Marin glared at him and gripped his trident tight. "You murdered my mate."

"Yes, I know." Urion sneered. "The leader of the guards, wasn't he?"

Marin hadn't thought he would remember one mer amongst the many he had attacked and killed. "Yes, he was."

"He was also a fool," Urion said, "as are you."

Marin bristled at the insult to Calder, though the one directed at himself didn't bother him in the slightest. "Choose the time and method of your death."

Urion chuckled again. "You mean the time and method of *your* death. I remember you from my time as a prisoner of the mer. The worst guard the city has ever seen, in any century since its inauguration. The only reason you were even accepted into the ranks is because you were spreading your legs for Calder."

"Choose!" Marin shouted.

Urion rolled his eyes. "Very well, if you insist on this foolishness, I'll be happy to send you to meet your lover. Dawn tomorrow, where?"

"Here in this clearing," Marin replied.

Urion appeared surprised. "You're mer, but you don't choose to fight in water?"

"No."

Urion studied him for a few moments. "Ah, I see. You think I will be unsteady on land after so many years in the ocean. An interesting tactic, but doomed to failure."

"Weapons?" Marin asked.

Urion went over to confer with his priests for several minutes. When he returned he had that same annoying sneer on his face. "I see you hold a trident, which would tell me you've been practicing with such a weapon. I therefore choose something different. I don't believe I've ever seen the mer fight with long and short swords, so that is the weapon I choose."

"Fuck!" Caspian swore behind him, loud enough for both Marin and Urion to hear.

Marin tried to stop the rising panic in his chest, but it only receded when Caspian touched him.

Medina stepped into the circle and gestured to Urion and the priests. "I will take you all to the Isle of the Gods until tomorrow. You may use your rooms in your former goddess' palace for the night." She turned to Marin and the others. "Be here in the clearing at dawn. Don't be late."

"I won't," Marin assured her.

The goddess and the priests vanished, leaving Marin to wonder how he was going to learn everything he needed to know about long and short swords in a single night.

"It'll be okay," Caspian said as he wrapped his arms around him.

"I don't even have those weapons to practice with," Marin whispered. "I'm going to die tomorrow and Calder won't be avenged at all."

He let Caspian hold him until he stopped shaking.

Fabian stood to the side. "I'll go to the Isle of Gods and get the swords from Andaman. I'm sure he'll have some in his stores."

"Thank you," Caspian said. "We'll be back at my place."

"Shouldn't we stay here?" Marin suggested. "There's not enough room to practice inside the house."

Caspian gave him a stern glare. "You are *not* practicing all night out here."

"But I—"

"No. You will need to be wide-awake and alert tomorrow. That means a good night's sleep is in order."

"I'm not going to be able to sleep. I'm too worked up."

"I know you are, but you're still not going to be training all night. I'll carry you back to the house over my shoulder if I have to."

"You wouldn't dare."

"Do you really want to test me?"

Marin sighed and shook his head. Caspian would carry out his threat. There was no question about that.

"We train until the light goes, then we go home," Caspian said.

"But it's already mid-afternoon."

"Then we go home, have dinner and go to bed."

"But—"

Caspian placed his finger over Marin's lips. "No arguments. If this is the last night we have together, I intend to spend it in your arms—not out here, stumbling around in the dark."

Marin could see there was no way he would win this argument. Somewhat begrudgingly, he nodded his understanding and agreement.

They waited for Fabian to return, which he did a short while later, with an armful of weapons.

"I brought you a selection of different lengths and weights," Fabian said as he placed them on the ground. "You should test them until you find ones that you're comfortable with."

"Thank you for this," Caspian said as he clasped Fabian's shoulder. "Please pass on our gratitude to Andaman when you see him, too."

"You can thank me yourself," Andaman said.

Marin spun around to see the god standing behind them.

"I thought about bringing you some armor," Andaman said. "Unfortunately, I don't think it will help you in a battle of single combat."

Caspian nodded. "Andaman is right. If you wear any protective gear, so can Urion, and when such items are made by the gods, they're nearly impossible to penetrate. Only weapons made by the gods can do so and even then it is difficult."

"Isn't that a good thing?" Marin asked. "If I'm harder to kill, I mean."

"Yes, but it means Urion would be harder to kill too. I think you'll agree that we want this battle over with as soon as possible. The last thing any of us wants is to drag it out even longer."

"Can he wear armor anyway?"

"Not if you don't," Caspian confirmed. "You either both wear it or you don't. When a challenge of this kind is issued, there must be a level playing field. Now, come and try out one of the long swords."

Marin studied the spread of weapons in front of him. "They all look the same."

Caspian, Fabian and Andaman gave identical sighs of frustration.

"Sorry, but they do." He picked up the nearest one and did a practice lunge. "It feels lighter than a trident."

"They all are," Andaman said. "That one is about in the middle of the weight range of the ones you have here. Is it good, or would you like to try one of the others? Remember, you'll have the short sword as well."

"Let me try with this one first," Marin said.

Caspian picked up one of the other swords and they stepped away from the others.

"Ready?" he said.

Marin nodded and they set to work.

Fabian and Andaman both stayed to offer tips and to switch places with Caspian, so Marin could practice fighting people with different styles.

Once they agreed Marin had done enough to get by with the long sword, he chose a short one too. He was never going to master them by dawn, but he hoped he wouldn't make a complete fool of himself.

"I think he'd do better to concentrate on the long sword alone," Fabian suggested.

"No," Andaman argued. "He needs at least basic training with them both or he'll find Urion's short sword in his gut within a matter of minutes."

"I agree," Caspian said. "Damn it? Why the fuck did he choose these instead of tridents?"

Marin assumed that was a rhetorical question, since Urion had made it very clear why he had chosen them at the time.

He checked the sky and figured they had at least another hour before they lost the light. He hoped it would be enough time.

Finally, Caspian called an end to their training. Andaman took the excess weapons back to his forge and wished Marin luck in the morning.

Fabian went home with Delwyn, who had stayed to watch after bringing them food when his lover hadn't returned for their evening meal.

Caspian kept hold of one set of weapons and Marin held on to the ones he had decided on.

"I thought we weren't going to practice any longer?" Marin asked. "Does this mean you've changed your mind?"

"No, but I'll warm up with you before the battle begins."

Marin tried to quell his disappointment. He didn't feel tired yet and there was so much he still had to learn.

"Come on," Caspian said. "Let's go home."

"You aren't going to carry me over your shoulder?" Marin asked with a teasing grin.

Caspian smirked back. "Well, you have a choice here. You can either walk with me and when we get back we'll have sex. Or I can carry you like I threatened, but be far too tired for anything when we get back."

Marin chuckled. "I think I'll walk."

"I thought you'd see it my way," Caspian replied. "Now, come on. I'm hungry."

"You're always hungry for sex."

"I was talking about food."

"Sure you were," teased Marin as he took Caspian's hand and they headed home. He tried not to think that this might be their last night together.

* * * *

After dinner—a quick microwave dinner each, since neither of them was much use in the kitchen—Caspian took Marin upstairs.

"The swords stay down here," Caspian said. "And we're not going downstairs until the hour before dawn. Understood?"

Marin nodded and sat on the edge of the bed.

Caspian stood in front of him and pulled off his shirt. "You want to fuck me tonight?"

Marin shook his head and smiled. "I want to make love to you. If it's our last night together, I want you to know how much I feel for you."

"I already know," Caspian replied. "So, what do you want to do?"

"I want to be inside you, but it won't just be fucking tonight." He held out his arms and Caspian came to meet him, toppling him backward onto the bed.

Marin laughed and rolled Caspian onto his back. Caspian chuckled as he ran his fingers down Marin's bare thigh.

"I do love the fact that you mer are so opposed to clothing," Caspian said.

Marin had been half hard most of the day. At times during their practice session, his erection had been almost painful, especially when he'd been up close against Caspian. He stroked his cock and stared into Caspian's eyes, watching the rising lust in them.

"Do you want this inside you?" Marin asked.

"Yes."

"How much?"

"More than anything."

"Would you beg for it?" Marin ran his finger over the tip and gathered the pearly drop of seed from the end. "For this?"

"Oh fuck."

Marin rubbed his finger over Caspian's lips. His lover licked up the cum before taking the finger into his mouth, sucking hard then releasing it with a pop.

"Get me ready," Caspian said.

Marin scrambled across the bed to find the lube, accidentally elbowing Caspian in the process.

"Ow," Caspian moaned. "How I miss being able to just produce things with a snap of my fingers."

Marin chuckled. "Want me to kiss it better?"

Caspian patted him on the rump. "Just find the damn lube and get back over here."

Marin rummaged through the drawer, wondering why the wretched stuff wasn't right on the top, since goodness knew they used it often enough. "Found it," he said as he spied it hidden at the back.

Caspian grabbed him halfway on his crawl back down the bed. "Come here and kiss me."

Marin laughed and pressed his lips to Caspian's. Any intention of keeping the kiss short and getting back to business soon flew from his mind. Caspian pushed his tongue into Marin's mouth and gripped the back of his head, holding him in place.

Marin moved slightly to improve the angle, without breaking the kiss. He rubbed up against Caspian's hip, slowly torturing himself with the increasing pressure to come.

Caspian's cock nudged him and a frantic need washed over him. The only time he had ever felt such desire was during the mating season, in another life. Yet he couldn't deny what he wanted, no more than he could pretend he wasn't hard and aching.

He broke their kiss and scooted down the bed. He dove on Caspian's cock like a starving man, taking it into his mouth with a moan of pure want. He sucked desperately, craving the taste of his lover's seed as he never had before.

Caspian cried out encouragement as memories of other times he had done this flooded his mind again. He knew every ridge of the member in his mouth. He knew exactly where to lick it and just how much Caspian could take before he spilled. With the knowledge from experience at the forefront of his mind, Marin pleasured Caspian with his mouth and tongue, eager for the moment his mouth would fill with the fluid he craved so desperately.

The moment Caspian climaxed, Marin's own orgasm crashed over him. He couldn't remember the last time he had come so hard just from sucking another man's cock. No, he remembered all right. It had been during the mating seasons he had spent as Phoebus.

When he came to his senses, Caspian was panting at the other end of the bed.

"Fuck," Marin mumbled. "That was something else."

"I'll say," Caspian replied, still somewhat breathless. "You haven't sucked me like that since..."

"Since I was Phoebus," Marin finished. "I know. I don't know what came over me. It's very rare I come just from sucking off someone else—and never this hard."

"You came too?"

"Yes. I guess we're going to have to wait a while if you still want me to fuck you."

"Don't you want to do that?" Caspian asked.

"I thought I did, but now I'm not so sure." Marin crawled back up the bed and snuggled against his lover. "I said I wanted to make love to you and I'm pretty sure I just did."

"You did indeed."

Marin sighed and ran his fingers over Caspian's chest. "Have you ever heard of a mer's mating trigger changing?"

"No, why do you ask?"

"I don't know, maybe I'm being foolish."

"I doubt that very much," Caspian replied. "Why are you wondering about that? You know I'm happy for you to fuck me whenever you want, mating season or not."

"I know." Marin kissed Caspian's chest. "Maybe it's my memories of my life as Phoebus merging with the here and now."

"But?"

"Just now, when I was sucking you, I felt the same as I do during the mating season—so desperate to come and knowing only your climax could trigger mine."

Caspian chuckled. "That describes us most of the time, you realize?"

"Well, now that you mention it..." Marin laughed at Caspian's observation. "Seriously though, I wonder if I have Phoebus' trigger, as well as his memories."

"You mean in addition to your own?"

"Yes. I guess we'll find out next solstice."

"Well, don't worry about it," Caspian said. "When the mating season comes around, you can do whatever you want to me, you know that. If your trigger *has* changed or if you have Phoebus' trigger too, it won't matter. I'm here for you."

"Thank you."

They lay still for a long time, just touching and being together. Neither of them even suggested the possibility that Marin might not be around for the next mating season.

Chapter Twenty-Four

Caspian nudged Marin awake. "Come on. You can't be late."

Marin grumbled as Caspian poked him in the ribs. "It can't be morning already."

"Not quite, but we need to be in the clearing by dawn, remember?"

Marin yawned. "Do we have time to shower?"

"Shower, yes," Caspian replied. "But if you're thinking about doing anything other than cleaning up, then no."

"You should have woken me earlier," Marin complained.

"I tried, but you were stubbornly sleepy. Besides, even if you could go a fourth round, I'm not sure I could. Go clean up and I'll make you a quick breakfast."

"I'm not hungry."

"You should still try to eat something."

Caspian didn't catch Marin's mumbled comment, but he could make a pretty good guess as to what it was. He ignored him and headed down to the kitchen. He'd persuade Marin to eat something. He couldn't fight Urion if he was weak and light-headed from lack of sustenance.

As it happened, it didn't take long for Caspian to convince Marin to have breakfast. All he had to do was tell him that the quicker he ate, the sooner they would be able to go to the clearing to warm up.

As soon as Marin was finished, they headed out of the door. They were the first to arrive at the clearing. It was still dark, but as the pre-dawn light spread over the horizon, it was bright enough to see by.

They did some stretching and lunges and Caspian drilled Marin on the basics they had covered the previous day.

They hadn't got through even half of what Caspian wanted before the others began to arrive. Fabian and Delwyn appeared first, followed by Jake and Kyle. Finn arrived shortly after his lovers, still eating breakfast.

Caspian was surprised to see Justin appear as well. The heir to the throne clasped Marin's shoulder. "Justice will be served this day."

Marin nodded and gave a small smile.

Medina was the second surprise witness. Although she had been instrumental in helping and seemed to genuinely care for Marin, Caspian had never known her to stand as a witness in such battles before. She wasn't a goddess who liked getting her hands dirty or watching others doing so.

Urion and the other priests arrived with two minutes to spare. They were laughing and joking, as though this were some kind of game.

"Over-confidence is a weakness," Caspian whispered in Marin's ear. "Play to it, if you can."

Marin nodded and stepped into the center of the clearing. Everyone else, except Urion, moved to the edge, staying outside the area that the arena would cover.

"Shall we get this over with?" Urion said as he swung his long sword in a wide arc. "I have a breakfast date, and it isn't wise to keep a goddess waiting."

Caspian wondered which goddess he was referring to. It couldn't be Mariana, but there were plenty of others who would be happy to invite Urion into their bed. He didn't care enough to ask.

The arena formed around the clearing and all Caspian could do was watch and hope that Marin came through this alive. He couldn't lose him again. The thought was unbearable. For the first time in his life, he wished he were human-born, with a god to pray to. "Please don't take him from me," he whispered. "I won't survive losing him a second time."

Marin held the long sword, leaving the short one sheathed at his side. The feel of the weapon in his hand was still strange compared to a spear or a trident. Nearly as disconcerting was the short tunic and belt, the latter being essential to hold the short sword, and the former needed to make the belt more comfortable. Maybe he should have worn clothing during more of his practices, but he had never imagined he'd need it. He put the strangeness out of his mind and faced Urion.

Urion laughed as Marin approached him. He turned around to his fellow priests as he pointed at Marin. "Place your bets now on how long it will take me to teach this creature a lesson."

"He won't last ten minutes," one of the priests shouted.

"I saw him practice with the guards," another replied. "He'll be lucky to last five."

They all roared with laughter as they contemplated how long it would take him to die.

Urion joined them in their jollity. "Which weapon do you think will strike the killing blow? The long or the short?"

His question prompted another round of betting and laughing.

Marin wished he would just get on with it, but he told himself to remember Caspian's advice. While Urion was playing to the crowd, over-confident and arrogant, he wouldn't be concentrating on the fight.

Finally, one of the priests declared that all bets were final and Urion returned his attention to Marin. He gave him a flamboyant, sweeping bow.

Marin offered him an abrupt nod in return.

"He can't even bow properly," Urion called. "Let's hope he at least knows how to die."

Urion swung around at a speed Marin hadn't anticipated, swinging his long sword in a wide arc. Marin barely dodged the blow.

He cursed himself. He had to make sure he was ready for the next one.

After the initial strike, Urion swung at Marin with rapid speed. He countered the blows with, if not ease, competence at least. Urion moved around a lot, dancing this way and that, while still playing to the crowd. Marin hoped he tired himself out quickly.

In between poking fun at his lack of fighting style, Urion also managed to slip in a few jibes about his taste in men. His insults about Caspian bothered Marin far more than the ones directed at him.

"You do realize you're only the latest in a long line of many men he's fucked?" Urion asked. "You're nothing special. Just another willing body to warm his bed."

Marin jabbed at Urion with his sword, but he easily stepped out of his reach.

"Did I hit a nerve?" Urion sneered. "For someone who is supposedly avenging the death of his lover, you seem awfully touchy about Caspian. Still, I suppose it can't be helped."

"What can't be helped?" Marin asked, even as he silently scolded himself for rising to the bait.

"You're *mer*," Urion said. "Everyone knows you're all sex-crazed and ready to spread your legs for anyone who asks. Tell me, Marin, which of them fucked you better — Calder or Caspian?"

Marin screamed and charged at Urion, heedless of the sword which swiped at his arm, drawing a thin line of blood where the edge of the blade caught him. Dimly he realized that if he had called the fight to first blood he would have lost, and it would all be over now.

Urion quickly regained his balance and pushed Marin back.

"You aren't the first mer he's had," Urion continued. "He had as many of those as he had Atlanteans. You don't think you're anything special to him, do you?"

Marin growled and swung his blade with as much force as he could. "You talk too much."

"Does the truth bother you, or are you simply incapable of carrying on a conversation and fighting at the same time?"

Urion turned to seek the approval of his priests for his latest attempt at a joke. Marin seized the opportunity to kick his legs out from under him. The idea was good, but unfortunately Urion was steadier on his feet than

Marin had anticipated. He barely stumbled and suddenly was paying far more attention to his opponent.

"I see someone has been teaching you some dirty tricks," Urion said. "Was it Fabian? That traitor never did know what a fair fight was."

Marin snorted. He unsheathed his short sword as they slowly circled each other. "If what I did wasn't allowed, I'd have been struck down. As for fighting fair, how fair was it when you killed Calder and those other mer?"

"They should have left the city when they were told," Urion snarled. "I was simply obeying the orders of my goddess."

"You murdered not only Calder but other mer, ones who had left the city or hadn't even been there."

"The mer don't deserve to live in the ocean. You're all unnatural creatures and we will rejoice on the day when the last of you dies and your species is extinct."

"That'll never happen," Marin replied. "My people will thrive long after you're dead."

"Your numbers decrease every generation. Maybe I won't live to see you gone, but it's only a matter of time and every true Atlantean will celebrate."

"Your people are gone," Marin reminded him. "Scattered around the world with no knowledge of their heritage. Atlantis is just a deserted island. Even the humans exploring it don't truly believe what it is, not even the ones who are descended from the Atlanteans. They have forgotten, your people are forgotten and so is your goddess."

Urion screamed in rage and came at Marin with both swords raised, a move leaving him dangerously exposed.

Marin thrust at him with his short sword, but instead of sinking the blade into the priest's chest, it only grazed his ribs.

Urion fell to the side in apparent shock at Marin drawing his blood at all. He stumbled on a piece of uneven ground and landed on his back. He had dropped his short sword when he'd clutched at his chest, but he still had a firm grip on the long one.

Marin kicked his arm aside, wishing he'd put on some footwear for the first time in his life. He dropped down onto Urion's chest and wrested the sword from his hand, tossing it well out of reach.

He could hear cheers of encouragement from behind him, but he didn't let himself be distracted. He couldn't hear Caspian's voice in the cheers, but he refused to turn around and see.

With his short sword in his hand, Marin glared down at Urion. For the first time, Urion looked at him with something other than contempt. He didn't think it was fear — maybe surprise.

"You won't kill me," Urion said. "You haven't got it in you. You're *weak* just like your lover was."

"Calder was *not* weak," Marin snapped. "He was the bravest merman I ever knew."

"He was a fool and you're an even bigger one."

Marin pressed the blade of his sword against Urion's throat. His hand shook and he thought for a moment he might drop the weapon altogether.

Urion chuckled. "What are you waiting for? You wanted a fight to the death, didn't you?"

"I did... Do."

"You don't sound so sure," Urion replied. "Didn't anyone tell you that if you declare a battle a death match, you can't then change your mind partway through?"

"I know that."

"Ah, but you thought you'd be able to go through with it. You've never killed anyone in your life, and you aren't going to kill me. You don't have the guts."

Marin faltered and a moment later Urion had bucked him off his chest and rolled on top of him, squeezing his wrist until he let go of his weapon.

For a second or two Marin thought this was it, then Urion seemed to hesitate.

"I'll be damned."

"What?" Marin whispered, though he wasn't sure he wanted to know what it was Urion had seen when he'd looked at him.

"You have different colored eyes."

"Yes, I know. What of it?"

Urion glanced behind him, in the direction where Caspian stood. "Our goddess spoke of another who had your eyes. He's the reason the Atlanteans were banished. She studied him when Caspian requested he be made immortal and curses the fact that she didn't kill him then, before he destroyed our people."

Marin shivered. He wasn't sure what his face revealed, but it seemed to be enough for Urion to guess the truth.

"You!" Urion jumped up and dragged Marin to his feet, yanking him across to the edge of the arena, where Caspian stood watching. "Is it true?" he screamed at Caspian. "Is this creature the one?"

Marin struggled to release himself from Urion's grip, but the hand on his arm was like a vise.

"This pathetic excuse of a fighter is what you chose over your own people?" Urion yelled. "Is he that good a fuck?"

Caspian's glare was icy as he looked at Urion. "That's none of your business." His gaze softened as he turned to Marin. "I love you."

Marin choked back a sob. "I'm sorry, Caspian. I'm so sorry."

"You have nothing to apologize for."

"But I failed. I couldn't do it. I couldn't kill him when I had the opportunity. I'm sorry I didn't listen to you when I had the chance. I love you."

"How sweet," Urion sneered. He pulled Marin in front of him and pushed him against the barrier surrounding the arena. "Take a good look at him, Caspian. Was he worth it?"

"Yes," Caspian whispered.

"Maybe I should find out for myself," Urion suggested. "I normally prefer to bed the fairer sex, but this creature is so pathetic, he's barely even a man."

"No!" Marin struggled as the memory of his last hours as Phoebus returned in a rush. Trapped with the barrier in front of him and Urion behind him, he screamed in panic, hitting out blindly.

Not again. Please, not again!

Urion grabbed at his crotch and Marin twisted and squirmed as he tried to free himself.

Marin was dimly aware of Caspian shouting but he couldn't make out the words. All he could focus on was Urion behind him, pressing against him, the stiff rod at his arse. He didn't even know if he'd lost his garments or whether they had been pushed aside by Urion.

"No!" he screamed again.

Suddenly he fell forward, the barrier gone. He stumbled toward the ground, but didn't hit it. Caspian caught him and they sank onto the grass together.

"It's over now," Caspian said. "It's over."

Marin choked out a sob and buried his face in Caspian's chest, gasping in gulps of air as he tried to calm his racing heart.

Finally, he drew back and chanced a glimpse over his shoulder. Urion lay on his back, a scorch mark in the center of his chest. His eyes were open, unseeing. "He's dead?" Marin asked.

"Yes."

"But how?"

"My father," Caspian explained. "As I explained to you before you issued your challenge, he oversees all battles such as this one."

"I don't understand," Marin said.

"Urion broke the rules of fair combat," Caspian continued. "The moment his taunts about fucking you became an actual intention to violate your body, he sealed his own fate. My father struck him down with one of his lightning bolts, his life forfeited."

Caspian helped Marin to his feet. "Come on. Let's go home."

"What about...?" Marin gestured to the body.

"His fellow priests will see to the funeral arrangements. All you need to do is come home with me and let me sort out your arm."

"Let me deal with that," Medina said as she approached. With a wave of her hand she cleaned away the blood and sealed the wound so neatly that it wasn't even visible.

"Are you supposed to do that?" Marin asked.

Medina smiled. "An injury suffered while seeking justice for your murdered lover. I would dare any god or goddess to tell me I have no right to heal it."

"Thank you," Marin said.

"You're welcome." Medina bit her lower lip, shrugged and spoke again. "By the way, Marin, you're right about your trigger."

"What do you mean?" Marin asked.

"Did you just pry into Marin's mind?" Caspian snapped at the same time.

"Occupational hazard," Medina replied to Caspian before turning to Marin. "You have Phoebus' memories, as well as his heart and soul. Now that you have accepted he is a part of you, you also have his mating trigger, in addition to the one you had already."

"How do you know that?"

Medina smiled. "I'm the Goddess of Love, Lust and Carnal Desire. It's my job to know. I could hear you wondering about it before the battle, but I didn't want to distract you—at least not any more than you already were while you were checking out Caspian's arse. I thought you might like to know, rather than waiting for the solstice to come around."

"Thank you," Marin said. "And for your help in getting Urion here."

"Yes," Caspian added. "Thank you for everything."

Medina smirked at him.

"Yes, for *everything*," Caspian repeated. "Even if your intentions were not always good, I know that without your interference I would never have known what it was to truly love someone."

Medina smiled and vanished without replying.

Marin looked around the clearing. Urion's fellow priests were still lingering some distance away and his own supporters were keeping back as well. He nodded his thanks to Fabian and the others, but he didn't want to be around them right now. He could see how pleased they were for his victory and he suspected they would want to celebrate his triumph.

Cheering and partying were the last thing Marin wanted right now. His memories of Phoebus and Rafe were too near the surface of his mind.

Caspian seemed to understand what Marin needed without him having to say a word, and he soon had him tucked into bed.

Marin yawned widely, only now realizing how tired he was. "Aren't you coming to bed?"

Caspian shook his head. "You need to sleep properly."

"Will you hold me?" Marin asked. "I don't want to be alone right now."

Caspian sat on top of the covers and opened his arms for Marin to crawl into. "You're safe now," Caspian assured him as Marin closed his eyes and let himself relax completely for the first time since he had lost Calder.

* * * *

Caspian left Marin to sleep and headed downstairs. He nearly didn't see the goddess sitting on his sofa.

"Cari, what are you doing here?"

"I grew tired of waiting for you to come and see me," his sister replied. "Now that Marin's quest is over, you have no more excuses to avoid me."

"Marin had nothing to do with my staying away from you," Caspian said as he walked over to the bar and poured himself a drink. He didn't bother offering one to Cari. He didn't anticipate her staying long.

"Why don't you ask me why I stripped you of your powers?" Cari asked.

"It was the decision of the pantheon, not just you."

"I had the deciding vote," Cari reminded him. "If it weren't for me, you'd still be immortal."

"I know." Caspian gulped down his whisky and poured himself another. He would probably regret it in the morning, but right now he didn't care.

"Damn in, Caspian, why don't you shout at me or something?"

"I don't see the point of giving myself a headache and it would wake up Marin."

Cari rose and joined him at the bar, perching on one of the stools. "You could at least offer me a drink."

Caspian planted a glass in front of her and poured her a whisky.

"You know I don't like that stuff."

Caspian rolled his eyes and went to find her a beer. "That's all I have. If you want something else, you'll have to conjure it yourself."

Cari took a drink and turned on the stool to face him directly. "I saw you age."

"In a vision?" Caspian asked.

"Yes."

"I suspected as much. It doesn't make it any easier to accept. You know as well as I do, the future can be changed. You made the decision to bring about the vision you saw, without even telling me about it. It never even occurred to you that I might not want to grow older."

"You were happy in my vision."

"I was perfectly happy as a god," Caspian reminded her.

"That's highly debatable."

"I *was*."

"You drifted through life without any sense of direction. The only time I ever saw you really happy was when you were with Phoebus—until my vision, that is."

"You saw me happy with Marin, didn't you?"

Cari nodded.

"Why didn't you tell me?"

"Because you and he hadn't worked things out together and I didn't want to risk changing things by giving you information that might alter your future."

"What makes you think that telling me now won't change things?"

"You and Marin are together now."

Caspian studied the dwindling contents of his glass.

"Caspian, what is it? You *are* a couple, aren't you?"

"I don't know. Maybe."

"Maybe?"

"Calder's murderer is dead now. Marin doesn't need me to train him any longer."

"I'm fairly sure that's not the only reason Marin spends time with you."

"Isn't it? My relationship with Marin consists of training and sex."

Cari gave an unladylike snort. "Well, that's more than your relationship with Phoebus entailed. I'm pretty sure that was all sex."

"No, it wasn't," Marin interrupted from the foot of the stairs.

"How long have you been standing there?" Caspian asked.

"Long enough to hear an awful lot of rubbish from both of you," Marin replied. "Do you really think that all we have between us is training and sex?"

"Well…"

Marin turned his glare on Cari. "And how dare you say that the only thing between Phoebus and Caspian was sex."

"She does have a point," Caspian said. "It's not like Phoebus and I had much in common."

Marin stalked across the room. "How can two beings who have lived so long be so ignorant?"

Cari stared at him, open-mouthed, but Marin didn't give her chance to say anything.

"Do you really believe that Phoebus — I — would have been prepared to give up my fins just because Caspian was a good fuck? That I would have given up my family and the sea for nothing more than sex?"

"Er…"

Caspian cringed at Marin's fury.

"And you," Marin rounded on Caspian. "We've barely trained in months."

"No, we were too busy having sex."

"And talking," Marin snapped. "Getting to know each other again, properly."

"I suppose."

Marin sighed and all his temper seemed to vanish as quickly as it had appeared. "You suppose? Oh, Caspian, what am I going to do with you?"

Cari placed her empty bottle on the bar and rose. "I should probably leave the two of you to talk. Caspian, I'm sorry I didn't speak to you about my vision before I cast my vote. Please believe me that I only wanted to try to bring about your happiness."

Caspian nodded and, after giving his sister a quick kiss on the cheek, she vanished from the room.

"What did she mean about her vote?" Marin asked.

"It's not important. I'm sorry we woke you. You should probably go get some more sleep. I know you didn't get much last night."

Marin shook his head. "I'm not tired."

"But—"

"And I don't need mothering. I had enough of that from Calder."

Caspian gaped at Marin. He had never heard him say anything even vaguely critical of Calder before.

Marin chuckled and shook his head. "Don't look so surprised. Calder and I quarreled, just the same as any couple does. Our relationship wasn't perfect. No relationship ever is. Surely you know that."

"I suppose I do, but you never said anything before to indicate that there were any sort of problems between the two of you."

"Why would I?" Marin asked. "Our quarrels were generally of short duration and soon forgotten. His overprotective streak didn't stop me loving him, just as yours doesn't stop me from loving you. You and Calder are very similar in that respect, though with one rather large difference."

"What's that?"

Marin smiled. "Calder would never have let me face Urion, not under any circumstances. He would have been furious at the idea of my challenging him. He'd probably have locked me up in the darkest dungeon of the palace to keep me from fighting him at all."

Caspian wanted to disagree, but he suspected Marin might have a point. Calder had been protective of all the guards under his command and Marin most of all.

Marin wrapped his arms around Caspian. "Thank you for having faith in me. I know you didn't want me to fight him."

"Watching you in the arena was one of the hardest things I've ever had to do. The thought of losing you scares me so much."

"You're not going to lose me. It's all over now."

Caspian led Marin over to the sofa. "So, how are you feeling?"

"I don't know," Marin replied. "I thought I'd feel different with Urion dead."

"You thought you'd feel better," Caspian said.

Marin shrugged. "I wanted justice for Calder."

"You have it. Calder would be proud of you."

"I know. I just never really thought I'd defeat him. I was prepared to die, but I'm not sure what to do now that I haven't."

"What we do now is live our lives, the best way we can," Caspian replied. "And let's not waste any more time with doubts."

"I don't have any of those."

"You're sure?"

Marin nodded. "Yes."

"Then you'll live here, with me? You'll have the conveniences of modern human technology but with the ocean and your people just a short swim away."

"You thought of everything when you decided to live here, didn't you?"

"You're mer and you're never happier than when you're in the ocean. I won't take that from you. I should never have asked it of Phoebus, and I won't ask it of you."

"You're wrong," Marin whispered as he leaned closer.

"What about?"

"There are times when I am happier than when I'm swimming...when I'm in your arms."

Caspian smiled and pulled Marin closer. He kissed him slowly, careful not to be too forceful, cautious not to scare him off. He didn't need to be told that the memories of Rafe and Urion were recent enough to be disturbing.

"I love you, Marin," Caspian whispered.

Marin smiled at him. "I love you too."

"I'm sorry I never told you how much I loved you when you were Phoebus," Caspian said. "I was a fool."

"I won't argue with that," Marin said. "But it's in the past. Besides, even though you never said the words, I knew you loved me, even back then. I wouldn't have agreed to give up my fins if I had doubted it. Now, I know it's early, but how about we have some lunch?"

"Okay, what do you want?"

"Something edible," Marin teased. "There may be a lot of reasons I love you and want to be with you, but your cooking skills have nothing to do with it."

Caspian laughed and the two of them headed into the kitchen in search of food. He wondered whether it was a scene like this that Cari had seen in her vision, but he supposed it didn't matter. She had always said that no person should know too much about their own future, and he found he agreed with her in that regard. He and Marin had a future together, and he intended to make the most of every single day.

Want to see more from this author? Here's a taster for you to enjoy!

To Change the Stars
L.M. Brown

Excerpt

"You were fired?" Jessiah groaned as Ashleigh delivered her bad news.

"I asked if I could change one of my days because it clashed with one of Blake's parties, and he kicked me out."

"He was our best shot at getting information about the laboratory."

Ashleigh snorted. "He wouldn't have told us anything. I think we should try a new target."

"Who do you suggest?" Jessiah asked. "Most of the scientists have live-in staff already. They don't need any extra help."

"This one does," Corrine announced with a smile. "His name's Garrett, and he could be the answer to our problem."

Jessiah and Ashleigh turned to see who Corrine was referring to. She had called up a new profile on her small tablet computer and the hologram of the man's head hovered above.

"He's dishy," Ashleigh said with a dreamy sigh.

"You're not his type, love," Corrine said.

"Always the way," Ashleigh muttered.

Corrine hit a few buttons on her tablet and Garrett's current advertisements appeared in the air. "He's looking for a part-time maid."

"What credits is he offering?" Ashleigh asked.

Jessiah glared at her. "Does it matter? You already have a job that pays pretty well. It's not as if you need the credits."

Ashleigh folded her arms across her chest. "If I'm going to be interviewed, I need to know what he's offering, and if it's too low, I intend to negotiate. I'll look like an amateur if I don't."

"Just don't negotiate yourself out of the job," Jessiah warned.

"I'd like to see you do better," Ashleigh snapped. "So far *I'm* the one doing all the work here."

"I'm not a maid," Jessiah pointed out.

"As anyone who's seen your quarters could tell."

Corrine clapped her hands together sharply, drawing their attention back to her and ending the squabble. "Ashleigh, go apply for the position. Jessiah, you should finish your errands before the boss gets back. Keep your eyes and ears open for anything useful about this Garrett, anything we can use to get closer to him. I'll keep searching for any other prospects, in case this one doesn't work out either."

Jessiah and Ashleigh hurried to do as they were told, leaving Corrine with her own job to do.

* * * *

"Absolutely not," Corrine stated with a shake of her head for good measure.

Ashleigh remained silent as she chewed on her nail.

Jessiah had known before he spoke that his suggestion would not go down very well. "AJ did it to get the credits for his sister's medicine," he pointed out.

"You're not AJ, and while he felt he had no choice, we do. Ashleigh got the job and has been working hard to find out whatever she can about the laboratories. She's already uncovered a wealth of information about rotas and current projects."

"It's taking too long," Jessiah said. "Hundreds die in the Labyrinth every day that we waste."

"Try to be patient," Corrine advised. "We don't want to ruin everything by doing something foolish."

"It's not foolish. You know there are only two things everyone who knows Garrett seems to agree on. He's a pretty useless scientist and he sleeps with more whores than most of the other scientists combined."

"I think the boss could give him a run for his credits," Ashleigh muttered.

Corrine sighed and shooed Ashleigh away. She took Jessiah's arm and steered him to a quiet corner in the staff quarters of their residence in the tower.

"You know it could be the answer to our problem of getting closer to him," Jessiah pointed out quietly.

"It could, but I still don't like it. We don't know enough about this man or how he treats the men he takes to his bed."

"Ashleigh doesn't think he's like the boss. She says he seems kind."

"I know, but so does Blake, when he wants to come across that way. Do you really want your first time to be with someone who's paying you?"

Jessiah wanted to deny his inexperience, but he knew it would be a waste of time. He had never been able to lie to Corrine, and she and Ashleigh knew him better than anyone else, except perhaps Ryder.

Once upon a time he had thought Ryder might be the one for him. He had harbored a youthful crush on him for years, though now he knew that was all it had been.

"I have enough credits to hire a collar," Jessiah said. "If it looks like Garrett might be interested in me, I can buy it after a few…err…"

"Fucks?" Corrine supplied with a grimace. "Is that the word you're looking for?"

Jessiah nodded as he tried to reconcile what he had heard with the fact that it had come out of Corrine's mouth. She swore so rarely that it always took him by surprise.

"For goodness' sake, be careful," Corrine warned. "If he treats you even half as badly as the boss treats his bed partners, promise me you'll walk away."

"I promise."

Corrine shook her head and pulled him into her arms. "I wanted so much for you to find a nice young man who'd treat you like you deserve."

"I'll be fine, and maybe when this is all over, I'll find someone in the past. The population was much bigger back then."

Jessiah left Corrine shaking her head.

"I hope you know what you're doing," she called after him as he reached the door.

"Of course I do," Jessiah replied. Privately, he hoped so too.

* * * *

Garrett swore as he tried to make sense of the equations on the hand-held computer in front of him.

"Have you got those results for me yet?" His father sounded even more impatient than he had been an hour ago, the last time he had asked for them.

Garrett sighed. "Nearly," he called back. The lie came with ease. After all, he'd had years of practice.

"Struggling?" Harland whispered from his terminal across the room.

"Is it that obvious?" Garrett replied as he pushed the computer aside. "I've no idea what I'm doing."

Harland took pity on him, as he almost always did. "Let me take a look."

"Thanks."

Ten minutes later, the report his father had been waiting for was spooling from the printer.

"How do you do that?" Garrett asked.

"I just have a head for science," Harland replied. "Some of us are lucky like that."

Garrett snorted. His father was similarly blessed, as had been his mother, his grandparents and great-grandparents before them. Garrett, on the other hand, had no business being in a laboratory at all. If his father hadn't been who he was, Garrett had no doubt he would never have been allowed entry into the inner sanctum.

Harland had earned his position, thanks to his brains. Garrett, thanks to his father's credits and influence.

Garrett's father appeared in the doorway. "Are you done yet?"

"It's just printing, sir," Harland said. "I think you'll be pleased with the results."

"Will I?" Blaine shot Garrett a hard glare. "And why is that, Garrett?"

Garrett had no clue, and when Harland tried to jump in to save him again, Blaine held up his hand and halted his words. Garrett hung his head, ashamed of his ignorance.

"You're a pitiful excuse for a scientist," Blaine sneered. "If you weren't my son..."

Garrett didn't need to hear the unspoken words. He had heard them many times before.

"Get out of here," Blaine snarled. "Harland, let's go over these results and see if we can boost the output from the generators."

It was tempting to offer to stay to help or at least try to learn something, but Garrett had figured out the hard way not to bother. Besides, right now he needed a drink and a willing arse to bury his cock in.

Garrett escaped from the stifling confines of the laboratory as fast as he could. His father had once again humiliated him in front of one of his co-workers, just as he seemed to do at every opportunity.

He headed down, not right into the Labyrinth but not far off, heading for his favorite watering hole. Everyone knew what happened in this sector. It was the worst-kept secret in the entire underground community. Garrett had been coming down here for years. It was the only place where no one would shame him for his lack of brains. They only saw his hard, trim body, his long blond hair and his dark blue eyes. Here he was judged on his looks and his sexual prowess, which was just the way he liked it.

Garrett scanned the tavern, avoiding the gaze of the whore he had fucked the previous week. He knew the man wanted to hook up with him again, but Garrett never went back for seconds, at least not knowingly.

He felt the gaze of the newcomer before he spotted him. The blue-eyed whore sat on the stool at the end of the bar, the flashing blue lights of his collar telling anyone who cared to look that he would take credits from men in exchange for sexual favors.

Garrett sipped his drink as he watched the prostitute from the corner of his eye. He wasn't as scrawny as most whores in this sector. He certainly wasn't starving in the bowels of the Labyrinth. He didn't seem to have as much dust on him as the lab rats did either. He must have cleaned up in the public facilities before coming to the tavern. His brown hair brushed his shoulders and Garrett recognized a professional cut when he saw it. He wondered if perhaps he might have a benefactor already, though the look of interest in his eyes was clear.

The whore watched him as he drank. He didn't approach, though Garrett couldn't tell if it was because of nerves or whether the guy was simply confident enough to believe Garrett would come to him.

He didn't have the look of a lab rat, nor did Garrett recognize him as one of the tower dwellers. Normally, Garrett could guess just by looking at someone where they had come from.

The whore who had caught his attention appeared to be in his early twenties, yet everything about him was a contradiction. To Garrett, that made him a lot more interesting than any of the other prostitutes in the place.

When it became clear the whore wasn't going to approach him, Garrett moved down the bar to speak to him instead.

"You busy?" he asked.

The whore shrugged. "Not right now. What do you have in mind?"

Garrett waved the bartender over. "I'll have another and whatever my friend here is drinking."

"Jesse," the whore said. "My name's Jesse. And I think I fancy something fruity."

"Garrett." He stuck out his hand for his new drinking companion to shake, glancing at his credit band as he did. Jesse carried just twenty credits on his band. It wouldn't last him more than a couple of days. "So, what's on offer?"

Jesse looked him up and down with a smirk. "Whatever you like, gorgeous."

"Prices?"

Jesse glanced quickly at the bartender who was pouring them their drinks.

"Oh, don't worry about him. The money he used to buy this cave and set up his tavern was earned by spreading his legs. He won't care if we want to do a bit of business here."

Jesse relaxed and picked up his glass.

"You're new to this, aren't you?" Garrett asked.

"No, I've just not been in here before."

"I didn't think I'd seen you around. So, that's enough small talk. Back to your prices?"

Jesse took a drink before he answered. Definitely nervous, Garrett realized.

"Virgin?" he asked.

"No," Jesse replied, a shade too quickly.

Garrett's cock hardened at the idea that Jesse might be untouched. It wasn't likely, of course. He had only ever come across one other whore who claimed he had never been fucked. He hadn't been a virgin, but his arse was. Garrett had bid in an auction for the pleasure of deflowering him but had been outbid by a man with more credits than Garrett could compete with.

"How much would you charge for me to bury myself in your arse?" Garrett asked. He stroked a hand over the backside in question and the whore named Jesse shivered at his touch.

"How about we discuss my prices at your place?" Jesse suggested.

The offer was tempting, but Garrett shook his head. "I don't take strange whores home with me."

"That's not what I heard."

Garrett gave him a questioning stare.

"Your parties are legendary," Jesse said.

"That's different. Those whores are sent by the agency, and they know damn well they won't be seeing any more work if anything should disappear."

"Are you calling me a thief?"

"No, but I don't take chances. Before I host a party, I make sure anything valuable is locked away and I know the agency will compensate me if something should go missing."

"I got this from the agency." Jesse toyed with his collar.

"I'm sure you did, but you're not on their clock at the moment, are you?"

Jesse seemed to realize he wasn't going to be invited back to Garrett's apartment and slid down from his stool. He was shorter than Garrett by nearly a head. "Where do you suggest we go then?"

"Your place?"

Jesse shook his head. Maybe he *was* a lab rat, then. Whores who lived down in the Labyrinth rarely took their clients deep down into the dusty realm beneath the towers. In the hierarchy of the Labyrinth, everyone seemed to want to look down on someone else and, unfortunately for the whores, they were at the very bottom of the ladder.

Garrett finished his drink and nodded Jesse back out into the main cavern.

"Where are we going?" Jesse asked.

"Not far."

Garrett led Jesse into one of the small caves off the main one, down a couple of twisting tunnels into the darkness, where there was at least the illusion of privacy.

"Here?" Jesse's eyes widened, the whites of them bright in the shadows.

Garrett nodded. "Now, about those prices."

"One hundred credits if you want to fuck me," Jesse said.

"A hundred?"

"Fifty," Jesse amended quickly.

Garrett smiled in the darkness. He might claim to be experienced, but only a newcomer to the trade would drop his price so quickly. "Done."

The lights on Jesse's collar stopped blinking the moment the deal was agreed. Jesse fumbled with his belt and dropped his trousers so they pooled around his ankles.

Garrett nudged him with his hand. "Turn around and brace yourself against the wall with your hands."

Jesse did as he was told without question. Garrett traced his hand along Jesse's spine, slipping his fingers between his buttocks, brushing the tip of his index finger against his hole. Jesse moaned softly.

"You can be as loud as you like down here. No one will care."

Jesse nodded, and the next time Garrett touched him, he moaned so loudly they probably heard him back in the tavern.

Garrett undid his trousers and pulled out his cock. He never came down here unprepared and this time was no different. He removed the bottle of lube from his pocket and coated his fingers. Now to see if Jesse was as untouched, as his reaction seemed to indicate.

He slid a single finger inside Jesse's arse and his cock hardened in anticipation when he realized how tight Jesse was.

"Tell me the truth," Garrett whispered into Jesse's ear. "Have you taken a cock up your arse before?"

Jesse shook his head.

"Good boy."

"I'm not a boy," Jesse snapped.

"How old are you?" Garrett asked. His curiosity was piqued, as well as a little concerned that his trick might not be legal.

"Eighteen."

Garrett crooked his finger inside him. "The truth?"

"Eighteen, I swear."

Garrett breathed a sigh of relief. He really didn't want to call an end to their play.

"How old are *you*?" Jesse asked.

"Old enough to know just how to pleasure an eighteen-year-old virgin."

"I'm *not* a virgin!"

Garrett chuckled. "You might not be, but your arse is. Now, stop being offended or you might just leave this cave with your anal virginity as intact as when you entered it."

Jesse frowned over his shoulder and Garrett kissed him lightly on the lips. He had no idea why he did such a thing. He never kissed his whores, yet he had been unable to resist the temptation of those pouting pink lips.

"Turn around," Garrett ordered as he removed his finger from Jesse's arse.

Jesse appeared confused but did as he was told.

Garrett pushed him back against the wall and kissed him again, harder this time, pushing his tongue into Jesse's mouth and tasting him. He could taste the fruity flavor of the wine Jesse had been drinking at the tavern. He moaned into Jesse's mouth and felt Jesse's erection rise between them. His own stiff shaft ached for attention. He tugged Jesse up and encouraged him to wrap his legs around Garrett's waist, grinding up against him until Jesse writhed in his arms, keening and groaning in pleasure.

He wasn't going to get inside Jesse. Garrett knew that for a fact, as surely as he knew Jesse was going to spill his seed between them as well.

Garrett pulled out of the kiss and concentrated on rubbing their cocks together. "Come for me, Jesse," he ordered. Even as he spoke, he wondered why he had started using his name instead of merely calling him his whore. 'Keep it impersonal and don't get involved' had always been his motto.

Jesse panted in his ear.

"Such a good whore," Garrett said, more to remind himself of who he was with than anything else. Jesse was just a whore. "Are you close, whore? Come for me, my dirty little whore."

The words sounded contrived to his own ears, though Jesse didn't seem to mind what he called him. He cried out loudly as he came in spurts between them.

Garrett followed him a few moments later, his cum mixing with Jesse's as they leaned against the dirty wall of the cave. "Jesse," he gasped into his ear.

Jesse seemed too dazed to pull himself together but Garrett recovered fairly quickly, and after cleaning them up with his handkerchief, he set their clothes to rights.

"You didn't fuck me," Jesse finally said. "We just…"

Garrett smiled and put their wrist bands together. "Frottage," he teased. "Sometimes it can be even better than fucking."

He transferred payment and led Jesse back into the main cavern. He heard Jesse's gasp and Garrett smiled to himself.

"I said fifty for a fuck and we didn't even do that," Jesse said. "I think you must have hit the wrong buttons in the dark."

Garrett laughed. "No, I didn't. Call it a bonus."

Jesse looked at him, completely stunned. Garrett suspected he had never had so much on his credit band at once in his life. He left the novice whore five hundred credits richer and returned to the tower. He didn't imagine he would ever see Jesse again. Someone else would no doubt have the pleasure of shoving their cock into his untouched — well, nearly untouched — arse for the first time. Garrett frowned at the thought of someone else taking what had been offered to him so eagerly. Maybe he should have fucked the guy, too.

He glanced back as he entered the elevator. Jesse had vanished from the cavern, no doubt searching for either his next meal or his next trick. Garrett hoped it was the former.

PUBLISHING

Sign up for our newsletter and find out about all our romance book releases, eBook sales and promotions, sneak peeks and FREE romance eBooks!

About the Author

L.M. Brown is an English writer of gay romances. She believes mermen live in the undiscovered areas of the ocean. She believes life exists on other planets. She believes in fairy tales, magic, and dreams. Most of all, she believes in love.

When L.M. Brown isn't bribing her fur babies for control of the laptop, she can usually be found with her nose in a book.

L.M. Brown loves to hear from readers. You can find her contact information, website details and author profile page at https://www.pride-publishing.com